THE
FIRES OF
VENGEANCE

By Evan Winter

THE BURNING
The Rage of Dragons
The Fires of Vengeance

THE
FIRES OF
VENGEANCE

THE SECOND BOOK OF
THE BURNING

EVAN WINTER

orbitbooks.net

Cover design by Lauren Panepinto
Cover illustration by Karla Ortiz
Cover copyright © 2020 by Hachette Book Group, Inc.
Map by Tim Paul

Orbit
Hachette Book Group
1290 Avenue of the Americas
New York, NY 10104
orbitbooks.net

First Edition: November 2020
Simultaneously published in Great Britain by Orbit

Orbit is an imprint of Hachette Book Group.
The Orbit name and logo are trademarks of Little, Brown Book Group Limited.

The publisher is not responsible for websites (or their content) that are not owned by the publisher.

The Hachette Speakers Bureau provides a wide range of authors for speaking events. To find out more, go to www.hachettespeakersbureau.com or call (866) 376-6591.

Library of Congress Cataloging-in-Publication Data
Names: Winter, Evan, author.
Title: The fires of vengeance / Evan Winter.
Description: First Edition. | New York : Orbit, 2020. | Series: The burning ; book 2
Identifiers: LCCN 2020009321 | ISBN 9780316489805 (hardcover) |
    ISBN 9780316489782
Subjects: GSAFD: Fantasy fiction.
Classification: LCC PR6123.I578 F57 2020 | DDC 823/.92—dc23
LC record available at https://lccn.loc.gov/2020009321

ISBNs: 978-0-316-48980-5 (hardcover), 978-0-316-48981-2 (ebook)

Printed in the United States of America

LSC-C

10 9 8 7 6 5 4 3 2 1

This book is dedicated to Neville Leopold Winter.

Quiet, stoic, impossibly hardworking, he was quick to laugh and had a joyous smile that crinkled his eyes. He was my father, and he passed away as The Fires of Vengeance *was being written.*

Married for almost fifty years to one of the most wonderful women on earth, Neville began his career as a chemical engineer and finished it as a high school teacher. He gave everything to his students, working tirelessly during the week and tutoring each weekend to make a difference in the lives that he could. He certainly made a difference in mine.

"One of the most important things in life is to complete what you start," he said to me right before I began to take my writing seriously.

He never gave me advice, and the one time that he did, it was surprisingly simple. Still, it stuck, and during the toughest writing days, when my story was wholly unwilling to be told, my father's words kept me going.

Two books came out of the strength that he gave me, and even with that strength, this novel was not easy to write. So much of this series is an exploration of the relationships between fathers and sons that sitting down to tell more of it often felt like I was being forced to face the fact that my father was gone, and losing him had already blown a hole right through me.

But reminding myself that my dad was there to raise me, teach me, watch me get married, and see me have a son of my own keeps me moving forward. He was there for me in every way that he could be, and I know that's not always possible. So, if this pain is the price for having had and being loved by a father like him, then I'll pay it gladly.

This book is for Neville Leopold Winter, whom I never stopped calling Daddy.

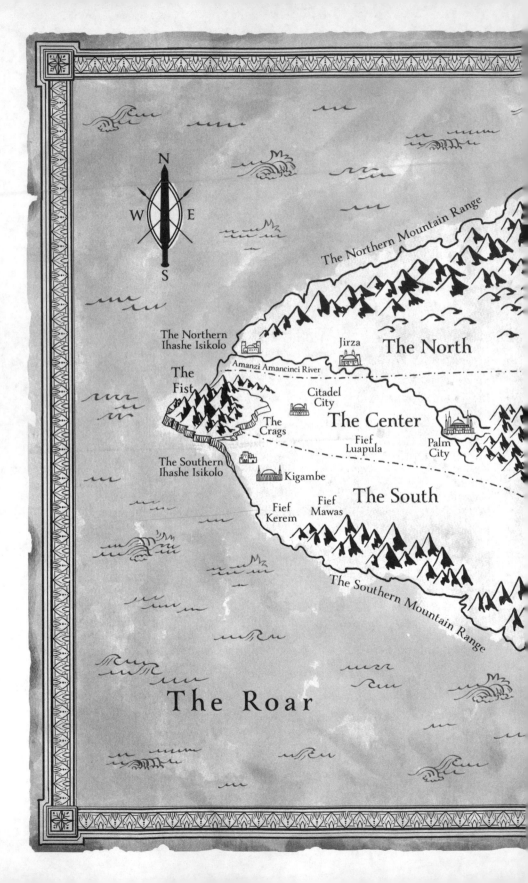

The Northern
Fortress

The Front Line

The Central
Mountains

The Southern
Fortress

Fief
Dakur

The Curse

THE
FIRES OF
VENGEANCE

CHAPTER ONE

JABARI ONAI

W ill he die?"

The voice woke him, returning him to torture. He knew he was in a hospital bed in Citadel City's Guardian Keep and that his body had been blasted by dragon fire, but Jabari Onai did not know why the Goddess would keep him alive in such misery.

He tried to open his eyes, and pain roared across his face in scorching waves. His eyelids had melted and fused together, leaving him to peer out at a world as if from behind a field of long grass.

He made to speak, to beg Tau or the Sah priestesses and priests to release him from his anguish, but he couldn't make a sound. His throat was too badly burned to manage it.

"I won't tell you he's going to die," Jabari heard a woman's voice say, "but I can't say that he'll live either."

The speaker moved toward the foot of his bed, and through the jagged gaps between his burned eyelids, he caught a glimpse of her standing next to Tau. She was a priestess of the Sah medicinal order.

"He's only survived this long because he's Noble," she said. "Their bodies can withstand more and they heal faster than us, but the damage that was done to him...it's a miracle he's still breathing."

"He's a fighter," Tau said. "He's always been one, and if you can give him any sort of chance, he'll take up the fight and do his best to win it."

"We won't give up...," she said.

Jabari heard a chair being pulled across the floor. It creaked when someone sat in it.

"I'm here, Jabari. It's Tau and I'm here."

"He can't hear you," the priestess said. "The pain...we're giving him herbs to help him rest. It's too cruel otherwise."

"Will it disturb him, if I'm here?" Tau asked.

"No," she said. "We should all be so lucky to have someone with us at the...at a time like this."

Jabari heard footsteps. The priestess was leaving, and when the sound of her shoes tapping against the floor faded, Tau leaned over him to take his hand. He did it gently, but it didn't matter.

Pain exploded from Jabari's burned fingers, and unable to make a sound or resist, he stared through the holes in his eyelids at his friend's scarred and worried face, hoping beyond hope that Tau could see enough of his eyes to recognize the light of consciousness in them. Tau didn't see—he kept hold of Jabari's hand—and desperate for any relief, Jabari sought refuge in his other senses. He caught the scent of leather, bronze, and earth from Tau and struggled to pull comfort from the familiar, but his agony made room for nothing but itself.

"I want you to know you did it," Tau said. "You're the man you always wanted to be. You don't need the blood of a Greater Noble to be an Ingonyama, not when you have their spirit, their courage."

He could hear Tau choking up, and that hurt too.

"Jabari, no matter what comes, I'll make certain the Omehi remember you for that."

There was silence for a while, and though his mind was slow, sluggish from the herbs, in his head, Jabari was screaming. The burns demanded it.

"It could have been different, neh? If not for the testing?" Tau said, whispering. "Feels like a thousand lifetimes ago. I just wanted to see you succeed, but when has the world ever cared what a Lesser wanted?"

Jabari would never forget that day. Tau had sparred with that spoiled brat, Kagiso, bloodying the fool in front of Guardian Councillor Abasi Odili. He'd been stupid enough to injure the Petty Noble, and Odili, intent on seeing the Lesser repaid for the insult, tasked Kellan Okar to remind Tau of his place.

Refusing to let his son face the already legendary Indlovu initiate, Aren fought Kellan Okar instead, losing his hand in the bout. It was a tragedy, but Jabari, like everyone else, could see that Kellan was trying to spare Aren's life, and it could have ended there. It should have ended there, but Tau picked up his father's fallen sword and aimed it at Kellan's back.

Stupid. There were Lessers and Drudge everywhere, and they all saw what Tau did. He'd threatened a Noble and Abasi Odili couldn't overlook that. The guardian councillor had Tau's father killed and then he called off the Indlovu initiate testing, threatening the stability of Kerem as a fief.

In just a few short breaths, a personal tragedy had become a disaster, and it only got worse. On the march home, Tau attacked Lekan, accusing Jabari's brother of being responsible for Aren's death, and twice in one day, Tau forced the hand of his betters. It had broken Jabari's heart to do it, but the only way he could save Tau from himself was to remove him from Lekan's reach, and so he banished his lifelong friend from Kerem.

Tau's voice pulled Jabari from the memory. "They killed my father and I was going to make them pay. I was going to join the military so I could challenge each one of them to a blood duel. I wanted to kill them and it was the only way I could do it without the Nobles coming for my family."

If Jabari didn't know how the story ended, he'd have sworn he was listening to the ravings of a madman.

"I thought I could become enough of a fighter to challenge and best an Ingonyama like Dejen Olujimi," Tau said, and as if the man's image was etched in his mind, Jabari could still see the soldier who'd killed Tau's father.

Dejen Olujimi had been more muscle than man. Dejen Olujimi had been one of the Omehi's best fighters. . . . Had been.

"I was so angry," Tau said. "I went to see Lekan before leaving the fief."

That part Jabari had not known, and he felt his breath come faster.

"I went to tell him that when next we met, I'd kill him for his part in my father's death."

For the first time since waking, Jabari's pain pulled back.

"Lekan came at me with a knife. He's the one who gave me the scar," Tau said, letting his fingertips brush the mark that ran from his nose to his cheek. "I fought him. I—I defended myself, and... he died."

He died. That was how Tau put it. He died. The words boomed in Jabari's head like a war drum.

His mother had cried for days when they found the body at the bottom of the stairs. An accidental fall, they'd been told, a slip after too much drink. His mother had cried and cursed and become withdrawn. She'd lost a son and a piece of her soul that day.

"I fled to Kigambe, tested in the Ihashe trials, and made it into Jayyed Ayim's scale," Tau continued. "I was lucky, and just like you said, there's no better umqondisi than Jayyed."

Jabari prayed for the strength to strangle the Lesser he'd called a friend and treated as an equal. His brother hadn't been perfect, but no one was. Lekan had just needed a chance to grow into himself and his responsibilities, but that chance was taken away when Tau stole him from the world and from his family.

"I gave my life to training. I was determined to be enough of a fighter to find justice for my father's death. It was the only thing that mattered before I saw Zuri in Citadel City."

Jabari's pain was back and the medicine in his system called to him, offering him oblivion, if he'd take it. He preferred the pain. He wanted to hear everything Tau had to say.

"She saved me, Jabari. The life I'd made wasn't worth living. Finding her in this city saved me." Tau paused.

Tau let go of his hand and Jabari thanked the Goddess. It galled him to lie helpless while his brother's murderer coddled him.

"It was here that I had my first chance at Kellan Okar. I was goaded into a fight with him in one of the city's circles. I wanted to tear his insides out and thought I could do it," Tau said. "I'd already learned to fight with two swords, and I was good, very good." Tau laughed, bitterly. "Kellan destroyed me," he said.

He should have killed you, Jabari thought.

"I'd given every waking moment to my training. I'd become the strongest fighter in the Southern Ihashe Isikolo, but I was still no match for him. Zuri had to save me from him, and I had to flee this city like a runaway Drudge."

Because you're no better than one, thought Jabari.

"I'd given my life to become the fighter I needed to be, but it wasn't enough," Tau said. "I had to give my soul to the cause too. So I did."

Jabari didn't understand, and he waited for Tau to explain.

"What I discovered is more curse than gift, and it's there, waiting for any foolish enough to reach for it. You see, we all have demons," Tau said. "I just learned to use mine."

He was speaking in riddles.

"My scale, we made it to the Queen's Melee, and it was the first time Lessers would compete in it in a generation," Tau said. "I was part of the improbable and, Jabari, I'd become the impossible. I was finally ready for Kellan Okar, and then I learned that Queen Tsiora had brokered a secret peace treaty with the Xiddeen, threatening everything I'd worked for."

Tau must have been uncomfortable with where his story was going. He kept shifting in his chair, making its legs scrape the floor.

"Scale Jayyed fought well and we made it into the semifinals," he said. "We were matched with Kellan's scale, your scale, and just like that, I had my first real chance. I could kill Kellan in the tournament and it'd be nothing but an unfortunate accident."

More chair shifting.

"You saw me there. You know I abandoned my sword brothers to get to him," Tau said. "I gave up the family I'd found at the isikolo for revenge, and when I held Okar's life in my hands, I hesitated. I didn't kill him when I had my chance, and then my chance was gone. Kellan Okar lived and we were knocked out of the melee."

Jabari had been stunned when he saw what Tau had done to Kellan. He'd thought the Greater Noble to be invincible, and the idea of the boy he'd grown up with doing that to Scale Osa's inkokeli was unthinkable.

"The men in my scale hated me, and Zuri and Jayyed tried to tell me that Kellan wasn't to blame for my father's death, but I wouldn't listen, and there was no time to be convinced. The Xiddeen invaded."

Jabari remembered it, the sound of the horns that night.

"It made no sense; peace was so close," Tau said. "It made no sense until I found out that the queen's Royal Nobles had planned a coup and betrayed her. They refused to submit their civilization to those they saw as savages. So, instead, they attacked the Xiddeen in secret, using a dragon to burn tens of thousands of their people to dust.

"The invasion wasn't the Xiddeen abandoning the peace treaty. It was them retaliating for the slaughter we visited on their women, men, and children," Tau said.

Jabari didn't want to hear about why the hedeni had done what they'd done. It didn't matter. He'd lost sword brothers that night. Omehi had died that night.

"In the battle in the Fist, Jayyed, Chinedu, and most of my scale went to the Goddess," Tau said.

It had been the same for Jabari's scale. They'd been massacred.

"The Xiddeen had us beat and we fled, retreating to Citadel City, hoping to find safety there. What we found were Odili and his traitors trying to kill the queen," Tau said. "You remember, neh? We fought alongside each other then, in her defense."

Jabari breathed out as hard as he could. He didn't want any grace from Tau, and it was a lie to say they'd fought together, as if they were equals in the act. He'd almost gotten himself killed several times over, and Tau had been forced to keep him alive each time.

"And we did it," Tau said. "We stopped Odili from getting to the queen, and I put an end to Dejen Olujimi."

Jabari didn't see their battle. He'd been in the room with the queen at the time, losing another fight to an Indlovu. He did, however, see the battle's aftermath. Dejen had been enraged when they'd dueled and Tau had blinded him, cut him to shreds, and stabbed him through the heart.

Tau had fought an Enraged Ingonyama alone and he'd butchered him. On its face, it was an impossible act, but then again, Tau had a secret. He had, Jabari thought, picturing his brother's funeral burning, a few secrets.

"Odili fled and we gave chase. He was trapped, but by then the Xiddeen were at the gates." Tau was speaking too fast. It was making it hard for Jabari to make sense of the words. "Zuri called a dragon to make the Xiddeen back down, and Odili had his men attack the creature, creating enough confusion to escape. Zuri, she...she couldn't keep the dragon under control and it went mad. It killed people."

Jabari wanted Tau to stop.

"It was going to kill my sword brothers."

Jabari had heard enough.

"But you didn't let it. It blew fire at good men and another good man shielded them, taking the brunt of the blast. You saved them."

It felt like Jabari was gasping for air, just like the night when the fires had embraced him, boiling away even his tears.

"The dragon turned on Zuri then," Tau said, his words coming out in a broken stutter. "It...it attacked her...it...she died that night, and Odili escaped, and the queen leashed the dragon. She leashed it, threatened the Xiddeen with it, and gave the warlord his son in exchange for their retreat. In exchange for a reprieve."

Jabari didn't know. He didn't know Zuri was dead. He'd grown up with her, even fancied her a little when they were too young for him to know she was just a Lesser.

"Before long, the Xiddeen will be back to finish what they started, and our people are split," Tau said. "The Royals have aligned themselves with Abasi Odili and the self-styled Queen Esi. Many of the other Nobles sided with them too."

We're all dead, then, thought Jabari.

"But it can't end this way. There's still so much to do...." Tau trailed off, and that's when Jabari heard the footsteps coming closer to them. "Keep fighting, Jabari Onai. I could use the help of a good and selfless man."

"Champion," a woman's voice said, "you're needed."

She stepped in and out of view. She was wearing a Gifted's robes. Zuri, was Jabari's first thought, but Tau had told him that Zuri was dead and it couldn't be her.

The chair beside Jabari's bed creaked and a shadow fell over him.

"Keep fighting," Tau whispered. "We'll get the man who hurt us both."

"Champion, we must hurry," the Gifted said.

"Abasi Odili won't escape what he's done," Tau told him. "Keep fighting, and I swear that before it consumes us, we'll burn our pain to ash in the fires of vengeance."

UNDENIABLE

W here are we going?" Tau asked the Gifted who'd called
him from Jabari's infirmary bed.

She hurried him along and back to his rooms, telling him that the
queen was preparing to attend a meeting with several Nobles and
that Nyah wanted him there too. The answer was not comforting. It
was late, and though Tau's experience with midnight meetings was
limited, he couldn't imagine they were a good thing.

Once in his rooms, the Gifted woman urged him to don the
dragon-scale swords and champion's armor that the queen had given
him. The black blades, mounted onto his father's and grandfather's
sword hilts, felt natural at his sides, but the armor, black-and-red
leather in the Ingonyama style, made him uncomfortable.

It wasn't the armor's fit or quality. The queen's latest offering was
a marvel that gave Tau greater freedom of movement and far more
protection than his old gambeson. The form of the thing wasn't
what worried him; it was its function.

Wearing it named him the queen's champion. It told all Omehi
that he was one of the best of them, and Tau had no illusions about
what the Nobles would think of that.

"Champion...," the Gifted said with a shiver as she looked him
up and down. "Champion Solarin." She raised her chin. "I'm Gifted

Thandi, but…I was a High Common before," she said with pride, though Tau couldn't be sure if it was due to her current station or some strange valuing of the one from which she'd escaped.

He still had trouble reconciling the idea of Gifted as ever having been Lessers. The woman in front of him looked strong, well-fed, and the robes she wore were pristine. The very essence of her seemed something other than Lesser, given the grace and confidence with which she moved, her smooth, unweathered skin, and the ease with which she let her beauty show.

Lessers didn't do that. They buried the fullness of what they were inside themselves because drawing attention to yourself around Nobles was a quick way to be reminded of where you actually stood.

"They'll think I have no right to wear it," he said, his thoughts spilling out before better sense could hold them back.

"They'll be wrong."

"How can you say that?"

"I say it because if there was any way to deny you, they'd have done it," she said. "The only way to get as far as you have, considering what they think of us, is to become undeniable." She waved him on. "Follow me."

Moving fast, they walked the halls, passing a few guards, who all saluted Tau, their military instincts overriding any reservations they might have about the man wearing the armor of an Ingonyama. Thandi led him to an unfamiliar and empty part of the Guardian Keep, where the walls were unadorned by tapestry or painting and the floors were bare, echoing the tip-tap of their footfalls. Leading him to the end of the undressed corridor, she stopped in front of a locked door that was little taller than Tau and reinforced by a bronze frame.

"I'm sorry for your friend, the Petty Noble who was burned," she said, revealing the key hidden in the bauble on her necklace and opening the door. "I heard he saved many lives."

"He did," Tau said.

Beyond the door were narrow stairs leading down to darkness, and Gifted Thandi led them on.

"A moment, Lady Gifted," Tau said, trying to keep the fear from his voice as he eyed the way ahead. "The stairs . . . you want me to go into the tunnels beneath the Keep?"

The robed woman looked over her shoulder at him. "Come, Champion," she said. "The vizier is waiting."

Tau took a step back. "I think I need to know more about what we're doing and why, or she may be waiting awhile."

Thandi tilted her head and blinked at him. She wasn't like the other Gifted he'd met. Most of them were ascetic in appearance and stern, but Thandi's face was round, and she had large eyes and a mouth that slipped easily into a smile. She looked young, honest, hopeful.

"The tunnels are the best way to move through the keep unseen," she said.

"Why do we need to move unseen? Are we in danger?"

She slipped into that easy smile, but it didn't extend beyond her lips. "Yes."

He was fine for the first two turns in the torchlit tunnels, but after that, with the exit far behind them, Tau's limbs began to shake and his mouth went dry. He hid his discomfort from the Gifted, unwilling to appear weak, but the nausea made him misstep and he fell against the nearest wall.

"Champion?"

"I'm well," he said over a tongue thick as porridge. "I don't . . . I don't like small places."

"Can I help?" she asked.

He waved her off and squinted his eyes. "I'll be fine," he said, imagining himself in the open air of Kerem's mountains. "I can do this . . . ," he muttered, pushing off the wall as a peal of thunder cracked loud enough to send bits of raw adobe raining down from the tunnel's makeshift ceiling.

Tau dropped to the ground and scurried to the wall, jamming his back against it while his heart leapt in his chest like a stick-poked frog.

"It's just the storm," the Gifted said, kneeling beside him and offering him a hand. "The tunnels are rough cut, but they won't collapse. I promise."

Tau stared at her but didn't see Gifted Thandi. He was remembering the last time someone had tried to comfort him in these tunnels. He was remembering Zuri and noting that the storm had raged since the night he'd lost her. He'd never seen one last so long and wondered if even the heavens mourned with him.

"Let me help," the Gifted said.

Like Zuri's, her eyes were brown, but that was the only feature they shared.

"I don't need it," he said, and though Thandi looked like she doubted that, she didn't get the chance to respond.

Nyah, looking like she hadn't slept in days, walked around the far corner of the tunnel.

"Gifted Thandi, you're late," the older woman said, spotting them both, and then, behaving as if it was perfectly normal to find Tau on his ass in the Guardian Keep's tunnels, she greeted him. "Evening, Champion."

"Vizier." Tau said, locking his eyes on her face so he didn't have to see the floor sliding back and forth.

"You look awful," she said.

"There's the sun chiding the cook fire for the hut's swelter," he said.

Gifted Thandi chuckled, Nyah turned to her, and Thandi pretended she'd been clearing her throat.

"Does this happen every time?" Nyah asked, swinging back to him. "Are you always unmanned by enclosed spaces?"

"It's uncomfortable but could be worse," he shot back. "I could be the youngling."

It was hot in the tunnels, but the temperature seemed to drop with the look Nyah gave him.

"Do you know why the youngling's presence and purpose are revealed to so few, Champion?" she asked.

"Because it's wrong," he said, working his way back to his feet.

"It's because the powerless, having no understanding or experience with how much real power can save or destroy, think too simply. They see things as either right or wrong, but the world and the purposes of those in it are distorted, misjudged when reduced to so basic a binary."

Tau shook his head, and testing his balance, he took a step toward Nyah. "Wrong is wrong," he said, needing to know what was around the corner behind her and seeing that, only a few strides away, the tunnel ended at a closed door. "It's in there, isn't it?" he asked.

"Turn around," Nyah said, pointing back the way he'd just come. "We're going that way."

He wasn't ready to leave. "They're intelligent, neh? It's why they can hold on to the Gifted when they're entreated. They're intelligent and you trapped one of them underground and behind locked doors for almost as long as we've lived on this land."

The vizier held his gaze with hers. "You think too simply, and you're wrong on the last count." She crossed her arms and stepped aside. "The doors to unwanted truths are rarely locked, since so few wish to face what's behind them."

Nyah didn't think he'd go in. She thought him unwilling to witness the cost of their survival, but Tau had seen the cost and suffered it. He'd been there, helpless, forced to watch Zuri spend her life to save others, and he'd be damned if he couldn't at least stand in the presence of the thing that had killed her. So without even a last look in the vizier's direction, he stepped up and pushed open the unlocked door.

TOOLS

The dragon's prison was hot as Hoard and cavernous. It stank like an inyoka's failed eggs and was lit by guttering torches losing a battle against the dark. The space, taken in its entirety, looked like the Goddess had inverted and dropped a rough-hewn bowl of hardened clay onto a cobbled path, and Tau stood on cracked, crumbling stones, smoothed by the passage of countless feet.

A few steps farther into the room, spread out around the cavern at equal distances, were six Gifted. They held themselves stiff as boards, hoods up, eyes closed, heads down, and most of them swayed with the unsteadiness of exhaustion. They were in Isihogo. Tau could tell. It was also the only explanation that could account for the restless slumber in which the beast before him was held.

With no more than forty strides separating them, it was the closest Tau had come to a dragon, and though it was far from grown, he was awed by the creature's size. The youngling was massive, and its scales, blacker than tar and harder than hammered bronze, blended into one another in a darkness so complete he couldn't hold on to their shape or depth in his mind.

In the prison, no one spoke, but it was not silent. The chamber rumbled and hissed with every breath the creature took, and with his back to the tunnels and the wide-open cavern in front of him, Tau's stomach had begun to settle, but trying to make sense of the dragon turned it anew. He couldn't focus on any part of it without the scales twisting the light and pulling his eyes this way and that.

"Goddess...," he said.

And behind him, Gifted Thandi whispered to Nyah. "There's been an edification from Palm. It's about the handmaidens."

"Are they well?" the vizier asked.

Ignoring them, Tau walked farther into the prison, trying to understand the thing before him.

"They rode past Palm's walls last night," Thandi told Nyah. "An alarm was raised over the missing horses, but the handmaidens were not pursued."

"They got out," Nyah said. "Praise the Goddess, the news will ease the queen's mind."

From muzzle to tail, the youngling was many times Tau's length. It was big enough to smash him beneath a single one of its claws, and being closer, he could see that it was missing scales along its body. The skin beneath the scaleless patches was gray, puckered, and angry, like the surface of a badly healed wound.

He looked back at them. "You've held that thing here for lifetimes, in an existence between dreaming and death. You've used it to control its kin and harvested weapons from it by ripping pieces of its body away."

"We've kept our people safe, Champion," Nyah said, letting her gaze fall to the guardian swords at his sides, "and none among us are innocent when all among us benefit from what is done here."

Unwilling to face her, Tau turned back to the prisoner. The heat, he realized, was coming from it. He went closer.

The dragon's eyes were closed and its mouth was shut, though he could see a few of its fangs peeking beyond the meat of its lips. Its teeth were coal black and scythe-like, tools for tearing flesh.

"Do you think this helps, being here?" Nyah asked.

He ignored her, letting the heat assault him, punishing himself for his inadequacies, and Nyah walked up to stand beside him. She stood tall and proud, even though her breathing was rapid and she had to squint against the invisible blaze radiating from the young-ling. "Our queen needs us."

Tau said nothing, his eyes on the dragon and its stirrings.

"While you've sequestered yourself these past few days, the remaining Greater Noblewomen in the city took it upon themselves to form a ruling council." Nyah's mouth twisted. "They think to 'advise' the queen."

"There's already a ruling council in Palm City," Tau said.

"The insects in Palm rule over none but the treacherous, and how can they be a ruling council when they bow to Odili?"

The sounds of the three syllables making up Odili's name felt like the tap of fingers wrapping round Tau's throat. They made it hard to swallow and harder to speak.

"Are all monarchies so brittle?" he asked. "Why can Odili claim that the queen's sister is our true ruler and get Palm City bowing to Queen Esi instead of Queen Tsiora?"

"It's a mistake to think this break the result of a single blow," Nyah said, shifting back half a step and wiping a hand across the sweat on her forehead. "In the moment, as the knife scrapes your spine, it may seem that way, but the ones who'd kill you from behind are not hot-blooded. They'd never trust your death to just one strike."

"So, there were other attempts to overthrow Tsiora?" Tau asked. "Well, you're the queen's vizier. Why didn't you stop it? Why didn't you see this coming?"

"It's always coming," she said. "The knife was no surprise, only its timing."

She wiped her forehead again and took another step away from the heat.

She tilted her head toward the dragon. "What you said earlier—you were right. We've enslaved this creature and kept it from its family."

Tau had his left hand on the pommel of his strong-side sword and his grip tightened. "Why say that? Did you let me come in here to taunt me with the things you've done?"

"Could I have stopped you?" she asked. "And why shouldn't you see how far we're all capable of going to keep those we love safe?"

He turned to face her. The skin on her lips was cracking from the heat.

"I love our queen, Champion Solarin, and this supposed ruling council meets without her," she said. "Can you understand what that means? Can you appreciate the position in which we find ourselves?" She turned away from him, the dragon, and its heat. "Come, now, we're needed."

Nyah wanted him to fight for the queen, and maybe Queen Tsiora was a better choice to lead the Omehi than the Royal Nobles or the Xiddeen, but Tau hadn't sworn the champion's oath because he thought it important to fight for Tsiora's throne. She'd been sitting on it when his father was murdered, and having her there hadn't helped Aren at all.

The queen's cause wasn't his. Tau was fighting to get to Abasi Odili so he could rip him apart, turn him inside out, piece by bloody piece, because that was what it would take for the Nobles to see and hear a man like him. To be understood, he'd speak the one language the powerful share with the powerless, the language of pain, fear, and loss. The powerful had to be shown that people can only be pushed so close to the flame before they catch fire and burn everything down.

He walked closer to the dragon.

"The Royal Nobles are the architects of the coup and are lost to us," Nyah said. "The few Petty and Greater Nobles who still side with the queen are restless, rudderless. We can't allow them to think that the queen is too weak to hold us together. We need to put this ruling council in their place."

Tau's exposed skin felt hot enough to burn. "You want to barge into their meeting and surprise them," he said. "You want me there, with my swords and scarred face, to remind them that the queen has both words and weapons."

"Every tool has its purpose, Champion," she said. "Will you serve yours? Will you serve her?" Nyah looked at the dragon and back to him. "Or only yourself?"

Without waiting for an answer, she walked away, leaving Thandi behind.

The younger Gifted pointed at the ground behind him and closer to the dragon. "Watch the blood on the floor, Champion. It can kill."

Tau followed her finger and saw the wet blackness staining the cobbles in streaks. "That's its blood?"

"The youngling was wounded when it went aboveground, and in any case, the blood is poisonous," she said. "The Indlovu came and gathered as much as they could, but the Guardian's heat prevents any from getting close enough to get it all. Have a care."

"I see."

She nodded to him, paused, and spoke. "You'll come, won't you?" she asked. "Nyah isn't telling you everything."

Tau had his back to her, but he was listening.

"We cannot rely on the loyalty of the others," she said. "The Nobles follow General Otobong. He's the highest-ranking Indlovu in the keep, and he's close with members of this...ruling council."

Tau said nothing.

"We do need your help," Thandi said before following the vizier.

Tau let her go and got as close to the creature as he could, close enough to reach out and touch it, the heat making it feel as if he were standing on top of a funeral pyre. Still, he leaned closer, letting his scalded lips almost brush the dragon's scales.

"She felt guilt for what's done to you, and I won't blame you for her death," he whispered to the beast. "I just want you to know that the Omehi intend nothing but this for you." The flesh on his cheeks began to peel. "They wouldn't forgive it if they'd been treated this way and so can't believe that you can either. They think you'd kill us all if you could and that's why they'll never let you go." He shook his head. "But Zuri believed that this thing we've done...that we do to you is a blight on our souls. She told me that a reckoning is coming, but I wonder if it must."

Unable to take the heat, Tau stepped back.

"When the time comes, I promise you freedom or a quick death," he said. "As soon as I'm able, either way I'll release you."

The dragon's eye snapped open. Its bloodred iris ringed a pupil so deep and dark it felt like he were gazing into an abyss. Then the pupil thinned vertically, focusing, and the dragon shifted its bulk, trying to stand.

Hearing something fall to the ground behind him, Tau leapt back, swords in his hands.

"Champion!"

Tau shot a look in the voice's direction. It was one of the Gifted tasked with keeping the youngling under control, and she was pointing to the woman next to her. The Gifted had collapsed, unconscious.

"Please," the pointing Gifted said, "your closeness to the Guardian makes the work more taxing. Pleas—"

The dragon roared, the sound cracking inside Tau's head like a whip, and the eye facing him rolled in the dragon's head as the creature scrabbled at the cobbled floor, trying to lift itself. Swords ready, Tau shifted sideways and away from its claws when movement from the circle of Gifted caught his attention.

The woman who had collapsed was on her knees, and she raised a hand in the youngling's direction. The effect was immediate. With the circle of Gifted complete again, the dragon could not fight its way free. Backing away, Tau watched as the youngling's pupil dilated and lost focus, and the eye finally closed.

"Champion," the one who had spoken earlier said, teeth gritted, the strain of manipulating her gift evident, "you must leave us to this."

With another glance at the Gifted on her knees, and wishing he had something more to offer the women whose work he'd made more difficult, Tau nodded and left the prison. His skin burned, but that wasn't what hurt. He was thinking about Zuri.

The days since her death had been impossible; the nights were worse. Like the youngling, Tau had been living a life little better than death, but unlike the beast behind him, he could still control the direction in which his fire flew.

He'd go to the queen. She needed him and he needed her. He'd go to the queen, because at the end of his path with her stood Abasi Odili.

REUNION

Tau found his sword brothers waiting for him in the hallway leading to the council chambers. He hadn't spent time with any of them since the night of the battle, and the faces of those present brought to mind the faces of those he'd never see again.

"Tau!" Hadith said, striding over and clasping him wrist to wrist before pulling him into a hug. "It's good to see you."

"And you," Tau said. His head was spinning. The tunnels hadn't relinquished their hold on him yet, and he wished he'd had a little more time to come back to himself before running into everyone, but even so, he couldn't deny how good it felt to see his brothers.

Uduak, waiting for Hadith to release him, wrapped Tau up in an embrace that pinched his still-healing ribs. "Tau," the big man said.

"Common of Kerem!" Themba, smiling large enough to show teeth and the gaps where teeth should have been, made a show of examining him from scalp to sole. "The new cloths and swords suit you."

Kellan, standing at attention a few strides back, saluted. "Champion Solarin."

Feeling awkward at having an Ingonyama showing him such respect, Tau returned the salute. Kellan had proven himself to be a decent man, but it was still hard for Tau to think of them as peers or as being on the same side.

"It's good to see you, brother," Yaw said, appearing out of the shadows to clap Tau on the shoulder. "You've been missed."

"And you, brother," Tau said.

"Any chance we were called from our beds to get fancy swords too?" Themba asked. "The color on those blades matches my eyes."

None of them had their swords, and Tau wondered if there was any merit to Themba's joke. "It wasn't me who called you."

"Themba is just joking," Hadith said. "Well, not about us being woken up. We were all in our beds when Nyah sent for us. You're not coming from your rooms, though. Where were you?"

"Neh?" Tau asked, knowing Hadith well enough to guess he'd not missed Tau's unsteady gait.

Hadith put a hand on Tau's shoulder. "You look like you've been spending time in tight spaces," Hadith said, too low for the others to hear. "Where are you coming from, Champion?"

The queen and her retinue saved Tau from answering. Queen Tsiora Omehia walked into the large hallway from a smaller side entrance flanked by her vizier and Gifted Thandi. Behind them marched four members of the Queen's Guard.

Tau and the men with him went to their knees.

"Rise," the queen said. "We thank you for leaving your rest so early, and you have not been called to us frivolously." She nodded to Nyah.

"We go to the council chambers," Nyah told them. "It seems several Greater Noblewomen in this keep have taken it upon themselves to form a ruling council. Their rush to do so I will attribute to a desire to offer our monarch aid and wisdom, since anything else slips dangerously close to treason." Nyah clipped the syllables on the last word, making it sound even uglier than usual. "You have been asked for specifically. Most of you are Lessers, but you fought for your queen when it seemed hopeless to do so. Greater Noble Kellan Okar, nephew to the last champion, stands with you. He came to his queen's defense when few other Indlovu would do so."

Kellan bowed his head, accepting her praise.

Nyah returned the gesture, then turned to Tau, staring him down. "We are also joined by the queen's anointed champion," she said. "Champion Solarin, who has sworn to serve his queen for the rest of his days . . . or for as long as she finds his service worthy."

Tau had little patience for the way she kept needling him, and he stared back, holding her gaze with his own.

A breath passed and Nyah looked away, speaking to the others as she did so. "I do believe this so-called ruling council hopes to tie the Omehi back together, and I find no fault in that," she said. "However, forming their council in secret and excluding the queen from this gathering suggests that ending our civil strife is not their only aim.

"It's only been days, but the Noblewomen in that council chamber have forgotten who fought and died to stop Abasi Odili's coup. Well, you're going to remind them," Nyah said. "You're here because they need to see that the blades that beat Odili back are loyal to Queen Tsiora Omehia II, and not to councils, whether ruling or guardian."

"They think us too young to lead," the queen said, stepping forward and catching the eyes of everyone present. "They think the damage Odili has done can only be undone by their hands, hands they'll call experienced and deserving. But the Omehi have been steered by hands claiming those merits for generations, and yet today, a greater number of our people starve, suffer, and perish than ever before.

"The ruling councils have had their chance," she said, "and it was squandered on a war without end that slowly grinds our people to dust. That's the experience to which they lay claim, and we say it's not enough. We say it was never enough."

The queen walked by them, leading the way in her midnight-black dress edged in patterns of gold. Nyah, Thandi, and the Queen's Guard followed, and the rest of them came after.

"From her lips to the Goddess's ears," Tau heard Yaw mutter to himself as if in prayer.

"Champion," Nyah said over her shoulder, lips tight. "Perhaps you'd care to walk alongside your queen, as is customary?"

Feeling a mixture of annoyance and embarrassment, Tau sped up, moving past Themba, whose arched eyebrow and twinkling eyes made his face look like it was begging to be slapped. He caught up to the queen and they left the hallway, entering the Guardian Keep's anteroom.

Tau hadn't been back to it since the day he'd fought alongside Champion Okar, and it was strange to see the large circular space empty, without the chaos of a dozen life-and-death skirmishes. Otherwise, the strange room was as he remembered.

It had thick columns supporting a high balcony with two staircases offering access, and though such ostentation was still a sight, the columns, staircases, and balcony were nothing compared to the anteroom's centerpiece.

The anteroom was anchored by a fountain made of chalk-white stone that was filled with a swirling red liquid. Standing in the blood-colored waters was a towering statue of Champion Tsiory, his sword plunged into its depths, and through some artifice, the carmine slurry was drawn up into the statue so it flowed to Tsiory's sword hand and down the hilt and blade of the statue's weapon. It was a gory reminder of the costly nature of the Omehi's first days on the peninsula, and it disturbed Tau almost as much as the memory of the lives that been lost in the room only a few nights gone.

Tau pulled his eyes away and they settled on the corridor where his predecessor, Champion Okar, had fallen. Half-formed figures of gray hid in the murk, and Tau's hands snapped to his blade hilts.

He thought to draw, almost did, but the shapes remained motionless and the queen placed one of her strangely cool hands on his. Tau had to force himself not to yank away from the unexpected touch.

"We asked a sculptor to render the scene of Champion Okar's last stand," she said. "When the work is done, anyone who wishes to enter that hallway must pass the statues of the Queen's Guard who fell holding it. They must pass the likeness of Champion Okar, who gave his life for ours."

She watched him as she spoke, and this time, Tau was first to turn away. There was something in the way she looked at him. They were strangers, but she had no trouble letting her gaze linger. It made him feel like less of a person and more of a thing, like a favorite toy, long misplaced and only just found.

"Do you find it fitting?" his queen asked as they walked past the unfinished statues.

"I do...my queen. You honor Champion Okar and all who fought beside him."

"He honored us," she said, moving down the next hallway and into a part of the keep that was new to Tau.

They were in a short passageway ending at a tall wooden door guarded by two Indlovu. The soldiers snapped to attention when they saw the queen. Tau didn't pay them much mind. He was looking at the door.

The wood was pale, and even in the dim torchlight, he could see that it was made from brittle Xiddan timber. For all its size, he could kick it down, if needed.

"Open it," Queen Tsiora ordered, walking toward the Indlovu. "We have something to say to those inside."

The soldiers hesitated, glancing at each other, but the queen kept to her pace, moving forward as if the door were already open, and the two Indlovu hurried to make sure it would be.

COUNCILS

When the door to the council chambers opened, Tau heard a man's voice, cave-deep, arguing the end of some unheard point, but the voice faltered when the queen walked in. Tau and Nyah were next through the door, and the rest of their group came behind them.

The room was circular, enclosed, brightly lit, but smoky from the burning torches, and its floor was painted black. Holding court in its center, wearing the uniform of an Ingonyama, was a boulder of a man. His freshly shaven head gleamed and he had thick eyebrows that sat on a forehead large enough to keep rainfall from ever wetting his nose.

Tau guessed he was the owner of the deep voice, but it was just a guess. There were eleven other Indlovu in the chamber sitting on rising rows of concentric benches, and as the queen's group entered, they'd all stood to salute her. The queen ignored the military men, so Tau did the same, letting his eyes flit about to take in the rest of the space.

At first glance, the circular room gave the impression of no beginning or end, a room without hierarchy. It was a nice idea, but not an Omehian one, and across the room in front of Tau, instead of another row of benches, there was a line of tall-backed chairs on which six Greater Noblewomen sat. Queen Tsiora focused on them.

"My queen," said the heavy-browed Ingonyama, saluting hard enough to crack his skull were it not slate thick.

She inclined her head but didn't look at him. Instead, she spoke to one of the two women seated closest to the center among the six in the chairs. "What do you do here in the dark, Mirembe?"

"My queen," Mirembe said, rising to bow along with the other Noblewomen, "your presence is an honor."

"Is it?"

Head low, eyes up, Mirembe smiled as if the queen had made a joke. The Greater Noblewoman, with hair the color of Ihashe grays, had walked her path for many cycles and was still handsome. Her skin, the color of fresh coal, was unlined, her eyes were bright, barely a crinkling at their edges, and when she smiled, her teeth were cloud white. "It's an honor, my queen, as always, to be near you."

"If the honor is so great, why not ask us to attend this...gathering?"

Mirembe took her seat, her lush dress billowing like a wave when she did. "We gather solely to explore the paths that lie before us. We gather to collect our thoughts so that, once they are collected, they can be presented to you, my queen."

Nyah took a step forward, drawing even with Tsiora. "By what right?" she asked.

Mirembe looked like she hadn't understood the question. "Vizier?"

"You heard me."

Mirembe flashed that cloud-white smile, and in Tau's mind it stretched wide enough to touch her ears. "Vizier Nyah, I did hear you but don't understand your concern. We're simply fulfilling our duty as the peninsula's one true ruling council."

Nyah waved a dismissive hand in Mirembe's direction. "You meet in the middle of the night with the queen's generals, vote yourselves to power, and have the audacity to—"

"Have a care, Vizier," Mirembe said. "You have a voice in council decisions, but that tradition is not enough for me to allow you to undermine us." She shifted in her chair, leaning forward. "We were unanimous without you, but if you'd like to vote against this council's formation, you can do so now, though it'll change nothing, given our majority."

The air was thick with tension. Tau could feel it like it was crawling over him.

"Majority? Who do you six represent but yourselves?" asked Nyah.

Mirembe's smile slipped. "We are the Ruling Council. We represent the Omehi."

"The unabridged title is 'the Queen's Ruling Council,'" Tsiora said, "and perhaps it's time your queen had her say."

Mirembe's smile came back, and when she spoke, Tau saw that her teeth had grown and curved like fangs. "Your Majesty, if it was my decision to make, your say would be all that counted."

Tau squeezed his eyes shut, doing his best to reject the hallucinations as the chairwoman continued to talk.

"It pains me to even mention it," Mirembe said, "but as we all know and accept, Omehi law dictates that the queen's will be balanced with the will of the Guardian and Ruling Councils."

Tau opened his eyes. The chairwoman looked normal again. He'd shaken the vision loose, but Nyah had noticed his behavior and was looking at him from the corner of her eye.

"Our war with the Xiddeen nears its climax at a time when our queendom has been sundered," Mirembe said. "Our existence depends on the choices we make these next few days."

The general nodded.

"Your Majesty," Mirembe said, "we're at war and war should not be the business of queens or ruling councils. We have our people to consider, which is why general Ade Otobong has been asked to lead our new Guardian Council and your military."

"So, you've selected and seek to raise to power the man who will act as the third balancing force in our queendom?" Tsiora asked in a way that reminded Tau of how he might stab at an opponent.

"We have and he will," Mirembe said, voice trembling as she swept her arm out in Otobong's direction. She sounded earnest to the point of being fearful, but her eyes told a different story. They were bright, sharp, and bold as bronze. "My queen, to end this civil strife, regain Palm City and the faith of all our Noble people, we need to be strong enough to show Odili that the cost of war is too great to bear. We need to present Abasi Odili with an opponent he has no choice but to respect, and this council, servants to you, one and all, have that person in General Otobong."

"In just one rainy night, you've decided all that?" the queen asked.

She was too far away to do so, but Mirembe reached out as if she would hold Tsiora, if only she could. "We have, my queen. My dear, we have. Tell her, General."

"The council has voted to give me authority over all the Ihagu, Ihashe, and Indlovu who remain loyal to Your Majesty," General Otobong said. "The path ahead will not be an easy one, but with the Goddess's blessing, I believe we can reunite our people and retain hold of the peninsula when the Xiddeen attack."

"With the Goddess's blessing..." Tsiora seemed to be speaking to herself.

Oblivious to her tone, Otobong charged ahead. "We believe Odili has the equivalent of one and a half dragons of fighting men with him in Palm City. He has five scales of Indlovu and thirty-something Lesser scales that are pretty evenly split between Ihashe and Ihagu. In this city, we have one military dragon made up of a scale and a third of Indlovu and twenty-eight scales of Lessers.

"The numbers make it clear that we can't take the capital before the Xiddeen return, so our first step will be to open talks with Palm City. I'm confident this will go well because Odili knows me. He knows my record and that I'm good to my word." Otobong clapped a fist to his chest three times. "He knows he's better off avoiding the fight I'd give him, and once he's offered a full pardon, we'll be able to negotiate reasonable terms with him and Queen Esi."

At the word "pardon," Tau's lips curled back over his teeth and his hands dropped to the hilts of his swords. The movement wasn't subtle, and the general's heavy brows pulled together as his eyes dipped to Tau's sheathed weapons. He was about to say something when the queen spoke.

"Queen Esi?" she asked, her words so quiet they were hard to hear.

"Ah... Your Majesty," Otobong began, "it is your sister's current styling, and with no offense meant, I simply—"

"Queen Esi?" Tsiora said, louder this time.

"Queen Tsiora," Mirembe said, emphasizing her name, "I believe the general only meant to suggest that, once talks begin, it will be prudent to extend every courtesy to the other side. Isn't that right, General?"

"As you wish, Chairwoman."

"Yes," Mirembe said, dipping her head low to the queen.

"Enough," Tsiora said. "Save such scheming for another day. We won't allow—"

"Scheming?" Mirembe said, voice high. "My queen, that's not a fair—"

"Your queen is speaking!" Nyah said.

Mirembe stood, feigning no subservience, and, instead of showing a lowered head or lipless smile, she flexed her hands into claws. "Vizier, you overstep."

"We said enough," Tsiora said. "This meeting rests on the mistaken belief that we cannot retake our capital and throne."

Keeping his hands on his hilts, Tau looked to the queen. He'd chosen her side and that was where he'd stay. She'd promised him Odili. But even without having laid eyes on it, he knew enough about Palm City, which had tall, thick walls and stood between the forks of the Amanzi River, to know that General Otobong was telling the truth.

They didn't have the strength of arms to wrest the capital from Odili's grasp and wouldn't without bolstering the number of soldiers they already had. To do that, they'd have to call up most of the Ihagu and Ihashe left in the peninsula.

As far as Tau knew, it was within the queen's rights to do so. She could order the fiefs to send their fighters to her, but if the other umbusi were anything like Jabari's mother, they wouldn't take kindly to orders that stripped them of their soldiers and left them defenseless. Worst of all, if they decided they were better off disobeying, it would weaken Tsiora. A leader whose orders aren't followed does not remain a leader for long.

"My queen, I'm afraid I haven't laid out our position clearly enough," Otobong said. "Please allow me to explain."

"Would you, General?" Tsiora asked, offering him a dead smile. "There are so many details."

If Otobong kept talking about pardoning Odili, Tau would be the first to gut the general, but given the queen's tone, his sense that the man was in danger was so strong, he almost wanted to warn him to shut up.

"Of course, my queen," Otobong said, nodding hard enough to make his jowls shake. "You see, we can't take the capital by siege. We don't have the numbers, and even if we did, we don't have the time. There's less than a moon cycle before our truce with the hedeni ends, and if the totality of our forces are not aligned by then, we'll be wiped out."

"Thank you, General. That's very helpful," Tsiora said. "Helpful, but wrong."

"Wrong? Uh . . . how's that . . . Your Majesty?"

"We don't need to siege the capital," she said. "When we go to take it, the gates will be opened for us."

Otobong narrowed his eyes, trying to understand what the queen was getting at. "If I may be bold, Your Majesty, I do not think Odili will surrender his life and the city to you, no matter how many times you order him to do it."

"We do not care what Odili will or won't do. We have agents in Palm City. They'll open the gates when we come."

Tau's grip tightened on his hilts when she said it. The queen had a way into the city and that meant they were going to take the fight to Odili.

Otobong shook his head, and the general began to speak even more slowly, enunciating each word as if Empiric wasn't the queen's first language. "My queen, I must take you at your word about these agents, but even so, you're asking us to take too great a risk. What we have are a smattering of Ihagu, some Ihashe, a few initiates from the citadel, and several loyal Indlovu who survived the invasion. Together they're a military dragon, but they just came out of a bitter battle. We can't expect to mobilize them, march to Palm, and win that fight, even if the gates are opened."

"You began this boasting of your capabilities," Tsiora said. "We've told you the gates will be open. Where is your faith, General?"

"They weren't boasts and I do have faith, my queen. I have faith that if we do the right thing, we can reunite our people and survive, but it isn't right to face Odili in combat, not as we are," he said. "He has too many Indlovu and Ingonyama. He has at least as many Gifted as we do, and Goddess knows, the Ihashe and Ihagu in Palm City won't understand our conflict and are likely to keep fighting for him too." Otobong turned his body to include Mirembe and the other councilwomen in the discussion. "To win this fight we need more soldiers but don't have the time to gather them. I'm telling you, if we wish to see another season, we have days to end this rebellion. Days."

Mirembe clapped her hands together, drawing the room's attention. "What can we do, then, General?" she asked. "What can we do to survive?"

"It's as I've said. We must compromise with Odili and…uh… and Princess Esi."

"This is your decision?" Mirembe asked. "The decision of the Guardian Council?"

"It is," Otobong said.

"No. Abasi Odili betrayed us," Queen Tsiora said. "He tried to kill us."

Mirembe nodded, put a hand to her chest, and closed her eyes as if in prayer. "His actions hurt us all. They are a stain on his honor and a blight on the history of our people." She opened her eyes, fixing them on Tsiora. "But that does nothing to change the facts the general described, the decision he's made, and the decision that we on the Ruling Council must also make."

"This is what you want?" Tsiora asked. "You wish us to forgive and forget treachery?"

"My queen, we're responsible for more than ourselves in this," Mirembe said, "and to carry out the duty we owe to those we lead, we have to forgive and forget, or everyone dies."

Someone behind Tau cleared his throat. It was Hadith, and although he looked uncomfortable when the faces in the room turned to him, he didn't wither beneath the gaze of his betters.

Tau was beside Nyah and saw her signal Tsiora. The vizier didn't want her to let Hadith speak, but Nyah's want wasn't enough. In the matter of Guardian Councillor Abasi Odili, Tau and the queen were cut from the same stone. They could not forget and they would never forgive.

"Ihashe," Queen Tsiora said to Hadith. "You have something to say?"

LEADERSHIP

There may be a way to delay the Xiddeen attack long enough to gather the forces needed to take Palm City," Hadith said, "but if we fail, the Xiddeen will send their full might against us immediately."

Otobong sucked his teeth and stepped farther away from Hadith, like the Ihashe's smell offended him. "You offer self-destruction?" he asked, before turning to the councilwomen. "I wonder, council, should we not bring in a few of the stabled horses to present their opinions as well?"

"General," Queen Tsiora said, "we have given this Ihashe leave to speak."

Otobong seemed to be waiting for Mirembe to do or say something. When she didn't, he frowned. "Of course, my queen. Why not listen? We have nothing if not time."

Tsiora looked ready to respond to that, but her next words were gentle, and they were for Hadith. "Go on, Ihashe. Describe the path as you see it."

"They haven't left yet," Hadith said. "The Xiddeen must wait out this storm before sailing, and that means they're still on our shores." A thunderclap boomed, as if to support his point. "There are only three beaches beyond the Fist where the Xiddeen could have landed as many raiders as they did. If we split our men into prongs, we can—"

"My queen," said Otobong, "I apologize, but must we listen to more of this madness? With no humor, I'd rather hear from the horses."

"General...," Tsiora said.

"The Lesser is going to suggest we attack the hedeni," the general said. "He thinks to void our truce by ambushing a force that out-numbers us. Why begin that journey when we can cut to the end of this path by slitting our own throats now?"

"Ihashe?" Tsiora said to Hadith.

She wanted an answer to the problems the general had raised. Tau worried there wasn't one.

"We don't need to kill everyone," Hadith said.

Otobong laughed. "That helps, since we can't."

"We just need to kill the warlord."

"Good thinking, Lesser," Otobong said. "We won't fight the other hedeni. We'll walk past them and only attack the warlord."

Hadith was becoming angry. His expression hadn't changed, but Tau had known him long enough to see it.

"We can wait until most of the Xiddeen have left our shores before we attack," Hadith said.

"Of course we can," Otobong said. "We have enough fight-ers to outnumber a single ship's complement. Our men can swim the Roar, blades held in their teeth, to attack Warlord Achak on his boat." He grinned at the Indlovu around him. "I see it better now."

"No, you don't," Hadith said, earning himself a sharp look from the Greater Noble. "The warlord is the Xiddeen's military leader, and by all accounts, he's a good one. He'll remain onshore as the majority of his raiders embark. We can attack when the Xiddeen remaining on our land are too few to stop us."

"Why in the Goddess's name would the warlord remain onshore while the strength of his force sails?"

"For much the same reason the Xiddeen fight women alongside their men," Hadith told the general.

Otobong waved away the explanation. "That's done because it's the only way they can field enough bodies to overwhelm us."

"They do it because they view one another as equals," Hadith said. "Women, men, soldiers, and leaders, for the most part each life is considered to hold equal value and ability."

Otobong squinted at Hadith. "What are you, Governor caste?" he asked, his eyes flickering to Tau. "Are you trying to tell me that a simple Low Common has equal worth in divining a fief's finances as you would? Come, now, you're grabbing a dull sword by its blade and naming it a hilt. The savages are unsophisticated, but even they know that a warlord's life, with his knowledge of their numbers, strategies, and tactics, outweighs the life of one soldier. He'll be protected."

"You're right on some counts," Hadith said. "The Xiddeen will protect him, but I'm telling you that, in this, they'll behave more like Lessers than Nobles."

Smiling, Otobong spread his arms wide. "Don't they always?" he asked.

Hadith turned to Tau. "Champion," he said, "a storm rages outside and no ships can sail the Roar for as long as it does. When the storm dies and the Xiddeen board their vessels, where would you, as their leader, be?"

Tau told the truth. "On the shore. If I lead men into danger, I must see them out of it as well."

Letting his eyes slide past the general and to the queen, Hadith dipped his head, the gesture taking them both in. "At its essence, isn't true leadership simply service?" he asked.

Tau didn't see the queen's reaction. He was too busy watching Otobong advance on Hadith.

"I'm right here, Lesser," the general said. "If you have something to say to me, have the courage to do it openly."

Hadith took a small step back while meeting Otobong's eyes with his own. "When the storm ends and the Xiddeen begin to leave our shores, we know they'll do it in several groupings. It's the only way they can be sure to avoid having their entire fleet sunk by a rogue wave." Hadith turned to the queen. "I think that the warlord will be among one of the final groups to take to the water, and that gives us our chance."

"You think?" Otobong asked. "You think?"

"I know it as well as I can know anything that hasn't yet happened," Hadith said, pushing on, "and I'm not saying it'll be easy to get to him. All the fighters in the warlord's sailing group will still be onshore. It's like you mentioned. The Xiddeen can't deny that Achak is important, and he will be protected, but we won't have to face the full strength of the raiding force." The general didn't seem convinced, and Hadith gave it one more swing. "Please, we'll never have a better chance."

Otobong closed the remaining distance between them. "You're saying that you understand our enemy because you're more like them than I am, and I won't argue that. On the other hand, I find myself revolted by the fact that you're using such base commonality as the foundation for your advice to our monarch. Goddess wept, you're asking your queen to break her sworn word. Lesser, do you lack even a Drudge's honor?"

Hadith drew himself up to his full height, coming just short of Otobong's neck. "If you do as I ask, Warlord Achak will never leave our peninsula. He'll die here and his death will throw the Xiddeen into disarray."

"I'll do no such thing," Otobong said. "I won't listen to plans for backstabbing and promise breaking when we have Odili and Palm City to consider."

"Odili stands behind the tall walls of a fortified city that is filled with Indlovu, Ihashe, and Gifted," Hadith said. "We don't have the strength to take him on without reinforcements from the fiefs, and we don't have the time to reinforce before the Xiddeen return to wipe us out. That's what you told us, right?"

Chairwoman Mirembe spoke then. "And that is why we must make amends with Odili."

"There will be no amends." The words were out of Tau's mouth before he could stop them.

"Champion," Nyah said, a warning in her tone.

"Champion...." Mirembe cocked her head to one side, saying

the word as if she'd never found occasion to utter it before. "Is there something you wish to add?"

"Odili is a traitor. He'll die a traitor's death," he said.

"Really? But isn't that something your queen should decide?" Mirembe asked. "Doesn't that decision fall under the purview of the one to whom you swore your oaths, and her councils?"

Tsiora answered and her words helped to calm Tau. "Abasi Odili attempted a coup and has thrown our queendom into a state of civil war. His crimes can have only one response."

"And in better times, we would respond exactly as you're suggesting," Mirembe said. "But, Your Majesty, we do not have the luxury of better times. We must do as we Nobles have always done. We must settle our internal differences peacefully so that we can face our enemies with the full might of our bronze and fire."

Tau couldn't believe what he was hearing. "Differences?" he said. "Odili tried to kill our queen and there are many others who no longer breathe because of him. He's a murderer and there's nothing but justice waiting for him."

"How dare you," Otobong said. "You're talking about a Royal Noble."

Tau could see where this was heading. They wouldn't listen. They'd planned it out so they wouldn't have to. The new Ruling and Guardian Councils intended to outvote the queen and welcome Odili back with open arms, and Odili would accept. He'd have to or he'd die like everyone else in the Xiddeen attack.

Then, once the rebellion was ended and Odili was pardoned, these Greater Nobles would get to keep their roles as councillors. Tau didn't know how a Noble might rise in caste, but if there was any way to do it, he imagined this was it.

"I think you mean to let Abasi Odili live," he said, putting a hand to his strong-side sword, "but so long as I draw breath, that won't be possible."

Nyah stepped close enough to be standing between them. "That's enough, both of you," she said, and, without giving either of them time to respond, she turned to Tsiora. "My queen, may we adjourn? These issues will be better discussed by the light of day, and—"

"You put your hand to your sword while we stand in council chambers with our queen," Otobong said to Tau, towering over him. "You lack the civility of an inyoka."

"Oh, you wish me to be civil?" Tau asked the larger man. "You want me to play the part of a Noble when you'll never give me the same consideration as one. Is that the game?"

"What are you talking about?"

"I can smile and talk as sweet as cane sugar. I can follow every rule you'll ever make, and it will never be good enough for people like you, because people like you don't see me as people," Tau said, pulling a handspan of black dragon scale free from its scabbard.

"Has this thing gone mad?" Otobong asked, backing away.

"General, that is our champion to whom you speak," the queen said.

It took him a breath, but Otobong tilted his head in deference. "Of course. He's your champion. Apologies, my queen."

Tau knew what was expected. He knew it was his turn to apologize, so they could both play the part of noblemen in good company, but Tau wasn't a nobleman. They'd never let him be one and he wasn't sure being one was better anyway. So, staring up at the general, he dropped his second hand to its corresponding blade.

"I need no titles to defend me," he said. "I can do it myself."

Otobong's nostrils flared at that and the queen raised her voice. "This meeting is over," she said. "Mirembe, if you are determined to see a new ruling council formed, we'll consider it at another time. For now, we'll retire to think over the advice that has been offered."

Tau let his eyes flit to Mirembe's face. The self-named chair-woman looked like she'd sucked something sour, and then she caught him looking at her.

"My queen," she said, "one last bit of advice?"

"If you must, Mirembe," Tsiora said.

"Whether we like it or not, we should speak with Guardian Councillor Odili. It's our duty to try to resolve this without Omehi spilling Omehi blood."

Tsiora could have been made from stone. "Is that everything?"

"Almost," Mirembe said, eyeing Tau up and down, "but I must

ask, would our queen not be better served by a champion like Kellan Okar?"

"As chairman of our newly formed Guardian Council," said Otobong, "I would like to second the chairwoman's thought. Indeed, Okar and Odili are also well acquainted and—"

Tau's twin blades kissed the bare flesh on Otobong's neck and the leather armor on his back, the dragon scale selling the man on silence.

"Thief," Tau said. "I warned you. You won't steal Odili from me."

"Champion." It was the queen.

"I will have justice," Tau said, keeping his blades in contact with the general's skin as the eleven Indlovu in the room moved to their feet and drew their bronze.

"Queen Tsiora, it appears as if you'd be well served to seriously consider my suggestion about champions," Mirembe said, her dispassionate facade thrown aside. Then, raising her voice, she spoke to Tau. "Put away your weapons, you insect."

"Champion Solarin, we have not yet asked you to kill the general," the queen said.

"This isn't the way," Hadith whispered. "It's not it, Tau."

Struggling to get his breathing back under control, Tau looked from face to face, seeing Hadith, Nyah, and at the last, his queen. He took a step back, lifting his black blades away from the general.

His life no longer in immediate danger, Otobong slapped a hand against his bleeding neck and pulled it away to stare in shock at the red smears on his fingers. "You drew blood."

The guardian swords were sharp beyond measure, and Tau was not accustomed to them.

"You attacked me?" Otobong asked. "You attacked me!"

"General Otobong," Nyah said, trying to take control, "do you honestly expect to heap abuses on others and receive none your—"

"No!" the general shouted. "It goes too far. This filthy half man shouldn't even be allowed near dragon scale, let alone to wield it." The general faced the queen. "Queen Tsiora, tell me, if you will, is this how you intend to rule? With blood drawn among those loyal to you and truces violated with assassinations? I thought you wanted peace. Why are you willing to offer it to our enemies but not to the women and men of your own kind?"

"General...," warned Nyah, but Otobong would not be stopped.

"I would like to know," he said, "will you rule with Lessers standing in the place of their betters?"

Nyah spoke first. "There's only one Lesser that the queen has elevated, and he's champion because of proven merit. Queen Tsiora has no intention of—"

The queen cut off her vizier. "We do what the Goddess wills and won't be second-guessed."

Otobong nodded. "Then we can expect more of them in these meetings, hmm? Whispering in your ear? Undermining your Nobles?" He sniffed. "Queen Tsiora, I understand that you didn't get to join yourself with a savage, but that shouldn't mean it must be done with a Lesser."

"General!" shouted Nyah, pointing an open hand at him.

Otobong eyed her. "You'll strike at me too, Vizier? Will you lay this Noble low with the Goddess's own gifts?" He licked his bottom lip and let his mouth twist like he was about to spit. "What have we become?"

Tau didn't know his queen a tenth as well as he knew Hadith, but he didn't need to, to know that she was furious beyond reasonable measure, and for some strange reason, seeing her that way made him calmer. It was as if he could sense that having the two of them in a state of pique would not end well.

"Apologize to us, General Otobong," the queen said, her voice as even and sharp as a newly made blade.

"Beg pardon?" the general asked.

"Apologize before you no longer have a choice in the matter," she said.

"With respect, my queen," Otobong said, "I wish to speak as honestly as I'm able before it's too late for any words to make a difference. You're too young to see the patterns in this, where it'll drag us." He looked down at Tau. "This person you want me to call a champion should be hung for even showing his blade in my presence, and if nothing is done about the affront, then we move in a direction that will eventually overturn the natural order. My queen," he said, "as perilous as the battles we face are to us, if we let the binds of civility and society slip, then, before long, we'll unravel everything it means to be Omehi, and when that happens, whether it's by our enemy's hands or our own, we cease to exist."

Tsiora said nothing and the room was silent.

Otobong pointed to Hadith. "And what of the whispers coming from this other Lesser's forked tongue?" He faced Mirembe and the rest of her ruling council. "Our queen is surrounded by base wretchedness. How can that not have a corrupting influence?" he asked, taking another step away from Tau and moving out of his reach as one of the eleven Indlovu came to stand between them. "My queen," he continued, "it worries me that you seem so ready to abandon the advice of your generals, councillors, and even your own sworn words of peace."

The queen's look was a hard one. "Are you finished, General?"

Otobong ground his teeth but held his tongue.

"The Xiddeen shul and several hundred thousand lost their lives in a torrent of dragon fire," Queen Tsiora said. "Peace died then, burned away in flames the traitor Abasi Odili fanned."

Otobong touched at his bleeding neck again and turned to the chairwoman of the Ruling Council. "I tried, Mirembe," he said. "The Goddess knows I did, but I can't be part of what she wants."

"You wish to be relieved of your duties, then?" Nyah asked him.

"Oh, it's far too late for that to be enough," the queen said.

Otobong's eyes widened at that.

"I understand, General," Mirembe said, "and, after hearing everything here tonight, I'm inclined to agree." She made a show of glancing to her left and right at the women sitting on either side of her. "The Ruling Council also agrees."

Tau wasn't sure what was happening, but he saw Tsiora's pupils shrink to pinpricks and he made himself ready.

"We're warning you, Mirembe," the queen said, "do not go down this path. You won't like where it leads, and we promise you, there's no way back from it."

"Queen Tsiora, we can't win a fight against Palm City before the hedeni attack us, and we won't survive their attack without the support of Palm City. Will you save your people and treat with Guardian Councillor Abasi Odili?"

Tau tensed.

"No," Tsiora said.

Mirembe blinked and leaned back, the edges of her mouth fluttering up and down before settling on an empty smile. "General Otobong, as chairwoman of the Ruling Council, I call on you to help us fulfill our obligation to keep our people and monarch safe from harm. Separate Queen Tsiora from the vizier and these Lessers."

The general had begun nodding halfway through Mirembe's little speech. "Indlovu, Queen's Guard, escort the queen to her rooms, and if any of the Lessers come between you, kill them."

The Indlovu readied their weapons, their eleven bronze blades reflecting the room's torchlight, and though she had every right to be scared, the only thing Tau could sense from Tsiora was fury.

Otobong turned his head to Kellan. "Okar, step away from them."

Kellan raised his hands, balled them into fists, and shuffled closer to Tau's sword brothers, placing himself in front of Gifted Thandi. "I don't think I can, General."

Otobong considered that, sniffed, and turned away. "Pity to lose you too," he said.

The gap between life and death, Tau thought, was closing. He saw a weaponless Kellan standing poised for a fight he couldn't win, while, beside him, Uduak breathed deep and widened his stance. Half hidden in the big man's shadow, Yaw flicked his eyes from Indlovu to Indlovu, and in front of them all, Hadith was frowning, as if regarding bad behavior he'd known to expect.

The odds were not favorable, and since his brothers had been called from their beds, Tau was the only one among them who was armed. It didn't help that his ribs hadn't had time to heal, three fingers on his right hand were too broken for a firm grip, and he couldn't be sure if the Queen's Guard would side with the queen they'd sworn to protect or the general who offered them a life likely to last longer than the next few breaths.

Someone laughed, and the sound was strange in the moment.

It was Themba. The Ihashe, grinning widely, winked at Tau and crossed his arms.

It seemed that the same man who'd once questioned Tau's ability to stand against a few Indlovu had become confident that he would beat eleven of them. Fifteen, if the Queen's Guard threw in with the general.

"Take them," ordered Otobong, and his men came forward.

Poor odds, thought Tau, leaping for the Indlovu standing between him and his target.

ODDS

The Indlovu was quick. He had one sword and no shield and still blocked Tau's weak-side strike as well as his strong-side follow-up. It was the third attack he couldn't stop. The Greater Noble brought his blocking blade up late and Tau's sword tore through his throat.

Tau didn't see him fall. He ran past the dying man as soon as his weapon ripped free of the Indlovu's neck.

"Kill him!" shouted Otobong, spit flying from his mouth.

The general needn't have bothered with the order because the ten remaining Indlovu were already moving. Tau had to dash past the nearest of them, shouldering the larger man aside, while hoping beyond hope that Hadith was right and that cutting the head from the inyoka would be enough to stop it from hurting them. He had to get to the chairwoman and make her call off the Indlovu.

Otobong was between them, though, and he swung his sword at Tau's head. It was a well-timed but obvious attack. Tau knew it was coming and dropped below the blade's leading edge, letting Otobong's wild swing shear through empty air, pulling the general out of position. Willing to end the Greater Noble's life, Tau went to counter, but the thing that Otobong had become made him stop in place.

Standing where Otobong had been was a two-armed demon with the turgid skin of a bloated tick. Tau was facing the creature's back, and without hesitation it swung round, sending a clawed arm for his face.

Skidding to a stop while trying to blink away the vision, Tau struggled to dodge the attack and regain his hold on the real. He couldn't do both and felt the bite of bronze as the front of his leather armor was caught and torn by a blade point. The contact yanked him to the side, threatening to take him from his feet, but he held his balance, letting the momentum whirl him around until he was facing his opponent again.

This time it was Otobong he faced and not the monster. The demon had vanished and the general was still resetting his stance, having swung at Tau hard enough to chop him in two. As Otobong righted himself, Tau sucked in a breath of smoky air and glanced down. A strip of leather hung free from his armor, and his chest burned from the shallow cut he'd received. The moment he'd lost to the vision had come close to costing him his life.

Roaring at Tau, Otobong attacked again, hauling his sword to purpose in a backhand swing. Tau parried with his weak side, staggering under the strength of the blow but stopping it. Without hesitation, Otobong jerked his blade back and stepped away, seeking to move beyond Tau's striking range while keeping Tau within his. But before he could do it, Tau ended the fight.

Using as much force as he could generate in close quarters, Tau slashed down with his twin swords. It wasn't necessary. The blades were made of dragon scale and when the one held in his left hand crashed into Otobong's sword, the one in his right chopped through the general's sword arm like it was a stalk of drought-withered cane.

It was Otobong's flesh that yielded first. It split, separating to reveal muscle, tendons, and the two thick bones that made up his forearm. The dragon scale bisected them both, and Otobong's hand, sword, and a cup's worth of his blood splattered across the painted floor. The general threw his head back then, screaming, howling in pain, the sound of it echoing through the council chamber from deck to dome.

No time to waste, Tau hopped back, ready to run to capture Mirembe or defend himself against the other Indlovu, but the Indlovu weren't attacking. They were staring at Otobong and what was on the floor in front of him.

The general was on his knees and using his remaining hand to clutch at his ruined arm as blood poured from it. On the ground beside him was his sword, and the weapon's blade had been cut in two. Tau's dragon-scale swords had struck Otobong's blade as well as his forearm, and they had destroyed them both.

Tau caught the movement as one of the Indlovu looked up at him from the kneeling general. The rest were also shaking off the shock. He knew he didn't have long, and he spun toward the chairwoman, racing for her. He got two steps before she took control of him.

It was like running into a wall of knives. His body felt like it had been shredded to bits, then put back together too quickly. Tau would have yelled, but he couldn't move his mouth. He could barely breathe, and even without having experienced it before, he'd seen enough with the dragons to guess what had been done. Desperate, he dove into Isihogo.

The gray mists and howling winds welcomed him home, and in front of him, exactly where the chairwoman had been standing, was an indistinct figure, masked by the shifting black opaqueness of a Gifted's shroud.

"This is how you die, Lesser," the woman behind the shroud said, her words faint in the underworld's endless storm.

"You'd entreat a man?" Tau asked.

She barked out a laugh. "Do Low Commons count themselves as such now?"

Though it was painful to even think her name, Tau thanked Zuri for her lessons. "We'll die together, then," he said, finding the tethers that bound his soul to the chairwoman's as easily as if the binds were physical. He pictured himself grabbing them, wrapping the tethers tight around his arms, and using them to hold her as firmly as she held him. "I'll keep you here, and when your shroud fails, we'll greet the demons together."

There was a pause. He'd caught her off guard. She hadn't expected him to know that Gifted did not entreat intelligent beings for exactly this reason. The tethers of entreating work both ways.

"You don't have the time," she said. "In Uhmlaba, my Indlovu will cut your head from your shoulders and I'll use it to feed the scorpions in the rock gardens."

Tau railed against her control, pulling and wrenching this way and that, looking for weakness or hoping to drain her power faster than he would if he let her control him. It was working. He could see her shroud quivering as he strained. He could also see that, even with the time difference between Isihogo and Uhmlaba, he had no hope of collapsing her shroud before the Indlovu killed him.

He fought harder. She laughed, and with the part of him that was still in his world, he heard her call out to the Indlovu.

"Kill...the...Common," she said, her voice deep and slow, like someone had poured syrup over the moments, stretching them like the gummy sap from the bramble bushes in Kerem's mountains.

He felt her then, in some part of his mind or soul or will. He felt her ooze her way over him and onto his arms. He felt her in his broken fingers and in his neck and face, too close, like a larger presence holding him, choking him, and breathing on him with fetid breath. She made him open his hands, digit by digit, and in a world far away from the mists that cloaked him, he heard his swords fall to the ground.

"Yes," she said, and it seemed that she was beside him, whispering, her wet lips smeared against his ear. "This is how it ends for you, freak. This is how it always ends for those who think to stand as tall as their betters."

She forced her way deeper inside his real body, the one in Uhmlaba. She moved his tongue between his teeth and made him bite down.

"How dare you speak to me," she said. "You don't have the right."

Tau pushed against her control, but she was too strong and he could taste blood as his teeth clamped down harder and harder on his tongue.

"How dare you," she said as blood began filling his mouth.

He tried to shout, to move. He tried to call for help, but the only thing he could manage was to hold on to the tethers of her soul as the Indlovu came to take his life. The only thing he could do was wait until it was over, but then came the pressure.

It was instant and crippling and Tau thought it was death. He thought either the Indlovu had killed him or the chairwoman had done it with her powers, but she shouted in surprise and he knew it was something else that had come for them.

"Mirembe!" called a new voice, heavy with power.

Tau battled the tethers, and in Isihogo, where they were looser, he was able to turn his head. Beside him was a darkness deeper than the blackest night, a shroud so thick Tau could see nothing of the person it hid. He knew them anyway.

"Mirembe, you have overstepped," his queen said.

"Tsiora?" Mirembe whispered, and Tau heard her only because she held him in her shackles, her voice sounding out like a bell rung in his head. "It's true?" she asked, and he felt Mirembe's fear as if it were his own. "Goddess wept...it's true?"

The bonds holding Tau slipped as Mirembe gave in to dread and Tau struggled against her. But before he could free himself, the globe of black beside him moved forward and a blinding bolt of light shot out from it, flying for the chairwoman. Mirembe tried to move, but the bolt grew in size, becoming too large to avoid, and when it struck her, the world exploded. Caught in the blast, Tau's consciousness collapsed, bursting like an overweight bubble and sending him spinning into nothingness.

When he could piece enough of himself back together, he found he was on his hands and knees in the council chambers. He spat the wad of blood from his mouth, thankful his tongue was still attached, and even that small act took most of his will. Tau's head felt like it held a hundred serrated dirks, and when he looked up, pain forked through him like a surgeon had pushed the knives deeper.

Across the room, Mirembe had tumbled backward over her chair and was sprawled on the ground, half senseless and moaning.

Tau growled and tried to get his feet beneath him. She'd been in his head, her oily grip sliding over and dirtying his soul. She'd held him helpless, used him, and he would kill her for it. He raised one knee, felt a presence near him, and jerked his head to see who was there.

An Indlovu was standing over Tau, sword at the ready, and Tau bunched his muscles, preparing to dive away, when he noticed the man was holding the blade defensively. The Greater Noble was in a standoff with two of the Queen's Guard.

Four of the other Indlovu were on the ground, felled, no doubt, by Thandi, who had her hands up and pointed in their direction. The remaining five were facing Tau's scale and the two other Queen's Guard as well as Nyah, whose hands were up and ready.

Tau sat back on his haunches. His odds had been wrong. His scale might have been weaponless, but the three Gifted with them were not.

"Be at ease, my queen," pled one of the councilwoman. "We are yours."

"No!" yelled Otobong, his face screwed up as he grasped the stump of his arm. "Don't do this. She offers nothing. She—"

Kellan slapped the general with the back of his hand. "General, you should step away now."

One of the Indlovu hefted his sword, but the same councilwoman called out. "Indlovu, do nothing! Queen Tsiora, this must end."

"And it will," the queen said. "Lay down your arms and none of you will be harmed."

"Don't . . . don't do it," Otobong said. The words, pushed past his bruised lips, were soft, shaky, and, kneeling in a growing pool of his own blood, he looked near to fainting.

"Do not make us rescind our clemency," Tsiora said, sweeping her eyes across the Indlovu.

In a clatter of bronze meeting stone, the general's men dropped their weapons and Tau's sword brothers snatched them up.

"Noblewomen, General Otobong, you're right, these times are trying," Tsiora said as Hadith helped Tau to his feet. "Our fight for survival grows desperate and it has been made very clear that if we are to survive we must move past compromise and councils. We must fight and burn as queens before us have done. We must be a Dragon Queen, and Dragon Queens keep their own council."

Otobong's head came up at that. "You? A Dragon Queen? You think yourself akin to Queen Taifa?"

Tsiora looked down on him. "We are kin," she said.

The general snorted. "And all this time we called your sister insane."

Moving with zeal, the same smile from earlier still on his face, Themba lifted his boot to kick Otobong. Tsiora stopped him with a raised hand.

"No," she said. "See that the general's wounds are tended and then imprison him with the rest who have defied us. They are not to be harmed, for they had our word."

Kellan saluted, pulled Themba back by his tunic, and signaled to Uduak, Yaw, and two of the Queen's Guard to help him remove the new crop of traitors.

Hadith, still helping Tau to stay standing, leaned close and whispered. "Care, Tau, care not to be used and thrown away in their schemes. What we do must benefit all, and things will happen fast now."

Tau shot him a look, but Hadith was focused on the queen, appearing for all the world as if he'd never spoken.

"Ihashe," the queen said to Hadith, "will cutting the head from the inyoka save us from its bite?"

"This creature has many heads, my queen," Hadith said, "but the one that has made clear its intention to strike is also the one we can stop."

Tsiora inclined her head and spoke to Kellan. "Be quick in handling these traitors, Kellan Okar," she said. "We believe that before this long day has ended, our champion will have need of his sword brothers."

Her gaze returned to Tau and Hadith, and though shadows of Mirembe's touch still ran riot through him, Tau stood straighter.

"Champion Solarin, you and your men have had too little time to grieve, too little time to heal, and we . . . we are sorry for this," the queen said.

There it was again, the strange intimacy. She spoke to him like he was a close companion who'd been gone too long. She spoke and he could almost believe she hurt for his pain, his loss. Her eyes told him she did.

"But time and storms wait for neither women nor queens, and there is work to be done," she said. "Champion, will you assemble your fighters and seek out the Xiddeen? Will you do what must be done to grant us the time to heal the rift in our queendom?"

"My queen, how can I leave you after what's just happened?" he asked. "How can I protect you if I go?" It felt strange to say it, but Tau felt it was true.

"You are gracious, but we have our Queen's Guard and we're never truly defenseless," she said, glancing at Mirembe cowering at the foot of two chairs. "We shall be careful until you return, Champion Solarin."

It was kind, the way she put it, but Tau felt a little foolish thinking he was the only sword standing between the queen of all the Omehi and those who might wish her harm. Even so, a part of him still wanted to stay with her.

"Champion Solarin, I'm asking you to do something horrible," she said. "Will you take Warlord Achak's life?"

To the queen he gave an answer. To the Goddess he offered his word. "That and more," he said.

CHAPTER TWO

HAFSA EKENE

The sun had yet to set and Hafsa Ekene was already of the opinion that the day was a flowering tragedy with more to come before its bloom was full. Her head swiveling left to right, she half walked, half ran to the keep's courtyard, looking for anyone important enough with whom to share the horrible news. She'd heard that the queen would be in the courtyard, watching the Ihashe and Indlovu readying themselves to leave to fight a battle somewhere, but, thought Hafsa, they might need to fight one in the keep first.

The general in her care had escaped. The same man whose severed arm she'd bandaged and treated just that morning, with the best of her considerable abilities, had left her hospital without a trace. The guards assigned to watch him were dead, and so were two of her finest physicians. Hateful, unbelievable, and still not the whole of it.

Hafsa had never seen it before, few had, but she'd read about it in her order's journals, and the twisted bodies of the dead, their mouths open in silent screams, had been the first clues. Then, when she'd discovered the nature of the weapon that had killed the guards and her physicians, her fears had been all but confirmed.

Feeling more desperate with each breath, she abandoned her half walk for a run and sped into the Guardian Keep's courtyard, frightened she might be throwing herself into the fray, and somehow even more afraid that she was already too late.

The damaged courtyard with its scorched walls and dirt-filled crevasse from which, apparently, a dragon had emerged, was an anthill of activity. Overhead, the sun was hidden by storm clouds and the yard was slick with pelting rain. The afternoon had a hazy, dreamlike quality as fighting men of all sizes in leathers, grays, and ugly bronze milled about in organized chaos.

A few of the soldiers watched her as she ran, but she had no time for priestly propriety. The queen was in the courtyard, she was still alive, and Hafsa wanted to keep her that way.

Queen Tsiora was with her vizier and Chibuye, the vizier's daughter. The queen was kneeling next to the child and smiling. That was a comfort, to see the love there.

Hafsa had never wanted children, but since the first moments of the chairman's coup, when the vizier had barreled into her hospital and thrust the child into her care, she hadn't been able to stop worrying over the bright and ever-smiling Chibuye.

She'd taken care of the girl for days while the vizier worked without end to put back together some of what Councillor Odili had broken. Far be it from Hafsa to tell any parent their business, but given the time she'd spent with the girl, she knew a portion of what parenting was and felt more than comfortable thinking that Chibuye should not be out here among these killers.

"Hafsa!" called the girl when she saw her.

Even with the horrors and lives lost that day, Chibuye's voice lifted Hafsa's heart, and she gave the little one a small wave before bending her knees and dipping her head to the queen.

"This is Priestess Ekene, Your Majesty," Nyah said, introducing her, and the question in her voice, wondering why Hafsa was there, was as clear as still water.

"My queen." Head still bowed, Hafsa chose to wade in immediately. "You're not safe here."

"Explain that," Nyah said.

"Rise," the queen told her at the same time.

Hafsa lifted her head. Nyah was staring hard, but the queen

watched her more...gently, considering her. She didn't look afraid, but that was because she didn't know.

"The guards and my physicians, they were murdered. The general..." Hafsa wasn't explaining it well enough. "Queen Tsiora, I have reason to believe that—"

Hafsa stifled a yelp. He'd appeared beside the queen as if from open air, but more likely she simply hadn't noticed him approaching. How could anyone not notice him?

He was black as coal, head shaved clean, and had a face that was unnaturally even, if one didn't consider the awful scar that ran from nose to cheek on his right side. He was clearly a Lesser, but wearing a champion's colors—black-and-red leathers—with two swords on his hips.

She'd heard of him, of course, and it should have been absurd, seeing a Lesser in champion's garb, but somehow it wasn't. It was terrifying.

His eyes, she thought. Something in them set her nerves on fire and her heart thumping. Something in them called on her to run away and never stop.

"My queen, we're ready to—" His voice was a rasp scraping down Hafsa's spine like a rust-pitted scalpel.

"Not now, Champion," Nyah said.

The man's face twitched and Hafsa stepped back.

"Priestess, speak quickly," Nyah said to her.

"I—I—" tried Hafsa.

"We're ready to leave, my queen," he said.

"Solarin!" Nyah said.

The champion's eyes slid from Hafsa's face, and only once they'd left her did she realize how tightly she'd bunched the muscles in her back and shoulders.

"The child?" he asked, looking at Chibuye.

"My daughter," Nyah told him.

The Lesser...no...the champion raised an eyebrow. "You've a daughter?"

"And you've eyes and ears," Nyah said. "Priestess Ekene, you spoke of danger."

Before he could look back and unsettle her, Hafsa drew breath and dove in. "General Otobong has escaped the hospital. The men guarding him were murdered along with my attending physicians."

The champion's swords were out and ready before she even registered the noise of him drawing the blades. She did yelp then.

"Uduak, Hadith, to me! To the queen!" he shouted as he scanned the courtyard for danger.

"There's more," said Hafsa, her voice lost to the flurry of heavy footsteps that came running toward the queen. "Beware their weapons. They're using poison."

"There." The single syllable came from one of the biggest Lessers Hafsa had ever seen. She might even have confused him for a Petty Noble if not for the Ihashe grays he wore and the absence of the supplementary musculature characteristic of Noble males. Long ago, in her final year of studies, she'd wanted to write a treatise on the physical differences between Lessers and Greaters, but her adviser had warned her away from the topic, telling her that—

"Up there!"

She followed the Lesser's pointing hand and saw the soldier on the keep's walls. It was an Indlovu and he had his elbows on the ramparts. He was leaning on it, steadying himself as he aimed a long hollow tube at them. The weapon he had to his lips wasn't common among the Omehi, but Hafsa recognized it and knew what was coming.

"No!" she shouted as the assassin blasted air into the tube, sending death flying through the night for one of them. Beside her, in a blur of black leather, the champion leapt in front of the queen and snatched Chibuye behind him. Hafsa heard the dart hit with a wet thud.

It hit like an oar smacking water and the sound made her tense up all over. She, however, was not hit, and the champion, teeth bared and eyes watering, grunted at the impact.

"Pull it out!" she said, feeling shame at the relief washing over her because she'd been spared.

He didn't, though. He was using his body to cover Chibuye and the queen, and Hafsa, frightened beyond thinking that the assassin might have more projectiles to shoot, rushed to his side.

"Hadith, stay with us," the champion ordered. "Uduak, stop that man!"

Immediately, the massive Lesser, along with one of the Indlovu in the courtyard, ran for the stairs that led to the ramparts. Carefully, very carefully, Hafsa grasped the tail of the dart that was sticking out of the champion's right thigh, tore it out, and dropped it to the ground.

She could feel him looking at her. She raised her head, saw him, and shivered. "Don't touch the dart," she said, pulling her eyes away from his and seeing the mix of red and black blood that oozed from the small hole in the champion's leg and leathers. Such a small thing to kill a man.

"Queen Tsiora, child, are you well?" he asked.

The queen, having been thrown to the floor by her champion, was holding Chibuye close. "We are fine," she said, more to the crying child than to the champion. "We are fine."

"Chibuye! Tsiora!" the vizier shouted, running up to wrap the child and queen in her arms.

Hafsa saw the vizier's distress, but given what needed to be done, it barely registered. She was looking for something sharp, and the closest things were the champion's swords.

"I need one of your swords," she said.

The champion glanced at her, and the weight of his full attention made her flinch. Then, dismissing her entirely, he called for more men to guard the queen, got up, and tried to run for the ramparts to accompany the other two. He stumbled, nearly fell, and grabbed at his leg.

"You don't understand," Hafsa said.

He looked at her again, shook his head, and limped after the massive Lesser, the one in pursuit of the assassin.

"What is it, Priestess?" the queen asked.

The champion didn't have long, and Hafsa couldn't comprehend why he felt it necessary to join the fight when the assassin was already trapped.

Up on the ramparts, there were four soldiers closing in on him from the right and three others from his left. He could get to the stairs before the soldiers stopped him, but then his path would be blocked by the Indlovu and the big Lesser. The assassin's choices were simple: remain on the ramparts and fight against seven or take the stairs and try his luck against two.

He chose the two.

It wasn't what she would have done. The champion was going to be at the bottom of the stairs, and though Hafsa didn't know why, exactly, she'd have taken her chances against the soldiers atop the wall.

"Priestess?" the queen asked again.

"There's poison in the dart, my queen," Hafsa told her. "It's dragon's blood."

On the stairs, the Lesser named Uduak met the assassin, and as much as she abhorred violence, Hafsa could not have torn her eyes away were she promised all the cures to all the world's diseases. Uduak struck first, swinging his great sword in a tight arc, but missed when the other man jumped back, landing two stairs higher and out of reach.

Shouting as he went, the accompanying Indlovu charged past the big Lesser and attacked. The two Indlovu, assassin and loyalist, exchanged strikes, both blocked. Then, using his higher vantage, the assassin kicked the loyalist below the neck, unbalancing him, and before the loyalist could regain his footing, the assassin hacked down with his sword.

Hafsa thought to look away. She didn't want to watch a man murdered, but the loyalist wasn't undone. He raised his shield and the assassin's blade smashed into it. It wasn't a good block, but it meant that the assassin was only able to shave a sliver of flesh from the side of the loyalist's neck and shoulder instead of stealing his life.

Having saved himself, the loyalist spun down and away, letting the big Lesser take his place to continue the attack. They did it as smoothly as if they were performing a practiced dance, and Hafsa felt her mouth drop open when, without a wasted step, the big Lesser moved up the stairs to whip his huge sword at the assassin's head.

Moving like a surgeon's stitching needle, the assassin darted in and out, and as weightless as the Lesser made his massive sword look, he could not wield it well enough to land a blow. The scream, then, from the loyalist, who was no longer in the fray or in danger, was a shock. The sound he made was so raw and ragged it had to have torn his throat to shreds.

"Goddess wept," Hafsa said, seeing the man stumble on the stairs.

He was doubled over in pain, his head thrown back at a near impossible angle, the veins in it full, tight, and visible even from a distance as he clutched at the cut on his neck. He staggered one step, two, then tumbled twelve strides from the stone stairs to the courtyard floor.

"The assassin's blade," Hafsa shouted to the big Lesser as she left the queen to run toward the fallen loyalist, "it's poisoned!"

Reaching the downed and writhing man slumped against the stairs, she skidded to a stop and dropped to her knees.

"Hold still," she said, grabbing his head in both hands to steady it as she examined the wound. "Hold still!"

The shallow wound the assassin's blade had shaved into the Indlovu's neck looked innocent enough, except for the tiny splashes of black dragon's blood that bubbled and festered at the edges of the lacerated flesh. Hafsa knew that the best method for saving those poisoned in this way was to amputate the infected area, preventing the poison's spread before it could reach the heart or brain, but the poison was in his neck and that left her with just one option.

"Listen to me," she said to the screaming man, trying to get through the fugue of his agony. "I'm going to give you something. It will taste foul, but you need to bite down on it and swallow the juices. It will take away the pain."

His pupils were dilated and his eyes bulged from his head, but she'd captured his attention, and he nodded at her, reaching for her with tremoring fingers, desperate for anything that could ease his suffering.

Leaving a hand on him, holding him as still as she could, Hafsa searched the inner pockets of her robe for the right pouch and tried not to see the hope in his face. She pulled free the pouch she'd been looking for, opened it up, and poured the contents into her palm. There was only one ball of oiled herbs left, a small one, too small. She wanted to cry.

The loyalist scrabbled for it and she let him take the ball. He put it into his mouth, chewed, and swallowed, and Hafsa sat with him. But she knew that what he'd taken wouldn't be enough. She'd been so busy dealing with the wounded from the battle between the queen's loyalists and Odili's traitors that it had been days since she'd last refilled her pouches.

His screams grew louder, his thrashings became worse, and the whole thing, from her running to his side to his dying, happened in just a few breaths, but it felt like she watched him suffer and spasm forever. When it ended, his eyes, glassy and unfocused, were fixed on her. She could see the accusation in them, damning her. She'd promised to take away his pain. She'd promised him a lie.

As if from a great distance, she heard bronze smash against bronze, and, too drained to feel fear, she looked up. The assassin was close, only a couple of stairs up from the courtyard. He'd fought his way down, forcing the big Lesser to give ground to avoid the poisoned blade.

Hafsa saw that more Indlovu, more loyalists, were running over, and that the seven soldiers from the top of the wall were on the stairs and almost down them. There wasn't much hope for the assassin, and the champion was waiting for him at the base of the steps.

The assassin must have realized this too. He glanced back up the way he'd come, saw it was blocked by men, and jumped down beside Hafsa and the dead Indlovu. He reached for her, she recoiled, more out of instinct than thoughtful action, and then she felt some-one pull her beyond the assassin's grasp.

The champion was there. He'd pulled her back, putting himself between her and the assassin.

"Breathe deep," the champion said to the poisoner, "it'll be the last one you take."

The assassin, seen up close, had a thin face that was prettier than any murderer deserved.

"Ukufa waits for us both," he said. "The dart pulled from

your thigh? It was coated in dragon's blood. Do you feel its fire, Lesser? Does it burn?" The assassin smiled and tilted his head at the dead Indlovu, coaxing them to note the body. "The pain is just beginning."

His gesture called Hafsa's attention to the dead man, and as soon as she looked he attacked. He'd tried to distract the champion, and the trick had worked on her. From the corner of her eye, she saw the killer thrust his poisoned blade for the champion's chest, and just as she drew breath to cry out a warning, Hafsa Ekene was showered with gore.

One moment the champion had been facing a mortal injury, and the next, he had one of his blades through the assassin's sword arm, pinning it and the man's poisoned weapon helpless. But it was the champion's second sword that had spilled the most blood. It was buried hilt-deep in the assassin's open mouth, and its point, having broken through the back of the man's skull, vibrated like an instrument's plucked string.

The assassin's dead body hit the ground beside her and Hafsa's attempted warning cry came out as a shriek.

"Stop that," the champion said to her. He was already crouched and breathing heavily. "Is what he said true? Was the dart poisoned?"

Noting to herself that she was likely in shock, she still managed a nod and a few words. "You killed him..."

"I did," he said.

"Champion Solarin!" yelled one of the men atop the ramparts. "Five horses and four riders are fleeing the keep. The general is one of them."

The champion shouted back, "Who else is with them?"

"Two Indlovu and a gray-haired woman."

"Mirembe," the champion said, sniffing as if in disgust. "She runs, abandoning the rest of her council."

Hafsa, shaken as she was, had to save the Lesser. "Give me your sword," she said for the second time that day.

"Why?" It was Nyah. She was a few strides distant and hurrying over.

"I must cut away the poison before it finishes its work."

"How are Queen Tsiora and your daughter?" the champion asked the vizier.

"They're safe. They're…thank you, Champion. They're safe," Nyah said.

The champion, shoulders slumped, nodded as if his head were a boulder.

Hafsa reached for one of his swords. The champion sheathed it and grabbed her wrist before she was even close. He was looking at the dead loyalist.

"Why should I trust you?" the champion asked. "You couldn't save him."

"It was too late," Hafsa said. "He was cut in the neck and the poison travels through the body. If it reaches the head or heart, it kills. There was nothing I could do."

"It burns," he said.

She nodded. "And it will get much worse."

"Save him," Nyah said. "Do what you must."

"It's in his leg," Hafsa said.

"Amputation?" the champion asked.

"You'll die otherwise," she said.

"You're not cutting off my leg," he said, looking over her shoulder.

She turned to see that the queen had come, and as if Hafsa had not just told him that he was within reach of the Goddess's everlasting embrace, he began speaking to the queen.

"Five horses left the keep," he said. "It's Otobong, Mirembe, and two Indlovu. The last horse is unridden. It must have been for their assassin."

Queen Tsiora was watching the champion like nothing else existed. "You're poisoned?"

"We have to stop them. They know you have agents in Palm. We can't let them get to Odili."

The queen turned to Hafsa. "I heard what you said. Save him." Then back to the champion. "Give the priestess one of your swords."

"No," he said.

"Champion, we are your queen and you will—"

"I will not."

Another Lesser had arrived. "Tau's right, my queen. We must stop Mirembe and Otobong." The new Lesser gave Hafsa a sidelong look like he was wondering if she could be trusted with what he was about to say. "They know too much."

"None of this matters, Hadith," the vizier told the new Lesser. "They're gone. You'll never catch them on foot."

"Then we don't chase them on foot," Hadith said. "How many horses are left?"

Hafsa wished she could shake sense into everyone. They didn't have time to talk about horses. The champion's leg had to come off.

"How many did they take? Five?" Nyah asked. "That leaves three. But few can ride the animals."

"I can, a little," said Kellan Okar, striding over. Hafsa knew him. Everyone knew him.

"As can I," Nyah said, "and, Ingonyama Okar, I know your reputation as a fighter, but we two are no match for their four. They have three Indlovu, and Mirembe is a powerful Gifted."

The queen, as if waking from a reverie, looked up and away from her champion. "We will ride the first of the three horses, Ingonyama Okar and Ihashe Uduak can ride double on the second one, and, Nyah, you'll ride alone on the third."

"What? No!" Nyah said. "Queen Tsiora, you cannot think to take part in chasing after—"

The queen raised a hand. "We find ourselves growing weary of being told 'no.'" Her gaze skimmed past her champion and landed on Hafsa. "Priestess Ekene, we will call over our Queen's Guard and they will hold the champion down. Save his life."

"I won't let anyone take my leg!" Tau said.

The queen rounded on him. "This is our order, Champion. How dare you. We will not see you die this day."

"Uduak!" the champion said.

"Neh?" said the big Lesser, drawing closer.

The champion pulled a dragon-scale dagger from his belt, struggled with the leathers around his poisoned leg, and pulled them down. Uncovering his leg had to hurt more than a salt scourging, but he bore the pain and maintained enough modesty to ensure his

manhood remained covered. The juxtaposition of insanity and propriety was enough to make Hafsa want to laugh, until the moment
grew more insane.

"Uduak, cut out the wound and poison," he said.

Hafsa sputtered; no matter the frequency with which she encountered it, the effortless idiocy of men always surprised her. "You can't
do that," she said. "It's been too long. The poison may have traveled.
We need to take the whole leg."

"Uduak, the priestess is concerned," the champion said. "Cut
away a large section."

The big Lesser grunted and took the black-bladed dagger.

"You don't understand," Hafsa said, trying to use words the Lessers were sure to know. "Even if you catch the root of the poison, the
edges of it will have traveled farther. What stays in you may not be
enough to stop your heart, but the poison causes unimaginable pain.
It'll drive you insane. You'll end your days begging for death."

The champion focused on her, and she blanched. He's already
mad, she thought.

"Pain?" he asked, spitting nonsense. "Pain lost its hold on me a
thousand lifetimes ago." Without looking away from her, he spoke
to the big Lesser. "Cut deep and true, Uduak. We've a warlord to
kill and a city to win, and I've wasted too much time already."

With not a word, the man named Uduak aimed the blade at the
champion's bare and bleeding leg while the champion kept his eyes
and scarred face on Hafsa.

She couldn't abide such stupidity. "Give me that!" she said, trying to snatch the dagger from the big Lesser, but his grip was like
granite and she came away empty-handed. "Listen," she said to the
champion, "your man will probably make your leg as useless as if I'd
amputated it anyway. Let me do the cutting. I'll go as shallow as I
dare and I can avoid the muscle and major arteries."

The argument worked, the champion grunted his assent, and it
was, as her old mentor had been fond of saying, time to twist the
knife.

"This is beyond foolish, but if it's all you'll allow, then I can get
you out of this with nothing more than a gory wound, a limp, and

the burning you feel in the leg now," she told him. "Well, that's until the traces of the poison spread deep enough to make you feel like you're being burned alive from the inside out." She paused for effect and to let her words sink in. "No matter," she said. "You have many sharp toys. It won't be hard for you to end things yourself then."

He nodded. "Shallow cuts, Priestess," he said. "My leg must work."

She hadn't expected that. She'd used the same tactic a hundred times on patients, and once she'd properly explained the folly of their preferred course, they always came round to her way. She wondered if the poison had already muddied his mind, but one look in his eyes told her that, muddied or not, his mind was made up.

The big Lesser handed her the dagger.

"Champion—" she began, trying again anyway.

"Shouldn't we do this quickly?" he asked.

"Bandages!" she shouted to a startled Ihashe. "Bring me bandages."

Blood poured from the leg as she dug into the champion's thigh, doing her best to picture the path the poison was most likely to have taken as it traveled through him. Someone handed her the bandages. She didn't know if it was the same Ihashe and didn't bother to look.

It might work, she dared to think. It might be enough to keep the champion alive, for a time. The blade was sharper than anything she'd used before, and the cut was clean. Indeed, it was distressing to think that they wasted so precious a material as dragon scale on swords instead of using it for surgical tools.

Then, finishing her grim job, she sawed through the last fibers of flesh and tore the ruined shank free. Someone retched. It was Chibuye. The child was watching the grotesquerie, her eyes wide and mouth open.

"Chibuye, you should not be here," Hafsa said as she flung the dead meat to the ground to free up both hands to fill and bandage the wound, but the child did not move and Hafsa was too busy to shoo her away.

The champion, who had remained silent for the whole of the

cutting, continued watching Hafsa. So when the queen laid a cool hand on her shoulder, she jumped.

"My queen?" Hafsa said.

"Will he live?"

"I don't think it'll be the poison that kills him, at least not directly," Hafsa said, tightening the last of the bandages and leaving the champion to groan as he pulled the leathers back over his leg. "But his pain will never end or abate, and I believe that when his will finally fails him, he'll die anyway, by his own hand."

"That's not how I go," the scarred swordsman said, as if his words were power.

Hafsa wanted to tell him that nobody cared how he thought he'd go, especially not the Goddess.

"Give him anything he needs. Do whatever you must," the queen told Hafsa. "Nyah, order the horses readied. We have traitors to hunt."

The vizier drew close to the queen. "You have to know that this is worse than unwise. If you chase Mirembe and are lost in the effort, Odili will rule and the Omehi will be no more."

The queen glanced at the champion before answering. "That's not how we go," she said.

The vizier pursed her lips tightly enough to kiss a beetle. "Tsiora."

"Nyah, can you handle Mirembe on your own?"

The vizier said nothing.

"Then ready the horses," the queen said. "We will not permit these traitors to get to Odili."

Nyah bowed to the queen and whispered to her daughter, who moved to stand beside Hafsa.

"Priestess," Nyah said, "I have another favor to ask...."

"Of course, she'll be cared for until you return," Hafsa said.

The vizier kissed the child on the forehead, mumbled a thanks to Hafsa, and went to do as she'd been bid.

As the vizier walked away, the queen spoke to the Ihashe and Indlovu in the courtyard.

"The man who fought and died for us will be honored," she said. "Burn a pyre for him. Let its fires consume the body and free his soul. Beneath tonight's stars, he goes to the Goddess, unfettered and unashamed."

Several fighters came forward to take and prepare their fallen brother.

"Kellan Okar, you told us you could ride, and you will. We need your sword. We need the man wielding it," the queen said, making the handsome Noble practically fall over himself in his hurry to salute. "Priestess, stay close. We find it likely that you'll be needed again before this is done."

The words made the day and its losses crash over Hafsa like white water. The sun had yet to set, too many had died already, and more were expected.

"I'm coming too," the champion said, struggling to his feet.

Hafsa made a funny noise in the back of her throat, and with as much authority as she could manage, she said, "Absolutely not!"

"Now it is our turn to deny you," the queen said to him. "No."

Hafsa's patient made it to his feet, though he was favoring his wounded right leg. "Am I no longer your champion?" he asked.

Hafsa blew air from her mouth, ridiculous! Then she saw the queen pause, and just as one didn't come to lead the medicinal order of the Sah without also understanding something of people, Hafsa could see, though she knew not why it worked, that the champion had said exactly what he needed to.

"Hurry, then, Champion," the queen said, walking away. "The traitors will not wait."

Limping terribly, with the same look on his face that her fief's umbusi would get before tearing the skin from the back of a Lesser who had displeased her, the champion followed the queen.

Watching him go, Hafsa Ekene placed an arm around Chibuye, worrying for the first time since becoming a priestess about how the Goddess would judge her, wondering if saving some lives made her an accomplice to the ending of others.

REINS

Tau was in so much pain he could barely think, and every step the running animal took made it feel like someone was chopping at his leg with an ax. It hurt almost as much as when the priestess had cut into him.

"I've found their horses in the mists," Nyah shouted.

The vizier was on his right, riding a brown creature with Uduak seated behind her. He was holding on to her so tight she had to bat at his hands, reminding him not to break her ribs.

"Where are they?" the queen asked.

"A thousand strides ahead and a little to our left," Nyah said.

Tau looked to his left. Kellan was on a white horse alongside him, but Tau didn't think he could call what Okar was doing riding. Kellan had a fixed stare, was hunched over his horse grumbling to himself, and looked like he might bounce up and off the side of the beast at any moment.

"A thousand strides?" the queen shouted back. "Show them to us, Nyah. We'll entreat Mirembe's horse and make it seem lame. We'll catch them."

"You think to entreat the horse the whole time it takes for us to catch them up? Not possible," Nyah said.

"We shall see," the queen said.

Finally, Tau thought, watching Kellan fumble about on the horse, something the great Kellan Okar was not so great at doing. He started to smile when his horse's feet hit the ground and the jolt sent a spasm of agony through his leg that was so powerful it threatened to make him lose control of his bowels.

"Cek!" he said.

"Put your arms around us," the queen said over her shoulder.

"I'm fine . . . my queen," Tau said, teeth clenched, face sweaty, and vision blurring.

"You are not. Put your arms around us before you fall. We cannot go faster like this."

Tau had been holding on to the sides of the horse's leather seat and intended to continue doing so, but the next jolting step sent such a shock through him that he cried out and snapped his arms around the queen. Her back went rod straight and Tau almost let go.

"No, hold on," she said. "Hold tight."

"Neh?"

"Hyah!" she shouted, speaking the beast's language and sending them faster and faster, the speed bringing tears to Tau's eyes and making him shiver from the wind's chill.

They raced across the earth, covering ground at an impossible pace, and though the wonder of it didn't stop Tau's pain, the pain ceased being his only thought. It was like flying, and when the sun set behind them, the stormy skies revealed a million stars flashing in and out of existence behind dark clouds.

"It's been too long," Nyah shouted after they'd slowed their tired horses to a canter. "Ask the queen how long before her shroud falls."

"Her shroud?" said Tau.

"She's been in Isihogo this whole time. She's slowing their horses for us."

Tau held more tightly to the queen, considering what a fall at such speed would do to them. "She's in the underworld?"

"And here," Nyah shouted back. "She holds her mind in both places, seeing in both realms."

Tau was behind the queen, but it still surprised him to think that she'd gone to Isihogo without him realizing. "Queen Tsiora?"

There was no answer and talking wasn't the fastest way to get the answer he needed anyway. He followed her into the underworld, where Isihogo called to his blood, begging him to stay, to fight, but he left before the call of the mists and the monsters it hid could convince him.

"Her shroud is collapsing," he shouted to the vizier.

"Of course it is. It shouldn't even be possible for her to use her gifts this long," Nyah said.

"We can hear you," the queen said, taking a deep breath as she came out of Isihogo and sagged against him. "We've done all we could, and the horse we entreated will behave as if it's injured for a quarter span at most. Care, they're close now."

And they were. It was dark, cloudy, and wet, but they'd been traveling east and the storm was moving in the opposite direction. Where they were it was barely raining and through the thin showers Tau could see his enemy.

"They're looking at one of the horse's feet," he said. "No... wait...they've seen us. They're abandoning that horse and one of them is getting onto another animal. I think...it's Mirembe. She's climbing onto the back of the spare horse, the one meant for the assassin."

"You can see all that?" Nyah said, riding hard, squinting, and leaning forward over her horse's neck. "What are you...Tau Solarin?"

"Sharp-eyed, Vizier Nyah," he said.

"The horse they left behind was their fastest," Queen Tsiora said. "We should take it, catch them, and force them to fight."

"Not you, my queen," said Nyah. "You've done enough and your gifts are spent."

"Who, then?" the queen asked. "Kellan cannot ride at speed. Ihashe Uduak cannot ride at all."

"Uduak and I will change to the fast horse," Nyah said. "Leave Okar on his horse to follow as he's able."

Kellan looked both angry and ashamed at the same time. He wanted to offer more than he was able to give.

"I'll ride with the vizier," Tau said. He needed to see Mirembe again, after what she'd done to him in the council chambers.

"It'll be me," Uduak countered.

"Those are Ingonyama and a Gifted up there," Tau said. "And the general can still do damage with a sword, even if he has to wield it off-handed. I can stop them."

Uduak waved a hand at Tau's thigh. "You've one good leg."

"Praise the Goddess, she also gave me two hands."

It looked like Uduak grunted, but Tau couldn't hear it over the wind and considered the discussion closed.

"What about the Gifted?" Uduak asked, reopening it and making Tau shiver at the memory of the hold Mirembe had had on him.

"She'll be busy," Nyah said. "I'll entreat her and she'll be forced to do the same to me."

"Champion," the queen said too quietly for the others to hear. "The fight between Nyah and Mirembe cannot last long."

Tau understood. Nyah and Mirembe would be fighting each other in Isihogo. They'd be pulling as much energy as they could and their shrouds would collapse quickly. The stronger one would win and the weaker one would fall prey to the demons.

"Nyah?" Tau asked as they pulled up to the horse the traitors had abandoned.

Nyah knew what he was asking. "Mirembe is stronger," she said, dismounting the horse she'd ridden with Uduak. "Let's go, Champion."

Tau took his arms from the queen's waist and she rocked in her horse's seat. She was exhausted and he delayed a moment to steady her.

"I won't let their fight last," he told her.

She nodded and he slid his way off the horse's back and onto the ground, almost collapsing when his wounded leg took the weight. Gritting his teeth and clenching his fists around his sword hilts, he let the wave of pain smash into and over him before making his way to Nyah, who was busy climbing up on the horse Mirembe had been riding.

"Tau...," Kellan said, worry in his voice.

"Come as fast as you can," Tau said. "I'll hold them until you do."

"Let's go!" said Nyah, offering a hand to help him climb onto the massive black horse.

Tau clasped Nyah's wrist, steeled his features, and pulled his way onto the seat behind her.

"Hyah!" Nyah said, the horse shot off like a spear, and they were flying over the ground again. Ahead, Otobong and Mirembe were whipping their horses with wooden switches, desperate to make the animals run faster, but the distance between the pursuer and the pursued continued to shrink.

As they closed the gap, Tau looked back. The queen, Uduak, and Kellan were falling behind.

"If my fight with Mirembe lasts too long, I'll fall to her," Nyah said, the wind making her sound tremulous.

"That won't happen," Tau told her.

She said nothing more to him, speaking to the horse instead, urging it on toward the small hill ahead.

Mirembe's party had just topped the hill and Tau could not see beyond it, but he did notice how much faster they were closing the distance.

"They're slowing," Tau said.

"They can't outrun us and they know that this is their best chance," Nyah said. "They hope to kill us before the others catch up."

Tau rotated his wrists, loosening them for the fight. "They hope."

FALLOW

Mirembe, Otobong, and the two Indlovu disappeared over the hill, and Tau worried that he and Nyah might be headed for an ambush. What he saw when they crested the hill was more surprising.

After a shallow dip, the sloping ground gave way to a thousand strides of farmland being worked by hundreds of Drudge with nothing but the moon's light by which to see. Nyah pulled their horse to a stop at the crop field's edge, and Tau winced as pain flared along his leg, locking his thigh in a spasm of cramps.

"I'll keep Mirembe out of the fight as long as I can," Nyah said.

Tau nodded, and with his leg still locked up, he heaved himself off the animal's back and onto the ground. He was not in good fighting shape. "The people, they can help."

"What people?" Nyah asked.

All around Tau were leafy stalks topped with rust-colored clusters of grain. The millet was arranged in neat rows taller than he was and they stretched off as far as he could see. The Drudge among them were still, heads down, as if they too had been planted in place.

Tau drew his swords. Without the extra height from the horse's back, he'd already lost sight of the Nobles, and they could be coming for him.

Not five strides away and closest to him was one of the Drudge. The man was old, his face lined, hair in knots, and skin peeling from too many days in the sun. He was wearing rags and holding a wooden crate, heavy with the grains he'd collected, clutched to his chest.

He was not looking down. He was staring, his gaze bouncing from Tau's scarred face to his red-and-black armor to his twin dragon-scale swords.

"Ukufa?" he asked in a whisper.

"Where are they?"

Still staring, the Drudge lifted a hand and pointed a bent and knobby finger at the packed stalks and leaves just to Tau's right. Tau turned his head, peering into the dark, and as he looked, the clouds parted just enough for the moonlight to glint off the bronze gripped in the hands of the two Indlovu hiding there.

"I see you," he said, and they charged him.

The old Drudge was in their way and Otobong's soldiers would cut him down first. To stop them, Tau hobbled to the Drudge as fast as he could, his right leg in agony every time he put weight on it. The first Indlovu swung his sword at the old man.

It was reckless, stupid, but Tau threw himself across the last two strides and into the Drudge, knocking the old man clear of the swing and narrowly avoiding losing his own head. They went down in a heap, Tau on the bottom, screaming. He'd landed on his right thigh and his vision pulsed with fat circles of red as the pain from his leg shot through him.

"Kill them!" shouted the slower of the two Indlovu, and the Noble standing over them was happy to oblige.

He sent a thrust for Tau's chest, and, unable to bring his own swords to bear, Tau rolled, dragging the Drudge with him. Instead of flesh, the Greater Noble's blade struck soil, kicking up a spray of dirt, and Tau, certain he couldn't get to his feet before hard bronze opened him up, dropped one of his weapons, scooped up a handful of dirt, and flung it at the man's face.

The Indlovu brought his sword up to deflect the dirt but still ended up taking most of it in the mouth.

Retrieving his sword, Tau half scrambled, half limped to his feet, turning in time to see the Indlovu spit out a thick gob of saliva-soaked soil. The slower Noble, having made it into striking range and hoping to catch Tau off guard, took a swing at him. Tau saw the attack, blocked it, and spun for the Noble covered in dirt, aiming to skewer that one with his other blade.

He didn't make it. His leg gave out and he had to hop on the good one to avoid tumbling to the ground.

"Cek!" he cursed as the soil-stained Indlovu came for him.

Tau parried, countered, and drew first blood with a vicious cut that ran the length of the Indlovu's sword arm. Yelping, the Greater Noble jumped back and then the second Indlovu was on him.

Hobbling and hopping, Tau whirled his blades at the second soldier's head, shoulder, hip, and leg, wilting the much larger man beneath the barrage.

"Help me!" the Indlovu shouted to the soil-stained Greater Noble, who responded by coming for Tau's back.

Tau spun on his left leg, away from the man he was facing, and crossed swords with the Indlovu coming for him. He cut him once, twice, and as he'd done a hundred thousand times in the mists when demons came at him from every side, Tau thrust the sword in his left hand forward, a feint, reversed his grip so the point faced behind him, and threw his arm back.

The black blade burned through the air until it met leather, flesh, the edge of bone, and finally, the softer stuff that tethers the souls of men. It plunged deep into the core of the Indlovu behind him, and the sword was almost pulled from Tau's grip when the man lurched, pawing at the thing that had killed him.

Holding his weapon tight, Tau glanced over his shoulder and saw the stabbed man slice his fingers to ribbons as they danced drunkenly along the edges of the dragon scale. The spark in the Indlovu's eyes dimmed, his legs gave out, and then he slipped off the weapon's point, onto the rare, rich soil of the peninsula's grain fields.

The remaining Indlovu, his face spattered with dirt, called to the fallen man with a tenderness that had no place on fields of blood. He spoke the man's name, invoking it like a prayer, but if that was what it was, it went unanswered.

"I'll leave your corpse here to rot!" the soil-stained Indlovu shouted, his muscles beginning to warp and multiply as the beginnings of the enraging took hold.

"Cek!" Tau cursed again, noticing Mirembe ten strides behind the Indlovu, her hands up and aimed at the transforming man. Otobong was beside her, holding his sword low in his off hand, his only hand.

"I'll shit in your dead mouth, Lesser!" the Greater Noble said, his voice so deep the words were barely intelligible.

"Tau!" It was Nyah from behind him. "You have to be quick," she said, her eyes losing focus on the world as she sent her spirit to Isihogo.

Mirembe stiffened immediately. "Kudliwe!"

The effects of the enraging slowed, halted, then began to work in reverse, and Tau heard the Greater Noble's bones creak and pop as he was returned to his normal size and strength.

"Watch the Lesser," Mirembe said through tight lips, and Otobong stepped in front of her, hefting his sword awkwardly.

Mirembe had the look of someone in the underworld. Her eyes flickered back and forth, not seeing the fields of grain around them, but something else. Then her gaze settled, locking onto something, someone. She clenched her fists and smiled, and Tau knew she'd found Nyah in the mists.

"I have you, nceku," Mirembe hissed, making a dragging motion with her hands that seemed to cause Nyah to stagger.

"Champion, hurry!" Nyah said, and before Tau could take a step, the Indlovu attacked, aiming for his wounded leg.

Tau used both swords to block the low strike. "Coward," he said.

"Lesser," the Indlovu answered.

And Nyah cried out, drawing Tau's attention. She was standing but bent over like she'd taken a blow.

"My shroud...it's gone," she said, eyes blank, still focused on the underworld. "They're coming. Oh Goddess...I can hear them coming."

Tau had to get to Mirembe, but his opponent knew it too and the Indlovu was backing up, doing just enough to keep him away from the chairwoman, and Tau couldn't move well enough to get past the soldier in the breaths that were left to do it. He needed help and saw it coming.

The queen, riding double with Uduak, along with Kellan on his white horse, had reached the hill's crest. They were close but not close enough. Time flowed differently in Isihogo, and Nyah would be dead before they could play a part.

Worry flooding him, Tau turned back to the fight. He couldn't get past the Indlovu and the general before Nyah died. He wasn't enough to stop them all. He knew it and was going to try anyway.

He raised his sword and gathered himself for a charge when he heard feet shuffling in the dirt, dozens of them, and Tau, like a cloth had been lifted from his eyes, remembered that the fields were not empty. They'd been so silent, so still and subdued, that the Drudge who'd gathered to watch the conflict seemed little more than the soil, stalks, and grains that surrounded them all. He'd paid them no mind, and the Drudge had been invisible to him. It was easy to forget that they were also Omehi.

"Fight the Nobles!" Tau shouted, shuffling forward on his good leg, ignoring the Indlovu's feint and ducking his real attack. "Fight them!"

Otobong, five strides distant, raised his sword higher and looked around for the new enemy. When he realized Tau was calling out to the Drudge, he laughed. "You think they'd dare?"

"Omehi, my name is Tau Solarin. I am the queen's champion and I call on you for aid!" Tau said.

He saw movement among the crops. It was the old man whom Tau had knocked to the ground. He was holding his large crate like it was a boulder, and when he was close enough, he brought it crashing down on the back of Mirembe's head. The basket smashed to pieces, Mirembe squawked, and the Indlovu whom Tau was fighting turned to her.

He would have seen Mirembe crumble to the ground. He might even have noticed Nyah do the same. There was, however, no chance he saw Tau lunge for him, because Tau's two blades took him in the back, killing him instantly.

Otobong swung at the old man, his sword, held in his off hand, moving in a crude arc. "Nceku!"

The old man, quicker than he looked, threw himself away from the blow but couldn't avoid it, and the sword sliced him from shoulder to navel. He dropped to the ground, cradling himself with his arms, and his ragged shirt grew stained with blood.

"Damn you!" Tau said to Otobong.

"Get back," Otobong said, pointing his sword at Tau's heart.

Tau began to circle Otobong, moving so he could check on the Drudge and Nyah. The Drudge wasn't moving.

"You're going to die on the end of my sword, Otobong," Tau growled, letting his eyes slip to Nyah.

The vizier was stirring, recovering from her battle with Mirembe, and at the same moment as relief flooded him that Nyah was well, Tau spun to block the blow Otobong had quietly launched for his skull.

Blade met blade, and Tau, ignoring his bad leg, stepped into the much larger general, moving Otobong's sword farther out of line while pressing his second sword to the general's armpit, aiming into his body and lungs.

"You think me a liar?" Tau asked. "I told you, it'll be my sword that ends your life."

"Champion Solarin, we must return General Otobong and Council-woman Mirembe to Citadel City to face justice." The queen had arrived.

"Champion?" Kellan had bumbled his way off the horse and marched over.

"What?" Tau asked, his body buzzing with anger. He wanted to spear Otobong like a fish for what he'd done to the old man. He wanted to gut Mirembe for what she'd done to him in the council chambers.

Uduak was there next, wide-legged and stiff from the riding. "I have him," the big man said, taking over from Tau by placing his great sword against Otobong's neck.

With another glance at Nyah, who was sitting up and holding hands with the queen, Tau went to the Drudge's side. The old man's eyes were open, staring sightlessly at the cloudy sky. He was dead.

It was torture to do it on his bad leg, but Tau knelt beside the man and gently closed his eyes.

"Champion," called Kellan, "we'll bind Otobong and Mirembe and throw them over the backs of the horses for the return ride. We need to get to the keep."

Tau ignored Kellan. "What was his name?" he asked the others. No one spoke, and Tau pointed to a woman in ragged clothes. "You, what was his name?"

"He was a Drudge," she said.

"Drudge have names," Tau said, persisting.

She backed away. "Please, nkosi, I don't want to be part of anything…"

"I'm not asking you to be."

"Please, nkosi," she said, slipping back into the stalks and the dark, disappearing.

Tau looked at the other Drudge, but they were leaving too. He saw a young man who still had some meat on his bones and made to speak to him.

The man dropped his eyes. "I'm sorry, nkosi," he said, shuffling back. "I can't."

"Can't what?" asked Tau, but the Drudge was gone.

Tau put his face in his hands, rubbing the skin there before standing stiffly and pointing to the old man. "He saved people tonight. He helped the queendom," he said to the ones hidden among the crops. "I need to leave. I have to leave. Will you take his body? Will you honor him and burn it?"

Silence.

"The old Drudge was the one who struck Mirembe?" asked Kellan, walking closer.

Glaring at Kellan, Tau struggled back to his feet. "You don't want him burned? What's fitting for a Drudge who struck a Noble instead? Should we eviscerate the body?"

Flexing his jaw, Kellan stepped past Tau to kneel beside the old man's body. He put his hands under it and carried him, moving closer to the row of crops that hid the nearest group of Drudge. As he went, Tau saw that the old man's blood had smeared and filthied Kellan's armor.

"If you do not object, I will carry him back to Citadel City," Kellan said to the Drudge. "We will give him full military honors. We will burn him and send his soul to the Goddess."

"If it please you, leave him, nkosi," said a thin voice, a woman's voice. "We will see to him."

"And who are you?" Kellan asked.

"He watches out for... he watched out for me, nkosi."

Kellan nodded at that, gently placed the man's body back on the ground, saluted in the direction of the Drudge, and walked away to help Uduak bundle the chairwoman and general onto one of the horses. Tau watched Kellan go, unsure how to feel, and, still unsure, he turned back to the Drudge.

"I should have been able to save him," he said to the women and men he could not see, and when no response came, he went too, giving the casteless the space to reclaim the man who was theirs.

"We worried about you," the queen said when Tau came close. She was next to Nyah. "We worried for your safety and Nyah's. She says you stopped Mirembe."

"A Drudge did that, my queen," Tau said.

"Queen Tsiora," said Kellan, "we should return to Citadel City. It's not wise for us to stay out here longer than we must."

Tau was tired, his muscles ached, and his leg burned. The ride back would be excruciating, but they might as well get on with it. He had hobbled his way past Nyah and toward the horses when she put a hand on his forearm, stopping him.

"I saw how hard you fought and know you're hurt and hurting. You saved me. Thank you."

Tau shook his head. "You almost died because I couldn't stop them. The old man... People keep on dying because I'm not enough to protect them."

Nyah seemed to consider him.

"I'll do better," Tau said. "I'll be stronger."

He didn't know why he said it, especially not why he said it to her, and she kept looking at him as if searching for something, but he was weary and in no mood for talk. He inclined his head to her and continued on.

"I think I can see why the queen picked you," she said.

Tau stopped without turning. He could have asked what she meant. That night, in that moment, she might even have told him. But he wasn't sure he wanted to know.

"The storm is weakening," Kellan called to them.

"No storm here," Uduak said.

"It's moving west, heading out to the ocean and beyond," Kellan said. "We need to get back to the city to gather our men for the attack. If Hadith is right and the warlord is onshore, tonight is our only chance. The storm and Achak will be gone come morning."

The queen, on her horse, held out one of her too-cool hands to Tau. He took it and fumbled his way up behind her.

"We ride hard and fast," she said. "We race a dying storm in hopes to trade it for Achak's life."

More killing, thought Tau, and his blades hadn't yet been cleaned from the last lot.

HOW

Mirembe and Otobong were taken to the keep's prisons, but not before the queen made them a promise: They would meet justice at dawn. Having given them her word, Queen Tsiora left the stables with Nyah, and Kellan and Uduak asked Tau to accompany them to the courtyard to finalize preparations for the attack on Warlord Achak.

Tau stayed behind, telling his brothers he had to clean his swords, and when they left, he dismissed the stable hands. Once alone, he clamped a hand over his mouth and screamed into it, desperate to expel the ball of hurt that seemed to live in his chest and heart.

The old Drudge had tried to help him and had died doing it. He'd gone to the Goddess in the same way that Tau's father had, that Oyibo had . . . that Zuri had. They'd all come to his defense, but when they'd needed him, he'd failed them.

Still screaming, Tau slumped against the door to the nearest horse pen and slammed a fist against it, hitting the weak wood hard enough to bruise his hand. His eyes were squeezed shut, and his head hummed in turmoil, but that didn't stop him from hearing it when the large black horse he'd ridden with the queen came closer. He heard its heavy steps on the hay-strewn floor and then its wet breathing, like it was blowing air against its cheeks as it exhaled.

Not knowing what the beast ate and unwilling to be bitten, Tau opened his eyes and stepped away.

"Don't even think it," he said to the black horse, showing it his strong-side sword. "I have teeth too."

Creeping closer, the horse paid him and the sword little mind. It had its ears back against its head, making them look small and pointed, but did the opposite with its eyes and nostrils. Both were wide, held open as far as possible. Tau was ignorant of the animal's typical behaviors but couldn't imagine these were signs of warmth and welcome.

"Leave me alone, nceku!" Tau said, raising his sword higher. "Ha-ya!"

The creature was on the far side of the low wooden wall of its pen, but the wood was weak and the horse could smash through the false barrier easily.

"What's the matter with you?"

The horse bared its block of teeth, rolled its eyes, and reared, feet kicking. Sticking to the wall of the pen, Tau backed away and to the side. The animals were priceless and he didn't want to hurt it, but he had both swords ready as he watched the crazed animal.

"Thought we were getting to be frien—" he began, realizing midthought that, when he'd moved to the side, the horse hadn't followed him with its head or eyes.

The horse, Tau realized, wasn't reacting to him, and with the hairs on his neck shooting up, he threw himself to the ground, rolling away as the wood where he'd been standing exploded in a storm of shards.

The howl he heard behind him was not a sound that could come from any animal he knew, and Tau lurched to his feet, tamping down the roar of pain in his leg as he spun to face the thing that had nearly decapitated him.

It wasn't tall. Which was to say, the demon matched him in height. It was heavier than he was, though, and had thick yellowish skin that was bumped and mottled like a toad's flesh. It stared at him with reflective eyes the size of fists and had the circular mouth of a suckerfish. Howling from that too-small orifice, it flexed the six clawed fingers on the ends of its short arms and ran at him.

"This can't be real. You're not rea—" Tau started, without the time to finish the thought before needing to jerk back and away from its slashing reach.

He made enough space to avoid disembowelment, hit his back against a wooden wall, and found himself facing the demon with less than two strides separating them. It leapt at him and Tau had nowhere left to go.

By this point, the black horse was in a frenzy, and though it looked to Tau like the demon was still howling when it jumped, he couldn't be sure. It was impossible to hear it over the braying and stomping of the penned-in horse.

Tau brought his swords up to stop the demon's claws from taking out his eyes and slid along the wall, hoping to get out of its way. The swords did their work. They stopped the demon from taking out his eyes and cut through the leather-thick flesh on its hands, but Tau couldn't get clear, the monster slammed into him, and he slammed into the wooden wall.

The wall behind Tau caved inward and he was sent crashing into the stall's hay-covered dirt floor hard enough to empty his lungs of breath. The demon was on top of him, its round maw slicing open and shut a fingerspan from his nose as he fought to hold it clear by pressing the hilts of his blades into its neck.

"How? How...," he growled at it as it snapped at him and scrabbled about, trying to bring it claws or teeth to bear.

Working fast, Tau slipped his knees beneath its bulk, leveraged his feet against what he considered to be its hips, and kicked out, pushing it down and away from him. He screamed as he did it, his leg protesting with a particularly vicious stab of pain.

The demon, thick but not slow, got its legs back under itself, and on all fours, it scuttled for him.

Scooting back, Tau slashed his strong-side sword into its shoulder and made to stab it through the face with his other blade but missed when the demon's head was trampled into the floor by the black horse's front hooves.

The demon, its eyes wider than should have been possible, spasmed like it was seizing, and the black horse reared and came down again. Its hooves connected, hammering into the demon's head, pulping it to mush and stilling the last of the monster's movements. The horse rose and came down a third time, its hooves hitting the hay-strewn ground and the demon-shaped pile of gray ash that had taken the monster's place.

The force of the blow scattered the ashes that had, one blink prior, been the demon, sending them swirling into the air, where each flake collapsed in on itself, falling out of sight and existence. Then, like sand flowing through the holes of an invisible sieve, the last of the ashes vanished until there was nothing of the demon left at all.

"How?" Tau asked again.

SHADOWS

Frantic and rushing, Tau limped his way out of the stables and ran for the courtyard. The rain had slowed to a drizzle and the keep's guttering torches turned the wet mist, slick cobblestones, and shining keep walls into an endless array of undulating shapes and shadows, each one capable of hiding a monster that could cut his throat before he had time to warn the others.

He ran faster, racing headlong into three shapes detaching themselves from the shadows up ahead.

"Found you," a voice said as the first of the three shapes stepped into the torchlight.

Cursing, Tau tried to stop but put his foot on a wet stone and slipped. To catch himself, he threw all his weight on his bad leg and the world contracted down to a singular, blinding point of agony.

"Cek!" he said, raising his swords.

"Tau, easy! What's going on?"

It was Hadith's voice. It had been Hadith's voice earlier as well, and as Tau's vision returned to normal and the pain subsided, he saw the others. Hadith was with Uduak and Kellan.

"We came for you," Hadith said. "The storm's heart has left the peninsula. It's already out on the Roar and soon the warlord's ships will be too. It's time to go."

Tau knew none of that mattered.

"They're here!" he said. "In the keep!"

As one, the three men drew their blades and closed ranks around Tau, expecting an attack.

"Where?" asked Uduak, looking left and right.

"Stables," Tau said. "It started there."

"How many of them?" Hadith asked.

"One, so far. It attacked me."

"One?" Kellan asked. "One Xiddeen? One of Odili's men?"

Tau couldn't catch his breath. "It's not a man."

Kellan nodded. "Xiddeen, then," he said. "A woman raider."

"It doesn't mean she's the only one here," Hadith said, pointing to an archway that led deeper into the keep. "Move to the archway. If there's many of them, they won't be able to surround us."

Uduak nodded and pulled on Tau's arm, and the four of them dashed to stand beneath and within the archway's protective walls, limiting the angles from which they could be attacked.

"Can we call to our men?" Kellan whispered to Tau. "Or do we risk bringing the Xiddeen down on ourselves?"

"It's not the Xiddeen," Tau said, peering out beyond the murk of the dark archway. There were so many shadows and they all stretched off in the distance, long as spears. "It was a demon."

Kellan's sword point bobbed in the air. "A what?"

"Did you say demon?" Hadith asked, his whisper more of a hiss.

Still scanning the pathway, Tau nodded. "It attacked me in the stables."

He heard Hadith sigh and then he heard him sheath his sword. "You fell asleep and were in Isihogo?"

Uduak and Kellan didn't put their weapons away, but both let their sword points drop toward the cobblestones.

No," said Tau. "It was here."

"Where, here?" Hadith asked him.

"Uhmlaba."

"A demon?"

"Yes."

Uduak and Kellan sheathed their blades.

"You need rest," Uduak said.

Hadith sniffed. "Tau, it's been a long day. You're wounded, exhausted. You probably fell asleep."

"No! I told you what happened."

Hadith put a hand on his shoulder. "And I'll do you the courtesy of pretending that you didn't."

"Don't you see?" Tau asked. "This could mean—"

"It could mean you get dismissed as champion. It could mean you and your story about stable demons contribute to the downfall of a queen whose rule already hangs by a strand as thin as spider's silk." Hadith shook his head. "Goddess wept, Tau, she made a Lesser her champion, a Low Common."

Tau bristled. "High Common."

"No one cares. Queen Tsiora is the monarch of a splintered queendom, ruling over a side populated by Lessers and the Nobility's castoffs."

Tau was losing them and he couldn't afford that. "I've seen them before. Long before today," he said. "It started at the isikolo. Sometimes in the shadows. Sometimes in the long grasses. Sometimes at the edges of my vision, disappearing when I turned my head. They'd put their faces on the faces of humans."

Uduak's breath rumbled in the back of his throat and the big man made the sign of the dragon's span.

"They'd come to me in—"

"Daydreams," Hadith said. "Visions brought on by overwork. You were not a healthy man at the isikolo, and because I must be honest with you, it's hard for me to believe you're one now. Tau, you've been through too much too fast. . . . We all have."

The words stung.

"You know me better than that," Tau said.

"I find you running through the keep with your sword out and you tell me you're being chased by demons."

"I didn't say I was being chased. I killed it"—Tau wasn't sure where to look—"with the horse's help."

For a long breath, Hadith simply stared. "Did it injure you? Do you have its blood on your blades?" Hadith said, eyeing his two swords.

Tau blinked and looked at the weapons he held. The blades were clean, bloodless. "I don't understand....I—I stabbed it. I—"

"Fine, we don't have any evidence here," Hadith said in a manner not unlike the way Aren would do after Tau had had a nightmare, "but we can go to the stables. You can show us the demon."

"It..." Tau sought help from Uduak or Kellan and found none. He brought his gaze back to Hadith's face, unable to meet his sword brother's eyes. "It turned to ash," he said. "It turned to ash and then the ashes vanished."

Hadith ran a hand over his shaved head. "Tau..."

Tau turned away from them and slammed his blades back into their scabbards. "I know what I saw."

"You need rest and probably a priestess."

Tau glared at him.

"For your leg," Hadith said, clarifying.

Tau closed his eyes. "I'm fine. I'm...I'm a little unsettled, that's all."

"Bleeding," Uduak said.

"What?" Tau looked down at his leg. The leather of his uniform was damp and dark around his wound.

"Need new bandages as well as rest," Uduak said.

"I will, when we're back."

Kellan cleared his throat. "Champion, we can do this. You need not come...if you're not well."

"He's right," Hadith said. "You're trying to do too much. Keep going this way and you'll be no use to yourself or anyone else."

"I'm fine," Tau said as an Ihashe walked into the archway and almost through the tip of the sword Tau had yanked out and up.

"Tau!" Hadith yelled.

Tau backed away. His sword was still up. He was having trouble lowering it. "I'm fine."

Looking ready to wet himself, the Ihashe swallowed, the stone in his throat jerking up and down. "The vizier sent me and a few others." He pointed in the direction of the courtyard. "The queen is ready to see the war party off."

"Thank you, Ihashe. We're coming," Kellan said.

The soldier saluted and left in a hurry.

"Do this for me and go see the priestess," Hadith said to Tau.

"No, I'm coming," Tau said, leaving them behind and walking toward the courtyard.

He tried to walk evenly, shutting out the burning from his leg and the shake in his nerves. The demon had to be real, but the doubt he'd seen on the faces of his sword brothers, his bloodless swords, and the demonless stables had already come together and conspired to make him doubt his own mind.

He heard the footsteps of his sword brothers behind him. Still, he didn't slow down and they didn't try to catch up, and when he got to the courtyard, he found it full of men in fighting gear and three Gifted, if the vizier and queen weren't counted.

The crowd turned to him, and though he didn't feel strong, Tau straightened his back while tightening his grip on the sword he still hadn't sheathed. He nodded to the fighters and every one of them saluted.

He walked over to the queen, who was smiling at something one of the Indlovu had said. The soldier bowed to her and left and Tau saw her smile slip. He wasn't the only one playing at strength he no longer had. He bowed his head to her.

"Champion," she said.

"My queen."

"We have come to wish you well. We are in your hands." She stepped closer, leaned in, and kissed him on the cheek.

It surprised him and he had to fight his instincts in order to hold still. He'd expected her lips to be cool, like her hands. They were not. They were warm, almost hot.

She kissed his other cheek and stepped back. "Come back to us."

Tau saluted, and from the corner of his eye, he saw Hadith tilt his head. It was the type of movement one made when being offered food or drink. It was the type of movement that asked, "A little more, please?"

Tau was thinking about the demon. He wanted to tell the queen and worried that Hadith was right and that telling her might brand him a madman, and he could see no way that helped him or her.

Hadith, Tau thought, was usually right, and with that in mind, Tau gave him what he wanted.

"We will return with the sun, my queen," Tau said loud enough for the courtyard to hear, "and when you see me again, the warlord will be dead."

CHAPTER THREE

EQUAL

Lightning forked across the night sky, tearing its blue-black infinity into brighter sections that outlined the claw of men trudging up the Fist. Pausing to see if the burning in his leg might lessen, Tau watched the lightning streak and disappear, plunging the world back into darkness, wet, and mud. He was having trouble keeping up and knew the claw were going slower than they would otherwise to accommodate him.

He'd have found that funny, if he wasn't in so much pain. Tau was born and raised in Kerem, in the southern mountain range of the peninsula, and no Kerem woman or man would deign to call the Fist a mountain. Yet, he was struggling to climb it, slowing down people who'd spent their entire lives in the flatlands.

"Like the view?" Themba asked, sliding up next to him and making a pretense of gazing out at the brush and blasted landscape he'd barely be able to see in the dark.

Not wanting to spare the energy for words, Tau grunted and marched on, the boots Jabari had given him squelching into the sucking mud.

Themba kept up easily. "Hadith wanted me to let you know the plan."

"It's changed from 'kill the warlord'?"

Themba chuckled. Cynicism seemed to tickle the man. "One prong for each beach. The prongs that do not find the Xiddeen are to make for the next nearest beach as reinforcements."

Tau offered another grunt. "Have you ever seen the beaches? Any of them?"

"Me? No," Themba said. "Kellan has, though. He says the Fist's peak is a few hundred strides back from the Roar and that there are paths leading down to the sand and waters." Themba looked Tau up and down. "Two of the paths require climbing."

"I'll make it."

"You won't need to."

"Neh?"

"Kellan will take one of the steep paths. He's leading his prong and will have a Gifted with him. Uduak has command of the other prong. He's got a Gifted too."

Tau grimaced. "They're giving me the easy way and Hadith to hold my hand?"

Themba smiled. "I'll be there too, and as I see it, we're the head of this dragon."

"I don't want soft treatment," Tau said, hating that the words sounded like they belonged in the mouth of a coddled Noble child.

"Suit yourself, but I'd rather you don't spoil it for those of us who don't mind a little soft every now and then. No sense in climbing up and down cliffs in the middle of the night if we don't have to."

Tau didn't answer that. He wasn't about to admit that he didn't think himself able to do much climbing. "Let's catch up," he said.

Eyeing Tau's wounded leg, Themba raised an eyebrow and pushed his lips to one side.

Having Themba judge him and find him wanting was more than Tau could take, and he shuffled past the taller man, marching as fast as he could without passing out from pain.

Themba, with his longer, healthier gait, caught up again. "Easy, Tau. You're already champion. Not much left to prove."

Tau, keeping his head down so Themba wouldn't see how much pain he was in, moved his hand to indicate the soldiers around them,

Ihashe and Indlovu. "It took twice the ability to get named it and it'll take thrice that for them to believe I deserve it."

Themba shrugged. "And their opinions of you are worth the pain, the sacrifice?"

The tone was so serious, it was hard to believe the words had come out of Themba's mouth, and Tau lifted his head to look at his sword brother. "I don't do anything for the opinions of others."

Tau knew the sentiment would be hard to accept, but with no smile, no mockery, and no insincerity, Themba asked, "Why, then?"

Tau kept marching, limping. "Because the limits to which we've been yoked were never ours, and the stories we've been told about our nature, our insignificance, and our lack, they were never true."

When Themba spoke, he did it quietly. "That's why, then? You think we can be Noble too?"

Tau's leg felt like it was being scourged, but he increased his pace, daring the pain to stop him. "That's not it," he said. "The lie isn't that we can't be their equals. The lie is that they were ever anything but our equals."

Yes, if the measure of a man was height, then Nobles were taller. If the measure of a man was physical strength, then Nobles were stronger. But Tau knew who decided what needed to be measured, and they'd chosen things in which they already had an advantage. They said, "This matters more than that," making it seem as if their edicts sprang from natural law when they were little more than self-serving choices. They wrote the rules in their favor, succeeded more often than others, and pointed to that as proof of their superiority. It was all a lie.

Meanwhile, the look on Themba's face was making Tau feel a bit foolish. The sarcastic Ihashe was being too serious, too intense. It wasn't like him, and, continuing to behave oddly, Themba nodded at Tau's words.

Tau had expected a rejoinder, a quip, a demeaning grin. What came instead surprised him.

"I miss it," said Themba.

"What?"

"On marches like this, he'd always be coughing."

"Chinedu?"

"I miss it, you know? I miss him coughing. It's stupid, neh?"

Tau caught Themba's eye and shook his head. "No, it's not."

Neither of them said another word for the rest of the march to the Crags, and when they arrived, the claw gathered in the urban battleground before separating into their prongs.

Uduak was already with his fighters and Hadith was speaking with him. They clasped wrists, Hadith said a few more words, Uduak waved to Tau, and Tau waved back. Then Uduak ordered his men to march, and just like that, they were gone.

Kellan was also with his men, and Tau saw that the Gifted in his prong was Thandi, the one he'd first met in the tunnels beneath the Guardian Keep. She was standing near him and gazing up at Kellan as he buckled his shield to his back, perhaps to keep it out of the way when he had to climb down the cliffs leading to his assigned beach.

As Tau stood there, feeling guilty that Kellan might have to climb because he could not, Kellan saluted. Hurriedly, Tau returned the gesture.

"Goddess go with you," Tau shouted across the distance between them.

"And you," Kellan called back.

Tau turned to Hadith, wondering why everyone was being so strange and formal, when he recognized where they were. He was standing in the same circle of the urban battleground where he'd almost killed Kellan not so long ago. He glanced back, seeking the Greater Noble, but Kellan had turned a corner and was lost to sight.

"Didn't think we'd be back here, especially not this soon," Hadith said.

"Looks different," Themba said.

"How so?"

"Smaller."

"Doesn't it just," said Hadith. "Come, now, let's go and see if we're the ones with the lucky beach."

"Why is it," Themba asked, sounding more like his regular self, "that with two of three beaches bound to be empty, I still think we'll be the ones to step in the scorpion's nest?"

"Ihashe, we should march in silence," said the older Gifted in their prong as she walked past Themba with her Indlovu honor guard.

"Couldn't have gotten us the pretty one?" Themba said when she'd gone from earshot.

"What's that?" Hadith asked, cupping his ear and looking in the Gifted's direction. "Speak up?"

Themba did no such thing, opting to give him a look and a few muttered curses instead.

The path they took up and out of the Crags was one Tau had never taken before, and they marched for the better part of a span before one of the Gifted's honor guard came to speak with them. He was big, a decent bit larger than Uduak, and he looked down his nose at them when he spoke.

"The beach isn't far now. We'll have to go in slowly and watch for scouts."

"I'll go ahead with Themba," Tau said.

Themba shot Tau a look. "What? Why? Uh... Champion."

"Because we are more than equal to the task," Tau told him. "What's the best way to the beach from here?"

The Indlovu explained the layout, drawing a crude map in the wet dirt.

"That can't be right," Tau said, having a hard time believing the man's map and maintaining an agonizing crouch so he could see it. "You've drawn it as if there's a forest of stone on the beach."

The Indlovu seemed to want to say something other than what he did. "It is right."

Tau stared at the lines in the dirt and then at the man. "Very well. If there are scouts, we'll handle them. Give us a quarter span and follow."

The Indlovu stood, saluted, and went back to stand with the Gifted. Tau prepared himself, exhaled, and straightened up too, closing his eyes and biting his lip as the spasm of agony blazed through his thigh.

"And with that leg, you want to go scouting?" Themba asked.

Tau opened his eyes. "I do."

Themba was pouting. "Stubborn as a dung beetle in an outhouse."

Hadith put a hand on Tau's shoulder. "Will you try not to do anything stupid?"

"I'll try," Tau said, taking some pleasure in the worried look on Themba's face.

Hadith clasped Tau's wrist and then it was time to go.

"Please be one of the lucky beaches," Themba said, following Tau.

"Are you often lucky?" Tau asked over his shoulder.

Themba sighed. "Since I met you? Never."

ORDERS

They encountered no scouts, but they did find the Xiddeen. The majority of the raiding fleet had set sail, and as far as Tau could see, a line of longboats snaked out of view behind the swell and crash of the Roar's eternal anger.

They had come in perfect time. The scouts had been recalled to board the last two ships, and all that remained of the largest invasion of Omehi land in living memory were two hundred hedeni, including their warlord.

A short run inland but still on the red clay sands of the beach, Tau and Themba hid behind one of the innumerable jagged pillars of stone that stretched for the sky like a maze of broken fingers. The pillars, white as chalk, began at the base of the Fist and extended out beyond the water's edge.

The sight of it had stunned Themba, and his mouth still hung open. "What in the Goddess's name?"

"It's exactly as the Indlovu drew it . . . ," Tau said. "The Roar actually did smash this section of the Fist into a cove of spires."

"This is no beach," said Themba. "It's the exposed and bleached bones of a dying peninsula."

Tau tilted his head at his sword brother. "Neh?"

"What? I can't be poetic too?" asked Themba. "You called it a cove of spires."

Tau shook his head at him. "The rest of the prong will be here soon."

"They'd better be. I don't think we have much time before the warlord gets on his ship."

"There's time," Tau said, pointing to the man in the distance, pointing to the warlord. "That's Achak, and the person he's speaking with is his son."

Squinting, Themba leaned forward, as if the distance gained might help. "That's Kana with him? You can see all that?"

"I can."

Themba eased back. "So what if he's speaking to his son?"

"He's wishing him a safe journey."

Themba eyed the rough waters. "I'm no coward, but you know, we could sit here and let them try the Roar. If we're lucky, they'll drown."

"Remind me, how often are you lucky?"

Themba spat onto the red clay. "Clean thrust," he said, conceding the point.

"If they're wishing each other goodbye, it means Kana is boarding the next ship. His father will be on the last one."

"They keep them apart?" Themba asked.

"Less likely to lose both that way."

"They'd lose no one if they kept to themselves and left us alone."

"The timing will be tight, but we should be fine," Tau said. "Kana will set sail, and before the warlord boards the last ship, we'll attack."

"Hold," Themba said, looking away from the beach and to Tau. "If the prong gets here in time, shouldn't we try to get both father and son?"

Tau shook his head. "We let Kana sail."

"Why?"

"It's a much easier fight without him on the beach too."

"Tau, most of Kana's fighters are already aboard their ship. They won't be able to get off fast enough to help anyway."

Tau shook his head. "We're here for the warlord."

"So you say, but I have trouble thinking that Hadith will agree with that."

Tau kept his eyes on the beach. "Kana isn't a threat."

Themba sniffed and looked behind them, toward the Fist. "Not yet. Anyway, it's not up to just us anymore."

That was true. Stealthy as they were trying to be, Tau could hear the rest of their prong approaching. Their soldiers were headed straight for them, which meant they'd found the guide marks Tau had drawn in the red clay. "Keep watch on the beach," Tau said, pulling his swords free and moving to stand in the shadow of the pillar behind which they were hiding. "If it's not them . . ."

Themba's nostrils flared. "Wait . . . what do you mean, if it's not them?"

Tau said nothing, tucking himself deeper in the shadows and watching the way behind them, when, a moment later, Hadith crept into view, the rest of the prong trailing.

He spotted Themba first and then saw the Xiddeen by the water's edge. "Looks like this is the lucky beach," he whispered. "Where's Tau?"

Tau stepped from the shadows. "Here."

Startling, Hadith snatched for his sword hilt. "Cek," he hissed. "Don't do that."

"Most of the ships have sailed," Tau said. "Two are left, and you were right. The warlord is still on the beach."

Hadith's mouth tightened. "He's a good leader, and we knew that."

"The son is there too," Themba said, and Tau shot him a look.

"Kana?" Hadith said. Themba nodded and Hadith counted the men on the beach quickly. "There's two hundred and twenty-three of them. We'll be outnumbered four to one, but if the son is there too, we should attack."

Tau remembered fighting alongside Kana on the Guardian Keep's ramparts against Odili's Indlovu. They'd guarded each other's backs. "We'll attack once the son and the raiders with him leave the shore," he said. "We're after the warlord."

Hadith shook his head. "The Xiddeen were willing to marry Kana to our queen. He's important enough that they might turn to him for leadership once the warlord is dead, and if that happens, Kana will have every reason to press for the invasion to continue. We can get them both and—"

"Kana isn't like his father."

Hadith's face was grim. "He won't get the chance to be," he said, turning to give the rest of the prong their orders.

"No."

Hadith froze midturn, like he were one of the pillars that were all around them. "No, Tau?"

"It's Champion Solarin," Tau said, "and we wait until Kana has sailed before we attack."

"That's not smart and I won't—"

"Those are my orders."

Hadith's eyebrows rose. "Orders? Truly?"

"Truly."

Hadith clenched his jaw, the muscles on the sides of his face pulsing. "As you say, Champion."

Tau nodded and turned back to the beach to wait for Kana to board his ship. The Xiddeen watercraft was larger than anything the Omehi bothered to build. It had masts and a slew of oars that made it look like the small water-walking insects Tau used to catch as a child.

He supposed the design made sense. The ships had to be beached and pulled far out of the water or the Roar would sink them. That meant they also had to have enough oars to row the ships back out to the open waters. The Xiddeen watercraft were cleverly done, looked very well built, and Tau still figured that one in ten sank on each voyage.

"Kana is boarding," Themba said.

But he didn't. Kana, halfway up the ship's walkway, turned, marched back down, and wrapped his father in a heavy hug. The two men clapped each other on the back and spoke.

"Ukufa's teeth, hurry up," Themba said.

The embrace ended, and the warlord, the dreaded Achak, held his son at arm's length and smiled at him. The others probably couldn't see the smile, but Tau did.

"Get on the boat, Kana...," Tau whispered, and as if he'd heard, Kana turned and boarded.

He embarked midships and walked to the longboat's rear, staying there while the sailors used long poles to push the ship into the water. The oars took over then, and the longboat shuddered, tossed, and fell among waves that crested and troughed like convulsing mountains. They were no longer allies, but each time Kana's ship dove down drops big enough to smash it apart, Tau held his breath, and he kept doing it until the longboat was safely beyond the point where the waves were breaking.

That was always one of the most dangerous parts of sailing the Roar, and having seen his son to relative safety, Achak raised his hand in a final farewell. From so far inland, Tau could no longer see Kana, but it wasn't hard to imagine him mirroring the gesture.

"It's time," Tau said. Kana was past the point of no return and it would be impossible for him to beat his way back to shore before the deed was done.

The Gifted with them lowered her hood. "Goddess go with us all," she said.

Tau nodded, caught the eyes of the rest, and, blood pounding in his ears, he pulled his black blades free. "Where we fight!" he shouted.

"The world burns!" his men screamed, rising from behind their pillars of stone to charge the beach.

LUCK

The Xiddeen on the beach seemed like a singular creature as they whirled to face an onslaught of bronze. Tau saw them heft their spears and hatchets and felt his blood run hot. He tried to run faster, but the rest of the prong were leaving him behind.

"Stay with him!" Hadith shouted at Themba as he raced along with the rest of the fighters to meet the hastily formed front line of Xiddeen.

The Chosen smashed into them and the Xiddeen front line snapped like dry twigs, women and men falling bloodied, dying, and dead. From the rear, Tau could survey the impromptu battle-field and he spotted the warlord.

"There," he said to Themba, and the two men veered for him and into their first fight.

Themba skidded to a stop, blocked a spear thrust with his shield, and took the one wielding the spear in the shoulder with his sword. With blood spraying from the wound, the spearman collapsed shrieking until Themba put his sword through the man's face.

Themba shot Tau a smile, pushed on, and engaged a Xiddeen woman with an ax in each hand.

Limping onward, Tau was attacked by a scarred Xiddeen spearman with long hair twisted into the whip-like cords that Kana wore. Bounding from foot to foot, the spearman threw himself at Tau, spear leading the way, and unable to trust his wounded leg, Tau leaned away from the strike and smacked it farther off target with his weak-side sword. Flowing with Tau's block and using the energy of it to give his attack momentum, the spearman spun, hoping to sever Tau's neck in a single sweep, but Tau's strong-side sword slipped into the spearman's spine, ripping up his insides before he could complete the move. He died on his feet and Tau limped on, trying to catch up to Themba, who had stepped over the axwoman's body and was fighting two Xiddeen at the same time.

Tau killed one of them, Themba stove in the skull of the other, and with no one else in easy reach, Tau searched again for the warlord.

It didn't take long to find him. Most of the Chosen were fighting their way toward him, and similarly, most of the Xiddeen were focused on keeping him safe so he could board the last longboat. It was, Tau knew, the most dangerous part of the attack. The Xiddeen had more fighters, and if they bunched up and fought together, it would be hard for the Chosen to win. Worse, if they got the warlord on the ship, they might be able to set sail and save him.

Hadith, however, had understood what the Xiddeen would need as well, because he was already coursing for the longboat, running through surf and sand to block the warlord's main hope of escape, and with him was an enraged Ingonyama. The Ingonyama's features were distorted by the enraging, but Tau recognized him. It was the same man who had drawn the map of the beach for him, and in another few breaths, the Ingonyama would be standing between the warlord and the warlord's ship.

Tau shook his head in disbelief at Hadith's insight. If he were to live forever, he wasn't sure he'd be able to think about the world in the same way that Hadith did.

Their prong had begun the charge from farther inland and Achak should have been able to get to his ship before they got to him, but Hadith had splintered the prong, taking a third into the surf. It made the remainder of their fighters look like they were too few to win a battle against the Xiddeen, and Hadith had guessed that the warlord

would not flee against a force he could destroy. True to form, Warlord Achak had ordered his raiders to attack, giving Hadith, the
Gifted, her honor guard, and the Ingonyama just enough time to cut
off his escape.

Tau watched as the bellowing Ingonyama used a single blow to
break the bodies of the first three Xiddeen to face him before bringing his sword back the other way, to split the next raider almost in
half. With his shield hand, the colossus grabbed a Xiddeen man by
the neck and snapped it in his grip.

The Gifted was twenty strides back from the fighting. She was
standing in the surf, and it swirled around her shoulder-width
planted feet, tugging at the hem of her saltwater-soaked robes as she
held her arms out to the Ingonyama and pushed Isihogo's energies
through him.

An axman came for Tau and died, and Tau wondered if the
warlord would be dead before he could get within a dozen strides
of him.

"Quickly, Themba!" Tau said as he sent another soul to the Goddess's embrace.

"Coming, coming…," Themba said, shouldering a wounded
Xiddeen fighter to one side before giving them the point of his
sword. "I'm com—" Themba's mouth dropped open as he stared in
the direction of Warlord Achak's longboat.

Tau followed his gaze and saw something right out of a fireside
story. Their Ingonyama was entangled with an enraged Xiddeen
warrior, and the two colossi bashed and battered at each other with
blows powerful enough to fell trees.

The Omehi did not train enraged Ingonyama against one another.
It was too dangerous. So Tau had never seen two enraged warriors
dueling to the death. It was a humbling sight, even more so when he
realized that the presence of just one enraged Xiddeen warrior had
managed to halt the advance of Hadith's splinter force.

The Omehi's way to Achak's longboat had been blocked, and
without Hadith's fighters to impede him, the warlord had not been
completely cut off. Achak, too clever to make the same mistake
twice, was already retreating farther down the beach.

At first, Tau didn't understand the point. They were in a cove and Achak's only way out was to fight past the Chosen's much larger force. Retreating bought him time, but because the cove ended at an outcropping of rock that extended all the way into the Roar, it also kept him trapped. He'd have nowhere left to run. Unless...

Tau checked the Roar and understood Achak's goal immediately. Several of the Xiddeen longboats were doing their best to beat a path back to the shore. Kana's was the closest, and the warlord hoped to get on that ship.

"Themba!" Tau pointed to the line of longboats and forced himself into a run, moving farther inland and around the press of warring bodies.

Seeing the incoming ships, Themba swore and sliced at the air with his sword like he wished he could cut it.

"Coming!" he said, chasing after Tau.

Tau ran and lurched along. If they could get around the fighting, they'd reach the end of the cove before the ships could make it back to shore. They'd have a chance at Achak.

Themba caught up to Tau. "We're far past our men!"

"Warlord!" Tau said, aiming his sword, and there he was, not thirty strides away.

Warlord Achak had made it to the end of the cove along with three raiders and his shaman. The rest of the Xiddeen were retreating while fighting, and Tau had made it between them and his target. Out on the Roar, Kana's ship was being hammered by the breakwater and looked in danger of sinking, but if the longboat made it past the point where the waves were cresting, it'd be a short journey to land and reinforcement.

Tau looked at Themba.

Themba took a deep breath. "Never lucky," he said, and together, they went in.

NAMES

Achak was watching the incoming ships, so it was his raiders who saw Tau and Themba first. The Xiddeen, refusing to risk letting them come within a sword's throw of the warlord, ran to meet them.

Themba crossed bronze with the first one, a tall, slim man with face tattoos marred by his heavy scarring. Tau, slower to join the battle, was left to deal with the other two. The one who got to him first let out an ululating cry and actually threw a spear at him.

Moving more on instinct than with sense, Tau dodged it, stumbled because of the weight he had to put on his injured leg, and straightened up, swords high, to block the hatchet hissing through the night toward his skull. He stopped the bronze-and-bone weapon from finding his face with one sword, but the collision of blades slammed his broken fingers together, and he nearly dropped his weapon. Teeth clenched against the pain, Tau cut down with his other blade and tore a hole through the raider's throat.

The dead man pitched forward, and before his body hit the red sand, the remaining warrior, a short and heavyset spearwoman, was stabbing at Tau.

Tau tried to dance backward, but his movements were more drunken gait than graceful steps. Advancing, she kept him at bay with her stabbing, and if her rhythm hadn't been so precise, he'd have had more difficulty shearing away her fingers.

She screamed and jumped back when her fingers and the spear fell free of her hand, and Tau limped past her, only twenty strides away from Achak.

The warlord was no longer watching the ocean. He was standing next to his shaman, his spear ready and his eyes fixed on Tau. Loosening his wrists, Tau twirled his swords and took a step in the warlord's direction, and then he heard the thunder of heavy footfalls to his left.

He glanced over. It was the enraged Xiddeen, and she was charging at him with her spear held high. She was moving fast but was too late. He'd get to the warlord before she could get to him.

He took another step, caught the word she was shouting at him, and stopped moving. The enraged spearwoman, running faster than any normal person could, was shouting one word over and over again.

"Jai-ehd!" she said. "Jai-ehd!"

His lips curling back to reveal his teeth, Tau turned away from the man who was his target and toward the enraged spearwoman. He remembered her now. It was the way she'd said his umqondisi's name. She was the one who had murdered Jayyed.

She staggered to a stop outside the reach of his blades, her chest heaving from the run and her eyes fixed on him. "Jai-ehd," she said again, hefting her spear.

Tau remained motionless, thinking about what was to come, and then, nodding more to himself than to anyone else, he spoke. "You've killed yourself," he told her.

She lunged at him, stabbing for his heart with superhuman speed. He expected the attack but not how fast it came, and to avoid being skewered, he leapt off the killing line. Pain shot up his leg as he did it, threatening to incapacitate him, but drowning out the agony with hate, he twisted away from the Xiddian's spear and whipped his weak-side sword into the small of her back.

The spearwoman was wearing unplated leathers, and though a weapon of bronze might have penetrated the animal hide, it would not have cut her enraged skin. But Tau was not wielding weapons of bronze, and when it struck, his dragon-scale blade parted her leathers as easily as a father plaiting his child's hair. The sword's edge dug into her flesh and caught there, dragging Tau forward as, crying out, she pulled away.

Flowing with her sudden movement, Tau cocked his left arm back and fired his other blade for her belly. She should have died then. She shouldn't have been fast enough to do as she did, but with Tau's sword a handspan from opening her middle, the spearwoman sliced down and struck his blade with the bone dagger she had in her off hand. The counter slammed Tau's sword down and away from her body, dragging him behind his weapon and shattering her dagger in an explosion of sharp fragments that sliced at the skin on his hands and face.

Turning his fall into a roll, Tau kept a tight hold of his other sword, the one still embedded in the small of the spearwoman's back. It pulled along behind him as he went, and he felt its edge catch and rake across her enraged skin, tearing a shallow line into her side as it ripped free.

Having moved past and behind her, Tau sprang to his feet and spun, his weapons ready to blow holes in her back. She was already coming for him, and with her spear leading the way, she threw the handle of her broken dagger at his head with her other hand.

Knocking the dagger from the air with one sword, Tau bent beneath her first and second spear thrusts, then slashed the sword in his right hand at the same cut he'd opened on her side two breaths earlier. His sword connected; she yelped and wheeled away, and, hunched over her twinned wounds, she backed off.

"Say his name again!" Tau shouted, going after her with his swords spinning.

She snarled, meeting him in kind, her spear streaking through the air. They clashed and she was bigger. They struck at each other and it was obvious she was stronger. They fought with wild fury, and anyone watching could see that she was faster. But against Tau Solarin, champion of the Omehi, none of it mattered.

Six, sixteen, then sixty wounds sprang up on the spearwoman's leathers, face, and flesh, until she was awash in blood and flailing about wildly, fighting from her back foot as her eyes rolled in her skull. Tau stalked her, tormenting her, and she staggered back, desperate to get away from the black blades that sapped her strength and razored open her skin.

"Say his name again!" he screamed.

And she screamed back. It was a guttural sound, instinctual, full of fear and anger. It was an admission of defeat and a refusal to surrender.

The enraged spearwoman, her body a wreck and at risk of killing the one empowering her, let the effects of the shaman's gifts leave her so that she might spare his life. It happened quickly, in a flash of light, and without the shaman's gifts to sustain her, she stumbled about, near collapse, her eyes so dull they looked lifeless already.

She was in a pitiful state, but Tau refused to feel pity. She'd killed people he loved and then dared to call him. Her end was her own doing.

"On the night you murdered Jayyed Ayim, you saw me," he said, taking a step toward her. "You recognized what I am and you ran."

She moved back, her knees buckling with every step.

"You should never have stopped running," he said, following her, the pain in his wounded leg masked by the anger in his heart.

She cursed him, spitting foul-sounding words as she struck out with thrusts too sluggish to land, and he knocked her attacks aside, casually, derisively. He hated her and he hated that she wouldn't give up.

She should have been born Chosen, he thought, though then they wouldn't have let her fight, and the spearwoman was born to fight.

She shouted again and charged with neither the strength nor the speed to have any hope of hurting him. He knew what she wanted. She wanted him to kill her as she ran at him. She was trying to have some small measure of control over her end, but she'd slain Jayyed and Chinedu, and Tau had no mercy in him to give.

His sword made the air sing before it smashed into her lead hand, splitting the limb in half and sending her spear flying away. Her cry then, as she fell, with her hand, wrist, and arm in flaps, was a cry not of pain, but of despair and loss. It was a cry to match the things Tau felt before sleep saved him every night. It was the cry he held inside himself whenever he thought of everyone he'd lost.

She was on the ground in front of him, her mangled arm cradled to her belly, and he stood over her, watching her struggle to reach into the pouch on her hip with the hand that remained whole. But there was no weapon left in the world that could help. The thing to come was inevitable.

"His name was Jayyed Ayim," Tau told her, "and you will never say it again."

He plunged his strong-side sword through her chest, pinning her to the red clay. She gasped, panting, the end near, and fumbled at her pouch, pulling something free from it.

It was a ragged square of folded papyrus. She tried to open it but couldn't do it fast enough one-handed. She died trying.

Tau brushed at his mouth with the back of his hand. He'd done it. He'd killed Jayyed's and Chinedu's murderer. He'd avenged them, and as he stood there over her body, waiting for the satisfaction to come and the weight in him to lessen, his mind kept filling with the memory of the light going out of her eyes.

But he didn't want to think about that, and shaking his head to knock loose the moment of her death, Tau focused on the papyrus she had in her hand instead. It could be important. It could be a map of Xiddeen territory or perhaps military orders, but the pain in his leg had returned and he wasn't sure that he'd be able to stand up if he knelt to retrieve it.

He told himself he'd come back for the papyrus when the rest was done, and he turned away from the spearwoman's body, trying to recapture his anger. It had kept the agony in his leg at bay, but Tau's fury had died with the spearwoman, and his leg ached.

The pain, radiating out from the wound and extending all the way into his core, felt like it was traveling to his heart, and for a moment, he worried that the priestess was right and that he didn't have much time left. But she'd also said that there wasn't enough poison in his body to kill him, just enough to make him kill himself.

Grimacing, Tau braced himself against the pain and limped onward. "That's not how I go," he said as he went to take the warlord's life.

SCARS

The remaining Xiddeen were fighting behind Tau, and they no longer outnumbered the Chosen, which meant there would soon be no Xiddeen left. In front of Tau, separated from the rest of the fighting, the warlord was standing at the edge of the cove, his feet in the surf.

In the time it had taken for Tau to kill the spearwoman, Kana's ship had made it past the breakwater, but Warlord Achak was not watching it. He had his back to the ocean and was facing toward Tau. Kana would not get to his father before Tau did, and clearly, Achak knew that too.

Eyes on Tau, the warlord handed his spear to his shaman and pulled two short-handled hatchets from his belt. The twin weapons of bronze and bone had oversized heads stretching two handspans from toe to heel, and their blades were curved as if to match the shape of the half-moon cove in which they both stood.

Achak's shaman, the one who had enraged the spearwoman, took the warlord's spear and leaned against it. The emaciated man looked drained but willing to fight, and placing a hand on the warlord's shoulder, he held his head high.

Achak reached over, took the shaman's hand in his, and squeezed it.

It was a moment of warmth between men who, in all likelihood, had shared a long history. It was, Tau thought, an assurance that, whatever came, they'd face it together.

They were wrong.

They'd come to his peninsula with their warriors and stolen the lives of those Tau loved. Like the spearwoman, they'd done things that had called him to them, he'd answered their call, and they would die, each man alone.

"You can wave to your son," Tau told Achak. "I'll let you say goodbye."

The warlord, with his half-burned face, gave Tau half a smile.

"Why," Achak asked in broken Empiric, "when I'll see Kana... after?"

Advancing, Tau shook his head. The fury was coming back. "After me, there is nothing."

The warlord laughed, flourished his hatchets, and charged. Without limping, feeling no pain, Tau raised his swords and kept walking, until his mind broke.

When the warlord was four strides from striking distance, he became two, then four, then six men. Tau was too close to get away completely, and when the six men raised their twelve hatchets to cut him down, he dashed to his left, out of reach of three of the six warlords, doing his best to block the attacks from the other six hatchets.

He couldn't stop them all, no one could, but turning his weak-side blade parallel to the ground and raising it like a shield, he barred the deadly arc of four hatchets. The power of them hitting his sword almost disarmed him, but Tau held on. He tried to do the same with his other sword but couldn't intercept the incoming attacks from that warlord, and a hatchet took him in the chest as the other one went through his neck... completely through his neck.

The hatchets in that warlord's hands moved in, through, and out of Tau, without him feeling a thing. Both ax-heads had "struck" killing blows, yet Tau was still alive.

There was little time to consider the miracle. The two warlords, the ones holding the hatchets he'd blocked, were attacking again. So were the ones he'd avoided, the ones on Tau's right.

With his mind overloaded, Tau gave his instincts the lead, turned his back on the warlord whose hatchets had gone through his body, and, using both swords, went to war with the closest two men. Those two Achaks, like the rest, moved in tandem, as if attached at the legs, hips, and arms by invisible cords.

That they were replicating each other's movements made it easier to block and counter them, but as Tau's sword went to meet the first of the hatchets, doubt plagued him. He did not understand what was happening, and if the warlord and hatchets at his back could become substantial, Tau was dead.

It being too late to adjust for that possibility, Tau did his best to avoid dying at the efforts of the two warlords directly in front of him. He sent up his swords to block, and dragon scale met bronze with full force.

Grunting under the power of the clash, Tau disengaged. He tried to make space, moving to keep all six opponents in front of him, but failed to track all six men and rammed right into and through one of them, as if the man was not there at all.

"Gifts," Tau spat, thinking he had some understanding of the things he faced. "Your shaman conjures soulless men with no substance to fight for you." Tau gambled, picking one of the two warlords he had crossed real blades with. "But I could feel the collision in my right when I blocked your real hatchet."

The warlord to whom he was pointing, the real Achak, tilted his head in acknowledgment and stepped back. The false men vanished when he did so, and Achak offered Tau another of his half smiles as the illusions re-formed in a single line.

The real Achak stepped among them, through them really, making it impossible for Tau to be certain that he still knew which of the six men was the real one. Then the newly formed sextet separated and brandished their hatchets, each copy wearing a perfect mirror image of Achak's broken sneer.

Tau tried to keep his confusion from his face, hoping Achak wouldn't attack if he thought Tau knew which of the copies was the real one. It made no difference. The six warlords attacked, and Tau, praying it would work and work in time—flung his spirit to Isihogo.

The mists of the underworld enveloped him, and Tau was in the prison Ananthi had made for Ukufa. Using his eyes in Isihogo, Tau saw the warlord charging him as if he moved through mud, and as Tau had gambled, there was only one Achak.

The illusions had no souls. They were the effect of energy taken from Isihogo and pushed into Uhmlaba. They could not appear in the spirit world.

The warlord, though moving at a crawl, was just to his right, and locking Achak's position in his mind, Tau fled Isihogo for the real world. His soul still somewhere between realms, Tau willed his arms to move, throwing up his swords to block two of the twelve hatchets chopping at him.

Ten hatchets slammed into thin air like they'd hit a wall, the illusory blades matching the height and angle at which Tau's swords had caught and collided with the real Achak's actual weapons. The block rocked Tau onto his heels. The warlord was powerfully built and he'd put everything into the twin strikes.

Tau pulled his swords and Achak's hatchets down and to the right, setting up a counter, but the warlord disengaged, slipping back and into position with the five copies.

He seemed to be able to draw them into himself and push them a slight distance away at will. It meant Tau couldn't keep track of the real man among the phantoms.

Tau heard the shaman say something in the Xiddeen language, and as if spurred to action, the warlord came on hard. Tau spun away from all six men, cast his soul to the underworld, caught sight of the real Achak, and was about to leave when he noticed the shaman in the distance. The shaman's shroud was a pale thing that, as Tau watched, vanished, revealing the eye-watering golden brightness of his unmasked soul.

Tau tore away from the underworld, blocked the real warlord's attack, and struck back. He whipped his weak-side sword at the warlord's left hand, and though he missed the man's wrist, he hit the hatchet's handle, sending it flying from his grasp.

The right-handed hatchet in each of the copies' hands did the same, flying away for six or seven strides before vanishing in midair.

Tau ran his gaze across the hands of the six men he faced. "He told you to finish me quickly, didn't he?" he asked, trying to distract Achak as he considered the discovery he'd just made, wondering all the while if he dared to trust it.

Ignoring Tau's jibe, the warlord let his copies vanish, hefted the hatchet in his left hand, and stepped back. Immediately, the five illusions began to re-form around him, and as they did, the warlord passed through them until Tau couldn't be certain he still had his eyes on the real man.

That done, Tau's opponents spread out, their six hatchets ready. Only, this time, Tau knew something important. By knocking one of the hatchets out of Achak's hands and seeing the illusions vanish and re-form, he'd learned that the replicas were not perfect. They truly were reflections.

"Your shaman's shroud has failed," Tau said. "And your spear-woman had courage enough to accept her end without killing her Gifted. She refused to trade his life for a few extra breaths. Tell me, Warlord, are you as brave?"

The warlord and his copies moved farther apart, encircling Tau as they spoke as one, their six voices overlapping. "In a few breaths, you won't exist," they said.

Once Tau was encircled, the warlords attacked, every one of them bellowing the same war cry. Tau was in Isihogo as they came, and looking straight ahead, he saw nothing. It meant the real Achak was one of the men behind him, but he didn't know which of the three was the real one and didn't have the time to turn, check, return to Uhmlaba, and block the real hatchet.

No choice remaining, Tau abandoned the underworld, spun round, and saw three warlords and three hatchets coming for him. The warlord to his right, the unburned side of his face closer to Tau and twisted in hate, swung the hatchet he had in his left hand in a blow that would kill Tau outright. The warlord directly in front of him was exactly the same, and that was why Tau turned to his left and stopped the hatchet that that Achak held in his right hand.

Catching the hatchet's bronze head a fingerspan from his temple,

Tau stabbed out with his other sword and took the warlord through the heart with his strong-side blade.

The illusions vanished, Tau jammed the blade deeper, and Achak's mouth dropped into a half O. His burned side, the side on his right, was too stiff to loosen, even as death spread through him.

"The illusions are reflections," Tau told the dying man. "They have your burns on the wrong side." Achak's eyes went dim. "And earlier, I knocked free the hatchet in your left hand."

The hatchet that the real Achak held in his right fell from his unresponsive fingers into the surf, where the churning waters dragged it into the ocean. Watching the weapon go, Tau tore his blade clear of the warlord's corpse, letting the man's body fall near the water's edge.

"Achak!"

It was the shaman, or what was left of him. The thin man, clutching the dead warlord's spear in both hands, rocked back and forth on his legs, which threatened to give out at any moment. The shaman couldn't see that his tribesman was no more. Blood, tinted blue-red by the night, seeped from eyes that could no longer see, and with each shout of the warlord's name, the shaman spat blood out onto the beach's sand.

"Achak!"

Tau walked over as the old man's knees gave out, dropping the shaman to the ground with a thud.

"Achak!" he called as Tau came to stand over him.

"Dead," Tau said, but the shaman couldn't hear him over his own screaming, and Tau didn't need to send his spirit anywhere to know that more demons had come to finish what one or two had started.

"Demon-death?"

Tau turned his head at Themba's voice. His sword brother had a hand to his side, squeezing a shallow cut there.

"Are you well?"

"Well enough," Themba said, gazing out at the water. "He actually came close to making it, the crazy bastard."

"Kana?" Tau looked toward the ship.

It had made it farther in than Tau would have thought possible and was less than a hundred strides offshore, but the longboat was paying the price for it. The ship was getting thrashed by the waves and at threat of sinking. Yet, Kana, flanked by two other Xiddeen warriors, stood at its prow with his body held stiff as an Indlovu flag. His hands were wrapped round the boat's railing hard enough to crush it, and his eyes were fixed on Tau.

"Guess he wants to die too," Themba said, smiling.

"What?"

"They're not stopping. He has to have told the ones piloting the ship to make landfall. Maybe he thinks his father is still alive?" Themba shrugged. "It's good for us. If they make it in, we can kill them too. "

Tau scanned the beach. There were no more Xiddeen alive onshore, and Kana's ship had too few fighters to challenge the Omehi who had reclaimed the beach. Themba was right: If Kana's ship did make it onshore, everyone on it would die.

"Just go, Goddess damn you," Tau whispered, willing it to be so. "Just go," but Kana and his ship battled forward.

Cursing, Tau strode over to Achak's body, bent down over it, his leg protesting the action, and filling his hand with Achak's hair, he wrenched the dead man's head up. Fighting back bile, Tau pulled free the guardian dagger that had belonged to his umqondisi and placed it against Achak's neck.

"Eh...what're you about?" Themba asked him.

Tau locked eyes on the ship and the man standing at its front. The longboat was close enough that he knew Kana could see him as clearly as he could see the hate on Kana's face.

"Your father's dead and you'll be too, if you come here," Tau said. He didn't shout it. There was no point. The words would have been lost to the Roar, but he didn't need Kana to hear the words. Their meaning could be sent another way.

Tau began to saw, sliding the guardian dagger back and forth over the meat, muscle, and tendons in Achak's neck with ease. The work was bloody, but the dragon scale made it quick, and the only part that took any time at all was breaking through the small bones in the back of the warlord's neck.

"Cek, Tau...," Themba muttered when the head came free.

Tau stood, his leg burning, and as he held the warlord's head aloft, showing it to the ship, showing it to the son, he began to believe that all the pain that wracked his body was deserved. Then, to finish it, Tau drew his arm back and flung the head out and into the waves.

"Leave," he whispered, not to Kana, because Kana would be incapable of doing it, but to the fighters who followed him. "There's nothing but death for you here," he said to those fighters, desperate for them to see that truth.

On the ship, Kana began to climb the railing. The warriors at his sides grabbed him. They held him back, perhaps thinking that he meant to retrieve his father's severed head from the roiling waters. Kana strained against them, the muscles on his arms bulging, but he couldn't get free and they wouldn't let him leap to his death, but Tau knew it wasn't Kana's intent to die in the Roar or to swim for his father's head.

Tau could see the hate in Kana's face and he knew that the whole of his being vibrated with it. It was fueling him, overloading him, and in that moment, it was not grief or suicide that compelled him. Kana didn't want to die in the waters. He meant to swim to shore so that he could kill Tau with his bare hands.

Whatever they thought of his purpose, the Xiddeen with Kana would not leave him to it, and though Tau could not hear their words, he saw them call out, shouting orders of their own to their sisters and brothers aboard the longboat.

Warlord Achak was dead, his son was not in his right mind, and the Xiddeen on the ship had no reason to come ashore. Tau watched as it struggled to turn, battered by wave after wave until it seemed it must capsize and grant the Roar claim over two generations from the same family in a single night.

It escaped, though. The Xiddeen oarspeople, its sailors, wrestled the vessel to rights and aimed its prow at the waves so it could cut through them again.

"Look at that. They're leaving," Themba said, "and I thought you sawing the man's head off would make them come ashore for sure."

Tau shook his head. "It's like Hadith said in the council chambers.

They're not like our Nobles, and the Xiddeen don't have castes. They won't follow an order just because of who gives it. You had the right of it too, Themba," Tau said.

"Neh?"

"They were coming back because they weren't sure that Achak was dead. I had to show them that he was."

Themba began walking toward the rest of their men and past the spearwoman's body. "You certainly showed them that," he said.

"The spearwoman," Tau said, feeling a mountain's weight in weariness setting in. "She's holding something in one of her hands. It could be important."

Themba grunted, bent over the body, and took the papyrus from her. "What's on it?"

Tau shrugged and Themba unfolded the paper. He whistled, then held it out.

Tau took it, and after a night of fighting one set of gifts, he saw a new and unexpected one. The papyrus held the image, made in coal, of two girls. Each one was holding a spear, and the girls looked enough alike to be copies. They looked enough alike to be more illusions woven by Xiddeen shamans.

"I've never seen—" Words failed him.

In the drawing, the girl on the left was smiling and looked so alive Tau swore he could see her eyes twinkling in the moonlight. Standing next to her was her sister, her birth pair, and she was stern, serious. She projected the aura of a grim warrior, but the solemn tilt of her lips and her knitted brows did nothing to hide the spark in her eyes.

Tau swallowed, took time to fold the paper over its original creases, and handed it back to Themba. "It's so real," he said, his eyes wandering to the spearwoman's dead hands, trying to picture them taking the time and care to create something so beautiful.

"Savage could draw, neh?" Themba said, dropping the masterwork into the surf and letting it wash away.

Tau watched the paper soak and sink, vanishing beneath the waves, and taking a deep breath, he lifted his gaze from the surf to look back to Kana's ship. The distance had grown too great for even his eyes, and he could no longer make out anyone on the longboat, but he imagined Kana at the ship's stern, watching him.

"It was the only way I knew to save your life," Tau whispered. "It was the—"

"Tau...," Themba said, pointing along the shore at the man thundering across the beach toward them.

"What is it? More Xiddeen?" Tau shouted to the Indlovu.

"No, Champion," he shouted back. "It's your sword brother. The one named Hadith."

"Hadith?" It was more an exhalation of air than a full-voiced word.

The Indlovu kicked at the dead spearwoman with his boot. "The Lesser...uh...your sword brother joined the men who fought this savage when she was enraged. By the time she came for you, she'd already killed our Ingonyama and put a spear in Hadith's chest."

Tau couldn't speak.

"Hadith's dead?" asked Themba.

"Not yet," the Indlovu said, turning and running back the way he'd come. "This way."

CHAPTER FOUR

SPEAR

The spear was still in Hadith's chest. He was on his back in the sand and the spear was sticking up and out of his midsection, its haft quivering with Hadith's every labored breath.

"By the Goddess, pull it out!" Tau yelled to the men around his friend.

"Can't," said the particularly stocky Indlovu kneeling by Hadith's shoulders and cradling Hadith's head. "He's only alive because that abomination left it in him. Even if we knew enough to pull it out clean, which we don't, he'd bleed to death without it plugging him up."

Hadith's eyes were open, but it didn't look like he was seeing through them. His every effort was dedicated to wheezing out the next battered breath.

"What, then?" Tau asked, seeing again the twin girls on the papyrus and wondering how hands that had rendered an image of such palpable life could be the same ones that had done this to Hadith. "What do we do?"

The Indlovu looked up at him. "We hold the spear as steady as we can, as close to where it's gone in as we can, and we break the rest away."

"With what hope?"

"With the hope that the spear's head, and the section of shaft we can't cut, will be stable enough inside him that he can last till Citadel City."

"You've done this before?"

"I have. I used to fight in the Curse. I've seen many men go down with spears still in them."

"And you've saved them this way."

The Indlovu spoke deliberately. "I've not been the last to see them alive . . . this way."

Tau turned from the man, desperate for someone, anyone, to fight.

"Champion?" the Indlovu asked.

"Get Hadith ready for travel," Tau said. "We're for the city."

"Your words, my will," the Noble said, signaling to two other Indlovu to lend him aid.

The two Indlovu knelt beside Hadith and put their hands on him, holding him down. Tau didn't want to watch. He'd have preferred to be anywhere else to avoid seeing his friend suffer, but he'd never leave Hadith alone to his fate.

"I'll help," he said to the men holding Hadith down. "Themba!"

"Champion?" Themba asked.

"Help us hold Hadith still."

"You sure you want to do this yourself, Champion?" the Indlovu playing the part of a Sah priest asked. "You can't let him move and we're . . . we're stronger."

"We'll be strongest if we do it together," Tau told him, kneeling beside Hadith.

"As you say." The Indlovu grunted. "Grab his shoulders and hips. Put your weight into it. Don't let him move. He'll rip himself open if he does."

Tau nodded and leaned his full weight on Hadith. Themba did the same and Hadith moaned, already trying to shift away from them.

"Good, good," the Indlovu said, finding a way to use the two Nobles whom Tau and Themba had freed up. He had one of them place his hands flat on Hadith's chest, around the spear, while the other one held the shaft above its entry point.

When he was satisfied that they were all in place and steady, the Indlovu leading the operation pulled his dagger free and placed it against the spear's bone shaft.

"Wait!" Tau said, stopping the man from making the first sawing cut. "With something sharper, you can cut through the spear more easily."

"I don't have anything sharper."

Tau handed the man the dragon-scale dagger that had belonged to Jayyed Ayim. "I do."

Bowing his head, the Indlovu reached out for the dagger. Even on a red sand beach, amid a forest of stone spires and dozens of the dead, the Indlovu couldn't shake his reverence for the priceless weapon.

"This could make a difference," he said as he began to cut.

The cutting went well until the dagger caught on a spur in the spear's bone shaft. The shaft shifted and Hadith cried out, trying to fight free of the hands holding him.

"Nearly done!" the Indlovu said. "Hold him, I'm almost there."

Tau clamped down harder on his semiconscious friend, speaking into his ear and saying words meant to give him comfort but that couldn't have made much sense at all.

"It's free!" the Indlovu said. "Don't let the shaft fall on him."

The spear was tossed aside and the Noble holding Tau's guardian dagger handed it back, his hands shaking when he did so. "We'll need to make a pallet to carry him," he said.

"It's here," a voice called out.

Tau looked over. Four Indlovu and two Ihashe were stringing leather armor, cloth, and Xiddeen spears together to form a many-handled bed. It struck Tau then, seeing both Indlovu and Ihashe working to save Hadith, that he had a duty to them all.

"How many?" he asked. "How many others can we save?"

That kicked loose the stone holding back the avalanche, and reports of the injured and their chances of survival came in fast. He listened, giving what orders he could to save as many as he could, all while worrying over Hadith.

He learned that their Gifted was still with the body of her Ingonyama, mourning him. He sent Themba to her, to tell her it was time to go, and ordered a few men to stay behind to burn the dead, reminding them to run in the unlikely chance that any Xiddeen returned. Then, taking up one of the handles on the bed on which Hadith lay, he gave the order to march, but Themba was back and he forced Tau to give up his place by Hadith's side.

"You're too short, and with that leg of yours, too slow," Themba said. "You don't need to do it all yourself."

"Look what happens when I don't," Tau told him, choking up.

Themba shouldered Tau away from the pallet and took his place. "It's not your fault."

Tau wasn't listening. "March! We go fast," he said, praying to the Goddess that Hadith could survive the journey.

THERE

He didn't think they'd make it. Hadith had wheezed and coughed and suffered for the first part of the march, but then he'd gone silent and limp for the rest. Tau had checked him often just to make sure he was still alive. He was, but he did not look good, and when they were within a sun span of the city, blood began to ooze from Hadith's wound. Tau brought it to the attention of the Indlovu who had cut the spear, and he had torn strips of cloth and bandaged them tightly around Hadith's torso to stem the bleeding.

Hadith hadn't moved or made a sound while it was done, and with nothing more than the expression on Tau's face, the Indlovu had known enough to tell Tau that his friend was still breathing.

"I can't lose him too," Tau said, or might have said. He couldn't be sure.

"The city!" The call came from one of their forward scouts.

"Send someone in for the Sah priests," said the stocky Indlovu.

Tau nodded. "Bring the priestess named Hafsa," he told the scout. "Find her and bring her."

The scout saluted and ran off, and they continued marching for the gates, when an alarm was raised.

A rear scout, an Ihashe, pushed his way through the crowd of soldiers to Tau. "We're being chased!" he said.

"By how many?" Tau asked.

"Maybe a unit," the scout said.

"Keep going," Tau told the ones carrying Hadith. "Get him and the wounded into the city. The rest of you, stand with me."

Swords were pulled free, the injured rushed on, and though their numbers were too small to do it well, Tau ordered a three-prong formation with which they would face the eighteen or so warriors running headlong from the base of the Fist and into the brief stretch of flatlands that stood between the mountain's base and the city gates.

"They're Omehi," Tau shouted, seeing enough in the low light to know that much. "Lower your weapons. They're Omehi."

"Where is he?!" one of the men running for them screamed. "Where is he?!"

"Uduak?"

The big man did not slow and the fighters with him could not match his pace. Uduak ran to Tau, grabbed him by the shoulders, and shouted in his face. "Where is he?!"

"Being carried into the city. He—"

Uduak pushed Tau aside and continued on.

"Tau..." It was Azima, breathless and looking near collapse. "Didn't find anyone on our beach," he said. "Came to yours next...Oh, mercy." He doubled over and retched, though nothing came up. "We saw the men you left to do the burning.... They told Uduak about Hadith. Been running ever since." Azima dropped to his ass. "Been running ever since.... Water?"

"Bring him water." Tau put a hand on Azima's shoulder, patting it. "Rest," he said, leaving the exhausted Ihashe and hurrying back to Hadith and Uduak.

Tau caught up to them inside the city gates. Uduak was walking beside Themba and the others who were carrying Hadith. He was holding one of Hadith's hands in both of his.

"Not good," Uduak said, when Tau was beside him. "Not good."

Uduak's face was tearstained, and seeing his friend so emotional, Tau dropped his head. There had been so much loss, and the weight of it kept trying to crush him.

"Put him down."

Tau looked up. The priestess, Hafsa, was standing in front of them, and as the men lowered Hadith, she unbound his bandages and examined him.

"You did well," she said to Tau and Uduak.

"I wasn't there," Uduak said.

"There's blood bubbling around the wound. It means the spear pierced his lung," Hafsa continued. "If you'd pulled the spear free or left it whole, he'd not have survived."

"Will he...will he survive?" Tau asked.

"You've given him a chance," she said, waving at the men to pick Hadith up again. "Bring him to the hospital."

"I wasn't there...," Uduak said.

"You are now," Tau told the big man as they followed Hafsa to the infirmary.

"You can't come in," she told them at the door to one of its rooms. Tau had seen inside that room before. It held all manner of small daggers, bronze pincers, and other instruments of seeming torture.

"I have to open the wound, remove the spear's head, and care for the lung. We'll need to keep the wound and the rest of the room as clean as possible. Wounded men die from filth almost as easily as from swords and spears."

Uduak grunted and tried to make his way past her.

"Uduak, let the priestess do her work," Tau said.

"I wasn't there, Tau!"

"I know, but we can't—"

"Where were you?"

The words hit like a fist.

"Where were you, Tau?"

"It won't be long," Hafsa said, her eyes shifting between them. "Within the span, the spear will be out. I'll have a better sense of his chances then."

She went into the room beyond, Uduak still tried to follow, and Tau took him by the wrist. Uduak shook Tau off, but he did stop.

"I didn't see it happen," Tau said.

"It was you who killed him?"

Tau didn't understand.

"The warlord," Uduak said, clarifying.

"I killed him."

"Still not worth Hadith's life."

"No."

Uduak nodded, like that settled it, and he sat on the ground in front of the closed door, head on his knees and hands on his head.

"I... Uduak, I have to speak with the queen."

Without looking up, Uduak flicked his fingers at Tau in dismissal.

"He'll be well," Tau said before walking away, no power in the words.

He didn't get far. He turned the corner in the infirmary, wondering where he might find the queen, and almost ran her over.

"Champion," she said. Her thick hair, pulled back behind a golden circlet, rose behind her head like it was part of a beautiful black shroud set to envelop and protect the rest of her at any moment.

Tau saluted, noticing the Queen's Guard as well as Nyah and Yaw. "My queen."

"One of your... brothers was injured?"

"Gravely, my queen."

She moved past him and around the corner, toward Uduak and the room where Hadith was being cared for. The Queen's Guard and Nyah followed, the vizier eyeing Tau as she went.

"What happened out there?" Yaw asked.

"Nothing good," Tau told him, following the queen.

Uduak was on his feet, holding a tight salute. His eyes were red, swollen.

"He is in there?" the queen asked, indicating the closed door.

"The priestess and her physicians seek to remove the head of the spear that felled him," Tau said.

"We had hoped to see him."

"And, my queen," Nyah said, "you may yet do so. Priestess Hafsa is as skilled a surgeon as exists on the peninsula."

Uduak looked at Nyah, hopeful for more, but the vizier had turned to Tau.

"I am sorry to push you at a time like this," she said, "but was it done?"

"The warlord is dead," Tau said.

"Goddess be praised," the vizier said. "Is it certain?"

Tau dropped his eyes. "His death came at my hands."

"I won't doubt it, then," said Nyah.

"You achieved all we asked and yet something troubles you, Champion," Tsiora said, "something more than worry over your brother's hurt."

Tau, unaccustomed to viziers and queens, decided, then and there, that he needed to learn to school his features to stillness. He did not enjoy people pulling his thoughts from his face.

"I fear I've failed you," he said.

"But you have not," Tsiora said.

"Kana is alive. . . . Hadith, my injured sword brother, he cautioned me to act swiftly. I—I didn't want to have to kill him too. I . . . Kana's alive and it's my fault."

"The son does not enjoy his father's support among the Xiddeen," Nyah said. "Kana is not his father."

"He saw what I did to him."

"What you did? What did Kana see?" Nyah asked.

"They were on their ships and trying to sail back to shore. I think they hoped the warlord was still alive. . . . I don't know. I—I gave them proof that the man was dead."

Nyah shrugged. "All the better. Kana himself can take the truth of his father's fall to the tribes. His own words will tear the alliance apart and give us the time needed to retake the throne."

"You didn't see his face," Tau said.

"Whose face?"

"Kana's."

"Why would I need to? The late shul, the first to set so many of the Xiddeen tribes to a common purpose, is dead, and now his greatest military leader is as well."

Tau shook his head. "You didn't see his face."

"Tell us what you saw," the queen said.

"Rage."

Tsiora blinked at him. "And what can one do with rage?"

"Everything."

"Is it like love, then?"

His father's face, Zuri's face, both flashed in his mind. "Rage is love . . . twisted in on itself," he said, using some of the words she'd spoken to him on the night Zuri died. "Rage reaches into the world when we can no longer contain the hurt of being treated as if our life and loves do not matter. Rage, and its consequences, are what we get when the world refuses to change for anything less."

The way she was looking at him made Tau worry he'd overstepped, but he was weary of making himself less than he was so that those cloaked in power might be comfortable.

"How can you have peace, if you think this?" she asked.

"Among the Omehi, I am called a Lesser, and failing that, I am made a Drudge," Tau said, thinking of the old man who had died in the fields. "What is peace to people like me?"

"Lessers can't know peace?" The queen asked it in earnest, her whole face the perfect picture of it, as if it was impossible for her to have known or imagined the damage that had been done to people like him.

"Champion. . . ." It was the vizier, warning him, but warning a man about the inyoka he's already stepped on is worthless. He must take its bite and pray he can survive the venom.

"We'll know peace," Tau said, "when we put an end to those who would deny it to us."

It was then that the queen's expression of cool neutrality slipped, and Nyah moved closer to her.

"A queen's champion fights for the queen's causes and those only," Nyah said, her small fists clenched.

Tau nodded. "True for all real champions," he said.

The vizier's hand twitched, like she wanted to hit him, like she wanted to reach into the underworld, snatch the power there, and hurt him with it. "After all that's happened this night, you speak this way?"

"You'd like me to wait for a time of your choosing to speak my truth?" Tau asked.

"We will wait," the queen said, spreading her skirts and sitting on the floor. "We will wait to hear about your sword brother, Champion Solarin, because rage won't help him tonight, but a little love just might."

Seeing the queen sit on the floor, Nyah made a sound somewhere between a strangled-off screech and a squeaked "meep!"

"Will you join us, Vizier?" Tsiora asked.

Nyah, nostrils pulsing like a pierced vein, behaved as though the ground might accost her, but she did, to Tau's surprise, sit.

"The queen is...sh-she's sitting!" Nyah said. "All of you sit, immediately."

The Queen's Guard were first, Yaw dropped into a cross-legged position, and Tau did the same.

"Too much talking," Uduak grumbled, head on his knees.

"It has been, yes," the queen said, leaving them with little choice but to sit in silence.

Tau hated it. He hated the thought of Hadith so close, but fighting alone. He hated the hurt that Uduak was in. And it was torture to sit so still. He had nothing to distract him from the agony of his leg and the call of Isihogo.

He closed his eyes and tried to be mindless, to let his miseries, hopes, losses, and pain wash over him, leaving him untouched. He tried, he did, and when it failed, the roiling inside him no less quiet, he made his choice. He did not think the others would notice much, if he went to spend his own palpable rage on the underworld's demons.

He readied himself. It had been too long. It was time to—

A door opened and Tau's eyes flew open. Hafsa was standing in the doorway.

Uduak was on his feet. Tau leapt to his. The queen was more dignified in the way she rose, and then Hafsa began to speak, addressing them all. Though, as was right, she gave Tsiora her focus.

"He'll live," she said.

Uduak cried. Yaw went to the big man's side. Tau nodded and wiped at his eyes, stripping them of the water that had formed there.

"The Goddess laid Her hand on him and his result is a promising one," the priestess said. "Yes, his lung is collapsed, but the spear only just pierced it and no other vital organs were hit." She smiled at them. "I wouldn't be surprised if he's able to be up and moving in a day or two, albeit slowly."

Tau swore he'd send a prayer to the Goddess that same night. "And fighting? How long until that?"

The priestess looked at him twice in rapid succession. "Fighting? He's alive, but as I said, with a collapsed lung. He'll never fight as he did."

"What? You said his was a promising result, that the Goddess had laid a hand on him."

The priestess's smile left her face. "Perhaps we see things differently," she said. "I consider the Goddess intelligent enough to find a purpose for men besides the killing of others."

Somehow he'd insulted her. "Of course," Tau said. "Alive is better than dead."

"Are you sure?" the priestess asked. "You don't sound sure."

Tau inclined his head to her. "Priestess, I am sure and I am grateful, but I've given offense, and for that I am sorry."

The queen glided over to Hafsa and took her hands. "Thank you," she said. "Thank you for saving him."

Not seeming to know what to do or where to look, Hafsa mumbled a thanks in return. The queen smiled at her reaction and gave her enough space to come back to herself.

"Alive is more than enough," Uduak said. "Much more than enough."

The smile returned to the priestess's face. "Perhaps it is," she said.

"I'll see him now?" Uduak asked.

"He's resting."

Uduak made for the door anyway; Hafsa raised a hand to stop him but then let it fall, allowing him to pass.

"No one else, for now," she said. "He needs to rest."

Tau wanted to catch the priestess's attention. He wanted to offer his own thanks. She would not look at him. Every time their gazes came close to crossing, she'd look away.

"I should get back in, if you'll excuse me, Your Majesty."

"We will, Priestess Ekene."

Hafsa bowed her head and went back into the room, closing the door behind her.

"Where is the sun, do you think?" the queen asked, turning to her vizier.

"Rising, my queen."

"We feared it so."

Tau didn't understand. "The sun?"

"We must gather the Nobles and Lessers in the city's largest circle. It must be public when we deliver justice to Otobong and Mirembe. We must show the people the Goddess's reward for treachery."

"That's to be done now?" Tau asked.

The look she gave him, though warm, was weary and pointed.

"It seems these two deaths and the message behind them very much need to be sent." She laid a hand on his arm as she moved past, her touch leaf light. "We must remind everyone what side they are on."

Shadowing the queen, Nyah breezed past as well, and after the briefest of pauses, Tau, champion to Queen Tsiora Omehia, followed them. He went to hear his queen's message and to watch a nearly unthinkable thing. He went to witness the execution of two Greater Nobles.

HANGED

The rain had stopped, the sun had risen, and Tau was standing next to the queen and Nyah in one of the larger circles in Citadel City. They were surrounded by the Queen's Guard, who served as a human barrier, preventing the mass of people who were coming into the circle from getting too close to the queen. The distance didn't stop the stares, and though he was next to the queen, it felt like everyone was sizing him up.

Tired of all the looks, Tau lifted his face to the sky. The clouds were thinning and the day was getting hot, but after so much rain, the city and its populace had yet to shake the damp. As the circle filled, the crowd's smell and murmurs washed over Tau, their individual scents mashing together in a swirl of sweat and stink while their words were garbled behind the clamor of carpentry hammers swung by the three Lessers finishing work on the gallows behind him.

Caught in his thoughts, Tau realized he'd missed the queen's words.

"Beg pardon, my queen?"

She tilted her head. "We seem to have forgotten. It's so rare we find cause to repeat ourselves."

"Apologies, I was ... I was thinking."

Nyah arched an eyebrow at that. Tau saw her do it, and that one pointed eyebrow felt like splinters in his skin.

"When this is...done," the queen said, "we will need a general to lead our forces."

Queen Tsiora had an impressive ability to hide the way she was feeling. On the outside she could appear as expressionless as stone, but however she'd learned to do it, the performance was meant to be viewed from a distance. Up close, the illusion was not as effective, and Tau could see how uncomfortable she was with what she'd decided to do.

"You will be our grand general," she said.

That startled Tau. "Neh? Uh...my queen?"

"You are our champion. You can be our grand general."

Tau shook his head. "I am...I'm honored, Your Majesty, but I am not a good choice."

"On that, I'll agree," Nyah said.

Queen Tsiora was not ready to release the argument's hilt. "We seem to be in a strange position where we find ourselves with few to trust and we would like to trust you, Champion Solarin."

"If it please you, Your Majesty, name no one for now," Nyah advised. "Give me time to determine the best remaining candidate from the Indlovu. I will provide a list of—"

"No, Nyah. We must begin our preparations to lay siege to Palm, and for that we need a general who can lead and motivate Lessers as well as Nobles. Our champion, as champion, fords the river between the two."

"My queen, he holds the title, but too many will see the Lesser in its place. I must still recommend—"

"We think this is the right choice, Nyah."

Tau was enjoying watching the vizier lose an argument, but if she lost entirely, they'd all be worse off. He was no general.

"I am not the right one to serve you in this way," he said to the queen, and Nyah waved her fingers in his direction, as if to say, "See?"

"We will not place one we can't trust in charge of our forces."

"You trust me?" Tau asked.

There was that look from her again, and a pause.

"We want to," she said.

It would have to do. "Hadith Buhari," Tau said. "He is your grand general."

Nyah laughed. "Solarin, you can't really be that blind. Choosing you would have been risk enough, and you are the queen's champion. In your place, you'd ask Nobles to follow a wounded Lesser? A Proven?"

"There's no one I know with a greater mind for strategy."

"You know too few people," Nyah said.

"Enough," the queen said. "Champion, we trust your opinion of your brother, but Nyah is right. We cannot risk the ire or open rebellion of the Nobles left to us."

Nyah crinkled her forehead and angled her body toward Tau. "You're young, Champion, and there are pieces within pieces, puzzles layered over puzzles, that must be considered when choices like this are made."

Tau adjusted his stance, trying to take weight from his burning leg. "I was asked to take up a task to which I know I am not equal. I gave the name of one who is the task's equal. You're right, Vizier. I know little of puzzles in puzzles, but I do know who I trust to get me out of a fight."

"And this is some of your problem," Nyah said. "You're still thinking about fights, when we need to win wars."

"The traitors," the queen said.

Councilwoman Mirembe and General Otobong had arrived in chains and under a heavy escort. Someone, Tau noticed, had taken the time and effort to redress Otobong's stump with clean cloths.

The cloths wrapped round Otobong's wrist were the cleanest thing about either of the Greater Nobles. It had been less than a full day since their attempted escape, capture, and imprisonment, and they were in poor shape. Mirembe held her head up, but her eyes were sunken, and Otobong's hunched shoulders told his story.

Tau had not considered the crowd's reaction to the sight of the two prisoners and found their silence unnerving. Perhaps for them, as it was for him, the execution of Nobles was also foreign.

"You cannot!" Mirembe shouted in Tau's direction, to the queen. The councilwoman, flanked by two Gifted women, had her hands tied behind her back, and in their place, she pointed to the gallows with her chin. "This is a Lesser's death."

Otobong, raising his head at her words, saw the hanging scaffold and came to a stop. The Indlovu behind him put a hand round his collar and pushed him onward.

"Do you see?" Mirembe shouted to the crowd. "Do you see the new world your child queen promises you? How long, do you think, until other Nobles stand where I do now?"

The crowd remained silent.

"You are traitors to the queen, to her people, to the Goddess!" Nyah said. "And you will be given a traitor's death."

Hanging, the punishment for traitors and disobedient Lessers, Tau thought, watching the soldiers pull a struggling Mirembe up the gallows stairs.

"Traitor, Nyah?" Mirembe said. "I am no traitor to my people or Goddess."

The noose was fitted round her neck and she flinched at its rough touch.

"Last words?" Nyah asked.

"I did all that I did for my people," Mirembe said, her voice rising in timbre, growing harder to understand. "When I saw that you would not listen, I did what anyone who loves their fellow women and men would do. I went to find someone who would."

"You think crawling to a man, to a man like Abasi Odili, would help your people? You lying wretch!" Nyah said.

Mirembe laughed, a hacking, desperate sound. "We weren't riding to him. We were going to General Bisi to ask that he bring his army back from the front lines and end your squabble," she said. "Odili and the child queen you support are the difference between the scorpion's sting and the inyoka's bite. Both will kill our people, though they take different paths to do it."

Tau saw Queen Tsiora send a look Nyah's way.

"Goodbye, Mirembe," Nyah said, lifting her hand into the air for the executioner to see. "May the Goddess greet you."

"Lie with a Lesser, nceku!" Mirembe turned her face to the crowds, staring them down.

And down came Nyah's hand, down came the executioner's lever, down went the floor beneath Mirembe's feet, and down she fell, the sound of her neck snapping louder than Tau expected. She died instantly, her legs swinging just above the ground, stalks in a gentle breeze.

She hadn't moved, but Tau could hear the queen. She was breathing too fast. He glanced at her and her pupils were tiny as pinpricks. He'd been there before, in Daba, when he'd come close to falling unconscious.

"Slow your breathing," he whispered to her, his mouth barely moving. "In through your nose and out through your mouth. Nice and slow."

She gave no sign that she heard him, but she did as he asked.

"Last words, Otobong?" Nyah said to the general as his neck was placed in the next noose.

"I am no traitor," he said, head still down. "I have always fought for my people and I go to my Goddess after a failed attempt at doing more of the—"

The wood beneath his feet creaked, broke, and collapsed, sending him falling after it. The rope round his neck drew taught, someone in the crowd screamed, and the wooden scaffolding to which the rope was attached crumpled under Mirembe's and Otobong's weight.

Mirembe's legs hit the ground and bent until she looked like she was kneeling. Otobong's side was higher up, and though he dangled, choking to death, his toes skittered across the ground, searching for some stable purchase to relieve the neck-breaking strain.

The general's face grew dark and swollen, his eyes bulged, and he shook this way and that, spasming on the end of a rope too long to kill him and too short to let him save himself.

The queen had her hand over her mouth, her fingers trembling like she was caught in the throes of a deadly fever. Nyah was frozen, except for her head, which she shook back and forth in silent denial of the moment.

The executioner scrambled around aboard the collapsing gallows, trying to bolster the post that held Otobong's and Mirembe's bodies. But he was not strong enough to lift it so that Otobong could die.

Seeing that, Tau broke through the circle of Queen's Guards, strode over to the suffering general, pulled free the black blade on his right hip, and with his left hand, he drove it through Otobong's straining heart. The general sighed and went limp, his torture ended.

Tau pulled his sword free and walked back to his queen's side. The quiet crowd did not need the Queen's Guard to keep them back. They gave the champion more than enough room.

"W-we need... we need to leave," the queen said to Tau. "We cannot... we..."

Her eyes were wet and her hands were still shaking. Her mask was slipping and Tau did not need to see all the layers to Nyah's puzzle to know that the crowded city circle was not the place for that to happen.

"Follow me, my queen," he said, walking toward the path leading to the Guardian Keep.

She did not follow. She was rooted in place, and not knowing what else to do, Tau reached out to her, took one of her too-cool hands in his own, and gently guided her to movement.

"If it please you, Majesty," he said.

She nodded and walked with him, Nyah joining them immediately, and the Queen's Guard shadowed them.

The crowds parted, letting them through, but Tau saw reluctance on many of the Noble faces around them. He saw a weighing on those faces as they considered the cost of stopping their queen in the circle.

"Let's hurry," Tau said, moving faster, getting them to the exiting path and exhaling in relief as they arrived.

"No," the queen said, taking her hand from his.

"My queen?"

"Not like this," she said, her back straightening and her mask sliding back into position, as if it had never moved at all.

She turned back toward the circle and the crowds and she called out to the women and men she ruled over. "Let it be known that we will retake Palm City and that all traitors, no matter their birth, will be given justice. This we promise you for we are the Goddess's voice on Uhmlaba and our will shall be done!"

The same silence from the crowd, a thousand mouths and not a tongue among them.

"We go to begin our preparations to retake our capital. We go to meet with our general, who will lead us all to victory and a return to the Goddess's grace. We go to Grand General Hadith Buhari to give him our orders that he may relay them to you!"

The queen gave the circle her back and walked out of it. As she went, the crowd found its voice and Tau could see the Nobles in it trying to confirm what they'd heard. Buhari? That was a Lesser's name. The women and men closest to the path the queen had taken moved forward like a cresting wave.

To discourage the crowd's advance, the Queen's Guard put their hands on their sword hilts.

"Stay back!" shouted one of the Queen's Guard, hitting someone from the crowd with the hilt of his sword.

The violence had the opposite of its intended effect, and the shouts and protests from the nearest Nobles were deafening.

Grimacing, but having had enough, Tau drew both his blades and stepped up beside the Queen's Guard.

"Let any who wish to discuss the queen's will bring their concerns to me," he shouted as loud as he could. "Come forward, Noble or Lesser, so that we may have this talk."

There was still pushing and rumbling, but it came from those farther back. The women and men in the front came no closer.

"Did she name a Lesser as grand general?" a woman asked Tau, eyeing his black swords.

"Hadith Buhari is grand general," he told her.

"And who is he?" another voice called out.

"The one chosen by your queen, and my sword brother," Tau answered.

"And your sword brother can take Palm?" a third Noble asked.

Tau sheathed his blades and let his eyes roam the crowd. "If you knew Grand General Buhari as I do, you would not need to ask.

Palm City was ours the moment Queen Tsiora placed him in command of her military. All that's left is that we go and take it."

In the sudden silence that followed, Tau turned on his heel and stalked out of the circle, praying that his belief in his friend hadn't doomed them all.

REST

Tau caught up to the queen and Nyah in the Guardian Keep. The Queen's Guard, who had followed her when she left the circle, had fallen into a two-columned marching line a respectful distance behind her, and as Tau made his way past the guards, he happened to catch one of their eyes.

The guard, an Indlovu, gave him a tight nod. "It was a mercy, Champion."

"Neh?"

"The crowd may not have seen it that way, but they are not military. You stopped General Otobong's suffering and it was mercy."

Tau watched the guard, unsure if the Indlovu's words were sincere. Choosing to treat them as if they were, he returned the man's tight nod and walked past, trying to catch up to the queen. He felt uneasy about having what he'd done called mercy. It had felt necessary, but Tau wasn't sure it'd been merciful.

"... need to know if it'll always be like this between you and the Lesser."

Tau didn't need to guess which Lesser Nyah was talking about.

"He's our champion," the queen said.

They were several strides ahead, their backs to him as they walked through the keep's hallways, and Tau knew he should announce his presence.

"He's little more than a boy."

"And Mirembe called us a girl. Do you feel she was right as well?"

"Tsiora..."

"Nyah."

"How can I keep you safe if you won't take my counsel?"

"How can we lead if our councillors doubt our every decision?"

"You let him make this decision."

"No, it was the Goddess's choice."

"Don't do this—"

"She brought him to us for a reason. Our faith is in Her, always."

"He docs not speak for the Goddess."

"He does not, but She chose, in that moment, to speak through him."

"Tsiora," Nyah said, "the more we want something, the harder it is to separate our own desires from Hers."

The queen stopped walking and turned to face her vizier.

"My queen," Nyah said, dropping her head and eyes.

Queen Tsiora opened her mouth, Tau saw her eyes slide toward him, and her head followed. "Champion," she said, "you are here."

It was his turn to drop his head. "I have just arrived."

"Of course you have," she said, turning from them both and continuing to walk down the hall.

Nyah hurried after her and Tau did the same, catching up to them in a few limping strides.

"We heard the crowd questioning you as we left."

"Yes, my queen."

"What did you tell them?"

"The truth," Tau lied. "I told them Palm City is as good as ours."

Tau could feel Nyah staring at him. He pretended she didn't exist.

"Nyah, Grand General Buhari will need time to recover, but we cannot wait long. You mentioned other potentials for the role of general. See to it that they are put in appropriate positions below our grand general."

"It will be done, Your Majesty," Nyah said.

"Also, send the rations master to the east council chambers. We will meet with her to confirm that we have the necessary supplies for the march and siege of Palm City."

"If it please you, I'll meet with her," Nyah said. "You need rest."

"An army lives and dies on its supply lines. We may be little more than a girl, but we remember that much from our studies, and so we will be there for the meeting with the rations master."

"Tsio . . . Queen Tsiora, you'll be useless to yourself and your people if you do not rest. When was the last time you slept?"

"We can go a little longer."

"But you shouldn't."

The queen offered her vizier a tight smile that did not reach her eyes. "And how will we sleep? How, when we see knives in every shadow?"

She was scared and Tau couldn't blame her.

"You'll be guarded," Nyah said.

"Where are our handmaidens?"

The shift from the queen's safety to her comfort threw Tau. Maybe he'd misread her intent and she wasn't afraid?

"They've yet to arrive, my queen," said Nyah.

"We won't feel safe without them, and that means we won't get any rest. So we may as well work."

Nyah looked down her nose at the young woman she was sworn to advise and protect. "Do you think to go without sleep until they arrive?"

Crossing her arms and staring back at Nyah, the queen was the picture of headstrong determination and youthful confidence, and seeing her like that gave Tau some small sense of what others might see when they looked at him.

To the Indlovu, to the councils, and to all the Nobles in positions of power, the queen and he were risky unknowns lacking the experience, and in his case, the right, to hold the roles to which they laid claim. The queen and Tau were climbing a rock face without rope, and they were a single missed handhold from a fatal fall. Climbs like that were far too dangerous to make when tired.

"The queen can rest safely," Tau said. "I'll guard her door."

He was exhausted, but it was more important for her to sleep. She needed to be sword sharp. Her decisions would mean the difference between life and death for them all.

"You will do no such—"

"Thank you, Champion," the queen said. "That would help."

"Queen Tsiora, I must insist that—"

"We thought you believed that we should rest."

Nyah balked. "I do, but..."

"But?"

Nyah's cheek was twitching and the queen turned down a corridor that ended in stairs to the keep's second floor. Nyah pointed to the Queen's Guard, indicating that they should follow the queen, and as she did, Tau noticed that Nyah's mouth had joined her cheek in its twitching.

"It's this way, Champion Solarin," the queen said, leading him to her chambers.

LOCKS

The hallways on the second floor were tight, cramped, and windowless. The inelegant design surprised Tau until the Queen's Guard joined them. The Indlovu couldn't stand two abreast, and that was the clue. The hallway to the queen's chambers was made for defense. Attackers would have to fight one by one, and if the defending swordsman was the stronger fighter, they could hold the passage until their heart gave out.

"What is it?" the queen asked.

"Why didn't you stay here, Your Majesty?"

Behind them, the Queen's Guard spread out along the thin hallway, securing its length.

"Stay here?"

"When Odili began the coup."

The queen pressed her lips together as her eyes moved up and to the left. She wasn't looking at anything in particular. She was remembering that night. "Days before his coup, Chairman Odili had scheduled an appointment with us in the sunroom. He pressed Nyah, pushing her to give him time with us. We believed he would make a final argument for rejecting peace. We intended to tell him that our decision was final."

"He made sure you were somewhere he could get to you?"

The queen blinked, perhaps to chase away the memory. "He did," she said, rounding a corner and stepping out of sight of the guards lining the hallway.

In front of Tau, five strides distant, the hallway ended at a small door.

"The door, it's made from Osonton wood," Tau said.

Her hand was on the door's latch, but she was looking at him. They were of a height, he noted as she nodded at him. She didn't move and Tau didn't know if there was something he should do or say, some ceremony or tradition he might be missing. He swallowed, and in the relative silence, he was certain she heard him do it.

"We shall go in now."

"Uh...of course, my queen. I'm with you." She tilted her head at that and Tau felt heat creep up the back of his neck. "I mean, I'll be out here for you. I'll be outside your door, guarding it...guarding you, I mean."

The edges of her mouth snuck upward, but she made the movement vanish and he couldn't be sure if he was seeing things.

"Thank you, Champion," she said.

"My queen."

She stayed standing there and Tau's scalp was itchy. He wanted to scratch but didn't want to do it with her there.

"We're going in," she said finally.

"My queen."

She manipulated the latch and pulled the door. It opened without a whisper and Tau saw that the wood was as thick as he was. The door's hinges had to be powerfully and expertly built. That much Osonton wood would weigh more than two Greater Nobles, and she'd moved it without effort.

She stepped past the door, and again, she waited.

"We are...we're going to close the door and you will hear it lock."

"Uh...yes, my queen." Tau didn't know what to say or where to look. She was being strange. Or maybe she wasn't and this was how she behaved. He didn't know her well enough to be sure.

"We trust you, Champion. Take nothing from us locking it."

"Of course, Your Majesty." Tau saluted. He had to do something.

She pulled the door shut. Tau sighed in relief and scratched his head, and the door swung open again. Tau froze, hand still on his head.

"Is it safer, for you to guard us, if we leave the door unlocked?"

"My queen?" Tau said, lowering his hand.

She brushed down the front of her dress, smoothing it. He didn't know why; it looked perfect. "That was a poor question," she said.

"No . . . it's a good one," Tau said. "Are there windows inside?"

"Windows?"

"Could someone access your room other than through this door?"

"Ah, windows. No. Do you need to see the room?" she asked.

"See it . . . uh . . . no. Not if there are no windows."

"There are no other doors either."

"Yes, that's good. I—I should have asked if there were other doors."

"So, we should lock it?"

"This door?"

"It's the only one," she said.

"Yes, I think perhaps you should lock it."

"We will, then. We're going to change and go to sleep."

Tau didn't think he should salute that, so he stood there, doing nothing.

"Um . . . continue on, Champion."

That didn't help. He didn't have anything to do but stand there. She seemed to realize that because she ducked behind the door and pulled it closed. A breath later he heard the lock turn.

"Cek, what was that about?" Tau muttered, scratching the rest of his scalp. His leg was hurting again and he'd have loved to take some weight off it, but he didn't dare lean against the door. Goddess forbid the queen hear him do it and come out again.

Instead, he shuffled the two steps to the wall and leaned against it. He tried massaging his leg around the bandages. It didn't help.

Tau grimaced as a stab of pain lanced through him. He couldn't imagine facing unending and unabated pain like this throughout his whole body. It'd drive him mad. It'd do that to anyone. The priestess, he thought, might have been right. Maybe he should have let her take the leg.

He closed his eyes, rejecting the thought. The dragon blood could spread, if it must. He didn't need to withstand the pain for long, just long enough to put an end to Odili. Tau opened his eyes. Just that long and he—

In front of him, five strides away, and immediately shy of the hallway's corner, so out of sight of the guards, was a demon. The creature sat on its haunches, its legs bent wrong at the knees, like a horse's back legs. On its flat face were three lidless eyes arranged vertically over a snarling mouth brimming with dagger-sharp teeth.

Tau pushed off the wall, swords already to hand when a waft of air struck him from behind. Tearing his eyes away from the threat in front, he swung round, swords moving, and seeing her, he had to wrench both blades upward and away.

Tsiora stepped back. She was wearing nothing but a thin nightdress of a shimmery opaque material. She looked...

The demon!

He whirled for the creature, swords back in position, and found there was nothing to fight. The thing was gone and the hall was empty.

Tau looked over his shoulder to the queen.

"It's only us," she said, eyes bouncing between his face and weapons.

Tau exhaled, still searching for the monster, but it was gone. Gone like it had never been. Shoulders slumping, he scabbarded his swords.

"I thought I—" First the stables and now the hallway. The visions were getting worse.

"We should have knocked before opening the door. To warn you."

The idea struck him as odd, her knocking to come out of her own room.

"I'm sorry," he said. "I-I'm not myself."

"Too much has happened in too short a time. It's not possible to be as we were before," she said, excusing him with grace.

Tau lowered his head, feeling shaken, doubting himself.

"We could not sleep," she said. "We tried, but...Champion, can you...will you come in?" his queen asked, stepping back into the room to make space for him as well.

GRIEF

It was true, the room had no other doors and was windowless, but that couldn't take away from the rest of its splendor. The ceilings were twice Tau's height and the walls had been painted a soft green, like new-grown grass kissed by rain. To his right, there was an ornate low table flanked by matching chairs, and the legs on all three pieces had been carved to look like they belonged to a dragon.

Across the room, beyond the sitting area, was a larger furniture piece Tau couldn't identify. The wooden thing stood as tall as he was and had two closed doors on its face, leaving its contents hidden to all but imagination. The other large piece of furniture was shorter and wider. It had shelves, and upon them lay more clothing than six women could need in three lifetimes.

It was wasteful, he thought, looking away and toward the bed. The bed, at least, he could understand, even if it was an odd one. First, it was huge, both wider and longer than the one in which he and Zuri had...

Tau tried to swallow, but his throat was dry. He turned away from the bed and the memories.

"You see the room, but not those within it," the queen said.

Her sleeping garb didn't leave him with many places that felt safe to look, so Tau kept his eyes on her face. "I've not seen much like it, my queen."

"The room, you mean?" she asked.

He nodded.

"It's uncommon to you, so it holds your attention?"

Another nod.

"Then your queen is already commonplace?"

"Commonplace?" If Tau didn't know better, he'd think her annoyed.

The annoyance, if he'd read it right, vanished behind that mask of hers. "You said you've not seen much like it, meaning you've been in rooms like this before?"

"Not like this," he said, "but... I'm reminded of the guest rooms in my isikolo."

"The... Southern?"

"Yes, my queen."

"But you trained there. It was your home. Why stay in the guest rooms?"

"Stay? No, my queen. I didn't stay there. No Lesser could..."

It was her turn to be confused. "Then?"

Joining his throat, Tau's mouth went dry. "I was in the rooms to see a friend." She tilted her head, waiting, and Tau cleared his throat. "I visited Gifted Zuri Uba in the isikolo's guest rooms when she rested there a night."

Her head untilted. "The Gifted who..." She blinked at him. "You were... close friends?"

This was not a discussion Tau cared to have. "As you say."

Her expression didn't change, but there it was again. He'd swear it—annoyance.

"We do not want it to be as we say," she told him. "We want it to be as it is. How would you name it?"

"How would I name it? What I have now?" Tau said. "I'd name it grief."

His voice broke on the last word, and he was done talking about this. She said nothing, neither did he, and the tension grew thick enough to touch.

"We're sorry," she said finally. "That was unkind." She paused. "It is not right to pry into your..."

Tau nodded and kept his head down, trying to keep the way he felt inside.

"Your leg," she said, the words bumping into each other in her rush to get them out. "It must hurt?"

"It all hurts."

"Please, you must sit," she said, drawing his attention to the chairs.

Tau was supposed to be guarding her and didn't think guards were supposed to sit, but he was too weary to worry about decorum. He sat in the chair, its cushions feeling softer than clouds must, and kept his eyes on the floor as he heard her moving the sheets on the bed.

"We are sorry for your loss, Champion Solarin."

Unwilling to trust his voice, he looked up. She was in the bed and under the covers, propped up by an army of pillows. She looked small, young, a bit uncertain.

He wanted to ask her why he was there, in her room. More, he wanted to ask her why she felt she could lead them all to a better future, and what in the Goddess's name she thought that future would look like. He didn't. He was there to guard her, not damn her.

"We want our people to have their proper place," she said, the words startling him with how closely they matched his thoughts. "We want to undo the mistakes that were made."

Perhaps she could do with a little damning. "Mistakes?" he asked.

"Our treatment of the Lessers, our treatment of the Xiddeen. It's not what the Goddess wants, and we barely survive because we do not live as we are meant to."

"No?"

"No."

"And you'll save us?" he asked.

She had a way with her eyes, a way of looking at and into him. He didn't like it.

"We'll save each other," she said.

He grunted as politely as he knew how.

"The queens before us, they didn't listen."

"To their councillors?"

She shook her head. "To their Goddess."

This talk always made Tau uncomfortable, and he'd begun to regret asking.

"Without truly listening, we almost took the wrong path," she said. "But the coup, the broken peace, and even the change in the Lessers, because of what they see in you, all are part of bigger things that will lead to a better world."

There couldn't be a better world without the people he'd lost, he wanted to tell her. "You really believe that?" he asked instead.

His question seemed to surprise her, too much for her mask to hide. "Yes," she said. "The world is broken and we must fix it."

"For who, my queen? For Nobles? For Lessers?"

She lowered her voice but kept it steady, as if telling a dangerous secret. "We are more alike than we are different," she said.

"What?" Tau asked. Those had been Jayyed's words.

"We are here to make things right," she said.

He began to shake his head, realized how that would look, and held his head still. He believed she meant the things she said, but that didn't count for much.

How long had things been as they were? Could a queen, a Royal Noble, be the one to change them? And what was a better world without his father, or Zuri, or Jayyed, or his sword brothers who had gone to the Goddess? Too much had been lost, and that hurt most of all.

Yet, Tau couldn't help but see the hopes of those he'd lost in this strange queen. She had strength, courage, and passion, and possible or impossible, he wasn't so callous as to let her chase the fantasy of a better world alone. He couldn't do that to the brave young queen and he told her so.

"You should rest," he said. "So long as I'm champion, I swear I'll keep you safe, and if there comes a day when I can't, I'll have men like me guard you in my stead."

He thought the words would comfort her, help her sleep. He even meant them. He'd see her through the siege of Palm. He could do that and thought that saying so would ease her worries. He'd forgotten that he was speaking to a monarch at war.

"Men like you, Champion Solarin?" Queen Tsiora asked, sitting up. "Can that be?"

Tau held his tongue, considering what could come from the truth, and then, with the love he held for his father, Zuri, and Jayyed close to heart, he decided to trust the queen and her hopes for a better world. He decided that, if her side was the one he was fighting for, they would smash all who opposed them.

"It can be done," he said.

She leaned forward, her mask of neutrality gone. "How?"

CHAPTER FIVE

WHOLE

"I have died more times than the days I've lived," Tau told the queen. "At the isikolo, I learned that..." He wanted to make it palatable for her. "The Goddess told me to go to Isihogo to find my true strength, and in the underworld's mists, I waited for the demons to come and I fought them."

She leaned in.

"The demons cannot be killed, or in the end, I am unable to kill them, but either way I can return to Isihogo time and time again, doing battle and learning all the ways a man, demon, or any being can seek to harm another. In this way, with time flowing differently in the mists, I could train harder and longer than any man living."

The queen had a handful of bedding gripped in one hand. "The Goddess, she sent you to us to be... this."

Tau said nothing.

"Tell us more," the queen said. "Isihogo takes your spirit but not your body, and the time you spend there will not make your arms or legs stronger here."

Tau nodded. "It was my training at the isikolo that honed my body, but the real difference isn't in my body. It's in my mind.

Her eyebrows pinched together. "Your mind?"

"My head is filled with... violence. Its patterns, its flow, the essence of it, and when I'm fighting"—Tau could feel his blood race as he spoke of it—"I can sense the way things will or should be. It's like I can remember the words yet to be sung in a familiar song."

The queen searched his face. "The Goddess shows you the future?"

"No, it's...I've lived so much violence it's become part of who I am," he said. "I can see its possibilities and their likelihood." He tried to be more clear. "Imagine you threw a stone to me—"

"A stone?"

"It has not yet landed and still has a distance to travel, but I can go to where it will be and snatch it out of the air, because with enough practice throwing and catching, I know what path the stone must take."

"Is there pain?" she asked.

He knew what she meant. "To do this is to suffer, my queen."

"Does the pain diminish? Do you grow...inured?"

"No."

"Then, what could possibly make doing what you do worth it?"

Tau took his time, thinking about the answer. "There must be consequences," he said. "Evil must be punished or it will continue undeterred until it consumes all that is good."

The queen wasn't convinced. "You do this as a holy mission to fight evil?"

Tau let his eyes roam the room, wondering what to say and how much of his truth to give her. "Abasi Odili murdered my father just to make a point," he said. "He did it with ease, because the life he was ending was not, to him, equally human. The Nobles think that we're born feeling less, loving less, worth less, but they're wrong, and I'm going to show them that."

"You'll punish them?"

"Him, I will," Tau said, his heart hammering as he told her what he wanted. "I'm going to break him in front of a crowd of Nobles. I'm going to strip him of his dignity and his humanity, because I want everyone to see how easy and vile it is to make a person seem less than fully human."

"You'll expose evil by doing evil?"

"No," Tau said. "I'll reclaim my humanity by destroying a man who would otherwise deny it. You can't talk people into giving up their hold over you. You have to make them do it."

"Tau"—it was unsettling to hear his name, unadorned, from her mouth—"aren't you simply justifying the right to do harm? And who but those who have succumbed to evil can believe they have that right?"

She was turning his words around. "You promised me Odili," he said.

"And we keep our promises, Champion."

"As do I. You have my loyalty," he told her, wishing the truth didn't sound so much like a marketplace barter.

She gave him a look that might have been pity, but it vanished from her face before he could be sure. "Allow us to ask our earlier question another way," she said. "How can you stand it? The fighting, the deaths, the horrors. How can you stay whole?"

The question cut too close to the spine, and Tau focused on her face, afraid to let his eyes wander, afraid of the demons he might see if they did. "I'm not sure."

"We may know," she said. "It is the Goddess who keeps you whole, and you need to honor Her faith in you. You say the Nobles want to make you smaller than you are, but in thinking only of revenge, you're also doing it to yourself. Tau Solarin, you're not here to kill one man," Tsiora said. "Ananthi isn't keeping you whole for that."

"Perhaps," Tau said, hoping to end the conversation.

"Tell me," the queen said, allowing the topic to shift, "you think you can take others to Isihogo, to do as you have done?"

"I do," Tau said, remembering the old Drudge whom he'd been unable to save from Otobong's sword. If Tau had more men with his training, then fewer innocents would die, more battles could be won, and together, they could make a difference to the world in a way that he could not on his own.

"Won't they break?" Tsiora asked.

"Not if I choose the right men."

"Did the Goddess speak their names?"

Remaining silent while people talked nonsense about the Goddess was one thing, outright lying about Her speaking names to him was another, and Tau wasn't about to do that. "I believe I know who to choose," he said.

"Do you hear Her voice?"

Biting the inside of his cheek, he shook his head.

"Then we cannot allow other men to do this."

"My queen—"

"The risk is too great. Without Her guidance, you could give this power to those unworthy of it. You'd create a group of Ingonyama killers. Imagine what would happen if these men turned away from our cause."

"My sword brothers can be trust—"

She shook her head. "If they understand the power you offer them and they are not worthy, we...you will have released more evil on the world than you could ever punish. The Goddess keeps you whole, Tau Solarin, and even so, there is still a terrible struggle in you. Swear to us that you will not reveal this path to anyone."

"Queen Tsiora—"

"Swear it."

Tau couldn't untangle his emotions fast enough to know if he was frustrated or relieved at the sudden turn. Regardless, the choice had been taken from him.

"I swear," he said.

She leaned toward him, her voice so soft he had trouble hearing her. "You are enough."

Not for Aren, he hadn't been, or Oyibo or Jayyed or—

"You are enough," she said.

—Zuri. His eyes burned and began to water. He wanted to turn away but couldn't because he was sure he'd see nothing but his demons.

"Tau," she said, and Goddess wept, the emotion she put into saying his name felt real and warm and kind. "You are enough."

His eyes stung and he lowered his head to wipe at them, thankful that Tsiora was perceptive enough to let him sit in silence awhile.

Then, after a time, she spoke. "We are sorry for all you've lost," she said.

Head still down, Tau nodded in thanks.

"We're glad you're here," she said, moving on the bed to lie down.

Tau raised his head, and even from across the room, he could see her muscles relax. She'd become at ease in his presence. Their talk, what he'd revealed, and her interpretation of it had done that. She truly believed the Goddess had brought him to her.

The queen closed her eyes, her breathing slowed, and before long she was asleep. The peace her devotion brought her made Tau wonder if he should take his prayers more seriously. The thought brought a small and sorrowful smile to his face. Prayers wouldn't bring him what he needed.

Closing his own eyes, Tau let his spirit spin loose. He'd been gone for far too long. He'd been gone long enough for it to feel as if the demons were seeking him out instead of the other way around.

He died thirteen times, each worse than the last, and every ending was excruciating. He could usually manage more before becoming hesitant, and he blamed the long night and longer day for his reluctance to keep fighting. But before they could truly sway him, Tau pushed away his fears and closed his eyes.

The fights that must be won come when they will, without care or concern for how tired, injured, or distracted a warrior might be. Tau knew that. He knew that the difference between the ones who stood and the ones who fell was that the truly triumphant taught themselves to meet all their fights, regardless of circumstance, in spite of the odds, and in defiance of fear.

So, he let his spirit fly free when, half a reality away, he heard the latch on the queen's door click. Mind and body protesting the rough treatment, Tau wrenched himself back to Uhmlaba and leapt to his feet, swords drawn, to stand face-to-face with the queen's vizier.

LOYAL

Strangling a yelp, Nyah jumped back, hitting her back against the half-open door she'd just walked through.

Tau sheathed his swords. "Vizier," he said, bowing so she wouldn't see his embarrassment and thinking that he needed to stop pointing blades at his allies.

"Give a Lesser a sword and before long he'll cut off his own manhood," Nyah said, rubbing her back with one hand as she closed the door with the other. "Why are you in here?"

"The queen asked."

"Asked? What did she ask?"

Tau straightened to his full height but kept his voice low. "I believe that's between me and the queen," he said, annoyed that he wasn't tall enough to look down at the vizier and feeling his face grow hot the moment the words left his mouth.

"How dare you even suggest...," she spluttered. "Who do you think you are, you—"

"This is not how we'd have wished to wake," the queen said, sitting up, stretching, and causing the arms of her nightdress to slip from her wrists to her elbows.

Tau looked away and stared at the floor, his face growing twice as hot when he realized the queen had probably heard him.

Schooling her features, Nyah bowed at the neck. "My queen."

"How long were we asleep? It can't be the next day. Is it even evening?"

"Apologies," Nyah said. "The sun still shines, and if there was any way I could ensure that you'd be left alone in this room for a few more spans"—Nyah's eyes slipped to Tau, and he could feel the sharp bronze in her look—"I would have done so, but this news cannot wait."

Tau risked a glance at the queen. Thankfully, her sleeves had fallen back around her wrists, but after seeing her face, it wasn't finding a safe place to look that worried him. Tsiora was exhausted and Nyah had come here to burden her further.

"The queen needs rest, Vizier," he said.

Tau wasn't afraid of Nyah, but she shot him a look that made him swallow.

"I have served Queen Tsiora since she was a child. I have been by her side through more than you will ever—"

"Nyah...," the queen said.

Tau could see that "saving" Nyah's daughter might have softened the vizier's view of him, but that simply meant that, in her mind, he'd gone from being an inyoka to being an imbecile. He might be less dangerous, but he was still a creature with no proper place in polite company.

Nyah turned her back to him, as if the quarter turn could erase his existence from the world, and spoke to the queen. "There's been an edification from the front lines. It's General Bisi."

"Were we too late?" the queen asked. "Did Mirembe and Otobong get word to Bisi?" Her eyes widened. "Is he marching for us?"

"It wasn't them," Nyah said, "and he's not marching, yet."

"What then?"

"It's Odili."

Tau's jaw clenched at the name.

"We see," the queen said, pulling the covers away and tossing her legs over the side of the bed. "Assemble the Guardian Counc... Champion, will you gather those loyal to our efforts? It seems even an afternoon's rest is too long to spare before we must fight our next battles."

Tau saluted.

"Vizier, please remain. Tell us what has happened as you help us dress."

"My queen," Nyah said.

"We will meet again in the stables in half a sun span."

"The stables?" Nyah asked.

Tsiora nodded. "Yes, there's something we need to do."

OPPORTUNITY

With no time to rest, a military meeting to attend in half a span, and feeling ill-equipped for the duty he'd been set, Tau went to the infirmary. Hadith was the queen's grand general, and Tau prayed he was awake. Perhaps it was cruel to need his sword brother less than a day after he'd been wounded, but Tau had no idea whom to gather, and he figured that Hadith could at least give him a few names to call on.

The closer he got to the infirmary, the more guilt he felt. He hadn't come to see Jabari in days. It was hard to be in his old friend's presence when the entire time he was he couldn't shake the feeling that he'd failed him.

"Champion!" The two Ihashe standing guard at the infirmary's doors snapped to attention when they saw him, their salutes crisp, proud.

Resisting the urge to look behind him to see if they were saluting someone else, Tau nodded to the two full-bloods, both older than him, and marched up to the door. The Ihashe on his left opened it for him and Tau walked into the sand-colored space.

The infirmary had beds lining the walls on either side of its slim width, with a series of lancet windows running along the left that looked out onto a shaded terrace. The first time he'd been in the infirmary, seeing to Jabari, he'd been confused by the build. The infirmary was a permanent structure designed to look like one of the tents the Ihashe and Indlovu used in the Queen's melee. Tau had mentioned that to Hadith, and Hadith had explained that all infirmaries looked that way.

For cycles after the Omehi had first landed on Xidda, they'd lived in tent camps as they struggled to survive and build. In the fighting that filled those early times, the medicinal order had saved and lost lives in those tents, and either hoping to honor those desperate times or simply because they could no longer picture it any other way, the Sah had given their permanent infirmaries the same shape as those tents.

The way things were becomes the way things are, Tau thought, and then he saw Hadith.

His sword brother was lying on a bed beneath one of the windows. His eyes were closed and his face was tight, as if even at rest it hurt him to breathe. Sitting on a chair beside Hadith's bed was Uduak. Uduak and Hadith had their arms clasped, wrist to wrist, and Uduak's head hung to his chest. The big man was asleep and Tau knew he hadn't moved since being allowed by Hadith's side.

"Brother," Tau said, laying a hand on the big man's shoulders.

Uduak opened his eyes and raised his head. "Mka."

"What?"

"You look like mka," he said.

"You think you look better?"

Uduak gave Tau a small smile and turned back to Hadith.

"I need to speak with him," Tau said.

"When he wakes."

"I need his advice."

"When he wakes."

"Yes, well, I'm awake now, aren't I?" Hadith said, scrunching his face as he moved a hand to touch at the bandages around his chest.

"What did you think you were doing, Hadith?" Tau asked.

"When?"

"You know when."

"When I fought the enraged Xiddian? I was thinking that our Ingonyama was losing and that he'd die if I didn't help."

"He did die."

"I know, but I tried to stop it."

"Foolish to fight an enraged—"

"I don't think you ever get to use that word when talking about someone else," Hadith said, earning a grunt from Uduak.

Tau opened and closed his mouth, nothing coming at first. "I know how I can seem, and I'm trying."

"Can't say I didn't learn from the best," Hadith said.

"You almost got yourself killed," Tau told him.

"Almost."

"You...you won't be able to fight again."

Hadith started to shrug, grimaced, and ended the shrug halfway. "Didn't particularly care for all the sword swinging. Waste of my talents, really."

The words were bold, but Tau saw through them. "I'm sorry," he said.

"Don't be."

"I am."

"It's fine. I'm Governor Caste and I'm sure that, given the last few days, the queen has one or two gaps in her bureaucratic administration."

Tau could feel the venom in Hadith's words and sought to draw some poison free. "No one's told you yet?"

"Told me what?" Hadith asked.

"The queen has a position in mind for you."

"Brave of her," Hadith said. "I might not have survived the night."

Tau shrugged. "The priestess says it's a miracle that you took as little damage as you did. Except for the lung thing."

Hadith was watching Tau from the side of his eyes. "Except for that."

"He needs to rest," Uduak said.

"What does she want from me, our queen?" Hadith asked.

"Rest," Uduak said.

"She made you her grand general."

Without thinking, Hadith tried to sit up, and Tau could tell exactly when the pain hit him.

"Sweet Goddess, that hurts!" Hadith groaned. "Did you say grand general?"

Tau nodded. "She declared it in front of most of Citadel City."

Hadith tried to laugh. "Hurts to laugh too," he said.

"Grand general?" Uduak asked. "Tell her he can't."

"Me?" Tau asked.

"You're champion," Uduak said.

"You can't be serious," Hadith said. "Does she want another coup? I'm a Lesser and the rebellion she hopes to quell is split across caste lines. Making me the leader of her military can only widen the gap she has to bridge. Why in Ananthi's love and Ukufa's hate would she . . ." Hadith tried to sit up again. "Tau!"

Tau raised his hands, palms out. "She asked my advice."

"No, she didn't," Hadith said, his eyes flitting back and forth. He was thinking. "She asked you to do it."

"Neh?" was the best Tau could manage.

"Don't 'neh' me. She asked you to do it and you told her that I would be better."

"Tau . . . ," Uduak growled.

"Well, it's the truth," Tau said.

"Nceku!" Uduak said.

"What's done is done, and I'll stand by the rightness of it," Tau said. "Within a season of me being grand general, we'd all be dead."

"I'm a Lesser, Tau," Hadith said.

"So am I, and you keep saying that we can't let the name they call us be the total of what we are. You keep telling me that things must change, and I know change is hard, but this is an opportunity to do it. Do you think to turn away just because it won't be easy? Are your ideals, your principles, only held when they don't inconvenience you? Can't you see that—"

"Enough."

"No! I'm right in this and—"

"Enough, Tau. Once you've won an argument, the most valuable thing you can do is shut your mouth and take the win."

"The win?"

"It's dangerous...even foolish, but you're right. There's a chance here to make a change, and what kind of person would I be if I didn't take it?"

"A living person," Uduak said.

"Not many of us will live through this anyway," Hadith said. "This way, at least we have some say in how our lives are spent."

Uduak lifted his hand and arm out of Hadith's.

"Uduak...," Hadith said.

"What kind of life?" the big man said, looking around.

Hadith reached for and took Uduak's hand. "One we'll make the best of."

"The queen is calling her...advisers," Tau said, guiding his sword brothers back to the current path. "Something happened with Odili and a general named Bisi from the front lines."

"Bisi? He leads one of our military rages. He's also our most decorated war hero," Hadith said.

"As you say."

"You don't know who he is, do you, Tau?"

Tau crossed his arms.

"How the...what were you doing at the Ihashe isikolo if you don't even know—"

"You know what I was doing," Tau said.

Hadith blinked slowly at him. "You're right. I do."

"The queen needs councillors, war councillors, and I'm to help assemble them. Well, you're her grand general. Who do I bring?"

"Me," Hadith said, waving with his free hand at Tau, asking him to help him up.

"No!" Uduak said.

"Help me, both of you."

"No!" Uduak said. "You need rest."

"I'll rest when I'm dead. Help me. That's an order."

"Order?"

"From your grand general."

Uduak laughed. "I'll call the priestess. She won't let you leave."

This wasn't Tau's plan, and with Hadith so soon out of surgery, he didn't want to rip up any of the work the priestess had done to hold his sword brother together. "Hadith, can't you just tell me who to bring or what to say?"

"Do you know what's happened with Bisi and Odili?"

Tau shook his head.

"Then, let's go find out." Hadith waved at Tau again. "Hurry. This will hurt and we need to go before I lose my nerve."

"I'm calling the priestess," Uduak said, standing.

"Priestess Hafsa Ekene seems to enjoy telling the same stories," Hadith said to Uduak. "Like Tau, she also told me how lucky I was in the way the spear cut through me. If I have her words right, she called it the Goddess's own miracle and said she expected me to be able to rise from this bed today. Well, I'm ready to do some rising."

Uduak stared at Hadith without a word.

"Goddess wept! Just help me," Hadith said.

"Stupid," Uduak said.

"It's mostly worked for Tau," Hadith said.

"What did you say?" asked Tau.

"You heard," Hadith said, waving Tau over to help him.

Shrugging, Tau walked to Hadith's far side to assist.

"Uduak?" Hadith said. "Help me, please."

Grumbling, Uduak moved to help.

Hadith smiled, but Tau could tell he was steeling himself for the pain.

"Good," Hadith said. "Let's find out what Odili has done now and how we can stop him."

COALS

With Tau limping and Hadith near immobile, it took all the time they had remaining to get to the stables. If anything, Tau had to caution Hadith time and again not to push himself. His sword brother, leaning on a crouched Uduak on one side and Tau on the other, remained stoic, even offering up the occasional joke. The humor, however, wasn't enough to hide the way he tensed and held his breath with every step.

"Can't you bend lower?" Hadith asked Uduak.

"Want me to crawl?"

"Tau?"

"I'm walking on my toes."

"Feels like I'm caught between a mountain and an anthill," Hadith grumbled as he nodded to Kellan, who was marching over at full speed.

"Grand General Buhari," Kellan said, saluting. "I came as soon as I received word you needed me."

Kellan's obsequiousness set Tau's teeth on edge. Hadith hadn't yet been a general for a full day and Kellan was already treating the change as if it had occurred a dozen cycles ago.

"There's a council meeting, my first as the queen's grand general. I wanted you with us," Hadith said.

Kellan's chin lifted and Tau could tell that with nothing more than a few words Hadith had earned a deeper loyalty from the Greater Noble. Tau watched his friend, trying to determine if Hadith meant the trust behind the words or if the words' purpose had been to make it seem as if he'd meant the trust. It didn't take long for him to realize he couldn't tell.

"We're meeting in the stables?" Kellan asked, glancing at the adobe-and-wood-walled building behind them.

In answer, Tau walked to the stable doors and reached for them. Before his hand could grasp the door's handle, he heard footsteps within and stepped back.

"There's someone inside," he said, hoping to sound normal and not as if he had any worries that it might be one of Isihogo's demons come to torment him.

The leftmost stable door creaked open, and out into the sunlight came Nyah and Thandi.

Seeing the four men, the vizier's eyes narrowed. "I can name several accomplished military leaders who still stand within this city's walls. I can name them, but I do not see them here with you."

"Vizier Nyah," Hadith said, "I came myself. I am new to my role, but if my counsel is needed to help set our direction, I'd prefer to come to an understanding with as small a group as possible."

"Well, you've brought one Noble with you, though I have doubts he's old enough to shave," she said. "Do you fear more experienced leaders might undermine your authority?" she asked. "If that's the reason for the presence of the men before me, I wonder if your authority might not need some undermining. The Indlovu you've excluded have fought battles and led warriors when you were still sitting on your father's shoulders."

"With respect, you're wrong," Hadith said.

"Am I?"

"I did not know my father and never sat on his shoulders."

Uduak stifled a snort.

"Ah yes, let's make light of our situation," Nyah said. "Nothing is serious until you watch everyone you love put to the sword because you valued your pride and humor over their safety."

"You misjudge me," Hadith said. "I value nothing more than the safety and lives of the people I love. It is because I value them that I do not invite more Greater Nobles to my first meeting with the queen. They will seek argument with me, not because of my ideas, but because of my person."

Nyah waved away his objection. "If your ideas hold merit, they'll win out in spite of your person."

"Yes, that's the lie everyone unaffected by hidden hardships believes."

"Hadith Buhari, you expect me to believe that, were you to present plans that would save us all, the Nobles would reject them?"

"Vizier Nyah, I think the world is too complex for most things to be purely right or wrong. Given that, the way words, actions, or even intent is viewed depends on who is doing the viewing and on who is being viewed."

She chuckled. "Is this why you think you can't achieve all you want? You think that just because you're a Lesser and they're Noble, they'd kneel on glowing coals for no better reason than to prove you wrong if you said the fire was still hot? Come, now."

"You're right, they wouldn't do that," Hadith said. "They'd have me walk across the coals with them as equals, me in my bare feet and them in leather boots."

Nyah sucked her teeth. "If you regard Nobles with such distrust, you'll see even the ones reaching down to lift you up as nothing more than hands trying to push you down."

"I presume the queen is already inside?" Hadith asked.

"That's it? Nothing more to say?"

"Not to those who can't hear," Hadith said, taking a step forward and getting Uduak and Tau to help him on.

Nyah was annoyed, but she also seemed done with the discussion. "Wait. I need to speak with the champion," she said.

Still holding Hadith, Tau looked over his shoulder at her.

"Alone," she said.

"Kellan, will you help me inside?" Hadith asked.

"Of course, General," Kellan said, moving to take Tau's place.

"Thank the Goddess," said Hadith when Kellan replaced Tau. "If

I had to take two more angled steps, I swear I would have been hunched to one side forever."

The three men walked into the stables and Thandi followed them, closing the stable door behind her.

When they were alone, Tau turned to Nyah. "Vizier?"

"I'm grateful. I want you to know that. You saved my daughter; you saved me. I am grateful."

Tau inclined his head.

"But my gratitude cannot offer you favor in matters that hurt the queendom."

"I don't follow."

"A champion is required to fulfill their martial duties," she said. "That is the only duty they must fulfill."

Tau frowned. "I think I know what you're suggesting and I'm insulted by it."

Nyah moved closer to him and lowered her voice, ensuring her words wouldn't carry to any inside the stable. "It hasn't been easy for her."

"Nor for any of us," Tau said.

"Oh, enough of that! Can't you leash your Lesser's self-pity for even a moment?"

Tau choked back the choice words he wanted to throw in her face. "What do you want?" he asked instead.

"Don't use her. She won't be able to take it."

"Use her? Are you mad?"

"She's strong, but so much is asked of her, and there's only so much any of us can take before we crack, before we break."

"Why tell me? Her Nobles resist her rule, she's disconnected from the lives of her Lessers, and she must win back a capital without the fighters to do it. Why do I rate in the list of obstacles to be overcome?"

"Because I know her strengths as well as her weaknesses, and because you don't know her anywhere near as well as I do."

"And I have no intention of doing so, Vizier."

"Liar."

"What did you call me?"

"A liar. She's told you that she thinks you're a gift from the Goddess, hasn't she?"

Tau clenched his jaw.

"Yes, I see she has. Don't think to use her faith to bind or bend her will. It won't go well for you."

That was a step too far, and Tau gave himself over to the man he was in the underworld. He locked eyes with the vizier and spoke with the same intensity with which he fought. "Are you threatening me, Vizier?"

She stepped back. "I will protect my queen."

"Is that what you think you're doing now?"

"She worships Queen Taifa and Champion Tsiory. You can tell that, can't you? She reveres the Dragon Queen's courage and idolizes the love that existed between her and Tsiory. She sees them as a model to be followed. You're not too foolish to see that, are you?"

Tau said nothing and Nyah nodded, as if he'd admitted guilt in a hanging offense.

"Queen Tsiora has been isolated her whole life. Every decision has been made for her, guiding her to these moments, and now, finally, she's come to power, and finally, she can make choices for herself. She's a good woman and she'll prove to be a great queen. She will because we've spent every day of her life getting her ready for what we knew was coming."

"Vizier, I'll help her win the fights to come, but—"

"But we didn't know you were coming."

"What?"

"A Lesser who fights like the Goddess Herself blessed him? A man who resurrects the legend of Champion Tsiory in a new image? We didn't expect you, Tau Solarin."

"I'm no Tsiory."

"No, you're not, and that's all I'm asking you to remember," Nyah said, walking away from him and into the stables.

"Are all Gifted and Nobles insane?" Tau asked under his breath, following her.

He wasn't a step past the doors when Kellan came over and placed a hand on his shoulder. "The vizier warns you away from the queen?"

"It seems I have my answer," Tau said to himself.

"Beg pardon?"

"Nothing, Kellan, nothing."

"You are the queen's chosen champion," Kellan said. "Out of everyone, she chose you, and that means she wants you to defend her queendom as well as be her—"

Tau put his hands up, palms out. "Kellan, listen to me. The queen chose me because she wanted me to fight. That's where I can give my all, and it's the only place I can. There's nothing else in me worth giving or taking."

Kellan squeezed his shoulder. It was meant to be comforting, but Tau had to hold himself back from shrugging Kellan's hand away.

"Champion Solarin," Kellan said, "don't give in to the lie that you honor the dead or Gifted Zuri Uba by closing your heart forever. Grief, anger, they'll hold you for a time. They must. But if you let them root and fester, they'll become a hate that will consume you."

Kellan patted him on the shoulder again, opened the doors wider, and walked into the stables to join the others as Tau seriously considered turning around and going to get some badly needed sleep.

"Champion Solarin," the queen called from across the stables. "Will you join us? We have something for you."

FURY

Feeling suspicious, Tau made his way to Tsiora and the others. The queen, dressed in an ocean-blue something that looked like a cross between a Gifted's robes on top and an Ihashe's pants below her waist, was brushing down the enormous horse Mirembe had stolen. It was the same animal that had smashed Tau's demon to ash. Though, in the time since, Tau had come to wonder if the memory was a true or false one.

"Where are they now?" Tau heard Tsiora ask Nyah.

"Riding hard for us," Nyah told her. "Don't worry about the handmaidens, my queen. They can take care of themselves."

The queen's hand, the one holding the brush she was using on the horse, hung in midair. She did not appear reassured. "Are they pursued?"

Nyah shook her head. "Lelise did not think so."

Tau wondered at handmaidens who could ride and who could create so much worry in the queen.

"Then the Goddess watches over them," the queen said, turning to Tau and gracing him with a smile. "Champion," she said.

Like Hadith, she had a gift with people. Tau couldn't deny that, but he also had no interest in playing the obsequious Kellan to her Hadith. Queen Tsiora had promised him more than smiles and sweet words for his loyalty.

"We lost our father to the war when we were young," she said, the conversation's sudden weight putting Tau off-balance. "At the time, it felt like his pyre's ashes hadn't even had the chance to cool before our mother's sickness returned her to the Goddess." The queen's smile fell away. "There were days we didn't think we could keep going. There were nights we thought it better if we didn't."

The vizier had looked away, as if she had no desire to remember or share in the queen's recalled pain.

"Nyah helped us through that time with her care and compassion. She could see the thread holding us to this life unraveling and she gave us something to keep that thread strong."

Aimed at Nyah, the queen's smile returned. The vizier met her queen's smile with one of her own, and for once, Tau had no doubts about intent. The two women cared for each other.

"Nyah told me that life, like love, is meant to be shared and that we are least linked to our own selves when we have no one with whom to share what we are. None of us are meant to go through this life alone." The queen continued brushing the warhorse. "When our mother died, Nyah brought us to the royal stables in Palm City and we walked its length, stopping at the last stall. Inside was a tiny foal, newborn."

"Foal?" Tau asked.

The queen's eyes crinkled at their corners. "A baby horse."

"I see."

"Nyah opened the stall door and we went inside. We sat with the foal until we were exhausted and hungry. We asked Nyah if we could come back on the morrow and she told us that we'd better, since the foal had lost its mother and was now ours to raise and shelter. We thought less about leaving this life after that."

Tau began to worry about where this was going.

"This is Fury," she said, patting the side of the coal-black horse.

"It has a name?"

"She does, yes."

"Fury?"

"Fury."

"Uh, does she live up to it?"

"You'll have to find out for yourself."

Tau's stomach dropped. "My queen?"

"Fury is yours."

His first thought, though it shamed him, was that he could trade the animal for enough rations to feed himself, his mother, his sister, and his mother's husband for the rest of their lives and the lives of all their children. But he was no longer Tau Tafari, the boy who needed to worry if he'd have enough to eat. For good or ill, that boy was gone.

"My queen, the gift is too great and I am not worthy," Tau said. "I have some sense of how rare these animals are and I have no knowledge of them or their care. I don't even know how to ride."

That smile from her again. "We will teach you," she said.

Tau shot a look at Hadith. His sword brother, allowed to sit on a straw bale due to his injury, mouthed the words "thank you."

"Thank you," Tau said to the queen.

"It pleases us to do this, Champion Solarin," she said. Then, turning to the rest of the women and men gathered before her, she sighed. "Now, gift granted, we must deal with less pleasant tasks."

Tau missed most of that. He was eyeing Fury, hoping the thing could continue to be housed in the stables, wondering what it ate, and worrying over how much it had hurt to ride a horse the one time he'd done it.

It could be, he thought, that most of the pain had been because of his injured leg, but that didn't account for why his ass and back were still so sore. Shaking his head, Tau surrendered the issue of the horse to another day and brought his attention back to the queen.

"Nyah will go over the rest," the queen said.

Bowing her head, Nyah spoke. "The Omehi have been split and the traditional ruling structure benefits the traitors. They sit in our capital city with the support of almost all the Royal Nobles, and we, a small group lacking experience and any authority but that which flows from our queen, hold council in relative exile. With every day that passes, the loyalty of the Nobles and Lessers who still call Queen Tsiora their monarch will weaken."

"You want to move quickly," Hadith said.

"It's not a want. It's a necessity," Nyah said. "Odili asked General Bisi to leave the front lines and march to Princess Esi's defense in Palm City."

The queen's face was stern. "This is a mistake we made. We should have requested the general's aid before Odili had the chance. To ask it now would give Bisi the chance to choose which command to follow. It would give him the chance to announce to all Omehi which side he views as the legitimate one without appearing partisan. He'd simply be following orders."

Never having had much patience for political maneuvering, Tau watched the faces of those around him. Of the queen, Nyah, Gifted Thandi, Hadith, Kellan, and Uduak, the oldest among them was the vizier. And out of the seven of them, three were Lessers, with one of those Lessers being their grand general.

The queen's hopes rested on the shoulders of a group comprised primarily of the inexperienced and the young, brought together by circumstance and plotting to retake a queendom from a stable.

Just once, Tau thought, he'd like to know what it was like to be on the side that wasn't being dragged to slaughter.

"Earlier today we received Bisi's response," Nyah said. "He sent the same edification to Citadel City and Palm, letting both Queen Tsiora and Guardian Councillor Abasi Odili know that he cannot leave the front lines because he must defend the paths into the peninsula."

"So, he'll wait for us to spend our might on one another before marching in to pick up the pieces?" Tau asked, thinking he needed to say something to show he was listening.

"Respectfully, Champion, I don't believe so," Kellan said. "General Bisi is a true soldier. He'll do what he believes is right to secure the future of our people."

"Yes, but what will that be?" asked Hadith.

"We cannot know," the queen said. "Perhaps we need not know. If the general comes to neither our nor Odili's aid, we have a chance to finish this without bringing the larger might of the military into the conflict. It will be a single battle instead of a true civil war."

"You still mean to attack Palm City," Hadith said.

The queen nodded.

"My queen, we don't have the soldiers to win that fight," Hadith said.

"We'll call upon the fiefs to honor their allegiance to us," the queen said. "We'll ask them to send their Ihagu and we'll commandeer the remaining Ihashe from the Northern and Southern Isikolo. With those forces, as well as the ones in this city, we can take Palm City and free our sister."

Hadith bowed his head to the queen. "If we can gather these forces, we'd have enough to defeat Odili in open combat, but it's still not enough to successfully siege the capital."

The vizier looked to the queen, as if asking for permission. Tsiora nodded, granting it.

"There is another way," Nyah said. "What was told to Mirembe and Otobong in the council chambers was true. We have agents inside Palm's walls who are loyal to Queen Tsiora."

"How can you be so sure they've remained loyal?" Hadith asked.

Nyah looked very much like she'd have preferred not to say, her mouth twitching before she managed to get the words out. "There is a group among the Gifted who are specifically chosen for their loyalty to the queen and the greater cause of the Goddess. We call them the Shadow Council and they have existed in one form or another since the time of Queen Taifa."

"Shadow Council?" asked Hadith. "Created by whom and for what purpose?"

"This is Royal Noble business and not something discussed beyond their circles, but Queen Taifa's rule ended when the Royals determined that her aims ran counter to theirs," Nyah said.

"Like us, Queen Taifa was betrayed," Tsiora said, "but the Goddess told her what was to come, and in preparation, the queen formed the Shadow Council."

"For what purpose, my queen?" Hadith asked.

"For our purpose," Queen Tsiora said, her words running a chill through Tau.

"The point," Nyah said, "is that we can communicate with the Shadow Council through edification and they can help us take the city."

"With respect and deference, how does it do that?" asked Kellan.

"We'll have them open the city gates," answered Hadith. "Then we can walk right in."

"You know the city, Buhari?" asked Nyah.

"On maps I've studied."

"On maps you've studied..." Nyah pressed her fingers to her temples and gave the queen a look.

Hadith turned to Kellan. "Odili's army will be at the main gates because Palm City sits between the two estuaries of the Amanzi. He'll probably destroy the bridge crossing the rivers when he learns we're on our way, but all that does is slow us down. The southern fork of the river is shallow and thin enough to be forded. So, he'll position his men behind the main gates because the main gates are the only ones we can attack."

"But then there's no way for the Shadow Council to open the main gates if the whole of Odili's army is standing behind them," Kellan said.

"That's not the gate they're going to open," Hadith said, and Tau saw Nyah's eyebrows lift. Hadith was putting the pieces together faster than she'd expected. "The northern fork of the river is the wider and faster-flowing one, but it was partially dammed so that a section of its waters flow through the city itself, yes?"

"That's right," Nyah said.

"And the waters that were redirected to run through the city, they enter it by way of an opening in the city's walls, an opening that faces away from the city's main gates."

"It sounds like you're speaking of the Port Gates, General."

"I am, but you already know this, because you've already come to this plan and wish to see if I can as well."

"Have I?" Nyah asked.

"We'll split our force into a main army, water army, and reserves," Hadith said. "Our main army will move on the city's main gates, ensuring that Odili and his fighters remain focused there. Our water army will be made up of Ihashe from the Northern Isikolo. Most men from the North know how to swim. They'll get to the Port Gates, which the Shadow Council can, I assume, open."

Nyah's eyebrows went from slightly lifted to fully arched. "The Port Gates are a massive bronze portcullis that a child could not slip through, and they can only be raised using the mechanism inside the city."

"And?" asked Hadith.

"And the Shadow Council can overcome the guards protecting the mechanism," Nyah said. "They can raise the gates."

Hadith nodded. "The water army will enter the city and make their way north. Their destination will be the much larger gates facing the northern fork of the Amanzi River. The water army will fight the few sentries Odili is bound to leave at the Northern Gates, and then...," Hadith said, opening his hands in Kellan's direction.

Kellan was grinning. "The water army opens the Northern Gates and our reserves can invade the city."

"Exactly," Hadith said. "In the days leading up to the attack, the reserves will build rafts large enough to hold every fighter with them. When we attack the west-facing main gates, they'll ford the river and enter through the ones in the north."

The queen was smiling at Nyah in a manner Tau might have called smug, if it weren't the queen doing it.

"We'll rip half the city from Odili's grasp before he even realizes it's gone," Hadith continued, "and then we have the choice to continue hammering against the reduced strength behind the main gates or we can march our main army around to the north side and flow into the city like a river of bronze."

Nyah inclined her head. She'd underestimated Hadith and was admitting as much to the queen.

"But," Hadith said, "there's still a problem."

"Yes, there is," the queen said.

"To make this work, we need Odili's forces concentrated at the main gates, and the best way to make him do that is to attack them. To stop us, Odili will have his Gifted call down their Guardians, and our men will die in dragon fire."

"Which is why we'll call to the Guardians as well," the queen said. "Some of them will fight for us, some for Odili. It means the

Guardians will have to turn their fire on each other instead of on our soldiers. The risk in drawing so much from the underworld is grave but necessary. We must pray to the Goddess that the Cull won't notice."

Nyah shot the queen a look at her mention of the Omehi's ancient enemy, and Kellan cleared his throat, seeking permission to speak.

"Yes, Ingonyama Okar?" the queen asked before raising a hand to forestall him a moment. "Excuse us, in this company we have little need to be so impersonal. Yes, Kellan?"

Having Tsiora say his name seemed to make Kellan forget what he'd wanted to say. "Ah...well...ah," he said, stammering, "don't Odili's Gifted outnumber our own?"

Nyah answered, but Kellan, Tau noticed, kept his eyes on the queen. "Our numbers are evenly matched, but, by and large, the Gifted in Palm City are better trained. They'll be more efficient with their powers and able to call to the Guardians for longer."

Hadith, sitting, leaned back and grimaced. He'd forgotten his injury. "This is where we fail, then," he said, placing a hand over the bandages beneath his loose-fitting shirt. "If Odili's Guardians outlast our own, we'll lose too many soldiers to dragon fire, and once our main force is decimated, he'll use his army to crush our reserves."

Perhaps the queen's talk of prayer had put him in a faithful mood, but for just the second time in his life, Tau felt as if the Goddess spoke to him, showing him the path forward. "Explain it again," he said.

"Seriously, Tau?" asked Hadith.

"Not the whole plan. The issue. What's the issue?"

Hadith's eyes thinned, but he did as Tau asked. "Odili's Gifted can field dragons for longer than we can, and the few dragons he has left, after we lose control of ours, will be more than enough to burn through our main force like a Hoard brushfire."

Turning to Tsiora, Tau captured her eyes with his and spoke quickly, trying to tell his tale before grief could stop him. "During the battle for this keep, I was in Isihogo with Gifted Zuri when her shroud failed." Saying her name hurt more than he cared to admit.

"The demons came for her, but I fought them away. It allowed her to draw energy from the underworld for longer than she could have otherwise."

"We see . . . ," the queen said.

Tau thought she might reach out to him, and he pushed on before she could, worrying that her pity would make him give in to his emotions. "I can train warriors to fight in Isihogo," he said. "We can protect you and the Gifted. We can give you time you wouldn't have otherwise."

Kellan gawked at him. "Train in Isihogo to fight demons?"

Tau nodded, trying to look calm as he waited to see if the queen would allow it. The evening prior, she'd worried that telling Tau's sword brothers his secret, before knowing if they could maintain their sanity in Isihogo, could lead to a group of unstable men using the underworld to become unstoppable killers. But now that they had another reason to commit men to the training, Tau's sword brothers would think they did it just to defend the Gifted.

The excuse gave Tau the chance to evaluate each man so that he could reject the ones in danger of losing their sanity before they could grasp what Isihogo really offered. Only the men able to withstand the underworld's torments, and whom he and the queen could trust, would be told the truth. It was perfect, unless Tsiora thought it wasn't.

"We see that you may have solved last night's dilemma," Tsiora said with a raised eyebrow, her words making Nyah glance at them with suspicion.

"Beg pardon, Your Majesty," Gifted Thandi said. "I'm worried that the champion is mistaken. As best we know, the underworld's demons can't be killed."

"We don't need to kill them," Tau told her. "We just need to keep them from getting to you."

"Have you, by any chance, discussed this before?" Nyah asked the queen.

"We saw our champion fight the demons in Gifted Zuri's defense," Tsiora told her.

Nyah appeared neither convinced nor satisfied by the queen's response but nodded as if she were both.

"Well, if it's true that the demons can be held back," Thandi said, her words coming faster as her excitement grew, "it's possible our Gifted could keep their Guardians in the fight for as long as Odili's Gifted keep hold of theirs."

"We'll be able to eliminate Odili's last advantage, and Hadith's plan to take the city can work," Kellan said. He was grinning, and Thandi, abandoning all reserve, grinned back at him for long enough that Nyah felt it necessary to clear her throat, startling Thandi back to the present.

Tau imagined the young Gifted's reaction to Kellan was the kind of thing that happened often. Okar's face and body were annoyingly symmetrical in that way that always drew attention. The man, thought Tau, needed more scars.

"A main army, water army, reserves, and men in Isihogo to protect the Gifted," said Thandi to the vizier, as if she'd had nothing on her mind but battle plans.

"And men in Isihogo to protect you," echoed Kellan, his words drawing Thandi's eyes back to him.

"Your Majesty?" Hadith said, asking for the queen's approval.

The queen had remained focused on Tau as the others talked. "Isihogo warriors," she said. "Very well, Champion. You'll have your way after all. Train them for us."

Tau's blood was up. He was going to do this. "Your will, my destiny."

"Take care in whom you trust," she said. "If those you train cannot stand with you, loyal to the end, we may lose more than our battle with Odili."

That seemed to deepen Nyah's suspicion. "Take Thandi for this training," she said. "She'll stand in for the Gifted you must protect. With her there, you'll see how long the shrouds of most Gifted can last."

Tau, who moments ago had felt near collapse, couldn't hold still. "We have our plan."

"We do," the queen said.

"And little time," Tau said.

The queen nodded.

"I'll begin immediately."

"What?" Gifted Thandi looked aghast. "When last did you sleep? What men have you chosen for this?"

"I go to choose them now," Tau told her.

CHAPTER SIX

NO

Tau had gathered his chosen in a small open-air circle tucked away behind the stables. It was quiet and the ground was soft sand, where a man in a panic could curl up in reasonable comfort. Most important, it was private.

He'd explained the basics to the five facing him, starting with how to enter Isihogo. They'd all done that several times already, leaving long before the demons could come.

As the queen had wanted, he'd told them nothing of his own training. The five fighters knew only that, if they could manage this, they'd be giving their Gifted a desperately needed advantage in the battle for Palm City.

"Not to be dense, but to confirm, we're going to Isihogo to fight demons that can't be killed and that will, without doubt, kill us?" Themba asked.

"Yes," Tau said.

"So, we're to be a meat shield and everyone is fine with this?"

"Lessers," Uduak said.

"Neh?" Themba asked the big man.

"We're Lessers," Yaw said. "We've always been a meat shield."

"He's not a Lesser," Themba said, pointing to Kellan.

Since Hadith had to return to the infirmary to rest and recover,

Tau tried Hadith's trick in his place. "I trust Kellan. That's why he's here."

The Greater Noble, standing tall, drew in a breath and held it, his broad chest puffing out, making Tau want to shake his head at how well some of Hadith's silly tricks worked.

It was true, though. Tau might not have wanted to admit it, but he trusted that Kellan would fight harder than any other man he could field, so he'd selected him. Kellan was also the only Noble he'd picked.

In fact, he was the only man in the circle who had not been in Scale Jayyed. And if that was favoritism, so be it. The queen had asked that this training go to no man Tau couldn't trust, and the five men standing with him in the circle were men he trusted.

"I've taught you to enter Isihogo and how to leave it," Tau said to them. "I've told you that, once the demons attack, you cannot leave and there remains only one escape."

"And you're sure they can't kill us?" Azima asked.

The drum player from Scale Jayyed was the last man Tau had approached for the training. He needed at least six men to be able to encircle the Gifted they would have to protect, and after the fighters who'd been part of Jayyed's six, Azima was the scale's strongest survivor.

"So long as you do not take any of the underworld's energy into yourself, your body here cannot be harmed by the demons there," Tau said.

"Note well, he said body," muttered Themba, tapping his head.

"Themba, I've done this before."

Themba opened his hands in Tau's direction, as if to say the point had been made for him.

"Would you prefer I select another in your place?" Tau asked.

Themba cracked his neck from side to side. "I'll fight."

Uduak nodded at that.

"We'll all fight," Kellan said.

"Then let's begin," Tau said.

"Aren't we to wait for Gifted Thandi?" Kellan asked.

"We don't need her for this."

"But Nyah said—"

"It's early in the training and we don't need a Gifted to act as our timer." It had bothered Tau, having Nyah force the Gifted on him, and after the frustrating conversation with her outside the stables, he was only too happy to get started without one of her Gifted looking over his shoulder.

"Sit," he told the men, and the five of them did so.

He joined them on the sand, letting his gaze touch the faces of the others. It was what Jayyed would have done. At the last, he came to Yaw.

"Where we fight," Yaw said, voice low.

"The world burns," Tau and the men from the scale said.

"Kellan?" Yaw asked. The Greater Noble hadn't offered the response. "You're with us now."

Kellan paused, then, making up his mind, he inclined his head. Yaw turned to Tau, waiting.

"Where we fight," Tau said.

"The world burns," came the call from the five warriors around him. "The world burns!"

Tau watched his sword brothers close their eyes, slow their breathing, and send their souls to suffer. He was about to do the same when he heard sandaled feet slapping against the sand. He looked over and saw Thandi running toward them.

"No!" she screamed. "No!"

"The world burns," Tau whispered, closing his eyes and joining the fight.

FINE

Tau, his swords out and up, scanned the mists. They were in the same circle behind the stables and yet they were not. The air was thicker, taking more effort to draw in and out. The ground was not the sand of the circle they'd left, but a shifting murk the consistency of wet mulch. And of course, Isihogo lacked true color. It was as if he was seeing the world through squinted eyes. The amber brown of the stable's rearmost wall had become the gray of decay, and the twilight sky lost its star-stained blue, replaced by an infinite black.

Isihogo was a realm with the substance of a waking nightmare, holding only enough detail to keep the mind captive. It was a quarter-formed world where the only things that seemed whole were the golden glows emanating from each of his sword brothers.

"They've found us," Tau shouted against the blowing winds, catching snatches of movement out in the deep mists.

"Goddess save us," Yaw said, pulling closer to Tau's shoulder.

"Do not take the power Isihogo offers you!" Tau reminded them. "Take it and you'll die back home as well as here."

Home, Tau thought. How much time had he spent in the mists? How much time before someplace foreign becomes home?

"To the left! I see it!" Azima shouted.

It was unfortunate. They'd hit a nest their first time in the under-world. That was what Tau called it, the times he came to Isihogo only to be overrun by a pack of demons. Typically, he'd run into nests toward the end of a long night of fighting, but looking to his left and right, he wondered if the glow of six golden souls might have drawn more of Ukufa's thralls than usual.

"Spread out," he ordered. "Form the circle. Fight them!"

Kellan was first to obey. His huge sword held defensively, he jogged several strides distant, covering Tau's back. Uduak was next, taking up a position to Tau's right.

Themba shook his head at Tau. "Madness," he shouted before running to stand near Uduak.

Yaw had his eyes closed, and his mouth was moving, praying. He finished quickly, his eyes snapped open, and with a nod to Tau, he moved into position.

"Azima," Tau said.

"I can't. Goddess wept, Tau, I can't."

Tau understood. "Stand with me. We'll do it together. Remember, take nothing from this place. The gift it offers is poison to—"

Feeling the presence appear beside him, Tau whirled, weapons ready. Her shroud was thick and thin, a multifaceted patchwork crystal that masked her features and hid her soul's glow.

"Thandi?" Tau shouted.

She ignored him, running straight for Kellan and trying to pull him back, but the Greater Noble wouldn't be moved. Tau couldn't see Thandi's face or mouth, but he knew they exchanged words. He saw Kellan shout his response to the Gifted, though his voice did not carry to Tau across the distance and gale, and then it was too late. The time for talk or retreat had passed. The demons had come.

"Umama!" cried Azima when the first demon leapt for him.

Tau shoved him clear, spun off the demon's killing line, and hammered his twin swords into its back, sending it crashing to the ground. It growled and began to rise, but the next demon, a centipede-like thing, had reared to attack, thinking to decapi-tate him.

Tau flowed beneath the creature's claws and came up stabbing, driving his black blades into its core. The demon shrieked and slashed at him with four of its legs. Tau was already out of reach, kicking the first monster in the back of its head and driving it back to the ground.

"Azima, to your left!" Tau shouted.

A thing on eight legs was charging his sword brother, and by the time Azima saw it, it was too late. The demon barreled into him, bowled him over, and drove the middle pair of its spiked legs into his torso. Azima howled and dropped his sword. His shield, still strapped to his arm, hung limp as he grasped at the demon's legs, desperate to pull the spikes from his rib cage.

Tau raced to help and skidded to a stop when the six-legged monster plowed its spiked forelegs through Azima's skull. Spinning, Tau took stock. Themba was on his back, kicking and slashing at the thing on top of him. Yaw was surrounded but moving too fast and fluid to have been caught yet. Uduak, mouth open in an unending war cry, fought a demon that had to be double his weight, and Kellan was in front of the still shrouded Thandi, trying to protect the only one among them who was actually safe.

The Greater Noble was facing two creatures working in tandem. He was determined that they would not get past him, not realizing that they had no interest in a shrouded Thandi, and as Tau watched, the demons attacked.

Kellan slammed his shield into the body of the first and swung his sword for the misshapen head of the other one. His sword found its mark and the demon collapsed, its head nearly severed from its shoulders. That surprised Tau. Isihogo's revenants were usually harder to hurt.

Thinking the demon he'd downed finished, Kellan turned back to the creature he'd stunned with his shield. Tau screamed a warning and started running to help, but he could not overcome the winds and Kellan did not hear. Still running, Tau saw the demon on the ground twitch and spasm while the sword-separated sides of its head stitched themselves back together. The process took no more time than a few short, gasping breaths, and then the demon rose.

Tau called out again. That time Kellan heard and the Greater Noble turned as the reanimated demon attacked.

He could have blocked the blow. Tau knew how well Kellan fought. He could have returned the demon's strike, but Kellan froze, unable to comprehend how the thing he'd destroyed could be standing against him, and with razored fingers the length of Tau's forearm, the demon latched a hand around Kellan's neck, driving him back as it throttled him.

Kellan's mouth opened to yell, and though Tau was close enough to have heard him, there was no noise. The demon's barbed fingers had cut through Kellan's neck in seven places, digging deep enough to sever the arteries in his neck, the muscles in his throat, and the cords that made his voice.

"Kellan!" Tau called, and the Noble's eyes rolled to Tau, terror in them.

Tau threw himself at the demon, chopping his strong-side sword into the appendage with which it held the Greater Noble. The demon reeled and lost its grip, and Kellan lurched free, staggering toward Tau, arms outstretched and fingers dragging at the air, begging for help. Kellan caught Tau's wrists and pulled Tau to his knees as he fell to the ground, dead.

Thandi, still hidden behind her shroud, went to her knees beside Tau. She was leaning over Kellan and Tau could hear her crying. As soon as the last of the Noble's golden light winked out, she vanished from the underworld too.

Tau had little time to consider her odd behavior. The two demons he'd fought at the start were coming for him again. The one Kellan had beaten down with his shield had regained its feet, and the thing that had killed the Greater Noble had recovered its senses and its arm was whole again.

Tau searched the circle. Azima was gone, Yaw too. Themba was dead and Tau watched Uduak deliver a sacrifice thrust into the chest of the demon he fought, forcing his sword through to the hilt. In turn, the demon wrapped its arms around Uduak and ripped away his face with its teeth.

And that left Tau.

He got back to his feet. "I know I can't kill you," he told them, his swords twirling in lazy circles as he spoke, "but I think you feel pain, and tonight, that will do!"

Snarling, laughing, jeering, the nightmare among them attacked and the demons fought back.

After falling to the monsters, Tau was forced back to Uhmlaba, where his mind pieced itself back together like it was made from demon flesh. When he was enough of himself again, he realized he was no longer sitting, but on his hands and knees. Still, he was doing better than his brothers.

Yaw was facedown in the dirt, breathing and snorting, creating puffs of sand with every exhalation. Themba was scrunched up against the stable's wall, mumbling and twitching as his eyes flitted back and forth, following afterimages of things that did not exist in the real world.

Azima was on his feet but in bad shape. The drummer moved like a drunk, shouting to no one and nothing. "They're not supposed to be able to kill us!" he said. "They're not supposed to be able to kill us!" Over and over again.

Uduak, near Tau, rocked himself from his knees, jaw clenched and hands running up and down his face. He looked at Tau, and though the big man's eyes did not seem able to focus, there was some clarity in them. He rocked and watched Tau, as if truly seeing him for the first time.

"You'll be well," Tau said to the big man as he got to a knee and then stood, shaking off the last of Isihogo's hold. He looked for Kellan last and found him. "Don't do that," he told Thandi.

She was kneeling next to the Greater Noble, cradling his head and whispering to him.

"He'll be well. Just give him time and space," Tau told her.

She turned to him, her eyes wild and face tear streaked, and that's when Tau saw the blood.

"I told you, you bastard," she said. "I told you!"

Tau ran over to them and saw that there was blood seeping from gashes in Kellan's neck. The worst of it was the arterial red spurting between Thandi's fingers. Kellan was awake, his eyes wide, and Thandi was telling him to be still. She hadn't been cradling his head. She was squeezing her hands and fingers against his neck to slow down the bleeding.

"No...," Tau said, "he can't be hurt. The demons, they can't—"

Her face was screwed up so tight she didn't look like herself. "Get help!"

The fear and fury in her voice jolted Tau from his confusion. "Help!" he shouted, running for the infirmary. "We need the priestess! Help!"

WOUNDS

C hampion?"

Consciousness came rushing back. "Kellan! Kellan?" Tau said, waking up disoriented.

"He's fine." It was Priestess Hafsa Ekene. She was standing over him and he was sitting, leaned up against the wall outside the infirmary.

He'd come here with Gifted Thandi and the Indlovu who had carried Kellan. Thandi was gone and he must have fallen asleep when they were waiting to hear Kellan's fate.

"How long?" he asked.

"Seven, maybe eight spans."

He rubbed a forearm across his eyes. "You shouldn't have let me sleep."

"I didn't," the priestess said. "I tried to wake you spans ago."

Tau's leg was throbbing and he shifted to ease the pain, touching above the wound with his right hand.

"I can take a look at the thigh, if it please you?"

"No," Tau said, waving her off and rising. "I need to see Kellan." It wasn't just his leg; he was stiff all over. He'd fallen asleep in his leather armor.

As he stood, a blanket fell off him. He looked down at it, surprised to think that someone had been able to get close enough to place it over him without his knowing.

The priestess bent over and picked it up. "You were exhausted."

"Long days."

"And nights, I suspect."

He nodded. "And nights."

"The vizier is coming. It's why I'm waking you now, but there's time to see your friend. Follow me." She walked to the infirmary doors, opened them, and led him inside.

Tau walked past the bed that held Jabari. It had curtains on all sides and he couldn't see in. He needed to visit him. It had been... Tau couldn't track the time. The last few days were a jumble. He also passed Hadith, who was sleeping. Uduak was doing the same, albeit in the chair beside the new general's bed.

"Uduak," Tau said.

The big man stirred, opening one eye and then the other.

"How are the others?" Tau asked.

Uduak turned to Hadith, saw him resting, and looked back to Tau. "Shaken."

"And you?"

"Shaken."

"It gets..." Tau let the words die on his tongue. He didn't want to lie. Instead, he nodded to the big man and moved on.

Kellan lay asleep in one of the last beds in the infirmary, and his neck had been swaddled in bandages that showed through with bloody streaks.

Gifted Thandi was with him, sitting on the edge of his bed, and the look she gave him, with her red-rimmed eyes, was not one Tau could call pleasant.

"I gave him something for the pain," Hafsa said. "It'll also help him rest."

"He shouldn't have needed it," Tau said, shaking his head. "He should be fine. He knew not to take the underworld's power."

Hafsa made the dragon's span with her fingers, to ward off evil.

"Do you know why this happened?" Tau asked, turning to Gifted Thandi.

The way she was looking at him, Tau half expected her to leap across the bed at him, but look was all she did. She'd behaved the same way when they'd brought Kellan to the infirmary; she wouldn't say a word to him.

Footsteps. It was the vizier. She was alone and walking toward them.

"Vizier Nyah," Tau said in greeting.

"Do all who deal with you end up in places like this, Champion?" she asked.

"It makes no sense," Tau said. "He shouldn't be hurt."

"Did you wait for Gifted Thandi as you were meant to? Did she say it was fine for Kellan to be one of your madmen?"

"Gifted Thandi has no say in who fights with me."

Nyah closed her eyes and kept them closed. "The queen wishes to see you."

"Kellan is the most disciplined man I know," Tau said. "He wouldn't have taken the underworld's powers into himself, and without them, the demons have no way to carry the harm they do in Isihogo to Uhmlaba." He pointed toward Kellan's neck. "Those wounds match the demon's claws that—"

"That's quite enough, Champion," Nyah said, tilting her head in Hafsa's direction. "Priestess Ekene is very busy and does not need to listen to us speak of fever dreams."

Tau glanced at Hafsa. Her eyes were round and they bounced between him and the vizier.

"The queen is waiting," Nyah said.

Tau lowered his head to rub at his face as worry and weariness set back in. "I don't know how this happened."

"Then let Kellan rest and come with me to the queen so she can explain it," said Nyah.

HANDMAIDENS

Tau pressed Nyah for answers, wanting her to tell him whatever it was that she knew, but she rebuffed him, saying over and over again that the queen would make things clear.

"What does the queen have to do with this?" he asked, struggling to keep pace with her. His leg burned and the night spent sleeping on the floor outside the infirmary hadn't helped.

"I told her Kellan Okar was injured and I explained how. She asked me to bring you to her."

"That doesn't answer my question," he said.

"No, it doesn't."

To take his mind off his frustration, Tau tried to figure out where they were going. They'd left the keep and were walking through the city's east side. It surprised Tau to find that, once he was away from the urban center, the buildings and homes got smaller, ragged, and the faces he saw staring back at him from behind crooked windows were the faces of Lessers.

"This is where those who serve the city live," he said.

"Yes, here and in the city's south," the vizier told him, glancing down at his injured leg. "We're almost there."

The adobe on the buildings around them was unpainted, paper-thin, and where it had worn away, poorly patched. The thoroughfare was in equally bad shape. Its cobblestones were loose and uneven and it intersected with many tiny paths littered with refuse or night soil.

It seemed that the Lessers who lived in the east side spent morning to night caring for the rest of the city, only to come home to a place where no one did the same for them.

"The conditions here are—" Tau began, when he heard shouting and running feet.

The sounds were coming from the intersecting path immediately ahead, and Tau watched as the first of several figures came into view. He thought them demons when they appeared, their smaller size and strange movements not matching his expectations, but it was children, four of them, playing.

They ran into the main path and were heading for the tiny one running perpendicular to it when they spotted him and Nyah. The lead child, clothes in tatters and face showing more dirt than skin, skidded to a stop. The two behind him crashed into his back and all three came close to tumbling to the ground. The last child had enough space to come to a standstill without incident, and soon Tau had four pairs of eyes locked on him.

"That a Lesser?" said the smallest of them, her voice thin as a river reed.

"Hush!" said the lead child, dropping his gaze to the ground.

"I am," Tau said to the children.

The lead child and the two closest to him kept their heads down. The smallest one was not so deferential. She examined Tau.

"Why you dressed like them, then?" she asked.

Tau wasn't sure he had a good answer for that. "I'm the queen's champion."

"Liar," the girl said.

"Goddess's bare ass, Nali!" the lead child hissed, making Nyah wince.

"I'm not lying," Tau said.

"But you're a Low Common, like me," the girl said.

"I'm a Hi—" Tau began before giving up. "Yes . . . like you."

"And you're champion?"

"Yes."

"Didn't know you could be both."

"Not sure I did either," Tau said.

"Champion is supposed to be the strongest."

"That's part of it."

"Big part," the girl said, looking him up and down.

Tau shrugged.

"Shouldn't you get back to your parents, child?" Nyah asked.

The girl's gaze bounced over to the vizier. "Ma's dead and Da's been fighting in the Curse since before I could talk. He'll be back soon."

"Shut it, Nali," the lead boy said.

"Come make me," she said, and Tau took a closer look at her.

She had to be eight or nine cycles, and if her father had gone to the front lines before she could talk, his mandatory service should have ended long ago.

"You have those black swords," she said.

"Yes," he said.

"Never seen someone with two before."

The lead boy gaped at her. "Nali, you can't just ask people why they have two swords."

"I can and I just did," she said, glaring at the boy. Returning her attention to Tau, she pointed at Nyah. "I'm going to be like her," she said.

"Her?" Tau asked.

Nyah shot him a look.

"Yes," the little one said. "I practice every day."

The girl had lost him. "What do you mean?"

"The black robes talk to the Goddess and She makes them strong," the girl said, speaking like she worried that he might be simple. "I practice by talking to Her too, all day and all night. When I'm older, I'll be Gifted."

"Uh... practicing is good," Tau said.

The vizier couldn't seem to meet the child's eyes. Tau knew why. Near three thousand Omehi women were born for every one who was Gifted. The girl could talk to the Goddess all day and every day and it wouldn't change how badly the odds were stacked against her.

"I wish you well, little one," Tau said. "I hope you grow to be very strong."

"I'm already strong," she said, chin out. "I'm still alive and most Nobles would be dead if they were me."

Tau blinked slowly, both acknowledging her words and wanting better for her than what was. She reminded him of his half sister. Well, she reminded him of Jelani on Jelani's good days.

"Nali, is it?" Tau asked, reaching for his belt pouch. "Come here. I have something for you."

Her eyes thinned and she took a step back. "Something like what?"

The distrust and fear, coming so quickly after her boldness, cut at him. A Low Common girl in a city full of Nobles, he could imagine her life.

"Here it is," he said, pulling his purse free from the pouch. "I don't need it anymore."

Her mouth fell open. "Anything in it?"

Tau nodded, and quick as a rumor spreading, she was next to him, hand out. He let the purse fall into her grime-lined palm and it landed with a clink, pushing her hand lower with its weight. She gaped. The purse contained the coin left over from his last pay as an initiate. It'd be spare change to a Noble, but more than what most Lessers saw in a moon cycle.

"Goodbye, Nali. Grow ever stronger and be powerful," he said.

"Bye, Champion Lesser. Goddess keep you close."

Tau smiled, and clutching her new purse, Nali ran off, the other children following close behind.

"They'll take it from her," Nyah said.

Tau watched until the children disappeared down the side path. "I don't think they can, Vizier," he said. "Which way now?"

She watched him like he was a map she might be holding upside down. "We're almost there. The queen will be at the city's eastern gates."

"The gates? Why?"

"In cities even the walls have ears," Nyah said.

Tau sighed. The gates couldn't be more than a couple of hundred strides distant, but he knew how much his leg would hurt, carrying him that far.

"Lead on, Vizier," he said, letting her move past him.

Within fifty strides Tau was sweating, more from the pain than from the heat. His leg and hip throbbed, both feeling three sizes too big, and he let his head hang down as they went, not wanting to see how much farther they had to go and finding it easier to keep his eyes on the swishing, dust-coated hem of Nyah's Gifted robes.

It was the horses and their noises that let him know they'd arrived, and raising his head, he noticed the queen first. He couldn't help it. She was mounted, sitting astride her horse beside four more of the animals, one of them Fury, and the queen was wearing a dress the color of fresh boiled maize.

Tau shook the thought away. The color that boiled maize brought to mind was the right one, but the queen's riding dress was more than that. Her dress looked like the cloth's dyer had stolen rays of sunlight just so they could be worked into the fabric, and seeing the queen in that fabric, it was hard to think of her as anything other than beautiful, which was the problem.

It was always easy to find Nobles beautiful. They were properly fed, they dressed in marvels, and they could move through the world with confidence, heads held high, treating the world as if it were fair and decent, because for them it was. Nobles had the better of everything and they wrapped themselves in that betterment, appearing to everyone else as beautiful, right, and good, just like sunlight.

The queen offered him a smile. Tau greeted her but couldn't find it in himself to smile back. Her smile weakened. He didn't let that get to him. He pictured how beautiful Zuri would have looked in that same dress and his heart had no room to worry over the feelings of a Royal Noble.

Having greeted his monarch, Tau gave his attention to the oddities standing next to the horses. Dressed in light, long-sleeved robes of pure white, belted at the waist, were two young women. Their hair was cut in matching styles, shaved on the sides with the middle wrapped around itself in twists that locked their tight curls into knots that ran down their backs.

The women were slim and hard, Tau's height, and they both had skin as dark as midnight. They had to be sisters, not born together, though. One looked a cycle or two older than the other.

Outwardly, they didn't look to have the same interest in him that he had in them. The sisters made it seem as if he was less interesting than a rock in a quarry, but he could feel their eyes on him whenever they thought he wasn't looking.

"Our handmaidens," the queen said. "Auset and Ramia." The women inclined their heads in turn, the movements slow but precise as a full-blood's salute. "They arrived not long ago from Palm City. They escaped to return to us as soon as they could."

"Should we begin?" Nyah asked the queen.

"We should," the queen said. "Champion, we know you have questions and we hope we have answers. We also promised to teach you how to ride, and those lessons may as well start now."

Tau glanced at Fury, wanting little less than to ride a horse after the painful walk he'd endured. "As you wish, my queen," he said, tamping down his unease with the handmaidens and limping the last few steps to the horse . . . his horse.

The handmaidens headed for their horses too, but the way they did it, moving with perfect balance, chilled the blood in his veins. They moved like fighters, like assassins, and they were closing the distance to the queen.

Tau turned to them to watch them more carefully, and the slightly taller one, Auset, the queen had named her, stared at him with red demon eyes.

"Stop there!" Tau said, pulling his swords free and dashing forward to put himself between Tsiora and the two women, who reacted as if expecting him to do just that.

Their expressions of disinterest vanished, replaced by snarls that showed their mouths to be filled with pointed teeth, and they assumed fighting stances, each of them holding two dragon-scale dirks snatched from the wrist bracers they had hidden beneath their sleeves.

The dragon scale surprised him. Demons didn't use weapons. He hoped the surprise didn't show.

"Run or die," he told them.

BLOODLINES

Enough!" Nyah said, the force in her voice pulling Tau's eyes away from the handmaidens. "No one is dying here."

"Damn you, Vizier, you don't understand. They're—" Tau returned his attention to the two, who had spread out to make themselves harder to fight. The pointed teeth had vanished, and the taller one, Auset, no longer had red eyes. Tau blinked, trying to clear his vision.

"All three of you, put away your weapons," the queen said.

Hearing their queen, the handmaidens whisked away their dirks, vanishing them up their sleeves as if they'd never been. As they did it, Tau considered killing them both.

"Auset and Ramia have been with us since birth," the queen said. "We trust them as we do Nyah, as we do you. We trust them with our lives."

It was shaming to hear her speak of him in that way, when Tau didn't think he'd have much to do with queens or queendoms after he was finished with Odili. "But they're..." He couldn't say demons. They weren't that. "They're fighters, warriors," he said, his swords aimed at the two women.

"Thank you for that," Nyah said. "We'd never have known if not for you."

"Humor, Vizier?" Tau asked.

The queen, speaking before Nyah could retort, did not look pleased. "We thought we'd asked for the weapons to be put away. Were we not heard?"

Tau eyed the handmaidens. They were back to playing the part of docile servants, and though he wasn't convinced there was no danger, he had to admit that what he'd seen, what he had thought he'd seen, was not real.

Grumbling, eyes still on the two women and making enough space to redraw, Tau slid his swords back into their scabbards. "I know handmaidens," he said. "I grew up around them, my sister is one, and those two are not handmaidens."

"They are the queen's handmaidens, part of the Shadow Council and charged with her protection," said Nyah.

"What does that mean? They're Bodies, like the Royal Nobles have?" Tau tried not to sound petulant. "I thought the champion fulfilled that role."

"Auset and Ramia are a less visible but needed layer of protection."

"Needed layer of . . . from whom?" Tau asked.

Nyah wouldn't say.

"Our Royal Nobles," the queen offered in the vizier's place.

"Apologies, my queen, you said these women have been with you since birth, and though the coup is much more recent than that, they move like they've trained for violence since they could walk. Why would that be, when the Royals have only just turned on you?"

He'd been flippant and the queen did not answer right away. She made him wait, like one would a naughty child, giving him time to stew and settle. When he did, she gestured in Fury's direction. "We'd hoped to explain further on our ride."

Still, Tau pushed. "And Kellan, my queen?"

"We'll offer one story and you'll have two answers," she said.

That felt a lot like a riddle and Tau wasn't fond of those, but he wanted to understand what had happened to Kellan. So, without giving the handmaidens his back, he moved to Fury's side and tried to climb aboard.

"Did Auset and Ramia explain the situation in Palm?" Nyah asked the queen.

"They did. Odili has been parading my sister in front of the Royal Nobles, forcing her to publicly proclaim her right to the throne. He gave the Royals just enough of an excuse to back him while holding their heads high, and they took it."

"Our plan is to fight," Nyah reminded the queen.

"And yet, we'd still hoped there might be another way, but that's gone now."

They stopped talking and Tau felt like everyone was watching him struggle with the horse.

"Watch how Auset does it," the queen said, after giving him another chance at clambering aboard the creature.

Face hot, Tau watched as the handmaiden flowed into her horse's seat. As she did, he noticed her robes were actually loose-fitting pants with wide bottoms. Auset's and Ramia's clothing masqueraded as the standard, constraining handmaiden's robes while actually allowing much more movement. Then Ramia was next in the saddle, making it look easy as spitting.

Sliding his jaw back and forth, Tau nodded to himself. He'd not be outdone by false handmaidens. He put his hands on Fury, to do as they had done, and the horse looked back at him, snorting. Tau jerked back, worried it might bite.

"Fury's just curious," the queen said. "Go on."

Wary of the horse's mouth and its large block-like teeth, Tau gave it another go, and to his own surprise, he swung up and into place on the first try. He was about to flash the handmaidens a look of victory, but Fury took a step, and he had to fall forward, wrapping his arms around the horse's neck to avoid toppling off.

"Relax, sit up. She'll sense your worry," the queen said.

"I am worried," he said.

Tsiora shook her head as if exasperated with him, but Tau could swear he saw the laugh behind her eyes. "Then, we'll start slow," she said, clucking her tongue so that her horse, a smaller, tree-brown version of Fury, moved off in that rolling gait the animals had.

Tau sat up, unsure if he should cluck his tongue too, when Fury began following the queen's horse. They rode to the eastern wall and through its gates. Ihashe were guarding them and they saluted the queen, the vizier, and him.

"Is it safe to travel outside?" Tau asked, looking back to the walls and gates that closed behind them.

"We have you and our handmaidens," the queen said. "Could we be safer?"

Yes, we could, Tau thought, back in the city.

"We're sorry about what happened to Kellan," the queen said, eschewing titles to speak of Okar in closer terms. "We assumed you'd choose only Lessers to train."

It was what a Noble would have done, Tau realized. They'd have picked people from their own caste and no other, and the queen was used to their way of thinking.

"Neither of you had any way to know what would happen to him, because that knowledge is a matter of history told only to Royal Nobles." The queen glanced at the handmaidens and Nyah. "Well, Royal Nobles and members of the Shadow Council."

"How can old stories hurt Kellan in Isihogo?" Tau asked.

"Because the stories are about his blood. Because Kellan Okar is not Omehi, as you are."

Tau squinted at her. "Not Omehi?"

"Not always."

"Apologies, Your Majesty," Tau said, "I'm not good at riddles."

The smile she offered him was a somber one. "It means that Lessers and Nobles were not always a single race of man."

Tau looked to Nyah and the handmaidens, trying to see if this was some game or trick. All three women were stone-faced.

"We're telling you the truth," the queen said. "Long before we sailed to these lands, there were Nobles and there were Omehi and these were two separate peoples. It is why the Nobles are bigger and stronger than you and everyone like you. It is their gift."

The land sloped down and Fury took a jolting step, shooting pain up Tau's thigh. He hardly noticed. "Their gift?"

"Men of the Noble race are all born Gifted, and that gift is a permanent connection to Isihogo. From the day they're born until they die, a fraction of their soul exists in the underworld, drawing a small but steady stream of power from it. The fraction glows dimly, unlike the souls of those wholly in the underworld, and the Nobles draw too little power from Isihogo to attract its demons. But what they do draw is enough, over a lifetime, to make them grow bigger and stronger than the women or men of any other race."

Tau's mouth was open. He could feel it was, but he didn't seem able to close it.

"Kellan Okar cannot fight the demons in Isihogo as you do," the queen said.

"Kellan always has Isihogo's power in him?" Tau asked. "When he fought the demons he was corporeal?"

"Somewhat, yes."

"Goddess...I sent him to his death."

"He did not die and you did not know."

"Two races of man? Is this why the castes aren't permitted to mix?"

"Some do," the queen said, dropping her eyes. "Almost all Gifted are Lessers, and they couple with Greater or Royal Nobles."

The thought hit Tau like a hammer. "Our Gifted...their gifts come from our race, the Lessers."

"Edification, enervation, and entreating are the gifts of the Omehi people," the queen said, "and long ago, we learned there was more that we could do. We learned we could enhance and multiply the natural gifts of the Nobles."

"Enraging," Tau said.

She nodded. "Enraging."

"How did we come to be...one people?"

Now the queen's smile held sorrow. "That is a hard story, and it was difficult enough, convincing Nyah to let us tell you as much as we have."

Tau swiveled to face the vizier. "I've heard half the tale. Give me the rest."

For once, Nyah seemed to treat Tau as an equal. "What you've been told is dangerous," she said. "Already a rift has opened in our queendom and stories like the ones you ask for are enough to turn that rift into a permanent sundering. You had to know this much because you had to know that a man who can be enraged cannot fight Isihogo's demons with impunity. The blood precludes it."

"Why tell me anything, then?" Tau said, better understanding the reason for a horse ride outside the city and away from everyone else.

"Because it's unlikely that we can retake Palm City without the benefit of your...project," Nyah said. "Because you need to understand why you can't use men like Kellan."

Tau thought the problem through, working out how to explain his position without telling Nyah and the handmaidens that the greater value of training men in Isihogo was not to enhance the powers of the Gifted, but to create men who were killers without peer.

"What I'm trying to do isn't easy," he said. "I need men I can trust, and there aren't many left."

Nyah sniffed. "You're short of Lessers? There's you, that big one, the light-skinned boy who's always sunburnt, the drummer, and Themba."

Tau narrowed his eyes. "Themba? Why do you know his name?"

"How could I not? He never stops talking nonsense," Nyah said.

Tau shrugged, ceding the point. "Your count puts us at five. It's not enough to form a protective circle around the Entreaters. I need more men, at least one more."

"Then pick one, anyone."

Tau let his gaze slip to the queen's face. Her features were placid, smooth as a mountain lake. It was a false calmness, similar to the false meekness of her handmaidens. The queen, Tau thought, had not told Nyah exactly what he was doing in Isihogo. So, he trod carefully.

"It's not as simple as choosing anyone," he said, thinking about how he sought to create and unleash men as deadly as permanently enraged Ingonyama on the world. "It takes time to develop the courage to stand when the demons come. It takes time to learn how to fight them." Tau gave his words a moment. He wanted Nyah to focus on the nightmare of having to stand and fight monsters and not on what one would have to become in order to do so. "To hold the demons back long enough for our Entreaters to gain an advantage, our fighters must be experienced at facing them. The only way to gain that experience is by taking men to the underworld night after night, where they'll fight and die to an enemy they cannot defeat, over and over again."

On some level, Nyah had to have understood this part of the plan, but he could tell that hearing him lay it out so plainly was unpleasant.

"I see," she said.

"I need men who can withstand the underworld's trials and I need enough of them to hold the circle," Tau told her. He needed men who could withstand the transformation into demigods without being driven mad.

"And there's no one else you can use?" Nyah asked.

"I have lost many of my closest sword brothers, but our family is not all gone." Tau turned to the queen. "Will you make time to teach me more of riding, my queen?"

"We will. Why do you ask?" she said.

"I'd like to ride back to the keep. I think I have a sixth man."

CHAPTER SEVEN

DUMA SIBUSISO

Duma couldn't be sure if he was lucky or damned. Night had fallen not long ago and he was sitting cross-legged in the dirt behind the building where they housed the horses. It seemed strange that the animals had a better roof over their heads than anything he'd had growing up, but a lot happened around Nobles that was strange, and Duma wasn't one to waste thoughts on foolishness he couldn't control.

Instead, he wondered if Tau...Champion Solarin had become some kind of Noble. He certainly looked like he had, sitting across from Duma in that red-and-black leather armor.

Scale Jayyed, Duma thought, had changed Tau. Well, it'd changed all of them, but him the most, and Duma knew himself well enough to admit that the man Tau had become was a frightening one.

Solarin had always had a way of looking at a man like he'd just as quick slit his throat as offer a word, but Duma had known that type back home, and there was usually something you could do to stop them from actually cutting your neck. The thing that made the new champion most frightening was that, as best as Duma could tell, there was precious little to be done if Tau got it in his head that someone had spent more than enough time living already. So, Duma wasn't sure if he was lucky or damned, but Tau Solarin had come to him that night to ask him to be the sixth man in his new unit, and Duma took pride in that.

He looked round at everyone, seeing Uduak, Yaw, Themba, Azima, that pretty Lady Gifted, and of course, Tau. Unlike Duma, they'd all done this before, and yet he could still see the anxiousness in their faces.

Given what Tau had told him to expect, it made sense, and Duma couldn't say he was looking forward to what they were set to do either. It also made his mouth dry, thinking that he was expected to do something Kellan Okar hadn't been able to handle. But the way Duma saw it, if Tau and his sword brothers needed him, he'd do his part.

"Remember what you've been taught," Tau said. "Take no power from the underworld."

Duma needed to piss. He'd gone just a quarter span ago and had no idea how an empty bladder could feel so full.

"Close your eyes and breathe," Tau said. "Let your muscles go loose, limp..."

It was hard to relax, and he thought the tension in him might keep him anchored where he sat, but Duma's head began to spin and he could tell that some better part of him was being taken from the world.

"Form the circle! They're coming!" Tau shouted, though his voice wasn't louder than a whisper.

Duma opened his eyes and looked around, seeing the sunlight glow of his fellows, bright and clean and so very different from anything else in the gloom pressing against him like a weight. He held his sword up and sent out a prayer as he peered into mist that was briar thick. His hands were shaking, and when the first monster burst through the fog, running for him, Duma's empty bladder opened right up and found itself some piss anyhow.

The demon, racing into range, leapt for him, and Duma screamed. He also slashed at it, catching it somewhere between its ugly head and gruesome body with the edge of his blade. The power in its jump and the angle of his swing took them tumbling into the muck that coated the ground, and then he was rolling and fighting, pulling his dagger from his belt.

He jabbed the small blade into the nearest part of the demon he could reach, and black blood belched out of it, the smell making him retch. They scuffled a little more, and the thing got its back legs onto one of his thighs and pushed off, ripping skin, muscles, and bone to bits.

Duma screamed again, pain and fear and the need to stay alive mixing themselves into an inseparable muddle of shit. He scooted back, scrambling to his feet, his torn leg ready to give out from under him, and the thing came at him again.

Duma knew he was dead, but he lifted his sword regardless. If he was going to the Goddess, he'd go with his killer's blood on his blade.

He didn't get the chance to do any dying. Before the demon could get to him, Tau was there, cutting at the creature faster than Duma's eyes could follow, until the thing was down and done, bleeding its life into the muck.

Tau grabbed Duma and pushed him back to the circle. Duma went, but he couldn't take his eyes from the thing Tau had cut down, because the cuts Tau had put in it were mending themselves.

"Keep holding!" Tau yelled.

Duma had lost his dagger, his sword felt too heavy to hold, and on his wreck of a leg, he was moving slow as new-made mud. So when the next monster came through the mists, fear had him clamped in its grip, but Tau Solarin had chosen him for this, his brothers needed him for this, and Duma would not let them down.

The demon attacked and Duma gave no ground. He fought it, shouted at it, and when they went to the ground and his sword slipped from his fingers, he pounded at it with his fists. It butchered him anyway.

"Duma, take your time. You're safe. You'll be well." It was Tau's voice. His normal voice, not the wind-dampened shout he had to use in that evil place.

Duma opened his eyes. He was on the ground. He was crying and couldn't stop. He had wet himself.

"Try to get your breathing under control first," Tau was saying to him and the others. "It makes the rest easier. Focus on your breathing."

Tau was pushing a small bowl at him. "Duma, here, drink."

It was water and Duma took it. It was good going down, though he choked a bit, since his breathing and crying made it hard to manage a clean swallow.

"It's not possible." That, he realized, was the Lady Gifted speaking to Tau.

Duma lifted his head and saw her. She was collected and calm and it shamed him to be out there on the ground in front of a woman like that with his pants soaked through.

"It's possible," Tau said to her. "It'll just take time."

"Champion Solarin, they fall immediately. We're asking too much of them, and for what? They're unable to offer anything beyond what my shroud gives me."

"I'm telling you, they need more time at it. Give them that and they'll be able hold the demons at bay."

"I worry that we're torturing these men in pursuit of a destination they can't reach. Every day, more fiefs and hamlets turn away from the queen in favor of Odili. If we wait for your men to master the underworld, they'll be the only ones left in our queen's army."

"We have enough time."

"Champion, the queen intends to march for Palm before the season ends. Look around you—your fighters need longer than that."

"You're thinking of it wrong," Tau said. "We're back in Uhmlaba at almost the same instant we left. Gifted Thandi, we have all the time in the world."

The Lady Gifted looked frustrated. "We have the time we need in the underworld, but look at how much is wasted here while they recover," she said. "How many battles do you think they can manage in a night? One, maybe two? It's not enough. We should tell Nyah and the queen that we need to find another way."

Tau sucked his teeth and turned to the Ihashe. "Men, gather yourselves. We fight again."

Duma heard someone lowing in fear, letting their cowardice show. When he took another swallow from the water bowl, the sound stopped, and Duma realized it'd been him making it. That alone told him they weren't ready to go again, not that night, maybe not ever.

He looked at the others, expecting to see similar thoughts writ large on their faces, but saw nothing of the sort. Uduak was sitting, looking worn but ready. It was the same with Azima, Yaw, and even Themba. And Tau—the champion could've woken from a nap a breath ago, the way he looked.

Duma didn't know what to do. He couldn't face the monsters again. There was no way he was—

"Ready?" the champion asked them. "Remember, hold the circle. Watch your brothers' backs. We can do this. Now, close your eyes."

Watch your brothers' backs. Duma saw everyone else close their eyes, and then the Lady Gifted was looking at him, the last man with his eyes open, and, Goddess, that woman was pretty as a new flower.

Watch your brothers' backs, Duma thought, nodding. Fear or no, demons or no, he could do that. He'd always do that.

He closed his eyes, battled his breathing, and, getting it close enough to controlled, he let his soul sink to that awful place.

"Form the circle!" Tau said.

"Watch their backs," Duma muttered. "Watch—"

"Move in, Themba! You're too far out," Tau said.

Duma had little enough idea where the others were. He knew they were near him and knew the Lady Gifted was in the center of their circle. He knew it as a practical thing, but he hadn't turned to see it for himself. He couldn't. His eyes were locked on the mists.

He heard them before he saw them. The demons had been drawn to the glowing of so many souls, and they came, screeching, howling, and cackling, disturbing the mist with their movements while staying hidden behind its ebb and flow.

Their sounds set Duma's nerves jangling, building a tension in him that stacked itself higher and higher until there was nowhere left for it to go but out.

"Nceku!" he roared at the roiling mists. "Why do you wait? Come out! Come out and fight!"

Two demons, small ones, raced toward the circle of men. The first one lunged for Themba, and the second angled for Uduak. Another demon, bigger than the initial two, charged at Tau, and then three more burst out of the mists, crooked things that came for Yaw and Azima.

Duma saw his brothers engage the monsters, and he knew he

should help them, but his feet wouldn't obey his commands. He remained in place and out of reach, letting Azima fight two of them alone.

The drummer was on his back foot, slashing wildly at the demons harrying him, and it was the reverse of the situation on the night of the Xiddeen invasion. Back then, it was Duma who'd been outnumbered.

He'd been caught out of position by two spearwomen and was mere breaths away from meeting the Goddess when Azima came along. Even fighting together, it was close. The spearwomen had been damned good fighters, but, in the end, Duma and Azima got to leave that battleground, and the spearwomen did not.

Using the memory of that victory to lend him courage, Duma finally got his legs moving. He ran to stand with Azima, but he'd delayed too long, and one of the creatures clawed the drummer's head clean off his shoulders.

Duma stopped in place, watching his sword brother's head roll around on the ground, Azima's eyes open but unseeing.

"No. . . . No!" The fear was back, and Duma turned to run, to flee this senseless battle with its certain outcome. He turned and saw the demon lord step from the mists.

It stood like a man but could never be mistaken for one. It had no eyes, and in their place were wide holes that expanded and shrank like nostrils tracking a scent. On the sides of its head were more holes, four on the left and four on the right. Those ears, if that's what they were, were sunk into its head instead of protruding from it, and on top of the thing's head were hardened spikes, ringing its skull like a melted crown held too long in a fire.

Fear took Duma's voice from him, but that didn't matter. The demon lord heard, smelled, or knew him anyway, and its head swiveled to face him. It came for him on two legs, spiked, malformed, and ending in two clawed toes that split from the main of each foot.

Panting, shivering, all hope stolen, Duma spun, searching for help, safety, anything.

In the eye of the maelstrom, he saw the Lady Gifted, hidden from the demons' view by her blanket of darkness. Behind him, his sword brothers fought and fell, their battles lost already. The only man not breathless from destruction was Tau, though the champion was besieged on all sides.

"Help me!" Duma begged, finding enough of his voice to call to the Lady Gifted. "Please!"

If she heard him, she gave no sign, and Duma turned back to the demon lord. It was almost on him, and he swung his sword.

The lord used its arm to block the blade, smashing into it with so much force that the collision sent Duma stumbling back. He swung again and the demon lord parried with the thing it held...with its sword.

In its claws, the monster held a weapon that looked like the dragon-scale swords made by the Omehi. It was a bastard brother to the blades Tau bore. The handle appeared to be twisted bone, it had no pommel, and the blade itself was unrefined, seeming for all the world as if the demon had torn it from the back of a dragon and fused it clumsily to its hilt.

"This isn't real," Duma said, pulling his sword away so he could swing it up and at the demon lord's neck.

The creature let him strike it, wading through a killing blow without reaction, and when it came within arm's length, it flung its free hand out, snatching Duma by his face, its rocklike grip scraping the skin from his cheeks. It pressed down with its claws, puncturing his flesh, and it lifted Duma from his feet, pulling him close.

He could smell it, and the reek was one he knew. The demon lord was a funeral pyre, its odor the foulness of the dead being burned.

Duma tried to call out, opening his mouth as wide as he was able, and in the space he'd made between his top and bottom teeth, Duma felt pain so pure it bloomed in his head like lightning. The lord's claws had pierced the meat of his cheeks, cracked through his teeth, and the thing's thumb and fingers had scissored together, slicing his tongue away.

The thing's palm was over Duma's face, he couldn't see, and that made the next shock worse. The demon lord drove its bastard sword into him, spearing him on its length, and Duma's soul, bright with suffering, collapsed in on itself like a dying world.

Eyes snapping open and mouth half filled with sand, Duma sputtered, clearing the dirt from his lips. He sat up, and, eyes wild, he scanned the yard. He was with the Lady Gifted, Uduak, Yaw, Themba, and a crouching demon.

Stumbling, Duma leapt to his feet. The mists were gone, but the kneeling demon with its yellow eyes fixed on him and its open maw, showing knifelike teeth, told him where he was. He was still in the underworld.

The thing in front of him rose from its crouch and stepped closer to Themba. Themba had his back to the demon and it was too late for a warning to save him, but there was still time for Duma to act.

He charged the creature, sword crashing through the air, and the demon, with its yellow eyes, watched him come, waiting too long before it tried to scurry off the killing line.

Too late, you're too late! Duma thought, putting all his weight behind the blow and feeling the blade bury itself into flesh and bone as he was spattered by the monster's blood. It raised a taloned hand for him and Duma swung again, blasting his weapon into its side.

"I won't let you have my brothers!" he shouted. "I won't—"

"Duma!"

The growl, bending sound unnaturally to form his name, had come from behind him. Duma spun and his knees buckled. It was the demon lord with its twin twisted blades. It was the lord, come for him again.

Duma sought his fellows, but they were unmoving, watching him with terror, undone by the moment.

Duma looked back. The lord was coming.

"I won't let you have my brothers!" he said, attacking it.

It moved out of the way, mocking him with his name. "Duma, stop," it said. "Duma!"

Fear lending him strength and speed he didn't know he had, Duma sent his blade streaming the other way in a backhand blow, but somehow the lord had known the attack would come and avoided it.

It was toying with him, Duma realized, toying with him so it could torture him again. It wanted to keep him trapped in Isihogo, and that's when Duma understood.

The demon lord had found a way to hide the underworld's mists and most of its demons. It had found a way to batter and torment him without killing him. It meant to keep him in the underworld forever.

Duma forced out a laugh. He'd seen through the deception, and, knowing what needed to be done to free himself, he dropped his sword.

"Duma!" the lord roared, rushing at him as Duma pulled his dagger from his belt and quickly, quickly plunged it into his chest, pain exploding through him.

The lord had him then, grabbing at him, but with the last of his strength, Duma shook the demon loose, ripped the dagger free, and slammed it home again, piercing his own heart. He lost control of his fingers when he did it, his hand fell away from the dagger, and with the sound of blood rushing through his head, Duma collapsed.

He was on the ground and the edges of his body seemed to be contracting. His sense of his fingers and toes, his hands and feet, his calves and forearms, vanished, and the vanishing kept going, hurting as it went, hurting as it erased him.

Standing over him was the lord, and Duma, time short, offered it a trembling smile. He'd won, he'd—

The demon's face fell apart like a city of sand struck by a wave. It fell apart as if it never was, and in the demon's place was Tau.

"Duma...I'm so sorry," his sword brother said. "I'm sorry."

Desperate and filled with horror, Duma lurched his head to the side, seeking the demon he'd felled. Azima was on the ground not far from Duma, his body broken, destroyed by sword cuts and awash with blood. Azima's eyes were open but soulless. His sword brother was dead.

It was then, staring into Azima's lifeless eyes, that Duma finally understood the truth. He was already in Uhmlaba, but he wasn't free. He was lost, and in the last beat of his broken heart, Duma Sibusiso went helpless, damned, and all alone into the dark.

LEGACY

They burned Duma and Azima in the eternal flames of the Sah Citadel's funeral pyres that same night. It was late, and with no words passed between them, Tau's brothers had gone to their beds. He stayed behind in the open-air circle of the citadel, watching the priestesses and priests, their features hidden behind sculpted nickel masks shaped to resemble the face of the Goddess, as they tended the twisting flames that they never allowed to die.

There were rumors, rumors about the two Ihashe from Tau's scale who had come to a strange end in the Guardian Keep. Some said it was a fight between friends turned deadly. Others said that Gifted loyal to Odili remained in Citadel City and that they had forbidden powers that could break a man's mind. The worst of the whisperers spoke the names of those they believed would be next to die.

Tau let the rumors run. They were no worse than the truth, and they were better than he deserved. As Hadith had once warned, he'd pushed too far and his brothers couldn't follow. Now two of them were dead.

Gifted Thandi came to stand beside him and he saw her mouth moving in silent prayer.

"I failed them," he said when she'd finished.

She turned to him. "Duma became demon-haunted. It can happen to women and men in their beds."

"He wasn't in his bed when he died," Tau said, thinking about the demon that had come for Duma in Isihogo. He hadn't seen it clearly, but it had looked like one he'd fought before. It had looked like it was carrying a weapon. "You were right," he said to Thandi. "I'm asking people I care about to take too many risks. I'm pushing them too far."

Thandi was quiet for a time. "Maybe I'm right," she said, "or maybe coming out of bad times has always meant pushing for a place that seems too far."

Lowering his head, Tau pinched the bridge of his nose, hoping to ease the ache in his skull. "I keep failing the people I'm supposed to keep safe."

Thandi didn't have words for him on that score and she turned away from the fire. "I'm going to see Kellan. Would you walk with me, Champion?"

Tau still wasn't ready to leave, but losing Duma and Azima was a reminder that the line between life and death was a thin one, and he knew he should see Kellan. More, he knew he should see Jabari. He'd not been by his friend's side for too long.

He nodded to her, and they left the priests, their citadel, and their eternal fires behind.

When they were alone, Thandi spoke. "Do you know why I'm on the Shadow Council?"

"No," Tau said, wishing they could keep walking in silence.

"It's because I believe in the things the queen is fighting for."

He grunted.

"She's fighting to give us back our legacy, and with that legacy comes freedom, real freedom, which will mean safety for the ones we love. Champion, I was born a Harvester. My family are all Harvesters... except my older brother.

"He was sickly and couldn't fight. He was made a Drudge, but a man too sickly to fight will be too sickly to labor as Drudges must. He died in a farming field and it took two seasons for the news to reach us."

Thandi's hurt remained fresh. Tau didn't think he was good at reading people, but he could see that much. "Goddess keep him," he said to her.

"I pray She does, but I'll also work toward the day when such fates cannot find my family or any others like it."

"Gifted Thandi, with respect, you and the rest of the Shadow Council serve the monarchy, not families like ours."

Thandi shook her head. "You don't understand Queen Tsiora's dream. She wants the Omehi to live as we were meant to." She smiled. "She's going to take us home."

Tau realized that the unending agony in his leg wouldn't have the chance to drive him mad. The fruitless hopes of religious zealots would do it first. "We have no home," he told her.

"We do and we always have," she insisted. "It's on Osonte."

"You think, after all this time, there's a place for us there?" he asked. "Will Osonte's women and men greet us warmly when we return? As warmly as the Xiddeen did?"

"The Goddess will see us through, and when that happens, we'll no longer be Lessers; we'll simply be Omehi. That, Tau Solarin, is what the queen wants. That is what I want."

"And now we're back to praying for change."

She actually laughed. "You think everything is so hopeless. What are you even fighting for?"

"I have my reasons," Tau said, thinking of Abasi Odili as he stopped in front of the infirmary doors.

"Are they good ones?"

"They'll serve."

She fidgeted with her belt. "I'd like you to know that I grieve the loss of your friends with you."

"And the grief is more bearable for that," he said, doing his best to be gracious.

"Tell me, will Duma's and Azima's passing be in vain?"

Tau took his hand from the infirmary door and faced her. "What?"

"Or will you honor them by finding others to complete the mission to which they gave their lives?"

"Lady Gifted," Tau said, "their funeral pyre is still burning and that's what you ask me?"

"Their funeral pyre is in the Sah Citadel. It will always burn."

"But must my brothers be its fuel?"

"Don't you see? Unless we take back Palm, everyone we love will feel the flames." She looked nervous and perhaps even ashamed. "Champion, I went to the queen. I had concerns and I raised them to her."

"Did you?"

"She told me to have faith. She told me that she believes in you, and because I believe in her, I choose to believe in you too."

Tau wiped at one side of his face in frustration. "It's nice to have your faith, but it doesn't change the fact that I have too few to hold the circle. There's four of us and that's not enough. I need more fighters."

"Then, find them," Thandi said.

He didn't mean to do it, but he sighed. "Lady Gifted, if you'll excuse me, I'm tired and would like to visit an injured friend whom I've neglected for far too long."

"You go to the burned Petty Noble? His survival is a miracle from the Goddess Herself."

"There's no give in Jabari," Tau said, reaching again for the infirmary door when the thought struck him: Some things are made stronger in fire. "Kellan can't fight in Isihogo because his blood prevents it, right?"

Thandi gave him a quizzical look. "Yes, you know this."

"What about the blood of a Petty Noble?"

Thandi's eyes widened. "Jabari? Champion, his body is a ruin."

Tau began to pace. "But he doesn't need his body in Isihogo. It's his spirit that will see him rise or fall." He stopped and turned to Thandi. "Can it be done?"

Thandi looked away. "Petty Noble blood is weak. It may be that he can fight in the underworld without suffering harm here, but why task him with this?"

"Because of the man that he is, because he's always wanted to fight for queen and queendom, and maybe I can give him something of that dream."

"You'll be asking him to suffer more than he already does."

"Lady Gifted, as far as I know, the only path to becoming what others cannot is to suffer what others will not."

She opened her hands, palms up. "I have no idea what to say to the queen about this."

"Tell her that we'll have five men for our circle."

Thandi tracked him with her eyes as he paced. "This is what you want to try, and you really think of yourself as a man lacking in faith?"

Tau refused to think of it as faith. "I know who he is and what he's capable of doing," he said.

"You believe in him."

"Of course."

"I understand," Thandi said. "It's how I feel about the queen and the Goddess."

Tau stopped midstep. "Clean thrust," he said.

Thandi gave him a small smile. "Yes, it was, wasn't it?"

Tau walked to the infirmary door and opened it. "Lady Gifted," he said, "can you tell the queen to meet us at midnight tomorrow?"

"What happens then?"

"She can watch us hold back the demons."

SEVEN

Tau was nervous. The night before, after deciding to ask Jabari to fight in Isihogo, he'd gone to his friend's bedside and explained everything. Jabari couldn't speak, not with the damage to his throat. It was likely he'd never speak properly again, but Tau had gotten an answer from him anyway.

At the end of his tale of demons, dragons, Gifted, and suffering, he'd placed his wrist in one of Jabari's bandaged hands and asked the Petty Noble if he would do this terrible thing with them. He couldn't believe Jabari would refuse, but as he waited for a response, he pictured himself in his friend's place and started to doubt.

Ashamed for putting his friend in such a position, Tau began to rise, intending to leave Jabari to rest, but Jabari squeezed his wrist before he could move away.

Tau looked into his best friend's eyes, the blacks at the center the only normal thing about them. Once the Petty Noble's condition had stabilized, the Sah priests had done what they could to make his body function as it once had. Early on in the process, they'd sliced away the fused flesh on his eyelids, permitting Jabari to open his eyes fully. It had been done long ago, but the whites around Jabari's pupils seemed to be permanently bruised and stained red.

"You're certain?" Tau asked.

Another squeeze. Jabari's eyes had a hunger in them.

So, on that next night, the night the queen was meant to see them fight the demons, Tau was at Jabari's bedside again. The curtains around the Petty Noble's bed had been pulled back, but there was no one to gawk at Jabari's condition. Priestess Hafsa, not knowing the reason for the request but grudgingly respecting the authority of it, had moved all patients except for Hadith and Kellan into another ward. The infirmary was Tau's.

Hadith, at the other end of the ward, his chest wrapped tight with bandages, was sitting up and watching them. The grand general had wanted to be moved closer, to observe. Tau told him it wasn't wise. He wanted enough space to stop another...accident, if one occurred.

Next to Hadith, Gifted Thandi was with Kellan. The Greater Noble had woken that morning, demanding his release from Hafsa's care and an immediate return to duty. The physician, declaring the worst behind him, had refused regardless. She wanted him in the infirmary for one more night.

Tau had already gone to Kellan and spoken with him. He told him as little as he could while still convincing him that he could not train in Isihogo. Tau had said that the same strength of blood that allowed the Gifted to move their powers through him meant that the demons could move the injuries they caused him in Isihogo into Uhmlaba.

It was basically the truth, but Tau knew that Kellan knew there was more to it. Thankfully, Kellan was too graceful to treat Tau's explanation as anything other than the whole truth.

Thandi had come then, telling Kellan that he'd been brave and lucky to survive Tau's foolishness. She told Kellan that her concerns about him fighting in the underworld had been due to her theory about his blood and the way it would interact with the demons.

Again, Kellan was graceful. He was always graceful, and the effect his good manners had was never more apparent than when women were present. Gifted Thandi hung on the Greater Noble's every mutter or mumble. So as Thandi and Kellan conversed, Tau took his leave, walking over to Jabari's bedside.

The sun had just set, the rest of the unit would arrive within a span, and Tau intended to work with Jabari until that time. He'd show him how to enter and leave Isihogo, and though he tried to hide his worries, Tau wanted this to work.

True, Isihogo had its price, but it was a rare thing of value that didn't. And if Jabari could withstand the underworld, he'd finally learn to fight as powerfully as any Ingonyama. Tau wanted that for him.

"You understand what to do?" Tau asked. "We'll enter and leave Isihogo a few times. I want you familiar with that before the others come."

Jabari squeezed his hand.

"You're sure you're ready to—"

Squeeze.

Tau smiled. "Of course. Close your eyes and listen to my voice . . ."

In all the times Tau had taken himself to the underworld, he had never entered it indoors and was unsure what he'd see. The mists, heavy, oppressive, and omnipresent, were there, and so were the infirmary walls, but they had been transformed, taking on the shape of outcroppings of gray vertical rock instead of the infirmary's cleanly scrubbed adobe. It was as if Isihogo denied the design of human hands, though that didn't explain how Tau's armor and weapons appeared to him exactly as they did in Uhmlaba.

Glancing about, Tau saw that there were no beds, tables, or anything else that could be easily moved. All that was temporary or unfixed was not replicated in the underworld's version, and the souls of Kellan, Hadith, and Thandi, the ones who had not joined them, could barely be seen. The souls' glow of those three looked more like afterimages of light than they did the real thing.

Then, afraid of what he'd see, Tau turned to the place where Jabari's bed would be.

"Tau . . ."

"Jabari." Relief flooded him. "Jabari!"

The Petty Noble was on his feet, his sword belted to his hip, and he had on the thick gambeson he'd worn to their countless training sessions back in Kerem, but none of that held Tau's attention. Jabari's face did. Tau's friend was unburned, uninjured, and it filled Tau's heart to see him so.

"There's no pain, Tau. Goddess be praised, there's no pain."

"Jabari, I—"

"Will it last?"

"Last?"

"I don't think I can go back," Jabari said, his voice breaking. "The burns, they hurt so much. And the priestesses and priests, they come to scrape at me, telling me they're removing dead and ruined flesh, but it feels like they're there to torture me, to pick at me like biting ants feeding on helpless prey. Tau, I spend my days in agony, and the nights are worse."

"I—I should have been here ... I should have come more often."

The Petty Noble's eyes were hard as he stared down at Tau. "Yes, you should have."

"I'm sorry."

Jabari shook his head. "It's no matter. You're here now, and you're giving me so much more than you know."

"I am sorry," Tau said, hearing a howl in the distance, out beyond the gaps in the rock that took the place of the infirmary's windows. "We have to leave."

"Leave?" Jabari asked. "No, I can't go back to that body."

"Jabari, the demons are coming."

"I'll hide. I'll hide and I'll stay."

"Look down at yourself," Tau said. "See the way you're glowing? It calls to them. They'll find you. They always do."

"Then I'll fight," Jabari said, touching the sword on his hip. "Isn't that why we're here? I'll fight to stay."

"You will fight, but not now. Come back with me, brother."

"To what, Tau? For what?"

The howls had multiplied. More demons were coming and they were close.

"We'll be back," Tau said. "Trust me."

"Trust you?" Jabari's smile was strange. "Of course, brother. Of course."

"You remember how to get back?" Tau asked.

Jabari nodded.

"Good. Free the air in your lungs. Let no more take its place. It'll feel like you're dying and—"

"Every moment I have feels like I'm dying," Jabari said, walking three steps away and exhaling.

Tau watched as Jabari's golden glow flared, dimmed, trembled, and vanished, taking Jabari with it. By then, the demons had arrived and it was too late to leave as Jabari had. Body itching in anticipation, Tau pulled his swords free.

Tau's eyes flew open and he was back in Uhmlaba. There had been three smaller demons at first and he'd held them off for a while. It was when the fourth had joined the fight that he'd fallen, and he was still coming back to himself when he felt Jabari squeezing his wrist.

Jabari's eyes and mouth, the only parts of his face not covered by bandages, were wide open and his back was arched.

"Jabari?"

The Petty Noble kept squeezing Tau's wrist.

Something was wrong and Tau began to rise. "I'll get Hafsa."

Jabari latched on to Tau's wrist, holding him in place and, given the state of his hands, Tau could imagine what it cost him to do it.

"You don't want the physician?"

Jabari, slowly, purposefully, shook his head.

"What then? What do you need?"

Jabari spoke one word, broken and hoarse, like the hiss of water thrown on a fire. "Isihogo."

Tau rubbed his neck with his free hand. "The demons will be closer. They are called to the places we go and they stay around them for a while after we're gone."

Jabari squeezed his wrist, one, two, three times.

Tau understood. "We have to be quick. No fighting. If you engage the demons, the only way to leave the underworld is through death, and, for now, it's more important to learn how to enter and leave Isihogo. Are you ready?"

Another wrist squeeze.

"Close your eyes and..." Jabari's eyes were already closed and he was working to bring his breathing under control. "Listen to my voice," Tau said, helping to focus and guide his friend to their destination.

"How long can we stay?" Jabari said, shouting over the underworld's mists.

"Not long. If we come back to the same place, there are always demons waiting."

"Can you move me? Move me in Uhmlaba? Then I can come back and it will take them longer to find me?"

Tau hadn't thought of that. "Perhaps," he said. "It might help a little, but it is never long before they come. The glow calls to them."

"Can we stop the glow?"

The question brought Tau's mind to Zuri, and the memory hurt. "No," he told Jabari. "We can't. Gifted can shroud themselves in the underworld, but only Gifted."

"How do you know? Have you tried?"

Tau didn't answer.

"You've tried...," Jabari said. "Maybe it's because you're a Lesser? Maybe I can—"

"You can't."

A demon roared from beyond the walls.

"I can't go back yet," Jabari said. "I need more time."

"We have to leave."

Jabari screamed in the direction of the roar. "Cek!"

Still angry, he turned to Tau and expelled the air from his lungs, holding his eyes on Tau's face as he did it.

They went back two more times. The last time they had only just stepped into the underworld when the demons had marked them. So after that they waited for the others, and without the need for words, Tau could sense Jabari's impatience.

Uduak was the first to arrive, and with a quick salute to Tau, he went to sit by Hadith. Yaw came next, bobbing his head at everyone, which made his necklace swing back and forth.

After the first fights in Isihogo, Tau's sword brother had taken to wearing the short necklace symbolizing deep faith in the Goddess. As best as Tau could tell, Yaw's necklace was typical. At the end of a short bronze chain hung a circle of wood that had been carved with the Goddess's likeness, and fingering the wood as Tau had often seen old Proven do, Yaw elected to stand a few strides away. He was trying to make it look as if he were examining the other infirmary beds, but Tau knew that Yaw simply wasn't sure how to be around Jabari, given the Petty Noble's particular state.

Themba was the last to join. He strode up, saluted Tau a little too sharply, and smiled down at Jabari.

"You're a fool to do this," he said to the burned man. "Brave, but a fool."

"Themba, bring Uduak and the Lady Gifted. We'll begin," Tau said, not wanting Jabari to have to wait any longer.

Themba's smile was back. "Can't even give him a moment, can you?"

"Who, Uduak? He's been a better brother than I have. He's always with Hadith."

Themba chuckled and lifted an eyebrow. "Well, that makes sense given ... everything."

Tau was feeling tender after worrying over Jabari and didn't need Themba piling on. "Given what, exactly?"

Themba let his eyebrow drop back in place and raised his hands, palms out. "Don't take me the wrong way. I've no problem with it," he said. "It's just that they got a lot more serious after Uduak was injured in the melee."

"More serious?"

"Yes, after Uduak was hurt and Hadith ..." Themba cocked his head. "Wait? You can't mean you didn't ..." The smile was back and Themba began speaking to Tau slowly, like he was talking to a child. "Why do you think I made all those jibes about Uduak and the pleasure houses or Uduak becoming the queen's champion and having to perform all his duties there or ... Goddess wept, you didn't know why I was always teasing him? How small is Kerem?"

Tau wasn't listening anymore. He was staring at his two sword brothers, Uduak and Hadith, clasping wrists and speaking in low voices to each other. "It's not ... uh ... Kerem isn't that small."

"So you say," Themba said, smirking at a straight-faced Yaw and then at Jabari, as if the three of them were sharing a joke.

"In any case," Tau said, "bring Uduak and the Lady Gifted. We should begin."

Reminded of their purpose that night, Themba grew serious and went to get them.

When he'd walked away, Tau turned to Yaw. "Did you know?"

Yaw shrugged, then nodded.

"I didn't," Tau said, watching Uduak and Gifted Thandi follow Themba back to them.

Themba's smirk was back. "Champion Solarin, may I introduce you to Uduak, an Ihashe of the Omehi military. I'm not sure you two ... really know each other."

Uduak glanced at Themba from the side of his eyes while Gifted Thandi ignored him outright.

Following Thandi's example, Tau left Themba to his smirking and got right to the point. "Lady Gifted, I hope to begin tonight's training immediately, but I'd like to know when we can expect the queen."

Thandi wouldn't look at him. "She's not coming."

"What? Why not?"

"The fiefs are sending far fewer Ihagu than the queen asked them for. So, she's meeting with Nyah and this city's umbusi to discuss how best to bring the rest of the umbusi in line, because we can't take back Palm without more soldiers.

"In any case, she thinks that you also need more fighters and that, even once you have enough to hold the circle, they'll need time in the underworld before they can actually do it."

They hadn't even begun the real work and already Tau was weary. "I told you there are no more men whom I trust with this, and why would the queen be so sure we need more fighters?"

"Hmm ... it could be because she asked my opinion on whether five fighters were enough."

Tau knew he was glaring. "And what did you tell her?"

"The truth."

Tau put his face in his hands and massaged his temples. "The truth? What is the truth, as you see it?"

"You can't keep the Gifted safe with just five men."

Tau didn't have time for this. "What happened to all your talk of faith and the Goddess and . . . char and ashes; Gifted Thandi, I won't have men I cannot trust face the underworld."

Thandi nodded. "The queen knows that."

"Then what do you expect me to—"

The doors to the infirmary opened, and lacking even a hint of their prior servility, in stalked Auset and Ramia, the queen's handmaidens.

NCHANGA

W ho're they?" asked Themba.

"Auset and Ramia, the queen's handmaidens," Tau told him.

"I thought this was secret training. Why are the queen's hand-maidens here?"

"I believe the queen wishes to bolster our numbers...and I think she finds it amusing to keep me off-balance."

The handmaidens were standing on either side of Gifted Thandi, and Tau had to admit, they looked intimidating when they weren't pretending to be otherwise.

"I'll teach you how to enter the underworld," Tau said to them, while worrying that Jabari would become impatient with another delay. "It'll take time from tonight's training, but what counts is that you're willing to do this with us. Thank you."

"We have been with the queen since the beginning," Auset said, her lips moving without seeming to affect the rest of her face. "We know how to come and go from Isihogo, Champion."

"Ah...of course you do. Apologies," Tau said.

"Wait, wait a moment." Themba was waving his hands like he was shooing flies. "Why are handmaidens coming with us?"

"They're not handmaidens," Tau said.

"Yes, we are," Ramia said, her voice sweet as the fruit from a masuku tree.

"See? Handmaidens," Themba said.

"Begin, Champion. Let's waste no time on the prattle of fools," Auset said.

"Fools?" Themba asked. "Do you know what we're doing tonight? I'm trying to help you."

"You can barely help yourself, Ihashe," Auset told him.

"Auset," Ramia said, "he doesn't know."

"He should. He has eyes. He's choosing not to accept what they tell him."

Themba walked up to Auset. "Listen, it's not my way to be rude, but you need to—"

"Step away from me, kudliwe," Auset said.

Tau tried to warn him. "Themba..."

"You may be a handmaiden to the queen," Themba said, pointing a finger in Auset's face, "but I'm a full-blood Ihashe and—"

Themba's words were replaced by his squawk when Auset snatched his finger, hooked the crook of her other elbow beneath the armpit of his extended arm, spun, and bent at the hips, sending him flying over her shoulder to land on his back in a heap.

"Goddess!" said Yaw.

"Big throw," Uduak said.

"Nceku!" shouted Themba, jumping back to his feet and putting a hand on his sword.

Tau didn't think Themba would have drawn the bronze, but Auset and Ramia couldn't know that, and the instant Themba's flesh brushed the weapon at his side, the two women had their dirks out and aimed, leaving Themba facing four black blades.

"They're not *only* handmaidens," Tau said.

"Dragon scale," Uduak noted appreciatively.

Themba was smart enough to lift his hand away from his sword. "What is this?"

It had been a trying time. Truth, it had been a trying life, so it lifted Tau's spirits to find he could still manage a grin.

"Themba," he asked, "have you never met handmaidens with

dragon-scale dirks before? How small is...ah..." Tau blinked. "I don't know where you're from."

Themba managed to look both shocked and hurt. "Nchanga. I'm from Nchanga, and I tell you stories about my home all the time. How do you not know where I'm from?"

"Nchanga. Yes, I remember," Tau lied. "Now, are we settled?"

The handmaidens made their dirks disappear and they nodded. Themba sucked his teeth, but he nodded too.

"Good, let's begin," Tau said, feeling the mood darken. He took another look at the women and men who would stand with him in this, his eyes alighting on Jabari last of all. "Everyone here knows our task and what must be done to achieve it. I'll see you in Isihogo," he told them, closing his eyes.

FRACTION

E ven though there were so many of them in the underworld, Tau didn't expect the demons to come as fast and hard as they did. His last thought, before drawing his swords, was that the trips with Jabari had agitated them.

"Tighten up! Get closer to one another," Tau shouted, hoping his voice was loud enough to carry.

On his right were the handmaidens, Ramia the closer of the two. Jabari and Uduak were to his left, and past them stood Yaw and Themba. Thandi was in the center of the circle of fighters and safe behind the shadows of her shroud.

"Jabari, the underworld suits you!" Themba shouted out, noting the Petty Noble's unburned body.

"Hush!" Tau said, peering into the rolling mists, trying to track the unseen monsters by their noises.

"This waiting is, I can tell you, my least favorite part," Themba said to the handmaidens. "I'd like to say I'll save you, if it comes to it, but I can't." He spat in the muck. "There is no saving the damned."

Tau saw Ramia's eyes widen at Themba's words. Auset was different. She showed her teeth to the mists as she swiveled her head to and fro, searching for the enemy.

"Tau!" It was Jabari. "The doorway."

He was right. In Isihogo, the infirmary's main entrance had no doors, and through the entrance rushed three demons.

"Waiting's over!" Themba said. "And I was wrong, it's not the worst part." The first demon leapt for him, and snarling back at it, Themba said, "The dying is!"

Themba and the demon met each other in a crash of bronze and claws. Tau's sword brother tore flesh from the monster's crimson hide, and it ripped three stripes of skin and leather away from his shoulder and chest.

Yaw dodged the second creature's lumbering assault and plunged his sword into what had to be its neck, causing the thing to shake its head, yanking his weapon away.

The third demon through the doorway attacked Ramia, or it tried to. The handmaiden was as slippery as a river eel, and the demon's teeth and claws found no purchase as she rammed the points of her dirks into it.

"More coming," Uduak said, lifting his chin toward four demons crawling through the underworld's version of the infirmary's windows.

One of them had four arms, walked upright, and had an elongated face that made it look like a feral horse afflicted with some wasting disease. Tau shouted at that one, drawing its attention. He found he got more out of the fights with the big demons. The four-armed grotesquerie spotted him, and its eyes, buglike, shone as it ran for him.

In the moments that followed, Tau saw Themba die, then Jabari was torn apart by a small but vicious thing, Yaw fell next, Ramia was cut down from behind, and Uduak dropped with a demon still latched on to his throat. Auset, bloodied, glassy-eyed, and with her left arm hanging uselessly, roared at the demons that had her surrounded as Tau fought his way to her side.

He'd dispatched the four-armed thing, sliced the legs out from under another one with the eyes and mouth of a hammer-beaten fish, and gutted the maggot-colored demon with the slicing arms of a mantis. Then, blasting his twin swords into the neck and spine of another upright, he dashed past its neighbor and next to Auset.

Their circle was no more, but it had gone better than all the times before, and just as Tau thought that, an idea came to him that filled him with hope.

"What do we do?" Auset asked, her voice strong but shaking and her pupils so wide they filled her eyes.

"We fight," Tau said.

"They'll kill us."

"They will," Tau said, launching himself at the nearest demon and admiring that Auset, in spite of her fears, did the same.

Back in Uhmlaba, everyone was still recovering as Tau explained his revelation to Gifted Thandi.

"We're doing it wrong," he said.

"Of that there can be no doubt," she said.

"What happened?" Hadith called from across the infirmary.

"They were slaughtered," Thandi told Hadith.

"Again?" asked Kellan.

"Same as always," she said.

"We're doing it wrong," Tau said loud enough for the two bed-ridden men to hear.

"Well, if you're getting slaughtered, you're unlikely to be doing it right," Hadith called back.

"Not the fighting part," Tau said. "We can't expect to hold for long, not in the beginning. Everyone still has to learn how to fight the demons. The issue is that the plan, as it stands, is unlikely to ever work," Tau said.

"Heartening speech," Themba muttered, his stomach pumping in and out like he might vomit.

"Goddess." Auset was standing on feet so unsteady Tau worried she'd fall and crack her head on the edge of an infirmary bed. "That was even worse than the queen said it would be."

"The champion thinks we're doing it wrong," Thandi said.

"Everything about this is wrong." Ramia was sitting, slumped on the floor and staring at the dirks she held in her hands. "Everything."

"Told you," Themba said. "I told—" His hand flew to his mouth, and through clenched fingers, he spewed the remnants of his evening meal onto the floor.

"Yaw, you're the one with the gift for stories," Hadith said. "What happened?"

Yaw's eyes jerked about like they couldn't settle on anything or anyone.

"Yaw?" Hadith asked.

Yaw shook his head, not saying a word.

"It's bad." Uduak said. The big man was on his knees, leaning against Jabari's bed. "The end."

Tau explained, "We don't have to hold the demons at bay for as long as we think we do."

"Why not?" asked Thandi as she checked on Yaw.

"Because the demons have no interest in you until your shroud fails," Tau said, "which means that our fighters don't even need to be in Isihogo until the Gifted are about to lose their shrouds. If we wait until then, the amount of time we need to hold the demons at bay is a fraction of what it'd be otherwise."

"What?" asked Themba, sounding hoarse from all the retching.

"We only need to enter Isihogo and fight once our Gifted are defenseless," Tau said.

"Good," Themba said. "Good."

Thandi clicked her tongue. "Of course! By coming in while my shroud is still up, you're drawing the demons and fighting them for longer than is necessary," she said, tapping a finger against her lips. "You really don't need to hold the demons for nearly so long as we thought. Goddess, we might actually be able to do this."

"I always had faith," Tau said with a lopsided smile and surprising himself when it was enough to make Thandi laugh.

"It can work," she said. "And while you train, I can keep a count. We'll see how long you can maintain the defensive circle and we'll keep trying to do better."

Tau nodded. He liked this. It reminded him of how he'd done things when he'd begun his training in Isihogo. "Yes," he said. "We'll keep a count, and by our efforts, that count will rise."

"Let's try it. Get them ready," Thandi said, waving at the others.

"Shouldn't we wait for you?" Tau asked her.

"I'm coming."

"It hasn't nearly been a quarter span."

"Our shrouds aren't depleted much simply by spending time in Isihogo. It's pulling power from the underworld that does it."

"Ah...," Tau said.

"Haven't you ever wondered how Edifiers transmit messages to one another over great distances?"

"Why would I do that?" Tau asked.

Thandi closed her eyes, breathed in through her mouth, and let the air out slowly. "Edifiers move through the underworld to distant meeting spots where they can deliver messages. If their shrouds depleted at the same rate as when Gifted are actively using their gifts, an Edifier would have no way to travel far enough to meet another Edifier."

"Hmm...," Tau said, turning to the others to get them ready.

"Then the Xiddeen can have Edifiers too?" Hadith asked.

Tau rubbed his bald head, frustrated by all the talking.

"No," Thandi said. "Our Gifted can hold their shrouds intact for longer than the other races of man. Back in the days when Xiddeen...Gifted were more common, they couldn't stay in Isihogo long enough to travel a great distance, even when they weren't pulling energy."

"But if the Edifiers travel through the underworld, would they not emerge where they—"

"Hadith...," Tau said.

"Apologies," Hadith said. "Time is short."

"It is," Tau said, facing his fighters and walking over to Jabari's side. He placed his wrist in the Petty Noble's hand. "If any of you cannot do this, let me know now."

Silence. It was an uncomfortable one, but it was silent, and Jabari's hand, holding Tau's wrist, didn't move at all.

The emotions running through Tau were in conflict. He felt sorrow, thinking about Azima and Duma. He felt concern, worrying that any of them could be next. He felt pride, that the women and men in front of him would not surrender, not even to unwinnable fights.

"Get yourselves ready," he said, finding it tough to talk. "Form a circle. We're going again."

Faces solemn, the six did as Tau asked.

"You're right to question it," Thandi called out to Hadith. "And, no, an Edifier doesn't return to Uhmlaba based on where she is in Isihogo." Thandi moved to the center of the circle of fighters and sat. "We send only our souls to the underworld, and our souls must return to our bodies."

"Close your eyes," Tau told the circle. "It's time."

They went back twice more, and the order in which they fell did not change much. Jabari, Yaw, and Themba were typically first to die. Ramia was usually next, and that left it a gruesome contest between Auset and Uduak.

Auset was a remarkable fighter, and Tau believed her a match for many Indlovu. Her existence and capabilities would have thrilled Jayyed.

"Who trained you and your sister?" he asked when he was back in Uhmlaba, sitting on the edge of Jabari's bed and waiting for Auset to be in a decent enough place to form an answer.

"Handmaidens to the queen," Auset said from the floor. She was holding her head in her hands and swallowing constantly, doing her best to keep her stomach's contents where they belonged. "We're not the first to protect the Omehian monarchs."

"I've not seen the like, in Lessers," Tau said.

"You, of all people, think of it as Nobles and Lessers?" she asked, raising her head to see him better. "Tell me, then, how did you come to be as you are?"

The room went so quiet Tau could almost hear everyone's ears opening up like flowers in bloom.

"Necessity," he said.

"Meaning?" she asked, unwilling to let his nonanswer stand.

"Auset . . . ," said Ramia.

"Form the circle, we'll go again," Tau said.

Themba shook his head. "I'll fight as hard as I can, Tau." He was staring down the length of the infirmary, looking at no one. "I'll do that for you, for Jayyed, for the queen, for each of us, but I've no desire to go the way Azima or Duma did. . . . I'm saying, I can't do more tonight. I can't."

"I can't either," Yaw said, quietly enough that it was hard to hear him.

Push too far and anyone can break—Tau knew that. "Very well, we'll stop for the—"

Jabari was squeezing Tau's wrist and moving his cracked and dry lips, forcing a word from his damaged throat. "More."

Looking down at his friend, Tau shook his head. "We can't. We're spent and the demons come too quickly. They're waiting for us. We'll continue tomorrow evening, at sunset."

Jabari released his wrist and turned away from Tau, hissing in pain as he did it. Jabari's reaction left Tau not knowing how to feel. On the one path, it was clear that Isihogo had given his friend a renewed sense of purpose. On the other, what did it mean that Jabari was suffering so greatly in Uhmlaba that he'd willingly turn to the underworld?

"We dismissed, then?" asked Themba.

"You are," said Tau.

Themba groaned and stretched. "Thank the Goddess for that mercy. Yaw, you headed back to the rooms?"

Yaw didn't answer. He just walked off.

"I think that's a yes," Themba said, whistling as he followed him.

The whistle was a nice touch, Tau thought, even if it wasn't enough to make him miss the looks Themba gave every dark corner and how he tight-knuckled his sword's pommel. Tau didn't blame him or Yaw or any of them for being unsettled. What they'd done, what they were going to do, it was inhuman.

Uduak came over and placed a heavy hand on Tau's shoulder. He drew close, speaking to him alone. "What do we become?" he asked.

"Neh?"

"In the end, what do we become?"

Tau looked up at the big man. "I don't know what you mean."

Uduak watched him, unblinking. "You do."

A secret shared was a secret no longer, but Tau wouldn't lie to Uduak. "I don't know where it ends," he said, "but I can tell you that whatever the end brings, we'll be its equal."

Uduak grunted. "Where we fight," he said, heading toward Hadith's bedside.

"If Uduak is looking to Hadith, maybe I'll see to Kellan...before I leave," Thandi said.

"Thank you for your kindness, Lady Gifted," Tau said.

She smiled and hurried across the infirmary to sit beside the Greater Noble. Tau watched her go and turned to the handmaidens. "You both saw that, right? I'm not imagining her eagerness, am I?" he asked.

Auset carried on like he'd not spoken. "You need to come with us," she said.

"Come with you? Where?"

"To the queen," Ramia said. She was always looking at his forehead or chin when she spoke to him. That time it was his forehead.

"You can't be serious," Tau said. He hadn't seen the queen since she'd explained just enough of Omehi history for him to understand what had happened to Kellan in Isihogo. "It's late."

"She told us to bring you to her when we were done," Ramia said, her tone shaded with hints of sympathy.

"I'll go in the morning," Tau said, the words leaving his mouth as he realized that seeing the queen so late at night was an opportunity to ask her questions without Nyah there to pinch her tongue.

"The queen wishes to see you. So, she'll see you," Auset said.

"As you say," Tau told the handmaidens. He was beginning to look forward to the meeting. It was time to learn what other hidden truths the queen knew.

CHAPTER EIGHT

ARMY

The handmaidens took Tau to the queen's chambers. They walked him to the door, and though Indlovu lined the hallway behind them, Tau thought the handmaidens might stand guard too, but they saw him to the door and left.

His mind tossing with the questions he'd ask, Tau knocked and heard the queen bid him enter. He walked in, hoping he wouldn't find her in a nightgown, and came near to running Nyah over.

"Vizier?" He knew he sounded disappointed.

"Champion," she said.

Nyah had quarter moons beneath her eyes, and tufts of her hair, typically pulled back perfectly, had escaped the golden band that held the rest. She'd been standing near the door when Tau walked in, and the queen, sitting cross-legged in one of the room's two chairs, was watching her.

Tsiora had to be tired as well but didn't look it. She seemed deep in thought and perhaps a bit distracted. Her brows were furrowed and she was wearing a flowing, amethyst-colored dress that was almost long enough to hide the bare foot she kept absentmindedly tapping against her chair.

"My queen," Tau said.

She looked up at him and smiled. "Thank you for coming. We'd like your help."

"How may I serve?" he asked, wondering if there was any chance that Nyah would leave.

"We need the rest of our army," Tsiora said. "We need the fiefs to send us their Ihagu, but the umbusi are not cooperating."

Unfortunately, Tau wasn't surprised. "You've already had time to speak with them?"

"Through edifications we have," Nyah said. "However, half the fiefs no longer send their Gifted to the meeting spots and the other half politely deny our requests for reinforcements." It didn't sound like she valued their politeness very much. "They say they can't send their Ihagu. They say they need them to guard the newly seeded fields. Their excuse is that if the Xiddeen attack the unguarded fields, we'll starve to death come Harvest and Hoard."

"A decent argument, neh?" Tau asked.

Nyah crossed her arms. "The best false-faith arguments often come cloaked in the cloths of greater concern. Yes, if the Xiddeen attack the fields we'll lose this cycle's harvest, but that's not why they resist us."

"The umbusi are Nobles," the queen said. "If they do not outright prefer that Odili and his Royals succeed in their coup, they certainly won't be heartbroken if they do."

"Have they turned against you, then?" Tau asked.

"Not yet, and not as a group," she said. "They're waiting to see which way the tree falls, and to avoid appearing seditious while they do it, they either keep their Gifted from receiving our messages or argue that sending their Ihagu risks the peninsula's crops."

"How do I help?" Tau asked, not sure there was much anyone could do.

"We need to be more convincing," Tsiora said. "So we'll see if the umbusi can deny their queen in person."

Nyah huffed. She didn't like the idea of the queen going to the umbusi but also didn't speak against it. Tau reasoned that meant she thought it necessary.

"Beg pardon, Your Majesty, but won't going to them make you look weak?" he asked.

"The umbusi can't be allowed to defy us," Tsiora said. "The ones who reply to our edicts with argument are alarming enough, but the ones breaking tradition, by no longer sending their Edifiers to meet with ours, they're endangering us all." Her foot stopped tapping. "We've held this peninsula as long as we have because of our ability to communicate across it, and no one gets to jeopardize that."

The queen's reasoning, cloaked in the cloths of greater concern, gave them not just the right but also the need to go to the fiefs and coerce them.

"I see," Tau said, not liking where this was going. "You wish me to accompany you?"

"We do," the queen said.

"As ever, I'll do as you say, my queen, but we need more than Ihagu to return Palm City to your control," Tau said. "I know the training in Isihogo has just begun, but by sending Auset and Ramia to us, you've made success possible. I don't want to stop now. The fighters I'm training won't be ready for the siege if we do."

"You don't have to stop," Nyah said. "You'll bring the ones you're training with you."

"While we wander from fief to fief? Eh... Queen Tsiora, one of them is badly injured—"

Nyah waved away Tau's objection. "We'll make a traveling cot for the Petty Noble, and Priestess Hafsa will accompany us to see to his needs."

"Champion Solarin, if we're to have our army, we must go and get it," Tsiora said.

Tau bowed his head. "Yes, my queen."

There was nothing to argue. The decision had already been made.

"Let's not forget," the queen said, a ghost of a smile playing across her lips, "this will mean you can practice your riding."

Tau tried to separate the fruit from the seeds. "I do look forward to riding with you, my queen. I know that my upbringing was not... typical for a champion and I want to fulfill the duties of my role to the best of my abilities. It will be good to have the chance to speak with you at length. I have so many questions."

He'd tried to be subtle, intending to hide his desire to learn more about the secret history of the Omehi behind flattery and courtly talk, but the queen spotted his destination like he'd marked it on a map.

"We won't keep secrets from you," she said, sitting forward in her chair. "You want to know who we are? You want to know our history? Our real history?"

"Queen Tsiora...," said Nyah.

"I do," said Tau.

"Then let's start with its most painful truth," she said. "The Cull are real."

TALES

They left the next day. Hadith was told to stay back and the queen instructed him to ready the city to receive the rest of her army. The grand general was to prepare for battle.

Nyah, good to her word, made it possible for Jabari to travel. He was in a covered palanquin carried by four Ihashe, and Hafsa, priestess of the medicinal order, accompanied him. Their first stop was fief Kabundi, the nearest and largest of the flatland fiefs.

Shocked to see the queen and an entire military claw at her keep gates, Kabundi's umbusi could do little but welcome Tsiora in, inviting her to a hurriedly prepared feast. The Lessers in the keep stared at Tau, reminding him of the Low Common girl he'd met in Citadel City. The umbusi's husband stared too, with hatred.

But his hate, the umbusi's fluster, none of it mattered. Queen Tsiora rode out and away from Kabundi with all its Ihagu in tow, and that night Tau joined the queen to hear more about the people the Omehi used to be.

"In the time immediately after Ananthi sealed Ukufa in Isihogo, the Cull were at their weakest," Tsiora told him.

Tau, Tsiora, and Nyah were in the queen's tent drinking from earthenware cups filled with watered-down olu and sitting across the fire pit from one another. It was a cold evening, and the pit and its glowing embers did more to create a comforting impression of heat than actually adding any. The space, smelling of charred wood, canvas, and flowers, reminded Tau of home, in the hut with Aren, and as Tsiora told her story, he fell into the tale, seeing its moments in her face, eyes, and lips.

"The Cull waited generations before their next attempt at conquest, and because the ones who waited were the same ones who had seen their master imprisoned, the waiting did nothing to weaken their resolve," Tsiora said. "They swore their souls to Ukufa, the Insatiate, in exchange for a never-ending existence. The Insatiate kept his part of the bargain, and it was time for the Cull to keep theirs.

"For the rest of us, time softened the memories of the war between the Goddess and the Insatiate as generation after generation lived and died, again and again until the races of man forgot to keep watch on the lands from which the Cull had come.

"They attacked the Ndola first. The Ndola, a peaceful people with gifts ill-suited to death and its dealings, were conquered, and the Cull became their masters.

"We don't know everything that happened next. What we can tell you is that the races of man did not retaliate against the Cull. Instead, they decided that their ancient enemy must have needed the Ndola's more fertile land for food and resources. They decided that the Ndola had none to blame but themselves for being weak enough to have been bested.

"The Cull, they told themselves, were after easy prey and would stop once the weak and the indolent had been dominated. But our ancient enemies did not stop, and by the time the other races of man had accepted that the Cull never would, they were too few to stop them.

"The Chosen were one of the last that the Cull attacked. They came to our homeland at the head of an endless host of the conquered. They came to destroy the Goddess's people, hoping to cast our gifts from the world, so that they might free Ukufa unopposed. It should have been the end of us, but the Goddess gave us her Guardians and we gave the Cull dragon fire.

"Where we fought, the world burned, and still it was not enough. The Cull led too many, and the ones who felt our fires in greatest number were the conquered, not the conquerors. It didn't take long to realize that we could not withstand the Cull's advance by ourselves, and there were few to whom we could turn.

"The strongest of the remaining free people on Osonte had always held themselves apart from the rest of the races of man, and in our desperation, we turned to them. We turned to the Nobles.

"They had always been warriors, and their gift was...uncomplicated. Their women and men were permanently connected to the Goddess's power in Isihogo. The connection meant that their women were stronger, faster, and bigger than most, and their men were mountains made flesh.

"We begged them to help us and they refused. We told them that when the Cull were finished with us, they'd come for them. The Nobles laughed at that. 'Blood will show,' they said, 'and no woman or man has blood as strong as ours.'

"We were desperate and we offered desperate things. We said that together we could defeat the Cull, take all their lands and the people they had conquered. Together, we said, we could rule Osonte. They laughed. 'If we wanted Osonte, we would take it,' they told us."

Tau rarely interrupted Tsiora's storytelling. He did then. "What did they want?"

"What does any such group, priding itself on being more than others, want?" she asked. "They wanted their claims and their beliefs about themselves to be true. They wanted to be more powerful and better than everyone else. So that's what our queen promised them."

"Enraging," Tau said.

Tsiora nodded. "Her name is lost to time, but she was one of the most powerful Gifted this world has ever seen. She could walk the mists of Isihogo for a quarter moon before her shroud fell, and she'd seen the weave and weft of gifts from every race of man. She understood the nature of the Nobles' power and she understood how to make it more.

"To convince them to join the Omehi, she offered the Nobles something they couldn't just laugh away. She said she would indenture the whole of her people to them if their greatest warrior, their champion, lost to her champion in a contest of single combat.

"They were interested but suspicious. They asked to see her fighter, and she stunned them by saying that they could choose the man from their own ranks. She asked only that they give her a night with him, and then he would return to challenge their champion at the next sunset.

"Agreeing immediately, they sent out one of their weaker men, a rabble-rouser who had been imprisoned for speaking out against Noble culture. They mocked him and our monarch both, saying that if the duel concluded in her favor, she would be their queen too.

"The queen welcomed the man the Nobles had sent to her, and when they were alone, he went to his knees in front of her, begging forgiveness. 'Though I will fight as hard as I'm able, I cannot defeat my opponent,' he said. 'He will kill me and you will lose your people.'

"The queen said this was not so. She told him what the Goddess had given her the gift to do, and the next day when the sun set, the queen of the Omehi took power from Isihogo and moved it through her champion. She enraged him and sent him to fight the greatest warrior the Nobles had ever known.

"The rabble-rouser, the reject, the man so weak his people cast him out, fought in the twilight of a day's end until his opponent, the Noble's champion, dressed in armor as black as night, fell. He was the greatest warrior the Nobles had ever known, and he died on Osonte's sands, his red blood staining the black leather armor that could not save him from the power of an Omehian queen.

"Seeing their strongest fall to one of their weakest, the Nobles knew the stories they told themselves about who they were would be nothing but lies without the power we could give them. For them, there was only one choice, and from the youngest child to the eldest warrior, the Nobles knelt to the Omehi queen and swore fealty to her, joining us in our war against the Cull.

"The fighting that followed threatened to bleed a continent dry, and though the war saw humanity embrace its worst instincts, it could not overwhelm the greatest gifts the Goddess had given to the races of man—love and life.

"The Omehi queen came to care for the Noble she'd enraged, and he continued to stand by her side. In time, their love brought life into the world. They had a daughter, and with her birth, the Omehi and the Nobles became one people.

"But we were losing the war. The Cull ravaged the Nobles' homeland, and with history repeating itself, we fled. The Omehi queen had promised victory and power. Instead, under her rule, the Nobles suffered a defeat beyond the scope of their cruelest nightmares.

"The queen faced threats to her rule, assassination attempts, and even open rebellion. They even called her a traitor, but how could anyone willing to suffer what she did be called that?

"When the Cull had the Omehi trapped, the queen called down a Guardian to protect the people she loved, and she set the earth on fire. It took days for her shroud to fade, and when it did, the demons that had been waiting tore her asunder.

"Her dragon, however, compelled by the memory of the queen's will, blasted any who sought to follow the Omehi as well as the battleground on which the two sides had fought for more than an entire cycle of the moon. It is said that the land where that battle took place still streams with rivers of fire that smoke and fill the air with fumes so acrid they kill any who breathe it. Where we fight, the world burns.

"Facing total defeat, the Omehi were in no position to dismantle and remake their monarchy. So, the queen's daughter took the throne, and though her father resisted it, a champion from one of the Noble royal families was chosen for her.

"The new queen tried to rule with her father's help, but she was young, her people were without a home, on the run, and she was surrounded by women and men who shared half her blood and less of her ideals. Power was stripped from her through councils populated by Nobles alone.

"Until, betraying his family's trust, her champion, having fallen in love with her, supported her against Noble interests, giving her the time she needed to become the woman she was destined to be. She was the last Omehi monarch on Osonte, and Queen Taifa Omehia was her mother's daughter.

"We'd been pushed to the edge of the continent," Tsiora explained. "There was nowhere left to go, and the Ruling and Guardian Councils decided that the Omehi would come to their end honorably. We'd die fighting so that even a history written by the Cull could not deny that, in the end, blood did show.

"But we didn't die in a last stand. Queen Taifa gathered allies in secret, calling them the Shadow Council, and when the time came to choose between fleeing the only land they had ever known and a fight to the death against the Cull, the Ruling Council, Guardian Council, Gifted, and Sah Priests, infiltrated by the Shadow Council, voted for something else."

Behind Tau, the flaps of the tent were pulled aside, startling him. It was Nyah. He'd been so wrapped in Tsiora's history lesson that he'd missed the vizier's approach.

"It grows late, my queen, and we've work to do this night," she said. "Perhaps we should let the champion rest."

It was a small thing, a turn of phrase, but Nyah knew he didn't rest when he left the queen's tent, and her words annoyed him. He tried to keep the emotion from his face, but the queen caught it.

"Remind us, Champion," she said, "what do you do tonight?"

"I go to Isihogo, where I will fight for my life," he told her.

"Normally, we'd wish you luck..."

"I thank you," he said, "but it'll make no difference to the outcome."

He stood, ready to go, and in a rare show of respect, Nyah inclined her head to him. Tau returned the gesture. The vizier was not easy to like, but she never had anything but the queen's interests at heart.

His head buzzing with the story of the Omehi, Nobles, and their queens, Tau left the tent to gather his fighters and lead them to damnation.

REBORN

In Isihogo it was always Uduak and Auset left with Tau. It was that way as nights turned into days, days turned into visits to fiefs, and the visits meant more and more Ihagu soldiers joined to their cause. It was Uduak and Auset as Tau's best fighters for a quarter moon that turned into a half moon and then into a full moon cycle. It was Uduak and Auset until, more and more often, they began to fall to Isihogo's denizens before Jabari, and Jabari began to fight like a demon himself.

Tau couldn't make sense of the change in his childhood friend, and one night, after his fighters could take no more and Jabari had been carried back to camp, Tau did not do as usual. He didn't return to the underworld alone.

Instead, he walked back to the camp, heading over to Jabari's palanquin. It was on the ground next to Priestess Hafsa's tent. Its curtains were drawn and Tau couldn't see inside, but if his suspicions were right, he didn't need to.

He moved between two nearby and tightly packed tents, sat on the ground where he would not be seen, and took himself to the underworld. He found Jabari there, fighting.

Jabari's surprise at seeing Tau almost got him killed when the demon he had engaged tried to claw his face off. He had to leap back to avoid its attack, and by the time he had his feet under him, the monster was charging. It swung for his head and he blocked with his sword, hissing through gritted teeth at the effort it took to keep the thing's hooks away.

Without a word, Tau joined him, cutting at the demon and slicing away one of its hooks. It howled and staggered away, but more demons came from the mists to replace it. As in training, Tau and Jabari went back to back, fighting like that until there were too many to hold and they were overwhelmed.

Jabari died gruesomely and Tau was torn apart not long after. It didn't matter. Tau went back to the mists and found Jabari there again. They fought together several more times, never speaking, and Jabari's will to continue was astonishing. Just as Tau wondered how much more Jabari could take, he went into Isihogo and did not find him there.

Tau fought and died for another two spans, and when he had nothing left to give, he floundered back to his tent, collapsed on his bedroll, and told himself that he would do the same the next night, to see if Jabari would be there.

The following evening, as Tau and his fighters gathered at the far edge of their ever-growing camp of Indlovu, Ihashe, and Ihagu, Priestess Hafsa came running over.

"You have to stop him," she said.

"Who?" Tau asked.

She didn't speak. She pointed.

In the distance and the dark, a burned and bandaged Jabari shuffled toward them.

"Jabari?" Tau asked the man shambling over, as if it could be anyone else in the bloodstained bandages.

"Goddess wept," said Thandi.

"Make him go back to the palanquin," said the priestess. "He won't listen to me and threatens anyone who tries to stop him."

Tau's shock had been so great that he hadn't noticed the naked bronze Jabari had in his right hand. "Priestess, he can barely stand. You're telling me no one could stop him?"

Hafsa spoke quietly. "No one will go near him."

Tau looked at her and then to his friend. "Jabari," he called. "Are you demon-haunted? What are you doing?"

The Petty Noble lurched over. He had on loose-fitting pants, Ihashe grays that had been cut away just above the knees, but wore no shirt. It wasn't needed. His torso and arms were covered in bandages, and on his shoulders he had a hooded cloak. The hood was up, hiding much of his face in shadows, and though it hurt Tau to admit it, he was thankful for that mercy.

Jabari's face was bandaged, but the walk over had caused several of the coverings to move and slip, and the things Tau saw underneath...

Tau crossed the remaining distance between them. "What are you doing?"

Jabari lilted to and fro, as he tried to stand steady. "Isihogo," he said, the word hard to understand coming from his ruined throat. He moved past Tau, and gurgling in pain, he bent over, putting his hands on the ground so he was on all fours. That done, he slid one foot forward and lowered himself onto his ass, a sudden cry escaping him as he did.

It looked everything other than easy, but he'd done it. Jabari was sitting in the circle with the rest of Tau's fighters.

"Tell him to go back where he belongs," Hafsa said.

Feeling his eyes grow wet, Tau went to join his sisters and brothers. "Leave us, Priestess," he said. "My brother is where he belongs."

The first time in the mists, on the night Jabari walked to their circle, Tau's fighters held the demons at bay long enough for him to see Thandi's shroud thin. To do it, the seven of them fought like they were Goddess blessed, and chasing the thought away as quick as it came, Tau wondered if something extra did guide their swords that night.

He didn't believe it, not really. But seeing Yaw and Themba fight with the desperation of the damned and Auset and Ramia moving through mist and demons like dancers following practiced steps made him proud enough to credit even the divine. He watched them with as much awe as he held for Uduak, the group's heart and hammer, who, roaring his fury, smashed through any demon foolish enough to come within his reach.

And, last to fall, as had become tradition, was Jabari Onai. In Uhmlaba, his birth marked him a Petty Noble, the blood moving through his veins too weak to be enraged, but in the underworld he fought as hard as any Ingonyama, and the Petty Noble was the most dangerous of the fighters Tau trained.

That first fight of the night, Jabari died on the barbs of a demon that towered over him. It had run him through and Jabari's mouth filled with blood as he cut at the creature with swing after swing of his sword. The beast ignored his weakening attacks, snarling and baring yellowed tusks at him. Jabari, his body dying, dropped the sword he was holding, and, hands free, he rammed his thumbs knuckle-deep into the thing's eyes.

Throwing its head back, the demon roared in pain, and Jabari began to laugh. It was a hacking cough of a thing, and he barked it in the face of the demon that had killed him.

"I'll be back. I'll keep coming back," he swore to the blinded beast, speaking around the blood that poured from his mouth before he died.

Tau had disabled two of the three demons facing him by then and had enough time to see that the towering tusked thing was coming for him. He looked back at Thandi, seeing her shroud shimmer and fail, noting the surprise on her face when she realized how long they'd held the circle. Then, before her golden glow could call more attention to itself, she left the underworld.

Twirling his black blades one way and turning on his heel in the opposite direction, Tau watched and listened as the creations of corruption and evil closed in on him from all sides. There were too many and he wouldn't last long, but his fighters had achieved more than their goal, and selecting the tusked one as his first target, Tau intended to celebrate before he suffered.

After that, Jabari walked to the circle for each night's training. He was stiff, moving like a man held up by wires of too-thick bronze and prone to crying out in pain without apparent cause, but he could stand, sit, and walk, which was more than Tau could have imagined after first seeing the damage the dragon's fire had done to his friend.

Hafsa, the priestess, told Tau that Jabari refused to let himself be carried in the palanquin and that she was worried he was pushing himself too hard. She worried his body was dying. She'd seen it before, she said. It often began with the body no longer able to perceive the pain it was in. That was, she argued, the only way that someone in his condition could be doing what he did.

Tau knew it wasn't the only way, but Hafsa had never seen Jabari in Isihogo. If she had, she might understand that, though the mind is chained to the body, it is not the body.

She couldn't understand a person doing as Jabari did, unless their pain was muted, but Jabari's pain was still there. He thrived not because his pain was gone, but because he had found a way to use it against the forces that were trying to break him.

Tau wondered if that was part of what it took to survive the underworld. He wondered if those who could stand Isihogo's privations were the same ones who had something to claim on the other side of the suffering it heaped upon them. He was still wondering it when he walked into the queen's tent to sit by her fire and learn how Queen Taifa Omehia and her Shadow Council had changed the course of life for every living Omehi woman and man.

OSONTON

It was another cold night, the third in a row, and after the diffi-cult day, Tau was glad the queen had the fire in her tent burning high. It crackled and hissed pleasantly, but also sounded too much like the noises the inkokeli from the fief they'd visited that after-noon had made when trying to breathe through the nose that Tau had broken for him.

The fief's umbusi had resisted the queen's request for her Ihagu, and when Tau stepped up to take command of the scale, the umbu-si's inkokeli, a Petty Noble, stepped up to Tau. They argued a little, and then Tau became impatient and pushed past the man. Taking it as an insult, the Petty Noble went for his blade, and Tau went for his, whipping his sword pommel into the Noble's nose and explod-ing it across his face. No one said much after that, and the umbusi's Ihagu joined the rest of the queen's growing army.

In the tent that night, Tsiora asked Tau to sit next to her so she wouldn't have to shout over the noise of the fire. He wasn't used to being so close to her but didn't mind because he never liked sitting with his back to an entrance. Still, it was strange to be so near her. It made him notice things he wouldn't have otherwise.

Her eyelashes, for instance, were surprisingly long, and the lines in her palms matched the skin there, making them almost invisible.

She also breathed with her chest more than her stomach and that made the small dip in her neck, the one sitting between her shoulder bones, rise and fall like a softer kind of heartbeat.

"Is it the necklace?" she asked, startling him.

"My queen?"

"You're looking at my necklace."

He was surprised to see that she was indeed wearing one. It was gold and ended in a wooden circle that had a woman's face carved into it, though she didn't look like anyone he'd ever seen in person. The face was too angular and its features were sharper than would have been typical on an Omehi.

"Yes, the necklace," Tau said. "The Goddess's face."

"A sign of our faith," Tsiora said.

"I'm used to seeing them on the Sah."

"A lot of Gifted wear them too."

"Yours...looks different," he said. "The wood, is it Osonton?"

"It is."

Tau looked up at his queen. "I've rarely seen anything so beautiful."

She took a breath when he said it, making the dip at the base of her neck dive, and then, as if she didn't know she was doing it, she reached up to touch the necklace. "Our mother gave it to us and her mother to her, and on and on."

Tau smiled. "I sometimes forget."

"What do you forget?"

"That you're descended from the same people in the stories you're telling me, that Queen Taifa's and Champion Tsiory's blood flows in your veins."

"We sometimes wish we could forget," she said.

Tau worried he'd said something wrong. "If you'd like to rest tonight instead of doing this, I could go..."

"No, we'd like you to stay, if you don't mind."

"I don't," Tau admitted. "I've been thinking about where we stopped and I want to go further."

Her eyes seemed to twinkle, but it had to be the firelight reflecting in them. "Do you?" she asked.

"I do," he said. "I know the Omehi left Osonte. I know we built ships and sailed the Roar, but what exactly did the Shadow Council push through with their voting? What did they vote for?"

Tsiora turned wistful. "Sometimes I wish I had happier stories to share, but this one will have to do," she said. "With the votes from the Shadow Council, Taifa Omehia was declared a Dragon Queen. They voted to hand her absolute power."

Tau chewed his lip. Voting to make Taifa a Dragon Queen hadn't been one of his guesses. "Why not simply win the vote to escape Osonte? Wouldn't that have been enough?" he asked.

"She didn't want to just flee. She wanted the power to change Omehi and Noble culture. She wanted to make her people strong enough to return to Osonte and stop the Cull. So, she became a Dragon Queen and that gave her the power to do what she wanted, but on Xidda, she lost something she needed."

Tau knew what was coming next. Any daughter or son of the Omehi knew what came next.

"On Xidda's white shores, Taifa watched her love, Champion Tsiory, fall. Yes, our beginnings here were soaked in blood, but perhaps there could have been an understanding with the Xiddeen, if only they hadn't killed him."

"Taifa turned to vengeance," Tau said.

"Taifa turned to slaughter," Tsiora said, touching her necklace. "She burned the beach and every Xiddeen on it to blackened glass, and in the season following our landfall, she called the dragons so often we lost every second Gifted we had.

"Queen Taifa Omehia found us a new world but couldn't escape the old one, and we fought the Xiddeen as hard as we'd fought the Cull. In those early days, when the skies rained fire, the people of this land died in the thousands, and desperate to stop the carnage, the Xiddeen sent messengers with gifts, overtures, and foreign words of peace. The Dragon Queen returned their messengers to them one limb at a time.

"But our brutality wasn't enough. We couldn't win, not without more Gifted, and as our losses to the Xiddeen increased, tragedy struck.

"The next Hoard was a season in which one in four starved and the Nobles began to whisper that Queen Taifa was leading the Omehi to another defeat. So, using the ire of starving people, they risked an attempt to depose her.

"They named her bloodthirsty, unfit to rule, and to appease those they'd taken to calling Lessers, they put Taifa's young daughter on the throne in her place."

"History shapes itself a circle," Tau said. "They wanted control of the queendom, and as was done to Taifa, they made a figurehead of her child."

"They thought this time it would be different," Tsiora said. "They thought Taifa's daughter was giftless. You see, the Nobles still needed to present an Omehi queen to their people. We were the dragon callers, the first Enragers, and the idea of us was what held our two peoples together.

"However, they'd never wanted and no longer needed their queen to have the power to bend the wills of men or bring down black death from above, and so they sought to weed the Goddess's power from the Omehia family line."

"But . . . you're gifted," Tau said.

"Yes, us, and all the queens before us. The Shadow Council protected the daughters of Queen Taifa's line across the generations, lying for us, training us, and preparing us. They've done it for every gifted princess."

Tau leaned back, taking in the secret's scope. "Did the child's mother . . . did Queen Taifa know that her daughter was gifted?"

"She planned the deception. The Goddess told Taifa that she'd be betrayed."

"The Goddess told her?" Tau said, thinking Shadow Council spies the more likely source of information about an impending betrayal.

"She did."

"And knowing the betrayal was coming, Queen Taifa let it happen?"

"It was necessary. She knew that. Her actions led to today, and in the tomorrows to come, they'll lead us home."

Tau wasn't about to give much weight to promised tomorrows. "What happened to Taifa?" he asked.

"They made an example of her," Tsiora said. "They made the price of ruling without Noble sanction as costly and as plain as they could."

As she was saying it, Tau realized he didn't want to know. He was speaking with Taifa's descendent, and it was too easy to picture Tsiora in her forebear's place, but he didn't want to do that. He didn't want to imagine what the Royal Nobles and Abasi Odili would do to his queen, if they lost the battle for Palm City.

"They eviscerated her," Tsiora said, unintentional in her lack of mercy. "It's where the tradition for the execution comes from."

"I see."

"Tau," she said, using his first name, "we are part of an unbroken line of Gifted that stretches back to the very first Omehi queen. Our kind was birthed on Osonte, and now it is time for us to go home."

"Go home? Why? Why now?" he asked. "Why does any of this need to happen now?"

"Because of my sister," Tsiora said.

THRONE

In the last fief they had to visit before returning to Citadel City, the umbusi made a terrible mistake. With the gates to her keep closed and bolted, the umbusi of fief Luapula stood on top of her keep's walls with helmeted and armed Ihagu lined up on either side of her, refusing the queen entry.

Nyah, riding up to the gates with Tau, addressed the umbusi from horseback. "In Queen Tsiora's name, I demand that you open these—"

"The queen, Queen Esi," the umbusi shouted down at them, "sits on her throne in Palm and makes no demands of me."

The umbusi's words made the central vein on Nyah's forehead stand out like a worm about to break ground.

"What did you say?" the vizier asked through gritted teeth.

"You heard me, you black-robed inyoka," the umbusi said. "The queen is in Palm City and I recognize no pretenders. Leave my fief."

It was a bad start. No denying that, and all things considered, Tau was surprised they hadn't encountered such recalcitrance before. Indeed, the more he thought about it, the more he wished they hadn't sent almost all the Ihashe and Ihagu they'd commandeered from the other fiefs to Citadel City.

He understood why they'd done it. They needed to give the men into Hadith's care as soon as possible so he could put them into scales and claws, assign inkokeli to each, outfit them, organize them, and otherwise prepare them for the upcoming assault. It made sense, but as he stood in front of a keep's closed gates and high walls, the sense of it didn't help much.

"What now?" Tau whispered to Nyah.

She didn't answer him, opting to call out to the umbusi instead. "This is your last warning. Open the gates while you still can."

"Fellate a scorpion's sting, you wingless kudliwe!" the umbusi shouted.

Tau tucked that one away for safekeeping. He'd trained among initiates, full-bloods, and Proven for an entire cycle and had never heard its like before.

Nyah, less amused, yanked on her horse's head straps, turning it back the way they'd come. Then, looking over her shoulder to the umbusi's Ihagu, she said, "Let none of you say she was not warned!" before riding off.

Tau considered saying something, anything, to try to convince the umbusi to listen to reason.

"Look," the umbusi said, raising the pitch of her voice to sound as if she spoke to a child, "the false queen dresses her Drudge in the armor of champions."

Tau shrugged and turned Fury back toward camp. Some people, he thought, can't be convinced by words alone.

It didn't take them long to come up with a plan to remove the rebellious umbusi from power. They based it on how they intended to attack and take Palm City. Kellan, leading the fighting men of their camp and with Gifted Thandi at his side, marched to the front gates of the keep. The queen remained near the rear with Nyah, protected and safe, though her champion and handmaidens were not with her.

Tau, the handmaidens, Uduak, Yaw, Themba, and even Jabari, who, without words, had made it clear he would not be left behind, had circled the keep and were standing in the shadows of its rear walls. Up above, on the keep's ramparts, were eight or nine distracted Ihagu.

They were trying to find out what was happening out front and kept calling to their sword brothers farther down the wall for news.

The attack on fief Luapula was going to be a test, and if the six others with Tau didn't necessarily think of it like that, he did. He wanted to see how the time spent in Isihogo had changed them, if it had at all. And breaking into a well-guarded fief to capture an umbusi seemed as good a test as any.

Part of him, however, wished that Jabari hadn't insisted on coming. The other part hadn't been able to order Jabari to remain in the camp. Tau's friend had made so many strides over the days or, rather, nights, and Tau didn't want to separate Jabari from the rest of the unit. He didn't want Jabari to feel...less than.

He would watch him, though. Jabari's recovery was nothing short of miraculous, and even though he was still stiff, the Petty Noble was mobile and had his sword on his hip wherever he went.

"I'm really meant to just throw this rope up onto the rampart and hope the hook catches?" Themba whispered.

"It worked for the Indlovu when they attacked the Guardian Keep," Tau said.

"If memory serves, there were a few more of them then than us now."

"We're plenty," Uduak said, his rope and hook in hand.

"Won't they just cut the ropes and we'll fall?" Themba asked.

"It's can't be more than twelve strides high, coward," said Auset, "and they won't get all of us."

"I know exactly who they should get," Themba muttered.

"Enough," said Tau. "On Kellan's cue."

They waited a quarter span or so in the dark before the cue came, and even on the far side of the keep, they could hear Kellan's voice, deepened and augmented by Thandi's enraging.

"*Umbusi!*" he bellowed. "*Your queen demands these gates be opened.*"

As expected, the Ihagu above turned their backs on the area they were meant to be watching, and Tau knew they'd be staring across the keep in the direction of Kellan's voice, even though they had no chance of seeing him or anyone else beyond and below the keep's main gates.

"Throw ropes," Tau said to his fighters, and they did.

Everyone's hooks caught and Tau began to scramble up the wall with the rest.

"Hear that?" he heard a voice ask.

Tau was three steps from the top of the wall and looked up to see a helmeted head pop out and over the rampart.

"Cek!" he heard the man squeal before calling to the other Ihagu. "They're climbing the walls! They've got ropes with hooks."

Pulling himself up faster, Tau watched the rampart closely. He had no intention of losing fingers to an overzealous guard.

"Here! They're over here!" the same voice called as the same head popped back out over the wall.

The Ihagu had a sword in his hand this time and swung it at the nearest rope.

"No! No! Don't you—" Themba said as his rope was cut clear, dropping him back to the ground with a thud. "Nceku!"

Tau hauled himself over the rampart and onto the wall. Yaw, ever a quick one, was already there, and they were joined by Auset, Ramia, and a grumbling Uduak. The thinking was that they'd take the ramparts, secure them, and then help Jabari scale them.

"Put down your swords and no one will be hurt," Tau said to the Ihagu guarding the ramparts. "Your umbusi is not following a lawful command from her queen."

"Ahhhhhhh!" screamed the Ihagu who had cut Themba's rope as he ran at Yaw. He swung at Yaw hard enough to kill him, but Yaw stepped out of range and let the man spin himself in a circle so he could kick him in the ass and send him crashing to the rampart's floor.

The other Ihagu—there were actually nine others—drew their blades.

"There's no need for bloodshed," Tau said, trying again.

"We put these down, you kill us," said one of the Ihagu.

"No, that's not true."

"It is," he said. "We have to fight for our umbusi. You're a Lesser, even if you dress like that. You know it's true. We put down our swords and abandon our duty and you and your queen will kill us for failing our Noble."

"We're not here to kill—"

One of the smaller Ihagu ran forward, hoping to surprise them. Two others, understanding the intent of the first, came with him. Yaw cracked the small one in the temple and he went down. Auset cut the other from shoulder to elbow with one dirk and was about to stab him with the other.

"Auset!" Tau called, and she turned her attack, slamming the guard in the gut with the flat of her blade and doubling him over.

The last man skidded to a stop and stared at Ramia.

"You...you're a woman," he said.

Ramia, dirks in hand, seemed to weigh the assertion. "Yes," she said finally, "a woman."

"What's going on up there?" shouted Themba.

Tau leaned over the wall and saw that Themba was halfway up and climbing Auset's rope.

"We're talking," Tau said.

"It sounds like fighting," Themba said.

"Nothing happening up here could be called fighting, fool," Auset said.

Tau looked past Themba and to Jabari. The Petty Noble had on Ihashe grays a size too large for him and a hooded cloak with the hood up. The oversized grays helped him move without the fabric tugging at his burns, and the hooded cloak was to hide his face.

"We're almost done, Jabari," Tau called, thinking he could see him nod, though in the dark it was too hard to be sure.

By then, Themba had made it up and Tau turned back to the Ihagu. "We're not here to kill you."

"Why are you here?" the same Ihagu as before said.

"There are traitors in Palm City. We need to stop them. We need Ihagu and Ihashe to help us take the city back."

"So, we'll die there instead of here. That's it?"

Tau made to speak and found he didn't have much to say.

"What happens if I say I don't want to fight for a city I've never seen?" the Ihagu asked.

Auset was moving toward the man.

"Hold, Auset," Tau said. "They'll put down their swords."

The Ihagu gripped his blade more tightly. "Didn't say I would."

"If you don't, you die tonight," Tau told him.

The man locked eyes with Tau, searching for something. He must have found it because he lowered his eyes, dropped his sword, and gestured for the others to do the same.

"You know, the umbusi was wrong," he said, continuing to avoid Tau's gaze. "She called you a Drudge. You're not, though." He jerked his thumb toward the part of the keep where the Nobles slept. "You've more in common with them."

The rest was easy. They helped Jabari up the wall, moving him slowly. They marched the Ihagu they'd disarmed down the ramparts and through the keep, opening the main gates for Kellan, Thandi, Nyah, the queen, and as many soldiers as the keep could hold.

Then they went to the umbusi's reception hall, Tau's seven, Kellan, Thandi, Nyah, and the queen. They found the umbusi there, on a chair on a dais.

"You denied us," Tsiora said, and to the umbusi's credit, she didn't wither beneath the queen's stare.

"You're not my queen," the umbusi said. "I accept no queen with gifts set to curse us and carry us down the path toward destruction."

"Is this the message Odili is sending to turn you against us now?"

"Don't change the topic," the umbusi asked. "Is it true? Are you gifted?"

"All true queens of the Omehi are gifted."

The umbusi laughed. "And, queen with gifts, is there any other title to which you lay claim?"

It was a silly game, Tau thought. A trap made of words among people for whom words held more value than deeds.

Tsiora lifted her chin. "We are a Dragon Queen," she said.

"That's all you needed to say," the umbusi told her as three full-blooded Indlovu burst into the room through a door just behind the umbusi's dais.

Shouting, the three men ran for the queen, swords out and ready. Without hesitation, Auset and Ramia moved to protect Tsiora.

"Char and ashes!" cursed Themba, reaching for his sword.

Yaw, Uduak, and Kellan were too far back to help.

"Out of the way, Goddess damn you!" It was Nyah. She was standing next to Thandi, and both women had their hands up and aimed, ready to fire off waves of enervating energy, but Tau was in the way, Jabari too, and the biggest full-blood, holding a shield and wearing armor, had come within striking distance.

The Noble slashed down at Tau with a sword so thick Tau wasn't sure he'd have been able to lift it, and as the blade cut a bright path for his skull, he flowed out and away, drawing his strong-side sword from its scabbard and across the man's armored chest. A season ago, a bronze blade would have met bronze plates and neither would have yielded, but Tau's sword was made of dragon scale and it split the Noble's leather armor, shrieking as it carved through the bronze beneath.

Clutching at his chest, the Indlovu wheeled back and glanced down at a hand already slick with blood. He grimaced, the pain of the cut evident, and intending to swing again, he brought his blade up. Intent was as far as he got.

Tau drew his weak-side sword and punched it into the man's stomach. The dragon scale missed the man's armored plates and was indifferent to the leather, meat, and muscle in its path. It went through the Noble like a shiver and he was dead before he could fall.

Tau spun to deal with the other two and bore witness to a miracle.

Jabari, his hood fallen back, revealing the mass of ruined skin upon his scalp and neck, was entangled with one of the Indlovu. Tau took a step to help and saw the Indlovu drop to his knees, his throat cut from shoulder to shoulder. The last full-blood still alive was yelling something, spittle flying from his mouth as he flew at Jabari.

Jabari pushed off the man he'd killed and bared teeth at the Indlovu coming to finish him, and they crossed blades.

"Out of the way!" shouted Nyah, but Tau heard it as a whisper. His attention, the whole of it, was on the fight.

The Indlovu's superior strength was apparent. Jabari had blocked correctly, but his blade was bashed aside. The full-blood, true to his training, carried his blocked attack through its natural length, then reversed his sword's direction, swinging it back for Jabari's core. Jabari reacted as he would have in the mists. He turned sideways, giving less of a target to his opponent, and the sword passed him by, a fingerspan from giving his insides a taste of open air. He was slower in Uhmlaba, and with each movement he scrunched up his bandaged face, showing his teeth beneath seared-away lips.

Tau thought it was a snarl or Jabari showing bloodlust. He realized it was Jabari fighting against agony, and he went to put an end to the match. The Indlovu saw Tau coming, and though he couldn't really manage it, he tried to keep Tau and Jabari between himself and Nyah and Thandi, who were ready to enervate him.

Jabari saw Tau coming too and waved him off.

"I'll finish it," Tau said.

Jabari shook his head.

"I'll finish it," Tau said again.

Jabari, with his free hand, thumped his chest with an open palm. Each hit hurt. Tau could see it, and he could see that Jabari didn't care. His friend was telling him to stay back. His friend was telling him that he would do this thing himself.

"Champion, this is no game," Nyah said.

"Does anyone look like they're playing, Vizier?" Tau asked, sheathing his swords.

The full-blood's eyes darted from Tau to Nyah to Jabari, and unwilling to test the good fortune keeping his odds fair, he attacked with an overhead swing. The swing was ungainly, impatient. It left him open. He couldn't have thought it mattered. He was fighting a Petty Noble so badly burned it was a wonder Jabari could stand. The Indlovu's assumption, blind to the facts facing him, was a fatal mistake.

Jabari was not just standing; he was fighting. That alone should have told the Indlovu that he was dealing with something he didn't understand, but it was already too late.

Moving like a creature held up by wires, Jabari jerked to the side of the Indlovu's killing blow and stepped forward, putting himself beside the full-blood. The Indlovu jerked his head, striving to keep his opponent in sight, and had just enough time to look into Jabari's bloodshot eyes before the Petty Noble's sword knifed into his side and gutted him.

The fight was over and the full-blood sagged, sighing like a farm-hand taking a seat at the end of a long day. His eyes fluttered, closing down, and Jabari ripped his blade free, letting the man take his rest.

Tau heard sobbing. It was the umbusi. She was standing, trembling.

"My sons," she said. "My boys." Her face was wet.

"Traitor," Nyah called her.

"You killed my boys!" The umbusi's rage was impotent, but frightening in its intensity.

It didn't mean much that Tau was no longer a child. His reaction to seeing a Noblewoman so incensed was instinctive. Lessers died when Nobles got that way.

Nyah turned to Tsiora, who'd been silent all the while.

"The punishment for treason is death," the queen said. "No one, Lesser or Noble, stands beyond reach of this edict. No one."

Her pronouncement made, Tsiora walked away with Auset and Ramia shadowing her.

"Tie the umbusi to the chair," Nyah said. "Tie her to it and get everyone out of the keep."

"Ukufa take you and everything you love, you silver-hearted wretch!" the umbusi said.

"Get everyone out...why?" Tau asked.

"We're going to burn it," Nyah said.

"Vizier...," Kellan said.

"Treason means death," Nyah said, the last word coming out breathless. "Tie her to the chair and burn this keep to the ground. Let the umbusi join her sons to find what mercy the Goddess wills. Let the story of what happened here be a warning to any who think to refuse their queen."

The umbusi began moving and Tau readied for more violence, but she went to the closest of the slain Indlovu and knelt beside him, hands hovering over the dead man as if she feared she might disturb him. Moving around her, Themba went to the door from which her sons had come and closed it, blocking the room's only other exit.

"I won't help," Tau said to Nyah as he waved Themba back. "Neither will my fighters."

Nyah didn't force it. "Get more soldiers in here," she said to Thandi. "Have them carry out my orders."

Crestfallen, Thandi nodded and left.

"Champion," Nyah said, looking to the three dead Indlovu and the weeping umbusi, "you and your fighters have already helped."

GIFTLESS

Tau walked into the queen's tent and noticed that there was no fire in the pit. It made sense. The fire raging outside, destroying what little was left of the umbusi's keep, burned hot enough.

The decision to set the keep on fire still didn't sit well with Tau. He wasn't foolish. He knew they couldn't allow open rebellion from Nobles like Luapula's umbusi. Doing so was the same as courting disaster, but the course they'd taken, after already defeating her, felt more personal than political.

"In the morning, we begin the journey back to Citadel City," the queen said.

"Yes," he said.

She'd changed clothes since he'd last seen her. Possibly to avoid the smoke's smell. If so, the new clothes wouldn't help. The stink of what they'd done clung to the skin.

"We imagine that this will be our last night of stories," Tsiora said.

"Yes." They'd beaten an opponent that night. They'd won. He didn't feel victorious.

"Where were we, then?" She was distracted. Perhaps she was asking herself some of the same questions he had.

"Princess Esi," Tau said, reminding her.

"Our sister."

He said nothing.

"We were born together. Most can't tell us apart. Our bodies, our spirits, they were fashioned from the same instance of the Goddess's will, and our births are a sign, because Esi is giftless," she said without inflection. "We were both tested by the Shadow Council, and when they believed Esi to be without gifts, she was tested over and over again." There was strain in her voice. "They had to be sure, Tau. They did what needed to be done to be sure, and Esi is the Goddess's warning that, even in the Omehia line, gifts can thin, they can fade, and they will vanish."

Tau didn't think he was going to like where this was going. "The Shadow Council taught you to use your gifts when you were still a girl, and that means they tested you when you were children. How many times did they send Esi to Isihogo?"

"It has fallen to us to act," Tsiora said, ignoring the question. "We must return the Chosen to their rightful place. If we don't do it, it'll be too late. It's why we wanted peace on Xidda."

"The Goddess didn't send us here to fight the Xiddeen. She sent us here so that we could fight with them against the Cull. Tau, the Xiddeen must be convinced that if the Cull aren't stopped, they'll unleash Ukufa on the world, and when they do that, we all die."

Tau searched her face, finding nothing but sincerity. To her it was true. If she failed to bring the Omehi back to Osonte, the Cull would win and the races of man would be no more. She believed it like he believed the sun would rise in the morning.

"I see," he said, trying to have even a fraction of her faith, while wondering where women and men like him fit in.

Where did Lessers stand in a world where dragon callers, colossal warriors, and illusion-wielding tribespeople went to war against immortals? He couldn't do it. It didn't make sense to see things that way, given the life he'd lived.

The powerful, in Tau's experience, kept seeing the loss of their desires as being world ending without ever once stopping to realize that for people like him, every day held that potential already. Thandi's brother, Anya and Nkiru's family, Oyibo, the old Drudge, and Tau's own father, they'd attest to it, if the world hadn't already seen them burn.

He couldn't look at it in Tsiora's way, and knowing that, he moved them onto safer ground. "Before we do anything else, we need to take care of Palm City and Odili, neh?"

She nodded. "Those things first." She still seemed distracted, disturbed by what had happened that evening and, perhaps, the talk of her sister. "Are your fighters ready?"

"They're ready," he told her.

"Then let us end the story of our history and begin writing one for our future."

She rose and walked to the flaps of her tent. Tau followed her outside and into the evening's oppressive heat, made worse by the keep's still-burning slag and the sweating bodies of the women and men they'd displaced. The crowd was held back from the queen and from him by soldiers, and he tried not to look at them. They made him feel guilty.

He tried not to look at the keep either. It made him picture the umbusi's end, and he didn't want to do that. His mind conjured the images anyway.

The umbusi, he knew, would have been roped to that chair, the one that'd been a symbol of her power. She'd have screamed as smoke filled her lungs and heat bubbled her flesh, the fires consuming her sons' bodies before coming for her.

Tau shivered in the warmth. He'd experienced more horrors than any single lifetime could hold, yet the ones he could create in his head still had the power to turn his stomach.

"You're sure?" he asked Tsiora, uncertain if his concern was for the queen or himself. "You're sure you want to go to Isihogo tonight?"

Tsiora stopped and gazed out at the keep's remains, a wall collapsing in on itself as she watched, its adobe crumbling to dust. "We're sure," she said, her profile limned by the fire's light. "We need to see what your fighters can do."

TRIBUTE

Discounting the battle for Daba more than two cycles ago, Tau had never been with so many souls in Isihogo. His six fighters had surrounded Thandi, and off to the side and observing were Nyah and the queen. Even with so many souls in the underworld, Tau had a hard time keeping his eyes off Tsiora.

Not that he could see her. That wasn't it. It was her shroud. She was enveloped in a globe so dark he could have held his dragonscale swords up to it and they would have matched. The queen's shroud reflected no light whatsoever, and looking at her was disorienting. It made him feel like he was falling into something immeasurably vast.

"They've found us," she said.

Tau couldn't see her through the shroud, but he'd have recognized her voice anywhere, and heeding Tsiora's warning, he looked to the horizon. What little of it he could discern through the shifting mists seemed to tilt his head like he'd a belly full of gaum.

Goddess blessed, indeed, he thought of Tsiora as he blinked away afterimages of her shroud.

"There," said Uduak. The big man stood to Tau's right and was using his sword to point.

Tau saw it, a big one, walking on two legs. "Mine," he called, flexing the muscles on his wounded thigh by habit, though his body was whole in the underworld.

"Welcome to it," grumbled Themba from Uduak's far side.

"Shhh," Auset said, fingers flexing over the handles of her dirks.

Themba said something else, but Tau couldn't make it out over the howling winds. He did, however, hear Jabari hiss. His friend's throat, like his body, was whole in Isihogo. Jabari could speak there, but he'd been doing it less and less.

Following Jabari's gaze, Tau caught glimpses of a short but thickset demon stalking along the edges of the mist, moving back and forth, parallel to them. It loped along on four legs and had a mouth that took up most of its bulbous head, a mouth filled with teeth like glass shards.

"I am Omchi. I am Chosen." Tau heard the words from behind him, from the other side of the circle. "I am of the Goddess and for the Goddess. Her will is my destiny. Her grace is my salvation." Yaw was praying.

"Her grace is my salvation," echoed Ramia.

"Hold the circle," Tau said loudly enough for everyone to hear. "Stand firm. Remember, the women and men to your left, to your right, they're your sword sisters and brothers. Keep them safe and they'll do the same for you."

Uduak grunted and squared his shoulders.

"I'll do that for everyone 'cept Auset," Themba said with mock cheer.

"Maybe I kill you before the demons," Auset said right back.

"They come," Tau said, and the big one burst through the mists, running alongside the thing with the teeth like jagged glass.

Feet planted, Tau twirled his swords, loosening his wrists. He was ready. His fighters were ready.

"Her grace is my salvation!" It was Yaw, screaming loud enough to be heard above the winds, and as he blasted his twin swords into the big demon's hide, Tau wished his sword brother well.

The demon, long-limbed and quick, struck out at Tau with the speed of a thrown spear. It used claws and fists, lunging with mouth open to bite and rip, kicking with legs tipped with hooked nails as thick and almost as black as his swords. It fought him with the fury of a wildfire at full burn.

But Tau moved like the mists, sweeping in and cutting with harsh blows before billowing away. He tore at the creature, paring it down with cut after cut, and like a carver whittling wood, he left the thing twitching on the murk of Isihogo's ground bearing little resemblance to what it had once been.

"Hold the circle!" Tau yelled, chest heaving from the fight, eyes fever bright. They'd lost no one in the first charge, but the second was already upon them.

Ramia was first to fall, dead to a blow that opened her up from groin to chest. Yaw was next, though Tau didn't see it happen. Third to be cast out from the underworld was Themba. He died fighting back to back with Auset, who was quickly overwhelmed after he fell. Uduak, battling like he was demon-haunted, was the only fighter to give no ground at all, and achieving the near impossible, the big man pushed the demons back toward the mists, churning through their number like a scythe until he went too deep and was surrounded and pulled down.

Jabari, having downed three or four monsters by Tau's best guess, was last to fall. He lost his life to the four-legged demon and its pack. They slashed him to ribbons with their glass-shard teeth, but Jabari was silent to the end.

That left Tau, Thandi, Nyah, and the queen. Thandi's shroud failed and she vanished. Nyah's shroud was thin, evaporating, dew under the sun. The vizier took her leave.

The demons encircled Tau. He was cut and hurt, limping and tired. He spared the queen a glance. Her shroud was as deep a black as ever. He could not see her face and knew, anyway, that her eyes were on him.

Tau brought his mind back to the task at hand, and the crowd of demons pressing in at him recoiled. They weren't human, but the language of violence is universal and their actions spoke of grudging respect.

It was going to hurt, Tau knew. There were too many and they had not swarmed him. That meant they wanted it to go slow, his end... and with a last look to his queen, Champion Tau Solarin hefted his swords and charged the thickest mass of the demons.

Demons and men had a language in common, Tau thought, and he meant to have a pointed discussion.

"It'll work," Nyah said. "Goddess be praised, it'll work."

Coming back to himself, Tau saw that the rest of his fighters were still in various stages of distress. On shaky legs and laboring to ignore the pain in his poisoned thigh, he stood.

"It'll work," he said to Nyah as the muscles controlling his mouth came under his command in sections.

"From your lips to the Goddess's ears," the queen said. "With warriors bold enough to brave what you have, there's nothing that can't be done."

The queen was behind Tau, and he turned to her. She looked concerned for him, but when he gave her a shaky smile, she offered him one in return that was so full and free it made her face glow. The warmth of her expression, the affection in it, made Tau feel more whole than he had in forever. It was just a smile, but it helped him shake off the rest of the underworld and reminded him that there was something to celebrate.

They'd done it. They could give the Gifted more time in Isihogo than Odili's Gifted would have. They could win the battle for Palm City.

He felt his body tingle with the idea of what they'd accomplished, and if Tsiora had been anyone else but his queen, he'd have wrapped her up in a big hug and twirled her around. The moment was too big for just words or smiles. It called for more.

Uduak clapped Tau on his shoulder hard enough to make him stumble. "That was a circle," the big man said.

Tau's smile broke into a toothy grin. "Yes, that was definitely a circle." They'd done it.

"We held for long enough, neh?" Themba said, looking a bit gray. He'd probably spilled his dinner into the grass.

"We did," Tau said.

"And we would have held longer, if Auset hadn't needed me to sacrifice myself for her."

"Kudliwe, you fight like a drunk child," Auset said over her shoulder as she helped Ramia to her feet. She seemed set to say more, but the queen was coming and Auset held her tongue.

The queen went to stand beside Tau, looking at the rest of the seven. Everyone was on their feet, and though Tau didn't want to get ahead of himself, the pride he felt when glancing at the faces around him took him by surprise.

There was Jabari, standing tall and impossibly strong. There were Yaw, Themba, Auset, Ramia, and Uduak, each of them doing the same. Tau knew that traditionally a scale was fifty-four men, but tradition had never met fighters like the six with him that night.

Cool fingers brushed his wrist, startling him from his thoughts.

"My queen?" he said.

She let her hand remain on his wrist as she spoke. "You have done more than we could have expected. You have taken our faith and returned it alongside hope, and for this we offer a humble gift."

Nyah came forward carrying something long and heavy wrapped in a roll of skinned and cured leather. She placed it on the floor in front of Tau.

"Some of you already have this gift," the queen said, "and now it's time for the rest to receive them."

"My queen?" Tau asked.

"Open it, Champion," she said.

Tau bent down, unrolled the leather, and gasped.

Themba's reaction was less restrained. "Nceku!" he said.

"Goddess be praised," Yaw said, rubbing a hand over the sun-flaked skin on his shaved head.

"So black," Uduak offered. "Beautiful."

"Champion Solarin, Auset, Ramia," the queen said, "you already have such gifts, but..."

"They're perfect," Tau said. "I can't tell you how perfect."

He picked up the first guardian sword from the roll of leather and knew it was Themba's. It was longer than the average sword the Ihashe wielded and thicker.

Themba knew it was his too. He stepped forward, as reverential as Tau had ever seen him.

"I am yours, now and forever," Themba said when Tau placed the blade in his hands. "You brought me here, Champion Solarin. I'll not forget it."

The next weapon was Yaw's, and it was so slender it was almost invisible. It was a weapon built for a master of precision and speed.

Yaw bobbed his head to the queen and to Tau. "The Goddess is too kind to Her humble servant," he said, taking the sword in shaking hands.

The third guardian blade could only belong to one person. No one there but Uduak would have been capable of wielding it. It was massive.

Hanging back, the big man stared at it. "How?" he asked.

"How?" Tau asked.

"How can I be worthy?"

"Uduak, you've always been worthy," Tau said, and the big man came for his gift.

"Jabari," Tau called, lifting the last dragon-scale sword from the leather wrap as the man Tau had known since he was a child ambled over on legs too stiff to bend well. Jabari came for his sword in a broken gait, but his head was held high.

Tau offered him the blade. It was an archetypal guardian sword and the dragon scale had been shaped to flawlessness. Jabari's sword was the type given to the greatest of the great Ingonyama.

Bowing his head, Jabari eased his way to his knees in front of the queen and Tau.

"Rise, Jabari Onai," the queen said. "Rise as a member of Scale Solarin."

That did it, and Tau felt water in his eyes. "My queen, if I may, there is another name."

"Is there?" she asked, eyes fixed on him.

He nodded.

"Tell it to us."

Tau looked to the two women and four men with whom he'd braved so much. He looked to the sisters and brothers who had followed him to death and beyond, and from his heart he spoke to them.

"Who I am, who we are, it began with an umqondisi. It began with Jayyed Ayim," he said. "His philosophies, his teachings, they brought us here. We are from him."

"You honor him, Tau Solarin," the queen said. "You honor him with this. Now speak it into existence. Speak it to the Goddess and the world. Tell them who you are."

"We are the Ayim," Tau said.

Yaw closed his eyes and lowered his head, overcome. Themba was grinning. Jabari, face hidden behind bandages, but eyes sharp, held himself at attention, and Ramia reached over to put an arm around her sister, holding Auset tight.

All that, and it was Uduak's words that broke through the shield behind which Tau had placed his emotions.

"Good name," he said in approval. "Good man."

Tau's tears spilled over and he closed his eyes, trying to keep himself together. It didn't work. Too much had been lost, too much sacrificed, and his shoulders shook as he wept.

With a kindness he didn't need to see to understand, he felt the queen's fingers intertwine with his, and holding his hand like that, she spoke.

"We welcome the Ayim," she said. "In the Goddess's name, we welcome you."

CHAPTER NINE

KEREM

A few days later, at the head of their modest host, Tau rode through the gates of Citadel City with Tsiora. The paths were lined with residents and soldiers cheering for their queen, greeting her like the civil war was already won.

The celebration, however, was not universal. As they rode the paths to the keep, Tau saw dour looks on many Noble faces. He didn't need to wonder why. No doubt the news about the fate of Luapula's umbusi and the burning of her keep had reached the city before they had.

Tau tried to shake away his worries. They'd not made friends in their travels, but the queen had her army, and the ecstatic members of the crowd, tossing talaki-dyed sand to celebrate them, were hard to ignore.

The sand, royal purple in color, dazzled the eye as it was thrown into the air in waves that crested in pace with the procession, and playing her part, Tsiora smiled and waved at the people. Tau found it odd to see the same woman, the one who had so captivated Jabari when she'd ridden into Kerem, from the perspective of his new role.

Her smile was still beautiful, no one living or dead could deny it, but Tau knew that this was her public face. It was the mask she wore when she needed to be seen as Queen Tsiora Omehia, first among the Chosen, and though he'd never think to call the queen a friend, he had spent more time with her. He knew the way she smiled around people with whom she felt safe.

That smile, the one that came from deep inside her, would first show at the edges of her lips, and they'd tremble like she was trying to stay serious. More often than not, the trembles increased, then gave way, and Tsiora would brighten everything around her with a smile that touched her eyes, crinkled her nose, and dimpled her cheeks.

He'd seen her smile like that in her tent amid unforgettable stories, the smell of honeyed wood crackling in the fire pit, and the choral sounds of male drum bugs. Those had been moments of calm, moments to hold close, and though Tau told himself it was well past time to be on the path to Palm, it didn't make him happy to think that those moments might be gone for good.

"Champion! Champion!"

A group of Lesser women were yelling his title, seeking his attention, and feeling a fool, he waved to them. Collectively, inexplicably, the women lost their minds, either reeling as if about to faint or screaming. One even raised her voice in the ululating cry often reserved as a greeting for couples who'd just sworn their marriage oaths.

Uncomfortable, he turned away, happening to catch the queen's look. Her almond-shaped eyes, the same brown as a mountain butterfly's wingtips, sparkled in the sunlight, and she looked like she was on the edge of laughter. It made his face grow hot.

Grumbling to himself, Tau shifted in his saddle and focused his attention on the back of Fury's head, choosing to count the hairs the horse had there.

It was easy for her, he thought, glancing at Tsiora again. She was born to this, raised for it, and looked the part of a story princess. He watched her smile and wave, and he tracked the recipients of her grace. Women or men, Noble or Lesser, it didn't matter. She drew them in and held them captive, making the men feel more handsome and bolder and the women wiser and more powerful. Tsiora enriched everyone with just a look, and Tau knew firsthand how beggared they'd feel by her absence.

Tau trained to fight. Tsiora trained to do this. It had to be why he missed the nights in her tent. He'd been under the spell of a lifetime of training that had taught Tsiora to be something for everyone. To him she offered peace, and in that tent, even if only for a span or two, he could forget the world with all its pain and strife.

He shook his head, hoping to knock loose such foolish wistfulness. Those nights and the peace they'd provided were never more than temporary. The world had too many people prospering from the pain and struggle of others to leave a man like him untouched.

And Tau had no intention of remaining a victim like the ones who closed their eyes to the whippings of their peers, thinking that because they were not yet the targets of the powerful, they would never be. The problem with feeling safe in a tent is that though it may hide the dangers outside, its canvas is no protection from them.

Fury tossed her head, and patting her neck, Tau liked to think it was her way of agreeing with him. They were close to the keep, and though the city had grown familiar, he considered how different everything looked. The past moons had seen Ihagu and Ihashe swell the city's numbers, filling it to capacity and returning Citadel City to numbers it had not seen in generations.

So many new bodies, coming so quickly, could have easily overwhelmed resources and resulted in starvation and disease, but Tau had seen the queen rise before dawn and go to her rest later each night in order to manage their mission to the fiefs as well as the efforts in Citadel City. She'd pored over reports and sent Hadith countless edifications, directing his efforts and ensuring that food, clothes, water, and other essential resources were carted into the city's walls in equal proportion to the newcomers.

The Dragon Queen and her grand general had prepared, outfitted, and organized her army so well that, in the days before battle, when everything was bloodless and defeat seemed impossible, Citadel City rumbled with chatter about the impending siege and inevitable capture of Palm.

"Citadel City welcomes Queen Tsiora Omehia," Hadith said, standing in the shadows of the open gates to the keep.

Tau stood in his stirrups, as he'd seen Champion Abshir Okar do what felt like a hundred lifetimes ago. "Queen Tsiora Omehia, second of her name, first among the Goddess's Chosen, and monarch of the Xiddan Peninsula, seeks the Guardian Keep's hospitality."

"I, Hadith Buhari, grand general to Queen Tsiora, would consider the Guardian Keep and Citadel City blessed by the Goddess, if my queen permitted me to wait upon her."

The queen's procession went on and inward as the crowd outside continued to cheer, and when the gates closed behind him, Tau breathed a sigh of relief and clambered down from Fury.

"Hadith," he called, "how long until we can—"

Hadith and Uduak were greeting each other with a warm embrace, and when they parted, Uduak tapped Hadith's face with an open palm. "Too long," he heard the big man say.

"At least it looks like they fed you well, and it seems that you have a new sword...," Hadith said, eyebrow raised at the black blade belted by Uduak's side. "Were you not sleeping, though? You look tired."

"Long nights," Uduak said. "Your chest?"

Hadith's mouth drew tight. "Long nights training?"

Uduak grunted.

"Is it worth the cost?" Hadith asked. "Will it make any difference?"

"It will," Tau said, interjecting. "It will make all the difference."

"Tau," Hadith said, reaching out to clasp his wrist.

"Hadith...Grand General Buhari."

Hadith blew air from his mouth. "Don't give me that."

"Why not? You've made it more than true. I heard a few of the reports coming in from the Edifiers. You've readied us an army."

"Well, something like that."

Tsiora walked up behind Tau. "General," she said.

Hadith bowed his head and bent his body a little, scrunching up his face as he did. "My queen."

"Rise, General. You're not well enough to go around bowing."

"Your Grace is kind."

"How do you fare?"

"I'll not win any footraces and need to be careful when I stretch in the mornings, but I'm better than I have any right to be."

She smiled at that. "We are glad to hear it. And our army? What of it?"

"When counting the soldiers with you today, we have the equivalent of four and a half dragons in Citadel City. There are eighty-six scales of Ihagu, twenty-eight of Ihashe, and we can field one scale and one unit of Indlovu. My queen," Hadith said, "your army is almost ready to march and it is ready to fight. The only trouble we seem to be having is coming from the—"

"Indlovu," the queen finished.

"The Indlovu," Hadith agreed. "If I can make use of Ingonyama Okar's services? I think the Indlovu will react more smoothly to him than me."

"You may have his services, General. However, we are tempted to deal with this another way. You are the one we appointed to lead our army and we are not amused by any resistance to that."

"Thank you, my queen. I appreciate the support, and in other circumstances, I might also recommend action in line with your thoughts. My worry, however, is over the small amount of time we have before we plan to march. Punishment may have less of a positive effect than simply giving the Indlovu what they want."

"And that is?" asked Tau.

"They want to still feel bigger than me," Hadith said.

"Kellan helps with that?"

"I'll let them feel as if Kellan leads them."

Tau shook his head. "Is this the nonsense you've been dealing with the whole time we've been gone?"

"This? This is nothing," Hadith said with a grin. "You should have seen the fuss that was made when I ordered all food given out equally to Nobles and Lessers. Some nights I wasn't sure I'd live to see the sun."

Tau was not amused. "You're laughing about treachery."

"The aches of growth, Tau. It's inevitable and expected. This is a lot of change in a very short time."

The vizier walked over with a heavy bag slung from her shoulder. "My queen, if I may..."

"Nyah, of course, see to Chibuye. She must miss you."

"I'll be there for the meeting after the midday meal," Nyah said. "It's just been so long, and truth told, I can't see Chibo soon enough."

The vizier's face looked . . . unarmed when she said her daughter's name. Tau didn't see her like that often.

"Maybe I'll even have enough time to unpack this bag," Nyah said. "I feel as if I've been living out of it for six seasons."

Tau saw the edges of Tsiora's lips begin to tremble, and he waited for it. She didn't disappoint, and her face broke into the warmest of smiles.

"Of course," the queen said. "We'll see you soon."

"Tau?" Hadith asked, leaning in.

"Neh?" Tau asked.

"Why have you got that silly smile on your face."

"What smile? I don't smile," Tau said, running a hand over his chin and cheeks. "I looked silly?"

"Like you'd forgotten where you put your swords or something."

Tau laid his hands on his hilts, making sure his blades were still there. "I'd never do that."

Chuckling to himself, Hadith walked over to the queen, who was watching Nyah leave. "My queen, though I won't impose on you for help with the Indlovu issue, there's another place where I would greatly appreciate your assistance," he said. "A few days ago, when the most recent food carts came in, we noticed that—"

"Queen Tsiora!" It was Gifted Thandi. She was with Kellan and practically running, making her Gifted robes swish back and forth like they were trying to dance with her. "Queen Tsiora, Vizier Nyah, you're needed."

Dropping her bag on the cobblestones, Nyah pivoted on her heel. "What's happened?"

"An edification from Kigambe," Thandi said.

Nyah strode over, the bag forgotten. "Saying what?"

Tau looked around them. Ihagu, Ihashe, and even Indlovu milled about, packing everything away, cleaning armor or weapons, and greeting friends they hadn't seen in more than a moon. It looked as tranquil as a courtyard filled with armed men ever could, and Tau had the awful feeling that it wasn't going to stay that way.

"It's a raid, a big one," Thandi said.

"On Kigambe?" Nyah asked.

"It won't be," Hadith said. "The walls are too big and the Xid-deen can't have the full strength of their old alliance. Even if they did, they couldn't sail and land enough ships to take Kigambe."

"It's not Kigambe," Thandi said, "and Umbusi Oghenekaro can't help. She sent all her soldiers here."

Tau's world was falling apart. "Who can't she help?" he asked, his flesh prickling.

"They're climbing the mountains," Thandi said. "They're making for—"

"Kerem," Tau finished. "It's Kana. He knows I'm called the Common of Kerem. He's coming for my home."

BOUND

"General Buhari, you told us the army was almost ready to march," the queen said. "Get them all the way ready."

Nyah moved very close to the queen. "Tsiora, we can't travel to the Southern Mountain Range and take a fight with Kana's forces. Don't let yourself get distracted, not now."

Tau saw the queen's eyes move between Nyah and him.

"How large is Kana's fighting force?" she asked Thandi.

It was like Daba, Tau thought, but this time the battle was coming for his home. This time the battle was coming for his mother, sister, and stepfather.

"It's almost too few," Hadith said, responding to whatever it was that Thandi had said. "Even though Kerem sent us their Ihagu, Kana will lose lives if he tries to take the fief with just a claw's worth of raiders. It has to mean that the Xiddeen alliance did crumble. It means Kana is here with the few fighters still willing to follow him."

"A claw of raiders," Nyah said. "We could wipe them out if our army were in Kerem, but it's not and we can't get it there in time."

"Two scales is enough," Hadith said to her. "With a hundred and eight soldiers, we can move quickly and Kana's raiders will outnumber us by less than fifty. We'll be too strong for him to face us."

"Why would Kana risk the few he has for vengeance on Tau?"

Kellan asked the group. "It makes no sense to make a sacrifice swing that won't end the fight even if it lands."

"I would do it," Tau said, seeing Kana's face the night that War-lord Achak died. "Were I Kana, I would go to Kerem and burn it to ash."

Hadith put a hand on Tau's shoulder but spoke to the queen. "It's not just vengeance. Kerem is a proving ground and if Kana razes the home of the man who killed the Xiddeen warlord, the victory will be a rallying cry." Hadith took a step toward the queen. "He's trying to re-form the Xiddeen alliance and this could give him the means to do it."

It was a convincing argument. It might even be true. Tau turned to the queen. She was already looking at him.

"No. We're not doing this," Nyah said. "Tsiora, tell them you're not doing this."

"Kana's ships were seen by Kigambe scouts?" Hadith asked.

Thandi's eyes slipped to Nyah first, but she answered him. "Yes, Grand General."

"Good. It means that Kana came ashore near the city. If we move fast, we can find the ships and sink them, preventing his escape."

"Kana will have scouts of his own," Kellan said. "When we attack the ships, they'll go to warn him. You'll be forcing him to flee through the mountains to get back to the Curse. He'll have to fight his way to freedom, killing hundreds more than he would if we let him have his boats."

Hadith shook his head. "He won't get the chance to hurt anyone else. We'll pincer Kana between us and the soldiers we'll call up from the Southern Fortress. We'll trap and finish him in the mountains."

"Do it, General," the queen said.

Tau released the breath he'd been holding.

"We're not thinking this through," said Nyah.

"Gifted Thandi," Tsiora said, "send an edification to the Southern Fortress. Tell the inkokeli that his Dragon Queen calls on him."

Thandi bowed her head.

"Hold, Thandi," Nyah said to the Gifted. "My queen, the for-tress's inkokeli is no friend of ours. What's to stop him from mimicking General Bisi and claiming that his men are duty bound to keep guard of the fortress? If he won't help and we sink Kana's boats, we'll be forcing the warlord's son to cut his way out of the peninsula. We could lose more than just Kerem."

Tsiora's mask was up and Tau had no idea what she was thinking.

"Queen Tsiora?" Nyah asked.

"Gifted Thandi," she said, "tell the inkokeli of the Southern Fortress that his queen rides to Kerem. Tell him she rides to battle and that he is honor bound to defend her." Her eyes found Tau's face. "Let's get you home," she said.

ALIKE

By nightfall they were marching away from Citadel City with three scales of the queen's army. Hadith was with them, and so was Kellan, though the grand general had wanted to leave him behind. Hadith had told Tau that he worried about the Nobles' loyalty and he thought leaving Kellan in the city with the Indlovu would help.

Kellan had been the one to solve the problem, explaining that they should take more than the two scales that were originally planned because the queen was going with them. To increase their numbers, he'd suggested they have all the Indlovu in Citadel City join them.

"Give us action and purpose," he'd argued. "Let us be part of the fight to which we have committed ourselves. You worry about loyalty? Let us prove ours."

"So be it, Inkokeli Okar," Hadith had told Kellan. "I'll admit, having all of you with us will make things easier, and the Ihashe and Ihagu we leave in the city should be able to keep things settled."

Tau had noted what went unsaid. If the Nobles living in Citadel City decided they were better off bowing to Queen Esi instead of Queen Tsiora, the city's Lessers, alongside the army stationed there, could make that decision a fatal one.

"If you and Kellan come with us, who leads the city?" Tau had asked.

"I wasn't idle the whole time you were gone," Hadith told him. "I've a decent chain of command in place."

Tau hadn't asked anything else. His only other concern was

getting to Kerem. So, for the second time that day, Queen Tsiora and Champion Solarin rode at the head of a small army. Beside them, riding together on a horse, were Nyah and her daughter. The vizier had been unwilling to leave her daughter again.

Behind them marched the Ayim, a few Gifted, the Indlovu, and two scales of Ihashe. They were moving fast, and the plan was to keep moving until they reached the beach where Kana had landed his ships.

It would be a long march, ending in a battle, and that came close to being too much to ask of their force. Still, Tau worried the extra efforts they were making wouldn't be enough, and he struggled against the urge to lean close to Fury's neck and let the horse run.

He wanted to leave everyone behind, race the sun to Kerem, and face the man who'd come to take vengeance on his home. He'd have done it too, if he thought his two swords enough to stop Kana and the Xiddeen with him. They weren't enough, though. Tau needed every single one of the people marching behind him, and that knowledge anchored him to their pace.

"We'll get there," Tsiora said, riding her horse closer to him.

Tau nodded, saying nothing, his worry battering him.

Two nights later, after marching almost nonstop, Tau was at the beach not far from the place where he'd nearly drowned as a boy, staring at the dark shapes of eight beached Xiddeen longships with Kellan and the Ayim.

"They burn no fires and light no torches," Kellan whispered. "Kana could have left ten or a hundred to guard his ships."

Tau, Kellan, and the Ayim had skulked through the dark and were lying on their bellies in the tall grass ringing the sands that led to the Roar.

"It doesn't matter," said Themba.

"What doesn't?" Kellan asked.

"Their numbers."

"Really?"

"However many they have, we'll come with our soldiers and do them."

"If they have any scouts out, and they should, we need to find them first. Champion, you agree?" Kellan asked.

Tau knew why they had to sink the ships, but he couldn't shake the feeling that they were wasting time.

"Whatever we do, let's do it quick," he said. "Kana will have gone with enough fighters to overwhelm Kerem's defenses, and they'll need our help."

Kellan nodded and went to work. "Yaw, you're the slipperiest of us. Head south, along the grass line, toward the mountains. The scouts are most likely to be positioned on the higher ground."

"Ramia, go with him, will you?" Tau asked. "There's not a scout alive who'd hear you coming."

The handmaiden gave him a slow blink, accepting the task.

"The rest of us should move north together," Kellan said. "We'll get as close to the ships as we can, and that means there's a decent chance we'll bump into more than just a few scouts." Kellan looked to Jabari. "You won't be able to keep up with us if we're crawling through the grasses, but that doesn't mean we don't need you. Return to camp and bring everyone here. By then we should have a better sense of what we face. If I give the signal, we charge the beach. Understand?"

Jabari, the hood of his cloak up, nodded without turning to face Kellan and skulked back through the grasses in that stiff-legged way he had.

"Goddess go with you all," Kellan said.

"May we walk ever in Her grace," Yaw said, before crawling off with Ramia.

"Let's go," Kellan said, leading the way.

As they crawled through the grasses, Tau kept thinking something wasn't right, and it bothered him that he couldn't figure out what that something was. He tried to recall everything he knew about the man he'd soon face. He'd known Kana only a short while, but the queen and Nyah often spoke about him. He was clever, they said, very much so.

"Found something," said Kellan.

"Something like what?" asked Themba.

"Three large bags. There's...food, clothes...a hatchet, water gourds. It's Xiddeen."

"Scouts?" Uduak asked.

"I don't think so," Kellan said. "Scouts wouldn't need this. There's enough here for days and days of ranging."

"Stay bright," Auset said. "The owners could be close."

Tau scanned the dark. "I don't see any. . . . "

Several strides away he saw a face in the grasses, and about to call out to the others, he reached for his swords; then it vanished.

"What is it?" asked Auset.

Tau stared at the spot where he'd seen it, the face. There was nothing, and his visions were becoming stranger. The face he'd seen had not been demonic. It had looked human.

"It's nothing, just the grass moving in the wind," he said. "Kellan, Uduak, Themba, take a bag each. If this is some kind of ration cache, we should deprive the Xiddeen of it."

"Done," Kellan said, keeping one of the bags and passing the other two to Uduak and Themba.

The task complete, the Greater Noble began to make his way forward once again, and doing his best to shake away the feeling that he was being watched, Tau returned to his earlier worries.

Yesterday, during the march, Hadith had been dictating notes to a Proven scribe. The notes held orders for the inkokeli in Citadel City. Tau knew that and none of the particulars. However, the vizier had been near them and the particulars impressed her.

"You remind me of Kana," she'd said.

"You know him well?" Hadith had asked.

"He was here to marry our queen. Do you think I let him have even one unwatched moment?"

"No, I don't imagine you did."

"Your minds work similarly," she'd said.

Kellan lifted a hand, calling them to a silent halt. He was peering into the dark, eyes squinted as if the issue was too much light rather than too little.

"Tau?" he whispered. "See anything?"

He kept whispering, and it was an unnecessary caution. This close to the Roar, the ocean's booms and crashes were enough to drown out anything less than a shout.

Tau scanned the beach, letting his gaze alight on longship after longship. They were built with unpainted Xiddan wood, reinforced heavily by hemp rope and what looked like leather hides, but that couldn't be right.

The Xiddeen would need to have access to the equivalent of hundreds of horses to have that much leather, and other than the few war lizards he'd seen them riding in the Fist, he'd heard no stories of them having animals. It occurred to him then that the ships might not be covered in animal hide. It could be human flesh instead.

The thought made his palms itch, and he had to forcibly cast it aside. He'd met Kana and fought others from the tribes. The Xiddeen were not like the Omehi, but they were also not like the stories he'd been told since he was a child. Given everything he'd been taught, it was easy to think they'd eat human flesh or skin one another for leather. It was easy to believe and extremely unlikely.

"Their oars are stowed and the sails have been lowered and wrapped around each ship's main mast," Tau told the others. "I don't see anyone."

"Hiding in the ships?" Uduak asked.

"Maybe."

"A trap, then," Kellan said.

Tau considered the possibility. "The trap is only worthwhile if Kana left enough fighters to successfully spring it."

"Well, that's exciting," Themba said.

Auset sucked her teeth. "He won't have left so many. Every raider he leaves with the boats is a raider he doesn't have for his attack on Kerem."

Tau was running short on patience. He wanted to pull his swords free and fight. "We don't have time for this."

"And, yet, we can't have our army charge into a trap," Kellan said.

Uduak elbowed Kellan in the shoulder. "Decoy."

"What?"

"Ride to the ships," Uduak told him, making the shape of a horse running with one hand. "Make them show themselves, then ride away."

"That could work," Kellan said, "but we'd have to go back to get a horse and—"

Tau stood up and walked out of the grasses, onto the sands of the beach.

"Champion? What's he doing?" Kellan asked the others.

"Here we go again," said Themba.

"Tau!" hissed Kellan.

Tau felt sick to his stomach. He'd known something was wrong and should have trusted himself. "Kana and Hadith...they think alike," he said over his shoulder, striding farther down the beach.

"I hate when he gets like this. What do we do?" Themba asked.

"Follow," said Uduak, and Tau heard the big man's steps behind him.

"They think alike," Tau said again, praying he was wrong.

"What does that mean?" Kellan had caught up. His sword was out and his head swiveled left and right, no doubt hoping to spot any movement among the ships while they still had the time and distance to run.

"Any fighters left with the ships would die, and knowing the ships were here, we had to come for them, to destroy them," Tau said. "It's what a good tactician would do and that's why it was Hadith's plan. Don't you see? We had to come for the ships."

"And?" Themba asked, jogging to catch up.

"And Kana knew it was what we'd do. He isn't going to sacrifice any fighters here," Tau said. "He's going to use every bit of strength he has to blaze and burn his way through Kerem. He's abandoned his ships because it was always his plan to fight his way back to Xiddeen territory through our mountains."

Tau was by the nearest longboat and kept his swords sheathed. He needed his hands because the side of the ship was too high for him to see over it, and though it could mean a spear through the eye or a hatchet in his skull, he jumped up, grabbing onto the boat's railing, pulling himself up and over.

Jumping into the belly of the longship, he spun round, the sick feeling in his stomach rising into his throat and mouth. "Empty...," he said.

"What?" Kellan asked from outside the boat.

"It's empty!"

"Check the others," Kellan ordered.

"They'll be empty," Tau said, not caring if they heard. "Kana took everyone. He's going to kill his way out of the peninsula."

BODIES

Fury's strides ate the ground beneath her as she coursed up the mountain's incline toward the plateau on which Keep Onai was built. Tau was bent over her neck, his eyes streaming tears caused by the wind rushing past him. He'd left the army behind. He couldn't stop Kana alone, but he couldn't wait either.

"Hyah, Fury! Hyah!"

She gave him more speed, enough to make it feel like they had taken flight, and they were on the last stretch of path before the keep would be in sight. He heard the clamor behind him and paid it no mind. Tsiora had sent Nyah chasing after him, and the vizier, a better rider than Tau, would have caught him already, if he weren't riding so recklessly.

"Hyah, Fury!"

The mountain air was filthy with thick haze that vibrated in the heat, and Tau didn't want to think what that might mean. He took the final bend in the path at speed, Fury's hooves kicking up dust behind them in a shower of sand and stone.

He had to be in time. He had to be. The keep came into view and the truth came with it.

Keep Onai was a smoldering ruin that smoked like a wet fire, and that wasn't nearly the worst of it. The women, men, and children of the keep had been placed on either side of the path leading to it. They were lying on their backs, each of them speared through the gut and held to the ground like a collection of beetles. Their hands had been tied to their neighbors', so they formed a chain, and every fourth or fifth person in the chain had had their arms cut off at the elbows. It was a broken chain of the dead. The reward for a queen's broken promises.

Before he could stop himself, Tau skimmed the faces. He saw Mistress Chione—the head handmaiden who'd often supervised Zuri's work—with blood spattered about her face. It looked like she'd taken a while to die, coughing up her last few breaths. Steps beyond her was Ekon. He'd become Aren's second-in-command, and then, after Aren was murdered, Umbusi Onai had probably made him the fief's inkokeli. If so, he hadn't held the position for long. Ekon was dead, and flies swarmed over his sun-bloated body, their maggots overflowing from his open mouth.

"No, no, no, nononono . . ."

Tau almost didn't recognize Ochieng. They'd beaten the keep guard's face so badly it didn't seem like any of the bones in it had held.

Tau threw his head back and yelled then. It startled Fury, she threatened to bolt, and he had to pull himself together enough to hold her steady.

"You're fine, girl," he said. "You're fine. . . ."

He heard the staccato drumming of Nyah's horse coming round the bend and drawing near. He heard the sudden dig of dirt and the animal's pained cry when the vizier jerked her horse to a halt.

"Goddess wept," he heard her say. "Come . . . come away, Tau."

Tau shook his head and urged Fury on.

"Tau . . ."

As much as it hurt, he studied the faces of the murdered. As much as it hurt, he looked left, then right, moving slowly down the path, looking for his family.

"Tau, don't go there," Nyah shouted to him. "It's what he wants. Don't look at it."

He was. He was looking, and hidden in the shadows of the keep's entrance were bodies piled up as if to serve as kindling for a bonfire, and in the middle of it all, a man had been lashed to an upright pole. His head was tied back and angled so it seemed he was admiring the thing he held in his upraised hand. He was naked and his belly had been opened up, spilling his entrails onto the bodies of those below him. He was dead, and that meant the Xiddeen had tied him such that his hand and the thing he held aloft would remain in place.

Tau dismounted, leaving Fury, and pulling his swords free of their scabbards, he stepped closer, peering into the shadows before wishing with every iota of his being that he hadn't.

"Makena?" he asked. "Makena!" he called as he ran his limping way toward his mother's husband, shouting the man's name as if the dead could hear.

He made it to the archway and into the shadows. He made it far enough to see what it was Makena held in his raised hand, and the bones went out of Tau. He collapsed to the earth on his hands and knees, his sword sheaths stabbing into the path's loose gravel.

He was panting and staring at the dirt below him. He was panting and getting no air at all. He lifted his head, unwilling to believe what his eyes had shown him, but nothing had changed and Tau's sharp eyes had never misled him.

Hanging from her hair, which had been tangled and knotted around Makena's dead hand, was Jelani's severed head.

Tau screamed and beat his fists against the ground. He tried to stand to take Jelani down from there, but he couldn't make himself do it. He tore his eyes away from the horror of it, and that's when he saw the umbusi and her husband. They were strewn among the other bodies in the heap of the dead, their throats slit, eyes plucked out, and hands cut away.

Someone touched his shoulder, and finding the strength to stand, Tau snatched up his swords and spun.

"Tau." It was Nyah. She had her hands up and out, empty. "Tau, please."

He didn't lower his swords. "My sister. My stepfather. Nyah, my sister."

Nyah looked up and past him to the monstrosity behind him.

She tried to draw closer. "I'm sorry, Tau."

"My sister," he said, his voice breaking. "It's Jelani."

"I'm sorry."

His swords were still up, but she walked between them and she put her hands on his face, holding his eyes with hers. "I'm sorry. This is an evil. I'm so sorry, Tau."

He was going to fall, when he heard a voice behind him call out. "Tau?"

The voice was weak, shaky, and hard to hear. It didn't matter. Tau knew the way his mother said his name.

CHAPTER TEN

WRATH

Tau was holding his mother in his arms when the rest of the army arrived. She was in horrible pain, but she told him what had happened. Kana and his tribespeople had killed person after person in the keep until the living broke and told him the names and likenesses of anyone related to Tau.

Kana killed Jelani and eviscerated Makena in front of Tau's mother. He made her watch it all and then he put out her eyes with fire-heated bronze, so that her daughter's murder and her husband's butchery would be the last things she ever saw. Blinded and bound to the bottom of the pole on which they strung up Makena, Tau's mother had listened to her husband dying for a day and night.

Tau held his mother, but he could hear Nyah explaining to the others what had been done.

He was still there, holding her, when Jabari came. Maybe he should have gone to his friend. He didn't, even when Jabari saw for himself what had been done to his own mother and father. Tau heard his friend's uncontrollable cries, but he was in too much pain to share in more.

"Can I see her?"

Tau looked up. It was the Sah priestess from the medicinal order, Hafsa.

"I should clean her wounds," Hafsa told him. "They could fester."

Tau nodded and made to move away. His mother clung to him. "Mother," he said. "This is Hafsa. She's a priestess from the medicinal order and has healed many of my sword brothers. She needs to look at you, to make sure you get better."

If she heard him, it made no difference. She held to him, and after a few more fruitless words, Tau had to pry his mother free so Hafsa could care for her.

"They're setting up camp higher on the mountain just beyond... this," Hafsa said. "We'll be in the infirmary tent, yes?"

"Yes," Tau managed.

The priestess nodded and guided his mother away, speaking to her as they went.

Tau picked up his swords from where he'd dropped them, and he sheathed them, sand and all. It felt like he was watching his life from a distance. He could sense the sun on his scalp, hear the voices of those around him, and see the efforts being made to clear the slaughter, but none of it felt like it was happening to him. He was removed and yet the pain of what he'd lost, whom he'd lost, sat in his stomach like a stone.

"Tau?"

It was another voice Tau would always recognize. It was the brilliant Grand General Hadith Buhari.

"There are no words, but you have my deepest sorrows for—"

Tau snatched Hadith by the throat.

"Oi!" shouted the nearest soldier, drawing the attention of others.

"He knew you'd make us go to the ships first," Tau hissed. "He knew it. It's why he beached them near enough to Kigambe to be found, and by doing it we gave him enough time to do this." Tau waved his free hand at the desecration that surrounded them.

"We'll get him. I promise you we'll get—" It was all Hadith managed before Tau shoved him away.

"Fail me again and it'll be your last time, Grand General," Tau said, turning away and heading up the mountain.

Kellan, in Tau's way, bowed his head and stepped aside. The other soldiers, who had been working to clear the dead, dropped their eyes, none daring to look him in the face.

"Champion." It was Hadith.

Tau stopped, listening.

"We've received our reply from the Southern Fortress. Thandi just gave it to me. They know the queen is with us, but they're not sending soldiers."

Tau turned, and in spite of the distance between them, Hadith stepped back.

"Does the queen know?" Tau asked, ignoring the demon at the edge of his vision.

"She does. I've never seen her so angry," Hadith said. "She wanted you to know because a choice must be made."

Tau blinked away the monster and fought to cool his blood. "What choice?"

Hadith tried to start his sentence a few times before settling on what to say. "Kana will do this again if we don't stop him."

"Can we stop him if the soldiers from the Southern Fortress aren't there to cut him off?"

"I don't know, but if we're to have any chance of doing it at all, we have to leave now."

"Now?" Tau asked, sliding his jaw from side to side. "And the dead? Who will burn them before the sun rots their bodies? Who will watch them burn and wish them well on their way to the Goddess?"

Hadith lowered his eyes.

"This is the choice you need me to make?" Tau asked, choking up. "A choice between woe and wrath?"

"Yes, Champion."

"And do you know what I'll choose, Grand General Buhari, when given such a choice?"

"Wrath, Champion," Hadith said quietly. "You'll choose wrath."

QUARRY

It wasn't hard to follow the warlord's son, because he wanted them to chase him. He wanted them to see the things he was doing.

Kana left a massacre in his wake, littering his path with the victims of his atrocities, and it was like marching through the after-effects of a plague.

Sichiwende, the hamlet to the east of what had been Keep Onai, was torn to pieces. Not a single hut was left standing, and the hamlet's tiny fields had been trampled, its people dismembered and scattered across the ground like seeds.

The mood as they marched was grim. Kana's viciousness was expected to grow more and more vile, and without help from the Southern Fortress, they might catch up to Kana, but how could they hold him? He'd simply retreat, never committing to an engagement, until he could slip into the Curse, free from their grasp forever.

"We split the army, sending half down the mountain to run the flatlands," Kellan suggested as they marched. "Then those men can climb back to us near the Curse to cut him off."

The only ones on horses were the queen and Nyah. Tau walked beside Fury, letting her rest after the strain of galloping to Keep Onai, and he needed to work off some of the anger that kept threatening to explode out of him. It didn't help his mood that the sun was setting, because the mountains were too dangerous for night travel and that meant they'd lose ground in their hunt for Kana.

They couldn't expect the warlord's son to slow down. If he wanted to get any of his raiders out of the peninsula alive, he'd need to spend some lives in exchange for speed.

"The trip down and up the mountain will take too long," Hadith told Kellan. "We'll deprive ourselves of half our strength, and I don't think the half crossing the flatlands can make good enough time to cut Kana off."

"We could take the chance," Kellan said.

"And what if Kana's scouts notice our depleted numbers? The Xiddeen could turn on us, decimating the half in the mountains, then doing the same to the second half, when they meet them outside the Curse."

Tau thought of his mother. She was back in the impromptu camp that had been set up before they'd begun the chase. She was with Hafsa and a few others.

"We're not going to divide our force. We'll just have to move faster," the queen said from her horse.

Tsiora looked tired enough to fall out of the saddle. She was unaccustomed to rough travel, the endless days, and poor food, but she hadn't complained. It was the opposite with her. She helped where she could, led at all times, and when she'd first seen Tau, after Keep Onai, she'd seemed so uncertain with him.

She'd approached him like he was a skittish horse and, after a time in silence, reached out, taking his hands. She'd spoken to him, soft hands holding his. Tau couldn't remember a word of what she'd said. They weren't what mattered. It was her presence that made a dent in his grief.

Thinking back on it, Tau wished Jelani could have been there to see him. Though they'd shared warmer moments growing up, she'd always been quick to treat him like a shameful secret in public, and he'd wanted to see the look on her face when she noticed him holding hands with the queen.

Tau laughed, startling Yaw, who was marching near him. He kept laughing, his tears flowing freely. He'd seen Jelani's face. He'd seen it exactly as Kana had wanted him to.

The sound of galloping hooves pulled him a small distance from the pain. It was Nyah, riding double with Thandi. They'd left the vizier's daughter in the camp with Hafsa, and Nyah had stopped off with Thandi a span ago. It had been time for Thandi to meet with the other Edifiers, and she couldn't do it easily if she was moving in Uhmlaba.

"What word?" Tsiora asked them when they were close. They'd been riding hard and Nyah's horse was slick with sweat.

"It's from the Shadow Council," Thandi said. "Lelise says Odili has restricted who among the Gifted can send or receive edifications for him. Lelise is no longer trusted enough to do it, but she managed to spy on one of the Gifted who is."

"And what did Gifted Lelise learn?" the queen asked.

"Odili told General Bisi that we have a Lesser as our grand general. He's asked Bisi to return to Palm so that he can be elevated to the Royal Noble caste and given the position of grand general under Queen Esi Omehia."

"And Bisi's response?" the queen asked.

"There was none, but he's begun marching for the capital at the head of three military rages."

Three military rages, Tau thought. His mind couldn't picture it. That was more than thirteen thousand soldiers.

"Bring us Buhari," Queen Tsiora said.

Hadith got there quickly, and he had Kellan with him. Night had fallen, the path they'd been following had become little more than a trail, and with steep cliffs to the south and crumbling ground beneath them, the decision was made to stop for the night. The terrain was too treacherous to navigate in the dark.

"I can think of two things it could mean," Hadith told the queen. "Bisi intends to accept Odili's offer and fight with him against us, or he plans to join us in the attack on Palm City."

"Which do you suppose it is, General?" Tsiora asked him.

"I suppose the general was purposeful when he didn't answer

Odili's edification because, if the thing he intends goes wrong, he can deny it was actually his intention."

"You think he's going to side with Odili," Tsiora said.

"I do, but he's guarding against the unknown. He's not even telling Odili his plan, but Odili should be able to come to the same conclusion as we do here."

"What does this do to the numbers?" she asked.

"Nothing good," Hadith said. "We have six thousand in our army, Odili has two, and Bisi is marching with thirteen."

Tau spoke then, getting to the crux of it. "What do we do?"

"Win Palm City," Hadith said. "We need to win the city and remove Odili from power. That leaves Bisi with no choice but to accept Queen Tsiora as the rightful monarch."

"Won't he just run us over with his thirteen thousand soldiers?" Tau asked.

Kellan shook his head. "General Bisi is known for valuing reputation, lawfulness, and discipline. He's a man who'd rather die than be shamed or thought of as having done something improper."

Watching Kellan, Tau thought he already knew someone who sounded like that.

"Bisi may take Odili's offer to make him a grand general and Royal Noble, if it can be done in a way that seems lawful," Kellan said. "But if we defeat Odili, the only avenue left to a man of Bisi's code will be to accept Queen Tsiora."

"How long will it take him to bring his three military dragons from the Curse to Palm?" Tsiora asked.

"Kellan? Is it half a moon?" Hadith asked.

"Half a moon to march them there," Kellan confirmed.

"How long for us to get to Palm from here?" Tsiora asked.

"Five days," Hadith said.

"Champion Solarin, a word," the queen said.

Tau and Tsiora went to their horses, and in spite of the dark, they rode them, at barely a walk, away from the rest.

"You're going to tell me that we need to send word to our army in Citadel City," Tau said. "You're going to tell me that we have to meet them on the path to Palm."

The queen played with her horse's reins, and she wouldn't quite meet his eyes. "If we let Bisi get there first, he'll decide our fates for us."

"If I let Kana go, he'll kill more people," Tau said, picturing the warlord's son burning his way across the mountains, turning fief after fief into slag heaps, just like the Omehi soldiers had done to Luapula.

"If we keep chasing him, we lose everything."

Tau slowed his horse. "I can't just let him go."

"You won't be the one doing it," she said. "Your queen will give that order. Come, Tau. Let's go back to Kerem and burn our dead."

He clenched his jaw hard enough to make his teeth ache. "It's blood I wanted, not tears."

"The Goddess knows that, and, sometimes, She gives us what we need instead of what we want." She reached out for him. "Shall we tell the others the decision?"

The anger Tau felt at having to let Kana go was close to being too much to leash. "My queen, would you go ahead?"

Understanding that he needed time, she turned her horse to return to the others. "Will you be a while?" she asked before leaving.

"It will not seem so," he said, taking himself to the demons.

PRICE

Only a few spans passed in Uhmlaba, but Tau hunted and butchered for days, fighting until his mind began to crack under the crush of the endless slaughter and torture. He fought until his rage burned itself out, its final blaze emptying his soul of everything he thought he was, leaving him with visions of a world that mixed the realm of his birth with the one that had forged him.

And back in Uhmlaba, curled up in a ball on the ground, he shook and sweated like he was fevered. He saw demons in every shadow, and the mountains were filled with Isihogo's mists, its fog grabbing at him with the edges of its smoky claws as he fought for sanity. It took more than a span for him to feel human again, and coming back to himself hadn't been so horrible since his very first trips to Isihogo.

Weak as a child, he tried to go to Fury, but she seemed to sense something on him and shied away, unwilling to let him get close. He made himself speak softly to her, and sick as he felt, Tau told her that he was fine, asking her not to worry and soothing her so that she'd let him ride.

Later that night, riding past the shell that had once been Keep Onai, he followed the glow from the funeral pyres. When he got closer, he could make out the silhouetted shapes of those who had gathered to see the dead take the last step on their path, and in the dark, backlit by flames, the mourners on the mountainside looked like weakening Gifted struggling to shroud their souls' glow.

One of the Indlovu who knew the horses took Fury, and with his mind blank, Tau walked over to where the funerals were taking place.

"Champion."

"Yes, Priestess," Tau said to Hafsa as she hurried over.

"I'm glad I found you." Her face, and the discomfort in it at being so near him, betrayed that lie. "I didn't think I'd be able to in the crowd. Your mother, she was determined to attend the burning. She's there now, with one of my aides, and she's asking for you...."

"Of course. Will you take me to her?"

Hafsa nodded. "Her...injuries, they've been cleaned and treated, but there was a lot of pain, as you can imagine. I've given her something for that. She'll be tired, weak, and when she can do no more for the night, I'd appreciate it if you brought her to the hospital tent. I'd like to continue her care."

"As you wish," Tau said, his relief that he'd be able to hand his mother back to the priestess steeped in shame.

The queen, shadowed by Nyah and the handmaidens, approached.

"May we accompany you?" Tsiora said, her eyes searching his. "We would meet your mother, and offer our condolences in person."

With no reasonable way to deny the queen's request, Tau mumbled his gratitude, and as a group, they walked up to the mass burning. It was taking place in the same large field where many of Kerem's celebrations were held. It was the same large field where Tau had danced with Zuri after being made a man, but it looked different that night with the crowds and, beyond them, the bodies.

The dead had been wrapped in lye-whitened linen and placed onto hundreds of unlit pyres surrounding the massive beacon fire that burned in the center of the field. Ihagu, Ihashe, and Indlovu stood at attention, ready to ignite the smaller pyres with the peat-moss torches they held.

The shifting firelight from the torches and beacon fire made everyone's shadows undulate. It looked like the spirits of the deceased moved among them, still clinging to some vestige of life and waiting impatiently for their release. Three fire-silhouetted figures, far off in the distance, even looked like they were Xiddeen—two warriors flanking a shaman. Perhaps they'd fallen in the raid and their spirits sought release too, Tau thought, blinking them away.

"She's there," Hafsa said, and she was.

Tau's mother, washed and dressed in a blue robe, was facing the beacon fire. She had a bandage wrapped round her head, covering the ruins of her eyes, and she held herself with her arms, as if it were possible to be cold in the night's natural swelter and so near the fire.

"Mother," Tau said, standing three strides distant.

"Tau..."

"The queen is coming."

Without moving her body at all, Imani Tafari turned her head to him, and even with the strip of bandage wrapped round her face, she was striking.

"The queen, Tau?"

"I—I am her champion."

"Yes, I'd heard but didn't believe." Imani turned back to the fire. "What could she ever want with you?"

Tau's neck and scalp felt hot. He'd never been able to face his mother, and when he tried to respond, nothing came out but more stuttering. The queen, who had held back to give them space, came forward, saving him.

"Imani Tafari, we are Queen Tsiora and we are here, feeling your great loss, our heart bleeding for you and yours."

Tau's mother turned to the queen, giving her a deep bow. "My queen, you honor me. My son and I are not worthy of your kindness and care. Goddess bless you, always."

"Rise, Imani Tafari," the queen said, taking Tau's mother's hands. "We are here for you. We are here for you and your son, our champion."

"It really is true, then?" Imani said. "He is your champion?"

"He is."

"It is my greatest hope that he serves you well. It is my greatest hope that he lives and dies for you, my queen."

Tsiora's eyebrows drew together, and then the queen's mask was back, and her face became placid. "Champion Solarin is a gift."

"Solarin?" Imani said. "Yes, it was his father's name. I thought it died with Aren, but what could be more wonderful than to honor that brave man?"

The queen inclined her head, and realizing Imani could not see it, she took one of her hands out of Imani's and used her free hand to pat the one that she still held.

"The Goddess will welcome your loved ones tonight," Tsiora said. "Your husband…"

"Makena Tafari, Your Grace."

"She'll welcome Makena and your daughter, Jelani."

"They were the whole of my life," Tau's mother said, and Tau noticed when the queen's eyes flashed to him.

"Of course," Tsiora said. "Imani, may we call you Imani?"

"Your Grace."

"Imani, we will leave you to grieve with your son, but know that you may call on us."

Another bow, this one deeper. "My queen. We are not worthy."

Tsiora began to leave, and though she did not dally, it seemed to Tau that she was hesitant to go.

"Give me your hand, boy," Imani said.

Tau did and she pulled him close, drawing him next to her.

"Where is she?" Imani said into his ear.

"The queen goes to begin the ceremony."

"How many can hear me?" she asked, tightening her grip.

Tau looked around them. "None, if you whisper."

She dug her nails into the back of his hand. "What have you done, Tau? What have you done?"

He tried to pull his hand away, but his mother's hold was hard as bronze.

"He asked for you," she said. "The man with his hair twisted and locked like a Sah priest." Her nails were drawing blood. "He made me memorize words for you. He made me memorize them as he sawed his knife through your sister's neck."

Tau tried to pull away again, and he was like a child to her.

" 'For my father, Common of Kerem.' That's what he said to me when he killed her. 'This is for my father!' "

"Mother—"

"What did you do, demon spawn? I gave you life and watched you grow. I know who and what you are. I know what stock you come from, and you are no champion."

Tau snatched his hand free and his mother scrabbled about, searching for him until she seized a handful of his tunic, pulling him back to her.

"I hear you're powerful," she whispered. "I hear you're strong, stronger even than your father was, and more powerful than any Lesser has ever been. Is it true? Is it, Tau?"

"Mother, please..."

"Answer me, boy. Is it true?"

"I can fight," Tau told her, tears springing to his eyes. "And I can kill, Mother. Oh, I can kill."

"Good," she said. "Good, because I want you to kill." She ran her hands up his arms, placing them on his shoulders and near his neck. "I want you to kill everyone responsible. You hear?"

Tau's mouth wouldn't work.

"Do you hear me, Tau...Solarin?"

"I hear you, Mother."

She leaned in farther and he could smell the dried blood beneath her bandages. She was so close their lips were near to touching.

"You made a deal with Ukufa, neh? You let him corrupt you, so you could be more than the Goddess intended. Well, the Insatiate has claimed his price and now I will name mine."

Tau pulled back, making as much space as he could with her nails dug in, clawlike, on his neck.

"You must burn them all for what they did to us," she said. "Promise it to me. Promise me you'll make the ones responsible for Makena and Jelani..." She made a strangled sound in the back of her throat. "Promise me you'll make them suffer!"

"Mother, I—"

"Promise it." She grew louder. "Promise it! Promise it, Tau! Help me hate you a little less and promise it!"

She wasn't going to stop.

"I promise," he said.

She showed her teeth, sharp and white. "Again," she said.

"I promise."

She pulled him against her, holding him there.

"We only have each other now, and we'll do it together," she said.

"Yes, Mother."

"Tell me when we leave."

The night flared with light from the pyres. The soldiers had lit them.

"In the morning," Tau said. "We leave in the morning."

She let him go and faced the flames, unable to see the fires that consumed the bodies of her husband and daughter and everyone from the life she'd known and lost.

"We'll make it worth it," she said to him. "I swear it to Ananthi and Ukufa, we'll make the power you were given worth its cost."

FAMILY

He came into the tent quietly enough that Tau wouldn't have heard him if he'd been sleeping, but after the burning and speaking with his mother, Tau couldn't rest. So when the shadow entered his tent and stood at the foot of his bedroll, hunched over to fit into the small, dark space, Tau knew it was him by the hooded cloak he always wore.

"Jabari," Tau said.

Nothing.

"I should have found you tonight," Tau said. "You were mourning as well."

The Petty Noble put a hand covered in burn scars to his neck, pressing his fingers there to help his throat make the right sounds. "Lekan," he said.

Tau sat up at the name, his eyes seeking his swords. They were in the far corner of the tent where he'd put them, but his guardian dagger was beside the bedroll and within reach. Moving slowly, he leaned on his elbow toward it when Jabari swung round and left the tent, his cloak billowing behind him.

Snatching up the dagger, Tau found his pants, buckled on his sword belt, and retrieved his swords. He wasn't wearing a shirt when he left the tent. He didn't think one would make a difference to what was coming.

Jabari was waiting a few strides away, and seeing Tau, he walked off. The Petty Noble moved stiffly, but Tau still had to rush to keep up with the taller man's shambling gait. He considered calling out to ask Jabari where they were going, but that would only confirm his guess. He knew where he was being taken.

When they got to Keep Onai, Jabari walked beneath the archway that had once held the keep's gates and into the keep itself. Tau went with him, the two men moving in silence until they reached their destination and were standing in the burned-down remains of what had once been Lekan's room.

"Why are we here?" Tau asked.

Jabari laughed. It was a painful, short-lived sound, and as he made it, he dropped a hand to his sword hilt. Tau matched the movement and the burned Petty Noble sneered before adjusting his sword so he could sit on the floor next to a bronze shield.

The shield couldn't have been there when the room burned. Its surface was clean of ashes and it hadn't been touched by smoke or fire.

Jabari closed his eyes and slowed his breathing.

"Isihogo?" Tau asked.

No answer.

"Isihogo." Tau nodded, more to himself than to anyone else, and he sat several strides away, facing Jabari.

He closed his own eyes but didn't need to slow his breathing or otherwise reframe his mind. One moment he was in Uhmlaba, and the next he was with Jabari in the underworld.

Jabari, his face whole and unmarred, was staring into the mists. "After I was burned, when you would visit me in the hospital, you spoke about so many things," he said, voice full and strong. "You spoke about the people you loved, the ones you'd lost, and all the things you'd done. You didn't think I could hear you, but I heard it all, Tau."

Tau closed his eyes for a breath.

"You killed my brother." Jabari said, pulling his dragon-scale sword free from its scabbard. "You killed him and I brought you here to accuse you of the crime with my own voice." He bent down to Isihogo's ground, retrieving the shield there. "You are here to be judged."

"Judged? And what sentence can you pass in this place?"

"I can't match you in Uhmlaba. My injuries prevent it." The Petty Noble licked his lips. "So, I was going to kill you in your sleep, slitting your throat and letting you die in your bed."

"Why didn't you?"

Jabari's nostrils flared. "Because I'm no inyoka. I won't slither into your room to take you quietly from dreams to death," he said. "I'm a man, and you, Common of Kerem, are not a better one than me."

"When did I say I was better?" Tau asked.

"When?" Jabari said, his tone dripping with scorn. "When you chose to show up Kagiso at the Indlovu testing. When you raised a sword to Kellan's back after he let your father live. When you attacked my brother on the path home, and when you murdered him in his rooms that same night!"

Tau stared Jabari down, unwilling to accept shame for the things he'd done. "In my place, would you have done differently? Would you let Kagiso maim you? Would you scrape and beg at the feet of the men who killed your father? Tell me, Jabari Onai, what makes me undeserving of the same humanity you claim for yourself?"

"Humanity? I saw what you did to Lekan." He was getting louder. "The back of his head looked like a hammer had been taken to it!" Jabari shouted. "You're a monster!"

"Did you know that Nkiru's family didn't make it to Dakur? Did you know that my father found their broken bodies at the bottom of a cliff in Kerem's mountains? Nkiru's wife was still holding the baby."

Jabari's sword dipped. He hadn't known.

"If I'm a monster, what was Lekan?" Tau asked.

"He was my brother!" Jabari said, cutting through the mists at his side with his sword. "And I've risked my soul for this moment."

"Enough," Tau said, trying to bring sense back to his sword brother. "There's no justice to be had in the underworld. Nothing you do here is permanent."

Jabari's smile was cold. "You're almost right," he said, stepping forward. "Dying in Isihogo isn't permanent, but it is disorienting, and even you need time to recover." He took another step. "I'll kill you here for what you did to my brother, and while you're coming back to yourself in Uhmlaba, I'll take your life there too."

With the blood in his ears booming, Tau tried to ignore the way his hands kept twitching closer to his blades. "I don't want to fight."

Jabari scoffed. "We both know that's not true," he said, raising his sword. "So, face me like you have some scrap of the humanity you covet, or die with your swords still in their scabbards. I'm sending you to the Goddess either way."

Jabari wasn't going to give him a choice, and along with that realization came a familiar longing. It was time for violence.

"Jabari, before we begin, I want you to know two things." Tau said as he unsheathed his black blades. "First, I didn't go that night to kill Lekan, but I won't lie to you, he was always going to die at my hands." He twirled his wrists, loosening them and making lazy circles with his swords. "Second, I want you to remember that you asked for this."

Jabari lunged, sending his sword cutting horizontally through the mists, and Tau leapt back, causing Jabari's swing to cleave air in place of flesh. When he touched ground, Tau pushed forward, thrusting for Jabari's chest with his weak-side sword and chasing the Petty Noble's blade with the one in his left.

Tau's chasing blade caught up to Jabari's sword and blocked its path, preventing the Petty Noble from bringing his weapon back to bear, but Jabari didn't need it to stop Tau's thrust. He repositioned his shield and Tau's sword point slammed into it instead of his heart.

With their swords still entangled, Jabari tipped his shield over the top of Tau's sword, driving the blade down. It pulled Tau off-balance and Jabari shot his leg forward to deliver a front kick to Tau's chest. Tau saw it coming, and instead of resisting Jabari's move with the shield, he let it yank him clear of the strike.

Missing his target, Jabari stumbled forward past Tau and Tau spun in a half circle to smash his elbow into the small of Jabari's back.

Arching in pain, Jabari staggered a few more steps, and when he turned, Tau was on him, swords whirling.

Jabari caught the first strike on his shield, blocked the second with his sword, ducked beneath the third, and, still ducking, he took the full impact of the flat of Tau's sword to the bridge of his nose. The Petty Noble pitched over and crashed to the ground, but rolling away and up, he threw his shield at Tau.

Tau bashed the flying shield from the air with one of his swords. "You should have done it in my sleep," he said, hearing demons howling in the mists.

Jabari tottered to his feet, blood pouring from his broken nose. "He was my brother!" he said, charging Tau.

Tau parried Jabari's swing with one sword, smashed him in the throat with hilt of the other, and kicked his legs out from under him, dropping him into Isihogo's muck.

Wiping blood from his face and limping, Jabari got back to his feet.

"They're coming," Tau said, waving a sword at the mists.

"I don't give a shit."

"My father might be alive today if not for Lekan," Tau said. "Nkiru, Anya, the rest of their family, I know they would be."

"He was my brother," Jabari said.

"He was cruel, callous, and selfish. Good people died because of him."

"Behind you, Tau."

Tau spun and crossed his swords, catching the demon's overhand strike. It was twice his size, it had four rear legs, but it stood tall and fought with its two much longer forearms. Its head and face looked like they were made from ruptured flesh stuck to rocky skin, and Tau drove a sword between the gaps in its stonelike exterior and into the soft stuff within.

The demon reared back, screeching, and Tau shot a look over his shoulder, expecting Jabari to stab him from behind, but the Petty Noble had his own demons to fight.

"Back to back!" Tau shouted, and Jabari nodded, grabbing his fallen shield on the way.

The rock demon, somewhat recovered, made an inhuman sound and attacked, forcing Tau to give it his full attention. He wasn't sure how Jabari was doing against the demons he faced, but if any in the Ayim could handle themselves in the underworld, the Petty Noble could, and they held the creatures off, until three more burst through the mists.

GRIT

Jabari died first, but Tau didn't last long on his own, and back in Uhmlaba, before Jabari had wholly come back to himself, Tau stood to go.

"We're done here!"

"No." The way it sounded, it had to tear Jabari's throat to shreds every time he spoke.

"I can't undo the night Lekan died," Tau said, working to rein in his own anger, "and I'm not sure I'd want to."

He turned to leave, and Jabari, still sitting, smacked the ground, disturbing the ashes there. "You're no champion," he coughed out, shaking his head in rebuke. "You're just a Lesser!"

Tau rounded on him. "Jabari Onai of the Nobles, what will you and yours have left, when it's no longer possible to pretend that you're better than people like me?"

"You didn't win!" Jabari said, coughing up blood and smacking the ground beside him. "I didn't ask for the Goddess's mercy!"

"You will," Tau said, joining him on the ground.

Jabari slammed his eyes shut, struggling to slow his breathing enough to switch realms. Tau closed his eyes and opened them in Isihogo.

When Jabari arrived, they fought. Tau beat him into the dirt, and when he wouldn't surrender, Tau drove his sword through Jabari's heart.

It was the first time he'd killed another human in Isihogo, and it worked just as Jabari had assumed. The Petty Noble died, his soul's glow went out, and he vanished.

Tau returned to Uhmlaba and waited for Jabari to recover. When he did, they returned to the underworld, and Tau killed him again.

They went back a fourth time, crossing swords as soon as they saw each other.

"They're here," Jabari said, hunching over his side where Tau had just cut him in their rapid exchange.

He barely had time to finish the sentence before a small horde of demons burst through the mists, and, howling as it jumped, the closest one launched itself through the air at Jabari. Tau blasted his swords into the monster's torso, knocking it off course, and Jabari followed up with a heavy cut that sliced the creature almost in two. The demon was down, but the others were on them, and the two Ayim, their black blades already slick with demon blood, went to work.

When they were killed, Tau and Jabari went back to the underworld and found the demons waiting for them. The creatures came in twos, prolonging the fight until Tau's and Jabari's mutilated human bodies could contain their souls no longer.

It was torment, that time, but after it was over, they went back anyway. Perhaps they hoped the demons wouldn't come and they could finish the fight they had with each other. But both men knew Isihogo better than that, and the demons gave them no quarter. Still, they kept returning to Isihogo, fighting and dying as many times as it took for them to remember that they must stand together against an implacable enemy. They went back as many times as it took to remember that, though they shared no blood, Tau Solarin and Jabari Onai had been and would always be brothers.

"There's no Goddess," Jabari said during their tenth or twentieth or maybe fortieth fight, his eyes wild and haunted. "How could there be, when this exists as well?"

The demons answered him, doing it with teeth and claws, and when they were killed and flung back to Uhmlaba, Tau realized that the sky had begun to lighten. They'd been fighting for so long, the sun was returning to the earth.

Jabari, not yet back to himself, staggered to his feet, and, eyes rolling in his head, he fell to his knees. Moaning from a mixture of the misery Isihogo had visited on him and the too-real pain of his burned body, Jabari crawled to the nearest wall and used it to work his way to a stand.

He remained like that for a time, then, finding enough courage or perhaps strength, he tried to leave the room, his walk a slow and lurching thing. But before he could disappear around the corner, his body gave in, and like a clutch of overripe fruit falling from a tree, he collapsed.

Fighting away his own fogginess, Tau looked to see if the Petty Noble was still breathing. Jabari's chest rose and fell fitfully, and, satisfied that he'd be fine, Tau leaned over to lie on his side amid the ashes. He was exhausted, the pain in his leg was back, and in the same way it worked with the demon's bodies, he felt as if his soul was stitching itself back to an imperfect wholeness.

"Lekan," Jabari said, his flayed voice startling Tau, "was an nceku."

Tau let his hanging head flop over so he could see his friend from the corner of his eye. Jabari was lying there in the same uncomfortable position in which he'd fallen, watching Tau.

"What?" Tau managed to say.

Jabari took a while to answer. "I loved Aren like he was my father," he said, the string of words sending him into a coughing fit that ended when he spat a glob of red phlegm onto the ash-filled floor. "But I had to fight you, Tau. Lekan was my blood."

"What now, then?" Tau asked. "You wait until I'm sleeping?"

Jabari shook his head. "No, never like that. But when I'm stronger than you, there'll be another fight." He coughed hard enough that his whole body spasmed, and when it passed, he sighed and let his head fall to the ground, still eyeing Tau.

Tau thought it over and nodded. Lekan's death was a wound between them that would never close all the way, but perhaps they could live with the scar. It seemed that Jabari was offering to try to do as much.

"You have my word," Tau said. "The next time you think you're stronger than me, there'll be another fight."

Jabari grunted his agreement. "Until then, sword brother," he said, closing his eyes and giving himself over to unconsciousness.

Tau counted Jabari's breaths. Doing it calmed him. Then, losing count, he watched the sun rise over the ruins of what had once been Keep Onai, and when the light became blinding, he blinked.

"Uh...Champion?"

Tau squinted, seeing the Ihagu soldier standing over him with the sun high overhead behind the man. Tau had been asleep.

"We...ah...Grand General Buhari sent me to find you. We've broken camp," the Ihagu said, swallowing nervously around his unusually large throat stone, the bulge in his neck bouncing up and down like a ball.

Tau sat up and the sudden movement sent shocks of pain reverberating up and down his leg. "Yes. Thank you, Ihagu," he said, rubbing around the wound in his leg.

The soldier glanced at Jabari's unconscious form, no doubt marking the bloody spit in which he lay. "Is...ah...is he well? I should call a Sah for him, neh?"

"He's well. I'll take care of it."

"As you say, Champion."

"Where's the army now?"

"Heading for Palm City and just a little ways down the mountain. They're not far ahead."

Tau nodded by way of dismissal, but the man didn't leave.

"Champion?"

"Yes, Ihagu?"

The soldier stood straighter. "What you've done for us Lessers, I...well, we're ready to fight against the Royals and what they want. We're people, same as them, and they'll see that when we beat them." The man seemed emboldened by his own words. "We have the queen, the Gifted, and the army. Nkosi, we have you, and that's all we need to crush them."

CHAPTER ELEVEN

INTRUDER

Tau and Jabari caught up to the army during the halt for the midday meal, and as they walked through the tail of the army, Jabari, hood up, brooded. It hadn't occurred to Tau before, but he could see why the Petty Noble hid as he did. Everyone they passed stared.

At first, Tau thought they might be looking at him, their champion, who was also a Lesser, who also wasn't wearing a shirt. It didn't take long to realize he was wrong. They were looking at Jabari, trying to see under the lip of his hood to gawk at the man so burned the whole of his flesh seemed to writhe with the searing imprints of a dragon's fire.

Feeling protective of his friend, Tau called to a few soldiers a little too brazen in their gawping.

"Have you nothing better to do, Ihagu?" Tau asked them, and, caught out, they bowed and apologized, looking mortified.

But Jabari put a hand on Tau's wrist and shook his head.

"Why shouldn't I say it?" Tau asked. "They've no right to stare or treat you that way. You, who saved lives by sacrificing yourself."

Jabari shook his head again and lowered his head, pulling the front of his hood farther down over his burned face.

"Fine, I'll do as you wish, but they shouldn't stare," Tau said. "Come, we'll get something to eat and find the others."

They didn't get the chance. Nyah rode up on her horse, and bringing the animal close enough to make them step back, she started in on Tau.

"How dare you! Where were you?" she asked. "When we came looking for you this morning, you were gone. Your swords were gone...." Nyah seemed to notice Jabari for the first time. "You cannot do that, not after the betrayals the queen has already faced. She carries too much as it is, without worrying over the loyalty of those in whom she places her trust."

It troubled Tau, how easily Nyah made him the one in the wrong. "Is she well?"

"I won't have her worrying any longer over where you are. Get on the horse—we're going to see her."

"I don't have a shirt," Tau said.

"Get on the horse."

Tau glanced at Jabari for help, but the Petty Noble gave no sign that he'd been listening at all. "I'll see you," Tau said to him, reaching up and clasping wrists with Nyah so she could help him clamber onto her horse.

"You smell like a rotting onion," she said, flicking the reins and setting them moving at a canter.

Tau wanted to say something about that, but after taking a sniff, he found his nose had taken Nyah's side. "Vizier, you can't really mean to take me to the queen like this."

"Hyah!" Nyah said, urging her horse to go faster and leading them to the center of camp, where Tsiora's massive tent had been put up. "Having you vanish shook her. I want her to know that you're still here."

Tau had no idea why a morning of absence justified anyone being out of sorts, but they'd arrived and he became more concerned about his smell and appearance than the moods of royalty. When Nyah slowed her horse to a stop, he climbed down, doing his best not to put any more weight than was necessary on his bad leg, while, beside him, Nyah hopped off, looking spry for all her cycles.

They walked past the Queen's Guard and he saw that Auset and Ramia were outside the tent, looking demure and handmaidenly, as they ate delicately from bowls of stew.

"Auset, Ramia," Tau said.

"Champion," they replied at the same time, though Auset raised an eyebrow at his appearance.

"Inside," Nyah said, and he followed her into the tent.

The queen, pacing with her back to the tent's entrance, turned as soon as she heard them. She did look worried.

"Did you find him...? Ah, Champion"—the queen blinked when she saw him—"Solarin."

Tau bowed, and awkward as he felt, he was determined to behave as if there was nothing out of the ordinary about attending an audience with the queen of the Omehi without a shirt.

"Queen Tsiora, please accept my apologies. I did not mean to absent myself these past spans. I...Jabari and I..."

"No, don't apologize. You've both been through so much. It's understandable that you'd need some time to..." She trailed off, considering his appearance again. "But...you're well?"

"Ah..."

"Excuse us, you don't need to answer that. Grief is personal, individual. We'd heard that time and again but only understood it after our mother and father went to the Goddess."

Nyah bowed and moved to the tent's flaps. "My queen, if you'll excuse me, you know how some seasons affect me, and it seems I must clear my nose."

Tau caught a trace of amusement in Tsiora's eyes, and it felt good to see it displace some small part of the worry and grief that they all held.

"Will fresh air help, Vizier?" the queen asked.

"I'll try, but I fear finding air fresh enough to do the trick," Nyah said as she left.

"My queen, please excuse my appearance," Tau said, his neck and scalp growing hot from embarrassment. "I was called from my tent late last night and didn't have time to make myself ready for an audience with you. If I could get to my...ah...I realize I don't know where my tent is."

"It's set up, with all your belongings, a few strides behind this one."

As she spoke, Tau noticed that Tsiora was doing a thing he saw most often when fighting someone. She was trying to keep her eyes on his face when she really wanted to look somewhere else. It was what poor swordsmen did when they wanted to strike for your chest but needed to make it seem as if they'd be aiming for your head. She was looking him in the eyes, but her gaze kept slipping lower. She probably couldn't believe how filthy he was.

"Thank you, my queen."

"Pardon?" she asked, her eyes shooting back up.

"For taking care of my tent and belongings."

"Yes, of course, that."

"May I, then?"

"May you?"

"Get dressed."

"Dressed? Yes, of course, why shouldn't we want that?" She paused, searching for her words. "We mean that we want you to get dressed, if that is what you want."

Feeling like he'd rolled in horse dung, then smeared it on for good measure, Tau couldn't wait to leave. He bowed and was about to go, until he saw the demon.

The queen noticed the change in him and her face fell. "We've been inappropriate, and at a most horrible time," she said. "It's our turn to ask for forgiveness."

"No," Tau said. "It's not you, it's me."

"Oh...that's a kind lie."

Tau wasn't listening. He was too worried about what it meant that he couldn't blink it away. No matter what he did, the demon crouched in the corner behind Tsiora would not vanish.

"Last night," he said, "I...Queen Tsiora, I fear I'm not in my right mind."

She lowered her eyes. "We did this," she said. "We know what the Goddess wants from us, but we're rushing it, asking for too much too soon. It doesn't have to happen the same way as it did for Taifa and Tsiory. They've been our example, but they don't need to be our template."

Tau was worrying over what Hafsa had told him about his likely end. "I think it's the dragon blood," he told the queen.

Tsiora gave him a look. "The dragon...wait, what?"

"Hafsa warned me. I didn't believe her, but it's happening faster and faster. I think I'm losing my mind."

The demon, a two-legged thing with its knees on backward, stood to its full height, its oversized jaws dripping ichor.

"Oh, Goddess...you're talking about the poison and your wound?" the queen asked. "That's what's worrying you?"

"It's getting worse, and after everything that's happened...I'm not well."

She stepped toward him and the demon came forward too. "We'll get through it," she said. "We'll do it together."

"I don't think I can. I see things," he said, "horrible things."

The queen stopped and tilted her head. "What things?"

Tau couldn't make himself say it, didn't want to say it. "I see demons, stalking me and those I care for in this world. I see demons, everywhere."

The monster behind the queen opened its mouth, revealing row upon row of pointed teeth.

"Demons?" she said. "When?"

"Now."

"Here? In this tent?"

"Yes."

"Where?"

Tau pointed behind her and Tsiora turned.

"Champion," she said.

"Yes?"

"We see it too."

LEASHED

The demon lunged for Tsiora, and Tau, flying through the air with only one sword drawn, grabbed her with his free hand and threw her back and down, causing the creature to miss her and hit him. It was heavier than him by far, and it bowled him over, knocking them both to the ground, where it slashed at him with claws and teeth, catching him in the side with the three razor-sharp talons on its right hand.

Tau was on his back when it ripped at him. He felt his skin tear, and not wanting to give the demon the chance to do more damage, he scrambled away from its clawed hands on his heels and elbows. Undeterred, the thing renewed its attempts, stretching its neck to snap its jaws near his throat. He pushed down at it, but with its back feet dug into the packed earth beneath them, it had more leverage.

He couldn't hold it back, and it climbed his prone body, drawing closer to his face. To stop it from killing him, Tau pushed his hand and the hilt of his weak-side sword into its neck, barely keeping its gnashing teeth at bay.

It was all defensive, and Tau couldn't use his other weapon. It was still sheathed, and the arm he'd use to draw it was pinned between their bodies in such a way that freeing it would mean slicing himself open. To make space, he drove a knee into the creature's side and pushed back, wriggling his body out from beneath it as the demon writhed on top of him, snarling and snapping at his hands, face, and body.

It should have had him. It would have had him, but Tau was shirtless, grimy, and in the heat, sweating already. He was slippery as a river eel, and wriggling loose, he kicked the beast back as he stood, bringing both blades to bear.

Something felt wrong, though, and he looked to his side. The demon's talons had ripped into the skin beneath his left ribs. The cuts weren't deep. Nothing vital had been pierced, but he was bleeding himself an ocean.

"Ramia, Auset!" Tsiora shouted, calling to her handmaidens but also drawing the demon's attention.

"I'm here, you bastard!" Tau shouted at it. "Look at me!"

It brought its giant head back to Tau, yellow eyes focusing right before it pounced.

His leg protesting and his side feeling as if it were on fire, Tau threw himself out of the demon's path, swinging both blades with all his might, blasting them into the back of the monster's head. The blades dug deep, opening up jagged gashes in the back of the thing's skull and spraying green corruption into the air around them.

The demon went down with the attack. Tau did too, but he rolled back to his feet, slipping a little on one of the tent's many embroidered carpets. Centering himself, he saw that the demon was up and ready as well.

The tent flaps opened behind him, the push of new air and added sunlight telling him the handmaidens had arrived before his eyes confirmed the fact. The two women, dirks to hand, saw the demon, and though they faced a nightmare made real, they did not falter. They ran into the tent in opposite directions, making a triangle with Tau as its head and Tsiora, most protected, behind him.

"What is this?" asked Ramia.

"You see it?" Tau said, beginning to feel faint from the loss of blood.

Ramia nodded, her eyes round as shields, and Auset gave Tau a look sour enough to curdle a mother's milk.

"Can it die?" she asked as the demon snapped its teeth in her direction first, and then in Ramia's, before leaping for Tau.

With Tsiora behind him, he couldn't get out of the way and leave her in reach of it. So he blocked the demon's swiping claw with one sword, stabbed it through with the other, and tried not to let its snapping jaws reach his face, but the demon was too big. It could still reach him, and it opened its mouth wide as it dove for the finish.

Shouting in horror, Tau left his sword in the creature and tried to twist away from its bite, when it froze, mouth open, saliva dripping.

"Goddess! Cek!" he swore, backing away from it and holding the sword he had remaining in front of him.

"Kill it. Kill it quickly," Tsiora said through gritted teeth.

She had her hands up and aimed at the creature, and though its eyes moved in its head, it did not, or could not, move. She'd entreated it, wrapping it up in the bonds of will that were the Omehi's greatest gift and the most direct expression of the Goddess's power. The queen of the Omehi had the demon in her grasp.

"Kill it!" she said again, and Tau obliged.

Taking up his weak-side sword in both hands, Champion Solarin swung as hard as he was able, connecting and cleaving through the demon's neck in a single stroke that took its head from its shoulders, decapitating it and denying it access to whatever foul power allowed it to be in Uhmlaba.

The monster's body and head crumbled in on themselves, losing color and form until they were nothing but ash, and even that vanished without trace, gone from the world as surely as it should never have come into it.

"Auset, Ramia, do you see others?" Tau's vision was closing in and he meant to bend forward to pick up his strong-side sword. It was on the ground, having fallen there when the demon was vanquished. He almost fell over in the attempt and abandoned the blade for the moment. "Do you see others?"

"No, no," said Ramia. "Should I be seeing others? Do you see others?"

"There's nothing else here, Champion," Auset said.

Tau nodded and looked to the queen. "You entreated it?"

"We did."

"Thank you for saving me," he said, his vision going all the way black as he dropped to the floor.

AUTHORITY

She was holding his hand when he opened his eyes. Squeezing it hard enough to hurt. His head was spinning and he was groggy, but not so much so that he couldn't place himself.

He was in the infirmary tent and could have recognized the bleached color of its woven roof anywhere. More than that, he knew and was made anxious by the smell of its grassy herbs and infected flesh almost as much as the constant susurrus of women and men in various states of misery.

They hadn't been in a battle recently, but moving people always meant accidents, arguments ending in violence, and the regular comings and goings of common and not so common illnesses. In any event, the infirmary tent was never empty.

The squeeze came again, hard enough to grind the bones in his hand against one another. He turned his head to her.

"You need to get up," his mother said.

"Mother..."

"The queen marches to join with her army from Citadel City. She's taking the war to Odili and Palm City, and if you don't get up you'll be left behind."

"How long was I—"

"He's awake!" his mother called to someone he couldn't see. "He just woke."

He heard someone approaching, and then Hafsa's head popped into view.

"That's surprising," she said. "Unless he was disturbed, the draught I gave him should have seen him resting for at least another few spans."

"He was born this way," Imani said. "Always stronger and more resilient than he appears. He should have been a Noble."

Tau could see Hafsa eyeing his mother.

"Well," the priestess began, "it's good he's up, but he needs to rest and recover."

"My side, how bad?" Tau asked, his tongue feeling as lifeless and withered as a salted slug.

"You were fortunate," Hafsa said. "It was just flesh I had to stitch. There was a lot of stitching, though, and you've got twine running from your hip to your ribs on your left side." She seemed to consider him a while. "Who cut you with such ragged blades? The hand-maidens asked me to purify the wound before stitching you, as if I wouldn't have anyway." The priestess licked her lips. "Champion, I do not mean to tell you your business, but you cannot continue to train so roughly. It makes no—"

"That's enough, Priestess," Tau's mother said.

Hafsa's chin almost tucked its way into the back of her neck. "I'm sorry, but in my hospital tent, I will speak as I see fit."

"You're speaking to the mother of the queen's champion and you will mind yourself." Imani was sitting and she was blind, but she also had a way of making herself seem tall enough to be a Greater Noble.

Still, it shouldn't have worked. Tau's mother was a High Common, and Hafsa, though born a Lesser, had to be at least a third- if not fourth-term Sah priestess.

But Tau could appreciate that the handholds this far up the mountainside were untested. He was the queen's champion, and champions were always Ingonyama, or in rare cases, Royals. That meant that the mother of a champion had always been a Greater or Royal

Noble as well, and he knew Hafsa was working her way through the societal puzzle Imani had posed.

"Enough wasting our time," his mother said. "Prepare him to leave."

Hafsa didn't look like she knew what to do with her hands. "I was told to let him recover. I was going to stay behind with him to let him rest when the army left."

"Who told you so?" Imani asked.

Here, Hafsa appeared to be on more solid ground. "Ingonyama Okar, and it is likely he received his orders from Grand General Buhari or..." She paused for effect. "The queen."

Imani waved the last away. "You were told this by Ingonyama Okar, and I'm here telling you that we're leaving."

"I don't see how you can—"

"'Champion mother' will serve."

Hafsa's lips pursed, but she acquiesced. "Champion mother, I cannot allow—"

"Tell her, Tau," Imani said, squeezing his hand again. "Tell her we're joining the army and marching with them to Palm."

Hafsa turned to him, helpless.

"We'll do as my mother says," Tau told her, no longer sure if he said it because it was what he wanted to do anyway or because he'd never been able to say no to his mother.

Hafsa wilted. "Yes, Champion. I'll come with you, of course. Just give me time to set the affairs here in order before—"

"That'll take too long," Imani said. "Help me stand him up."

"You can't be... Champion mother, your son is in no shape to go traipsing... Listen, his wounds aren't a danger, but the blood loss, he'll be weak for a while and it would not do to have him tear the stitches before his body can heal."

"Come, now, Priestess. With others we are coy, but you, of all people, must understand that his strength does not come from that body."

Hafsa stuttered at the start. "I assure you, I do not know what you mean."

"Mother—"

"He's a match for Greaters and Royals," Imani said. "You've heard the stories?"

"Mother—"

"How long have you been a priestess? How many Lessers and Nobles have you examined, stitched back together, watched heal? How many Lessers should be able to defeat a Noble?"

The conversation was taking place over Tau, and the two women were so intent on each other, it was as if he were not there.

"You are one of the leaders of the medicinal order, neh?" Imani asked. "No normal Lesser can match Nobles. You know this."

"I'm not sure what you wish me to say, Champion mother."

"I'm after no less and no more than the obvious truth," Imani said, leaving the actual words that made up her truth unspoken.

"Mother, enough," Tau said. "Priestess Ekene, when in the day is it?"

"You fell unconscious from blood loss only yesterday afternoon," Hafsa said, emphasizing how recently he'd been injured. "It's now morning and most in camp will just have broken their fast."

"Good. Help me up, both of you. Before we march, Queen Tsiora will meet with her council for war. Things have changed, and our plans will as well. I need to be part of that discussion. Take me to them."

BATTLES

It didn't matter that she was blind. Tau's mother insisted on helping the priestess take him to the war council. She stumbled a bit, and though he was the one being helped, Imani was the one slowing their pace. But soon after they arrived, Tau realized why she'd insisted on coming.

Imani wanted to get to know the players in the game. She'd done the same in Kerem, and almost impossibly for a High Common, she'd risen from being just another handmaiden to becoming one of the fief's chief administrators in less than a cycle.

The large tent, intended for the army's military leaders, was close to the same size as the queen's own. It was, however, dyed black, matching the Indlovu's sense of aesthetics and pride over sense. Dyed black canvas in the broiling heat of Xidda made the interior of Indlovu campaign tents feel more like humid caves than shaded relief from the day.

When Hafsa and his mother walked him in, the heat hit him like an adobe wall.

"They sent no Edifiers to the last two meetings," Nyah was saying. "No one from Palm's Shadow Council came, and that worries me."

Everyone in the room was sitting on thin cushions set around a low table, but Tsiora had a thick, plush cushion that raised her higher than the rest.

"Tau?" asked Hadith, turning on his cushion. "You're up already?" He caught Hafsa's attention. "Please, leave the tent flaps open. It's already too hot in here."

Sitting closest to the door was a grizzled full-blood Ihashe who, though freshly shaven, had the type of face that never seemed clear of stubble. Beside him was Uduak, and Tau figured that Hadith had put the big man in charge of the Ayim while he was recovering. Uduak was next to Kellan, who would lead the Indlovu among them, and beyond them were Thandi, Nyah, and the queen.

"Should you not be resting?" Tsiora asked. She'd leaned forward on her cushion when he'd walked in.

Instinctively, Tau began to bow but abandoned the attempt when his stitches pulled. "My queen," he said, one eye pinched shut against the stinging in his side.

"Should he not be resting, Priestess?" Tsiora asked Hafsa.

Hafsa glared at Imani, and though his mother could no longer see, Tau would have wagered that she knew exactly what the priestess was doing.

"There was insistence that he attend," Hafsa said, bowing.

"I'm fine," Tau told the room while still speaking mostly to Tsiora as he limped to the unoccupied cushion to her right and lowered himself to the floor. "Scratches, nothing more."

"Scratches!" Hafsa said. "Those are a good deal more than…" The priestess seemed to recall the company in which she found herself. "Your wounds are not life-threatening, I'll grant that, but how can you expect to heal properly without rest? You want so badly to rush back to battle, but your body is not at its best."

"Perhaps the priestess is right," said Nyah, from the left side of the queen. "Queen Tsiora…as we'd discussed, it may be better if the champion does not—"

Tau couldn't let Nyah sway the queen but also didn't want to challenge her directly. So he used Hafsa as a proxy.

"Priestess, a fighter who will only go into battle when they're at their best fights for pleasure and not principle," he said. "The things worth fighting for die in darkness if we'll only defend them in the sun."

He kept his eyes on Hafsa, purposefully not looking at Tsiora when he said it, and saw his mother nod at his words.

"I...those are pretty words, sounding true on their face," Hafsa said, "but my life has been spent learning that those who argue for the moral necessity of a fight are far better at spending lives than they are at saving them. Won't enough people die in the battle that's to come? What difference can one more body make in it?"

"On occasion, the whole of the difference."

"Queen Tsiora," said Nyah, interjecting, "we now have a patient arguing with their priestess, and I'm not sure they'll come to terms on their own. What say you?"

But Hafsa wasn't done with Tau yet, and after a glance at Tau's mother, she questioned him. "How highly must one think of themselves to believe that they are the difference in a battle of thousands?"

"You mistake me, Priestess," Tau said. "I don't believe that I'm the difference that matters, but I am the only difference I get to control. So I'll fight, because it's the only principled choice I can make, and doing anything less is the same as an acceptance of defeat and the admission that it's deserved."

Uduak grunted, and from the corner of his eye, Tau saw Tsiora nod and shift on her cushion.

"Thank you, Priestess, for everything," the queen said. "We are blessed by your talent and passion, but the champion and the rest of us on this council must now continue to plan for what's coming."

Hafsa was about to say more, seemed to think better of it, bowed to her queen, and turned to leave.

"Priestess Ekene, would you be kind enough to guide Imani back with you?" Nyah asked, coating her tongue and words with nectar.

"Please do, Priestess," Tau's mother said. "The vizier speaks with the queen's authority, and those who rise so high do it because of their vision and wisdom. I am tired, but, somehow, I didn't realize it until now." Despite being blind and bandaged, Imani locked onto Nyah's face. "Vizier, I aspire to become much more like you."

Tau shivered at his mother's tone, and Nyah's eyes narrowed, but the vizier had no chance to respond. Imani took the priestess's hand and let Hafsa guide her from the room.

"Well, having settled those skirmishes, shall we return our attention to the battle?" Hadith asked, teasing a hint of a smile from Tsiora. "But, excuse me, I'm uncouth," he said, opening his hand toward the rough-faced Ihashe sitting near him. "Tau, this is Inkokeli Wanjala. Just before you and the queen returned to Citadel City from gathering the rest of our army, Wanjala arrived from Jirza with a wing of Ihagu to fight for his queen. And, remaining unbribed by even so gracious an offering, I can say with sincerity that it has been my good fortune to get to know him over the past season. He's a diligent, brilliant, reliable commander, and I've set him the task of leading our Ihashe and Ihagu."

Tau inclined his head toward the man. "Well met, Inkokeli Wanjala."

"It is an honor, Champion."

Wanjala had that way of speaking that instantly placed him as a northern-born Lesser. It was tongue-tip heavy, though the words still sounded like they were coming from the back of the mouth.

"Everyone introduced and comfortable now?" asked Nyah, looking around the table. "Good, because we need to decide how to proceed since I haven't heard from anyone in Palm. Our Shadow Council Edifiers have always kept a strict schedule, but they've missed the last two meetings."

"You think they've been discovered?" asked Hadith.

Nyah had her hands clasped and was chewing on the inside of her cheek. "I'm not sure what it means," she said.

"Until we know more, we should keep faith that they'll be able to open the gates for us," Hadith said. "We should continue with the attack as planned." He glanced at Tau. "Our army has left Citadel City. It's marching for Palm, and if we're going to catch up with them, we need to do the same, but there's still that other issue to discuss."

"The stables?" asked the queen.

"The stables," Nyah confirmed. "Grand General Buhari told us what happened there," she said to Tau.

"Did he?" Tau said. "Strange, he didn't think the tale worth repeating when first he heard it."

"Tau, you told me a demon attacked you in a stable," Hadith said.

"Because one did."

"Well, yes, I believe you now, though I think I was happier when I didn't."

"I worry that Ananthi's prison has begun to crack and that the cracks begin with you, Champion." Nyah let her eyes drift to the queen as she said it.

The vizier might also hold the role of KaEid, but Tau had known Nyah long enough to doubt she was that religious. She was trying to get the queen to agree to something.

"What do you want, Vizier?" he asked.

"The Ayim must suspend their training in the underworld until we know more about why this is happening."

"No," Tau said. "We've proven what we can do in Isihogo, and the other six need more time to master it."

"I'm talking about all seven of you."

Tau felt his eyes go wide before he could stop them. "You want me to stop?"

"What if the things you're doing are opening holes between the realms?" Nyah asked.

Tau sucked his teeth. "You can't really expect—"

"What do you think happens if Ananthi's prison collapses entirely?"

Tau was going to say more, but Nyah's words horrified him.

"We'll still use the Ayim in the attack," Hadith said. "We don't have a choice, if we hope to retake the city, but the vizier's right. There's too much we don't know and the risks are too great."

"The queen has already been put in danger," Nyah said, "and now there's the dead Ihagu."

"Dead Ihagu?" Tau asked.

"He was found in camp a few spans ago," Hadith said. "The back of his head caved in. It could have been a fight among the men gone wrong, or someone managed to get into our camp, kill the soldier, and escape unseen, or..."

"Or?" Tau asked.

"A demon. It could have been a demon that crossed into our world," he said. "Tau, it's safer to do it the way the vizier suggests and stay out of the underworld. We trust that the Ayim will do what they must, when the time comes."

"You can't return to Isihogo until the attack, none of you," Nyah said. "We need to understand what it is you've done first."

The queen nodded. "Ukufa is imprisoned in Isihogo, and it is harder for him to reach you if you stay in Uhmlaba."

"That can't be all we do," Nyah added. "The champion should be guarded, and he can't be allowed near you, Your Majesty."

"We can defend ourselves from the demons," the queen said.

"From one demon, Queen Tsiora. You can entreat only one of them at a time," Nyah said.

"We're not afraid."

"It's not about fear. It's about what makes sense."

"The answer remains no, Nyah, and as much as you may wish we had chosen differently, you don't get to decide this part of our life for us."

Tau looked from the queen to Nyah and back again. It didn't feel like they were talking about the demons, exactly. Also, though Nyah's points were good ones, the queen seemed set in her decision, and not really wanting to examine why, Tau was glad for it. He was her champion and didn't like the idea of not being able to see her. It felt important to be near her.

"So, to confirm, the Ayim training stops now," Hadith said. "In a few days, we'll be in front of Palm's walls, and that will be the next time they return to the underworld."

Tau said nothing.

"My queen, do you think us ready?" Hadith asked, taking Tau's silence as agreement.

"Yes, General Buhari, we do," she said.

Hadith nodded. "Kellan, Wanjala, call the march for Palm City. Odili's civil war begins and ends now."

CHAPTER TWELVE

PALM

Palm City, capital of the Xiddan Peninsula, sat between the fork in the Amanzi Amancinci River with the Central Mountains as its cloak, stone walls the height of seven Greater Nobles as its armor, and the rivers themselves as its shield. The city, extending from the base of the mountains, stretched to the river shores to the north and south and was designed to be defended.

Indeed, if not for the soft contours of its domed buildings and the palace, with its massive central dome and spires, it would be easy to call Palm City a fortress. Whatever one called it, it made Kigambe look like a Drudge's hut after a rainstorm.

"She really lives in that city?" Themba asked.

"She rules it, Themba. It and everything and everyone," said Hadith. "Now, stop staring and help the rest make camp."

They were a couple of thousand strides west of the south fork of the Amanzi with three-quarters of Tsiora's army behind them. Meanwhile, leading close to ten military claws, Wanjala's second-in-command had separated from the main army a day's march earlier to ford the river, crossing to its north shore. The fifteen hundred Ihashe and Ihagu he had with him made up the water and reserve prongs.

As Tsiora's main army set up camp in view of the capital and any scouts Odili had watching, the water and reserve prongs were hiding to the north of the city. There their engineers were completing the rafts that the water prong would use once the attack was underway.

And while Odili defended Palm's main gates with the majority of his forces, the water prong would sail to the city's Port Gates and the Shadow Council agents would open them. Once inside, the soldiers would race to the city's Northern Gates to overwhelm the few guards Odili would have there. That done, the Northern Gates would be opened, Wanjala's second, at the head of more than a thousand men, would come charging in, and they'd be able to take half the city before Odili could even react. The scales, claws, and wings were ready, and before long, Tau expected to be standing in the palace in Palm.

"I can't believe I spent night after night listening to her tell me stories in a tent, like we're two old friends," Tau said, tracing the palace domes and spires with his eyes.

Hadith was also eyeing the capital. "You knew she was a queen."

"I didn't know it meant this," Tau said, waving his hand at the metropolis in the distance.

"Really?" asked Hadith.

"Look at the size of it."

"You know, if the stories of Osonte are true, the cities there are much bigger."

Tau shook his head. "And that is exactly why most of the stories have to be more myth than truth," Tau said. "We're supposed to have built this in the time we've been on Xidda?"

"It wasn't built in a day," Hadith said.

"I can't understand how it could be built in a million million days. Are you really so unimpressed?"

Hadith looked over at him. "I'm trying not to fall over in fright, Tau. I came up with a plan to capture this city and I think it's a good one, but when I look at Palm..." Hadith gave a mirthless laugh. "Who do I think I am to stand against that?"

"It's good to see the capital again," said Kellan, walking over.

"You lived here before the citadel, right?" Tau asked.

"I did, but no longer. Even my mother and sister are gone."

"Gone?"

"Not like that. They fled Palm when they heard about the coup. My uncle was the queen's champion and my mother is political enough to know what that could mean for her and my sister."

"Where are they now?" asked Tau.

"I don't know," Kellan said, "but when word spreads of our victory here, they'll be able to come back."

"Yes...our victory," Tau said as he stared at the most intimidating stronghold he could fathom, wondering if he'd have had the audacity to think he could bring justice to Odili if he'd properly understood the world the man came from. Without looking away, he addressed Hadith. "Honestly, is there any chance? Won't Odili simply conscript Palm's residents and make them fight us? We'd lose to sheer numbers."

"What?" Kellan asked.

"It doesn't work that way," Hadith said. "The big cities, Kigambe, Jirza, Palm, they don't face the war or the raids in the same way our fiefs, hamlets, and villages do. Yes, they send men to train and join the army, and the women test to see if they're Gifted, but the citizens who've completed service, or avoided it because the city needed their particular skills, they won't pick up arms and fight."

"And Odili would have a revolt on his hands if he tried to conscript city Nobles," Kellan said.

"So we only have to worry about Odili's actual soldiers?" Tau asked.

Hadith nodded. "At last count from the Shadow Council, he had something like two thousand men to our six thousand two hundred and twenty-six." Absentmindedly, he touched the space just below his chest, where the spear had gone in. "That's one of the many problems with treating Lessers the way Nobles do," he said. "There's more of us than them, and when we finally refuse to survive on the scraps they throw us, our numbers will make all the difference."

"We have more fighters and we're about to attack an Omehi city. Aren't we playing the part of the Xiddeen in this?" Tau said.

"We should be good at it, then. It's a role we're used to playing, neh?" Hadith said.

Kellan frowned. "You think the skirmishes make you out to be the Xiddeen?"

"I do, Kellan," said Hadith. "We Lessers have the numbers advantage and we're set up to fail against you. It's a nice, tidy lesson on all counts. It teaches us that rebellion against the Nobles would result in our defeat and it encourages the Nobles to make war and never peace because they've seen, firsthand, that they can win against superior numbers."

"Grand General, you're making it sound like there's a secret group of figures plotting the way our society runs and controlling our treatment of one another."

Hadith raised an eyebrow. "How long have you known about the Shadow Council?"

"Ah...That's...that's not the same," Kellan said.

"In any case," Hadith said, "after we delayed the Xiddeen attack, Odili was free to sit behind Palm's walls. He knew the queen would have more and more difficulty arguing that she rules the peninsula when she doesn't control its capital. He knew we'd have to come here to fight, and it's his hope that our greater numbers won't mean much against his stone walls."

"Can we even get to the walls?" Tau asked, pointing to the rivers. "He's destroyed the bridges."

Tau didn't grow up near rivers or other passable bodies of water, but the mass of stone and wooden debris half damming the waters, where cobbled paths met the riverbed, had to be where the city's bridges had once stood.

"The man spits on our history," Kellan said. "The Trident stood for a hundred cycles."

"Trident?" Tau asked.

"See there, where the river's two tributaries join up and flow into the main of the Amanzi? The Trident is...was an engineering marvel. It was a bridge that landed on the north side of the northern fork, the southern side of the southern fork, and it also carried traffic onto the city's side between the two forks. It had three points, like a trident.

"A trident?"

"Yes, it's an . . . ah . . . an old weapon. Osonton, I imagine. It's like a spear with three points."

Tau tilted his head. "Why would you want a spear to have three points? That's like a sword with three points," he said. "It makes no sense."

"I didn't say it made sense," Kellan said. "It's just the name of the thing."

Tau looked to Hadith. "You see? All the old stories are like this."

"This, Chibo, is what men call leadership," Nyah said, walking up with her daughter. "You can tell they're doing it when you see several of them standing around not doing any work."

"Vizier, Chibuye," Tau said, his attention making the girl look down at her feet.

"Good day, Champion," the child said while staring at her feet.

Tau smiled. He was pretty sure those were the first words she'd said to him.

"The queen's tent is up and the council tent is ready as well," Nyah told them.

"Any word from . . ." Hadith looked to Nyah's daughter and then back to Nyah. "From inside the city?"

"None yet, but we're next to meet at sundown. I hope to make contact then."

"We need to know if they can still open the Port Gates," Hadith said.

"Trust me, General, I know." The words were bold, but Nyah looked worried.

"A rider," Kellan said, pointing to the main gates of the city.

They were too far away to have heard them open, but the gates had been opened, and a rider was galloping out from them, holding a long black pennant that snapped in the wind behind him.

"I'll get the queen," Nyah said, taking Chibuye's hand.

"The black cloth, what does it mean?" Tau asked.

"It means they want to talk," said Kellan.

NEED

Tau, the queen, Hadith, Nyah, Kellan, and Wanjala met the messenger near the ruins of the Trident Bridge, and Tau saw that he'd been wrong. The rider wasn't a man. It was a tall woman, middle-aged, pretty, with a purposeful air of self-assurance.

She yelled over the river's waters from her side. "I am Councillor Yamikani Owanu and I come to tell you that our queen is willing to grace you with her presence. She is willing to tell you the terms that will allow us all to avoid unnecessary bloodshed and death."

"Yamikani, we know your daughter," Tsiora said. "Is she well?"

The Royal Noble across the river had a mask of her own but did not wear it like Tau's queen, and her confidence crumbled. "I am Councillor Yamikani Owanu and I come to tell—"

"Are you forbidden to say anything else, Yami?"

The councillor's horse skittered on the stones by the riverbed, sensing its rider's discomfort.

"Will you speak with the queen?" the councillor asked.

"We are the queen."

Yamikani blinked, her face moving like she had a tic. "Will you speak with your sister?"

"Has Odili made her memorize lines too?"

"I know the truth about the two of you. We all do now. Your

sister was born to this duty, and she's acting in the interest of the Omehi."

"The truth? Don't make us angry, Yami."

The councillor swallowed so hard that Tau saw her do it from across the river. "You refuse to meet, then?" she asked.

Tsiora flicked her fingers at the councillor. "Bring Esi to us."

Yamikani's mouth and cheeks fluttered again. "I will convey your words and leave it to the queen to meet with you or not, as is her right."

She turned her horse.

"Yami," Tsiora called. "Give little Nuha a kiss for us. We miss her."

That set the Royal Noble's face flickering like sunlight through tree leaves, and without waiting to get herself under control, she rode off.

"Why send that one?" Tau asked Kellan.

"The Owanu are one of the peninsula's wealthiest families," Kellan whispered. "Odili is showing us the depth and breadth of the alliance he's strung together. He also honors Councillor Owanu by selecting her as his emissary."

"Will they really let her come to us, Nyah?" Tsiora asked. "Do you think they will?"

"If Esi comes out here, Abasi will be with her," Nyah said.

"We don't care. We'll have the chance to see her and make sure she hasn't been harmed."

"Tsiora...," Nyah said, without using the queen's honorific, "it may not be what you want it to be."

"She's our sister. He's using her against us."

"The whole of my heart wants that to be true, my queen."

"It is true," Tsiora said.

Bowing her head, Nyah changed the topic. "The next meeting with the Shadow Council is to be at sunset, and I'll need to be in camp by then. I'm not sending Thandi. I want to attend this one myself. By now, the Shadow Council knows that our army is outside the city. They'll know we're running out of time and they'll find a way to get to the meeting.

Hadith glanced up at the sun. It was low in the sky. "Odili might make us wait," he said.

They needn't have worried. A few moments after disappearing beyond the city's gates, the messenger came out again with a Queen's Guard of Greater Nobles running alongside four horses.

The first two animals carried Gifted with their hoods up, and the third was ridden by a veiled woman in a dress of morning-sky blue. It was Tsiora's fabled sister and in any other circumstance she would have held his attention, but riding beside her was Abasi Odili, and Tau was focused on the man he'd sworn to kill.

As they approached, time broke down more completely than it did when moving between realms, and though Tau's mind raced, the five horses and running Queen's Guard seemed not to move. Yet in a blink, they'd arrived, bringing Tau face-to-face with the only demon that had ever mattered.

Tau felt like he'd succumbed to a fit. He was burning up, trembling, and squeezing Fury's reins so tightly the leather was creaking. Meanwhile, Abasi Odili, murderer, traitor, and coward, sat comfortably astride a white horse across the pebble-bottomed river not twenty-four strides away.

The scum was wearing the armor of a champion and had a guardian sword belted on his hip, and his black-and-red bronze-plated leathers matched the black cloak draping behind him. He looked the part he was playing more surely than Tau ever could.

"I present Queen Esi Omehia, ruler of—"

"Shut up, Yamikani, and let the sisters talk," Nyah said.

"Don't do anything stupid, Tau," Hadith whispered from the ground beside him.

"He's across a river," Tau said, still staring at Odili.

"A river that's too deep to ride through," said Hadith. "A river that's separating us from a dozen Indlovu and two Gifted."

"I have eyes, General."

Kellan was close enough to hear the conversation and took a couple of steps forward, putting himself in front of Fury.

"Esi, we'll help you," Tsiora said.

In response, the queen's sister lifted her veil, drawing her hands up and over, so that the gauzy material fell behind her head and shoulders. Tau, letting his eyes slide to her for a moment, was knocked down and drowned in the shock that washed over him.

Esi's skin, the same dark velvet as the space between the stars, glowed with an allure matched only by the curve of her lips. Her cheekbones and chin were graceful, her nose the perfect place for gentle kisses, and she had eyes the sugared brown of a honeycomb. It was like looking at Tsiora, but because it wasn't actually his queen, Tau's defenses were down, and the thought surfaced before he could stop it—she was beautiful.

"Goddess wept," Tau said.

"Sister, you're the one who needs help," Queen Esi said. "End this madness before it's too late."

"You don't need to tell his lies for him," Tsiora said to her sister. "He doesn't dare harm you. If he did, even the Royals would turn on him."

Tau looked down at Kellan, who was standing at attention just past Fury's nose, and whispered at him. "The sisters, I know they're a birth pair, but have they always...have they always looked so much alike?"

Kellan didn't turn. He just nodded.

"Abasi is my champion, sister," Queen Esi said. "He does my bidding."

"He's a traitor to us and our rule."

"Stop it. Just stop. You're one person, not many. You don't speak for the Nobles and Lessers or the Goddess. You speak for yourself and yourself alone. You speak without the authority of a Ruling or Guardian Council. Tsiora, look at yourself, standing on the wrong side of the Amanzi without a capital, palace, or mandate. You're the traitor, Tsiora. It's you. It's always been you."

"What has he done to you, sweet sister, to make you say such things?"

Esi ignored that. "Surrender your army into my care and I'll grant you mercy."

"Surrender? Mercy? We surrender only to the Goddess, and mercy comes from Her, nowhere else. Sister, we will have Palm City and we beg you not to test us."

"I'm wasting my time with you, aren't I?" Queen Esi said. "You're so mired in the stories they fed you, you can't see the truth for the tale. Tsiora, you're not special. You're not great. The Goddess doesn't speak to you or through you, and if you attack Palm, your army will be crushed and you'll die." She pulled on her horse's reins, turning it around. "Champion, I've said all I can. She won't listen."

"Please, my queen," said Odili, the sound of his slippery voice taking Tau back to the day his father was murdered. "Many lives hang in the balance. May I?"

She seemed to sigh, though the distance separating Tau from her made it hard to know for sure.

"Tsiora... Queen Tsiora," Abasi Odili said, "are you willing to burn Palm City to the ground? Because you'll only get what you want by destroying what you need. Can you see that?"

Tsiora gave Odili the full weight of her attention, and though Tau found it difficult to disagree with Esi's words about the Goddess, there was power in his queen's words.

"Councilman, you think we'll balk over one city?" she said. "We'll burn the whole world to ash, if it's what the Goddess wills."

Odili watched her awhile, then lowered his eyes. "Yes, I can see that you would," he said, turning his horse and waiting on his queen.

Queen Esi rode away first, Odili followed with Yamikani and the Gifted, and then the rest of the Queen's Guard went as well.

"He turned her against us," Tsiora said, dropping her mask and letting tears fill her eyes.

Tau moved Fury next to her horse. "We'll save her," he said, picturing himself standing over Odili's corpse. "Just like you said, we'll get her back."

She reached for him, taking his hand. "Thank you, Champion."

"The sun goes to meet the ocean," Hadith said. "Nyah, will you ride ahead to camp?"

"I can't make it back in time," she said. "I'll need to enter Isihogo here."

"When you meet with the Shadow Council, tell them the rafts will be finished in one more day. Our men will sail for the water gates on the morning that follows, two spans before dawn. Whoever the Shadow Council plans to send to the water gates must be ready then," Hadith said. "Two days from now, two spans before dawn."

"I'll remind them," Nyah said.

Wanjala cleared his throat, surprising Tau. He'd forgotten the quiet inkokeli was with them. "Excuse, but I worry we'll draw attention if we remain here."

"That's 'cause we will," Hadith said. "Tau, can you come down from the horse and examine its foot?"

Tau knew Tsiora liked to wear riding gloves. She'd had them on that day, but when she'd taken his hand a few moments earlier, she'd removed her glove. It was her bare hand in his, and in spite of the day's heat, her skin was cool.

"Champion?" Hadith said.

"Neh?"

"Would you mind pretending that your horse has hurt its leg? It'll give us a reason to stay here."

"Oh, of course," Tau said, dismounting and feeling the day's heat come rushing back when Tsiora's hand slipped from his.

He crouched beside Fury, wincing at the pain in his leg when he did. "Don't kick me, girl," he said to the horse as he rubbed, then lifted one of her feet.

"It's time," said Hadith, checking the horizon and disappearing sun.

Nyah dismounted, moved a few steps west of Fury, and sat. The warhorse's bulk would keep her hidden from the view of anyone in the capital.

"I'll see you soon," Nyah said, closing her eyes.

"Give them our blessings," Tsiora said.

Nyah nodded, her face went slack, and Tau knew she was in the underworld.

Hadith was speaking with Wanjala, and Kellan kept looking at the queen, perhaps to make sure she was well. Tau, meanwhile, considered asking her about her sister but was concerned that any talk of Esi, while she remained within Odili's reach, would do Tsiora more harm than good, and as they waited, the sun set, exchanging its presence for twilight and a growing darkness.

"Something's wrong!" Nyah said, her eyes snapping open.

Hadith stepped toward her. "Vizier?"

"Nyah, what's happened?" asked Tsiora.

"Lelise, they have Lelise," Nyah said. "She was trying to shout something to me. She was with two Gifted and then they all vanished from the underworld. Tsiora, the ones who had Lelise, they weren't Shadow Council."

"If they have her, Odili knows everything," Hadith said.

Then Wanjala was shouting. "They're on the walls!"

Tau and everyone with him looked as the long line of torches atop the nearest wall of Palm City was set burning. It was dusk, but the blazing peat moss provided enough light for them to see it when several poles of thick bronze were held out from the top of the wall's parapets like fishing rods. The poles were spaced evenly and had ropes attached to their ends, and if they'd been spears, they'd have been pointed right at them.

"What are they doing?" Wanjala asked.

"Goddess, no!" cried Nyah.

She'd been the one to see Lelise in Isihogo. She was the one to figure it out first.

"Look away, my queen!" Hadith said, catching up to the events.

Tsiora's brows furrowed. "Why, what is—"

The rest of her sentence was lost to the sound of her own scream as the still-moving bodies of a dozen Gifted women, with ropes wrapped round their necks and sacks over their heads, were thrown from the ramparts to fall until the nooses pulled taught, snapping spines and killing every last one of them.

Tau was up immediately. He lifted Tsiora from her horse and held her tight, muttering empty things about how it would all be well.

He tried to calm her. He tried to turn her away from the executions, but she was rooted to the spot, still as stone, her eyes fixed on the walls and the dead swinging from them.

BURN

Nothing and no one," Nyah said, returning from her third trip to Isihogo. It had been several spans since the hangings, dusk had become night, and Tau, along with the queen and her council, were in the war tent back in their camp.

"How many Shadow Council were in the city?" asked Hadith.

"Fewer than the women he killed," Nyah told him.

She was sitting cross-legged on a cushion, rubbing her temples. Hadith was pacing. Kellan and Wanjala were standing, but still. The handmaidens were also in the tent, and so was Uduak. The queen, sitting on her cushion, had her head in her hands, and Tau was kneeling beside her, listening to the conversation swirl around him.

Hadith spoke slowly, like he didn't want to ask the question. "Could you identify any of them by—"

"No," said Nyah.

He nodded. "That's intentional. Odili hid their faces so we wouldn't know if he'd really captured them all."

"Yes," said Nyah.

"It means we must behave as if he has."

"Yes," said Nyah.

"It means he knows about our plans for the Port Gate. It means he knows about our splinter army on the north side of the river."

Nyah nodded and closed her eyes.

"So be it. . . . We'll . . . ah . . . we'll have to—"

"Call the water and reserve prongs back to the main army," the queen said, head still in her hands.

"My queen?" asked Hadith.

Tsiora looked up and Tau saw that her tears had tracked a path all the way to her chin. "Call the whole of our army to us, General," she said. "We have had enough of Odili, his treachery and cruelty. Our army will attack before the light of the new day. We will burn down the walls with our Guardians and we will drag that insect from our palace."

"Queen Tsiora, I'm not sure we can win that way. Odili will call his own Guardians, and our losses, the loss of life on both sides, will be terrible."

"There is only one side, General," she said, before turning to Tau. "Champion, it falls to you and the Ayim now. The difference in victory or defeat depends on how much time you can give our Entreaters. Give us enough and Palm's walls will come down."

"Then they'll fall, my queen," Tau told her.

"Vizier, have you nothing to say?" Hadith asked, begging her to help him make his argument.

Nyah had not cried, but when she looked to Hadith, Tau saw that her eyes were red, swollen. "The walls will fall and Odili will die," the vizier said.

The nod from Hadith didn't come quickly. "Wanjala, order the water and reserve prongs to cross the Amanzi and join forces with us here. Ready our ponton bridges. As before, the supporting boats go in the water two spans before dawn and our army will cross each bridge as it's laid."

"Your word, my will, Grand General," said Wanjala, turning for the tent's entrance at the same moment as a thunderous boom shook the earth.

Shouting from outside followed the blast.

"What in the Goddess is that?" asked Kellan.

Not waiting for an answer, Tau moved in front of Tsiora, hands on his swords, and the handmaidens dashed to the queen. He could hear that the shouting outside the tent had given way to panicked screaming.

"An attack," said Uduak as a closer boom hit hard enough to make it feel like Tau's very bones were vibrating.

"We'll see how they like it when we fight back," said Wanjala, opening the flaps of the tent to step outside.

Past him, Tau could see a thick line of fire burning across the ground like a giant had raked a flaming torch through the dirt.

"Goddess," Wanjala said, his eyes on the night skies and his voice faint. "They've called their dragons!"

The next blast hit then, strafing across the tent's entrance and burning through Wanjala like he'd been made of wizened straw.

The aftershock and eruption of dirt from the firebomb threw Tau back as the air in the tent flared with sparks and evaporated, sucking the structure in on itself and collapsing it on them. One moment Tau was standing, seeing Wanjala die, and the next he was on his back, ears ringing like in Daba, wrapped in burning canvas.

"Tsiora!" he yelled, cutting his way free of the tent's remains. "Tsiora!"

He saw a form writhing beneath more burning cloth, and ripping it away, he pulled Nyah clear.

"The queen," she mouthed—or shouted. It was hard for Tau to hear anything over the ringing in his ears.

He spun round, looking for Tsiora, and felt his stomach clench. The area of the camp closest to the river was on fire. Three or four of Odili's dragons were already in the air, blasting fat gouts of twisting flame into their army's midst, and though the city was too far away for Tau to see its gates, he knew Odili had ordered them opened.

There was no other way to explain the mass of Palm City's soldiers running straight for the Amanzi, the ones in the forefront carrying the tools to cross it. They ran in groups, holding either ponton boats or the hemp-strapped wooden planks that would be placed on top of them to make temporary bridges.

Odili's army was coming for them.

POWERFUL

Tau turned away from the approaching disaster. "Tsiora! Tsiora!"

Nyah grabbed him by the elbow, pointing and shouting something he could only half hear in one ear.

Following her pointing hand, he felt relief flow through him, and Tau ran to help Auset and Ramia cut themselves and the queen out of the mess that had been the war council's tent.

As soon as she was free, Tau wrapped Tsiora in his arms, lifting her clear of the smoking canvas.

"Are you well?" he said, holding her.

She shook her head, worrying him until he realized it was because she couldn't hear.

"Are you hurt?" he asked, exaggerating the words so she could follow the shapes his mouth made.

Understanding flooded her face and she shook her head again. She was fine.

"Tau!"

With the ringing in his ears subsiding, Tau looked over his shoulder. It was Hadith with Uduak and Kellan. They were making their way over the embers and disarray of the toppled tent.

Tsiora, still in his arms, pressed her lips to his good ear and came close to deafening him when she shouted in it. "We need to call to our Guardians!" He flinched and her eyebrows shot up. "You can hear?" she shouted.

Nodding, he turned to the rest. "Vizier, bring the Entreaters. Uduak, gather the Ayim and meet us in front of the queen's tent," he yelled. "Hadith, Kellan, Odili's army is crossing the river. He knows the rest of our soldiers are on the river's north side. You need to defend the camp with what we have."

"They've got us, Tau. We have to run!" Hadith said, half his words lost beneath another burst of dragon fire.

"No!" Tsiora shouted, hearing enough of what her grand general had said. "Do as our champion commands. Fight back."

"Uduak, go!" Tau said.

The big man saluted and ran off through the haze of gathering smoke to get the others.

"Mama!" called a thin voice.

Tau swung round, pulling the queen behind him, and saw a small girl running for the vizier, her arms spread wide. Seeing her, Nyah gasped, dropped to her knees, and embraced the child, crying as she held her. "Chibuye!"

It was Hafsa; she'd brought the girl, and Tau's mother too. "The hospital tents were hit...they're burning...not safe. I brought... I'm trying to save as many as I can. There's nowhere else to—"

"You've done well, Priestess," said the queen. "Thank you."

"I—I have to go back and try to get more out."

"Go," Tsiora said. "And when you've done what you can, meet us at our tent."

"Tau?" His mother, hearing that Hafsa was about to leave, cast about with her free hand, trying to find him.

"He's here," the priestess said, handing her over before running back the way she'd come.

"What's going on?" Imani asked, latching on to Tau's wrist. "What's happening?"

"We're under attack," he said. "Odili sent dragons and his army against us."

"Guardians will do his bidding?" She was rattled but shook it off.

"It doesn't matter. You were given your strength for a reason. You'll see us through."

The queen touched the back of his mother's shoulder. "He was and he will."

"Nyah, the Entreaters," Tau said, hemmed in by their closeness and expectations.

But the vizier didn't move. "My daughter..."

"She'll be with us," Tau said. "Call the others or we all die."

"The queen's tent?" Nyah asked.

"Yes, there. Meet us, with the Entreaters."

"Take my daughter, Tau."

"Vizier..."

"I want you to take her. You."

"We'll take her, the champion and us," the queen said. "Go, Nyah."

Nyah stood, holding her daughter's face in her hands. "They'll keep you safe."

"I'll come with you, Mama," the girl said. "I'm safe with you."

Nyah gave the child a smile. "Trust me, Chibo. Hold tight to the queen and her champion. There are no two people more powerful in the whole world."

The words were spoken in earnest, and Chibuye gave Tau a sideways look, wanting, he knew, to believe her mother, but the dragons made mock of Nyah's talk of power, pounding the ground mere strides away with enough fire and fury to kill more than two dozen women and men cowering behind a train of supply wagons.

The girl jumped in fear, crying out and clinging to her mother's robes, but Nyah pried the small hands open and thrust them at Tau.

"Take her."

"Vizier...," Tau said, unable to tear his eyes from the burning bodies not a spear's throw away.

"Keep her safe."

He looked at Nyah. "I will," he said. "I will."

Breathing out and letting go of some tiny part of her worry, Nyah gave the girl a last kiss before disappearing into the smoke as Uduak had done before.

"Mama!" the girl yelled, trying to pull away from Tau.

"Kellan goes for the officer's tents," Hadith said. "Tau, I can't move as fast and feel a coward for even saying it, but I told him to send runners back to us. I'll come with you and use the runners to relay orders. I swear I'll be more use that way than trying to set up a command position out there."

"You're no coward, Hadith. You've never been and you're not one now. If that's the way to do it, then it is. Let's go," Tau said, eyeing the horizon and seeing the dragons banking for another pass. "Auset, Ramia!"

"We have the queen," Auset said, and the two women flanked her.

"Take my arm, Mother," Tau said, moving his mother's grip away from his wrist. "I've got you, Chibuye. Your mother will be back, she knows where we're going."

They went as fast as they could, running from the chaos and the dragon fire. Behind them, the camp had turned into a stampede of people trampling one another in their attempts to flee the flames. To stay ahead of the madness, Tau pulled his mother and Chibuye along, while, over his shoulder, he saw people knocked down and crushed by their fleeing fellows. No one helped, and whether hurt or dead, the fallen remained where they fell to burn either way.

In the tumult, Tau thought, the army would kill as many of their own as the dragons would, but in the long term, if they did not find a way to contest the Guardians, the civil war would be over in a single span.

"He found them!"

Hadith was pointing up the low hill on which the queen's tent had been pitched, and Uduak was in front of it with Yaw, Themba, and Jabari. The Petty Noble, freshly bandaged and hood up, was watching the skies. He was watching the dragons.

"Quickly," said Tau, urging more speed from the girl and his mother's stumbling steps. "Almost there."

"They attacked us at night," said Themba when they were close. "What kind of inyoka does that?"

"We were going to do that, you simpleton," Auset said.

"Ours was predawn. Predawn, not night," Themba told her. "What now?" he asked, turning to Tau.

Tau didn't answer right away. He handed his mother and Chibuye into the care of the nearest of Tsiora's actual handmaidens. "Take them inside the tent, but all of you, stay near the entrance. If we need to run, you have to be close at hand."

The handmaiden, a wisp of a thing, bobbed her head and took hold of Chibuye and Tau's mother. "Your word, my will, Champion," she said.

"Close, neh?" Tau reminded her. "If I open the tent flaps, you all need to be right there."

The same head bob and she was off with them, leaving Tau feeling guilty. He'd promised Nyah he'd stay with Chibuye, and though she was just a few strides away, he worried about protecting her if she was beyond arm's reach.

"They're as with us as they can be, Tau," Tsiora said, reading the emotions behind his face. "We have our own fighting to do, and if we fail, it won't matter how close we keep them."

"Incoming...," muttered Themba.

"What?" Tau said, finding the answer himself.

Two more dragons had joined the others.

"Tau, tell me something good," Themba said.

Tau shook his head. "They're not ours."

Hadith pointed to a group running toward them. "But they are," he said, and Tau had never been so relieved to see Nyah in his life.

CALL

Nyah was not alone. Behind her and Thandi were seventeen Gifted, and without a word, they arrayed themselves into four groups, Nyah leading one, the queen another, Thandi the third, and in the fourth grouping, two Gifted, whom Tau did not know, stood apart from the rest. Each Hex, each grouping of six, linked arms.

They'd not done that in Daba, but Tau could imagine that it helped their nerves if not their powers. After all, though some had their hoods up and others not, the one thing they shared was something with which he'd become intimately familiar. They were afraid.

"There are three Hexes and two additional Gifted," Nyah said to him. "The two will not call to the Guardians. Instead, they'll remain in Isihogo to watch for the strength of our shrouds. When our shrouds fail, they'll come to you and you must join us."

"We'll come when called," Tau said, thinking of the dragons that would do the same.

They'd race from their nests in the Central Mountains to see if it was actually their youngling crying out to them.

The dragons were intelligent; they had to be to hold the Gifted in Isihogo. They must have some sense that the calls they answered were a trap, and they came anyway. Without regard for themselves, they answered every cry, holding hope that one day it would be their missing child they found instead of bondage.

"Chibuye?" Nyah asked, drawing Tau from his thoughts and sounding frightened of what he might say.

"Inside the tent, right by the entrance. She waits for us. She waits for you."

"Thank you," Nyah said, inclining her head, surprising Tau with the show of respect.

"You know what it is we must do," the queen said to her Gifted, "but there is something you have not been told." The Gifted were trained and disciplined. There was not even a shuffling of feet as they waited for their queen to say more. "We have trained warriors to come into Isihogo as our shrouds begin to fail. They have trained to face the demons, match them, and hold them back."

That caused some shuffling. The news was too big to be heard in stillness.

"When our shrouds fail, we will remain in the underworld. When our shrouds fail, we...will...not. We must hold to our Hex until the demons break the circle of warriors, and then and only then may we return to our world. Is this understood?"

They answered as one. "It is," they said.

"May the Goddess give you strength, courage, wisdom, and love," Tsiora told them. "May She accept the sacrifices we make tonight in Her name and for Her glory."

"May She accept us as we are," the nineteen Gifted intoned.

"Her grace, my salvation," muttered Yaw to himself as the twenty women closed their eyes and sent their spirits to the underworld.

"Are you ready?" Tau asked the Ayim.

Themba spoke before the others. "Does it matter?"

"Not even in the slightest," Tau said, clapping his sword brother on the back.

"Then," Themba said, "we're ready."

Auset snorted. "The Goddess is great. She gives even the lowliest among us a chance to speak Her truth."

"She is great," said Yaw. "She'll help us."

"Good," Themba said, lifting his chin to point toward the front of the army. "We'll need it."

Odili's dragons were coming in for another pass, and under the cover of their constant barrage of flame and smoke, Odili's army had completed their ponton bridges and were crossing the Amanzi.

"We can't fear them," said Yaw. "Odili and his followers move behind the Goddess's back. We stand in Her grace." He called their attention to the bottom of the hill on which they stood. "Look, a sign. The runners arrive with messages."

Lightly armored Ihashe and Indlovu ran up the small slope and saluted Hadith, taking turns to give him their reports, and he, in his turn, gave them orders to send back to their scales or claws, and, in a few cases, wings.

"The reserve and water prongs are crossing the Amanzi from north to south," Hadith told Tau. "We'll have them with us in a couple spans."

"Tonight, a couple spans is a long time," Tau said.

"It's faster than I'd dared hope," Hadith said.

Tau took his friend by the shoulders. "Then it's fast enough, neh?"

He didn't look convinced, but Hadith returned the gesture, putting his hands on Tau's shoulders, and the two men bolstered each other with shared strength. "We'll make it fast enough."

"You'll hold Odili back with our Indlovu?" Tau asked. "Where will you have Kellan and his men fight?"

Hadith paused, took his hands from Tau's shoulders, and shook his head. "Kellan should have his scale ready soon, but I can't risk losing them to dragon fire. They won't engage until our Guardians are in the air too. They won't go in until the Guardians aim their fury at each other instead of our soldiers. If we're going to win this battle, we need our Indlovu. I can't risk them needlessly."

Tau didn't understand. "Needlessly? Without Kellan's Indlovu to blunt the strength of Odili's soldiers, we'll lose hundreds of Lessers."

Hadith's eyes dropped, settling on Tau's chin. "The Ihagu, they'll hold until our Guardians are in the air."

"What? The Ihagu can't hold against Odili's Indlovu. They'll be slaughtered."

There was silence as Tau realized he was talking through things Hadith already knew. The Ihagu were the cost to be paid to buy the time they needed to get their dragons in the fight. The Ihagu would stand, fight, and fall, so that the reserve and water prongs, filled with Ihashe, could cross the river and join the rest of the army.

"Hadith...," Tau said, the despair on his friend's face stopping him from finishing the thought.

"We need the time," Hadith said, his voice shaking as he turned to issue the order for the Lessers to hold.

Tau didn't stop him. The grand general had his duty and Tau had his. "Ayim," he shouted, wondering if the Ihagu with the unusually large throat stone who had found him and Jabari after their night in Isihogo would be among the ones ordered to stand and fight, "form our circle!"

The six moved to his side. From his right it was Jabari, Yaw, Auset, Ramia, Themba, and, immediately to his left, Uduak. The seven of them sat on the mix of dirt and dead grass that had been tromped into nothingness by the passage of thousands of feet.

"Care," Hadith said to them all, his eyes on Uduak.

"You too," Uduak said, and then more messengers had come and Hadith was with them, and the Ayim, surrounded by twenty Gifted, military runners, Queen's Guard, and the tumultuous fear and fervor that were ubiquitous in war, were somehow still significantly alone.

Tau let his fingers play across his sword hilts, passing time as he waited for his turn to take part in the fight. Then, when he was almost too nervous to stay sitting, he heard a single shout that joined with other voices to forge the riotous sound of hopeful cheering.

He raised his head to the skies and was just in time to see three black dragons dive through the evening's clouds and into the same air as Odili's beasts.

Tsiora's Guardians had come to call.

DRAGONS

Beneath the dragons' swooping bulk, Odili's soldiers, having crossed the river, sprinted over the deadened grasslands. Fastest among them were the Indlovu, and in their hundreds, they ran for the men Tau had spent a season gathering for this very battle.

The two sides met in a cacophony of bronze that resounded across the plains like a mountain echo, and Tsiora's Ihagu and Ihashe never had a chance. Their battle lines dissolved under the weight, strength, speed, and ferocity of their Noble brethren, and the Lessers were cut down.

Tau watched them drop, dead or soon to be, while backlit by torrents of spiraling fire that shot from the mouths of flying monsters. Odili had five Guardians in the air, Tsiora three, and in a scene better suited for the mind and memory of bards or sculptors, Tau witnessed what it was to see the gods at war.

The largest of the dragons, a newcomer and so one of Tsiora's, launched itself at a smaller beastling, leading with a blaze of wildfire so vast it etched motes of flickering lights into Tau's vision. The dragon, the black wrath, buried the beastling's body in an inferno, and over the shouts of the men and the clashing of their swords, Tau heard the beastling scream.

Careening out of control, the burned dragon burst clear of the fires in which the black wrath had engulfed it. Tau tried to track the falling creature, but his eyes kept jerking and slipping away from the beastling's light-absorbing scales. He did catch its end, though. He saw it plummet to the ground and smash into the grasslands, obliterating tents, wagons, women, and men.

It had to be dead. Nothing could survive that, Tau thought, but the beastling struggled to its feet, scanned the skies, and saw its true death coming.

The black wrath, diving too fast for Tau to see, struck the beastling with it claws, driving talons through the body of the smaller dragon and into its neck, forcing the beastling's head to the dirt. The bigger dragon roared, the sound setting Tau's heart to pounding, and then, maw wide as the gap between the living and the dead, it snatched the beastling's head in its jaws and cracked its skull, breaking the smaller dragon's bones, scales, and face to pieces.

"Goddess wept," said Tau, watching as the beastling's body caved in on itself, collapsing like an unstable cliff that turned to ash and then vanished. "Goddess wept," he said as the black wrath beat its edgeless wings and hauled itself back to the skies to rejoin the stars and the storm of savagery taking place among them.

Airborne again, Black Wrath blew gout after gout of columned fire at its new target, a dragon of near equal size. Nearby, two others were entangled in the air, spinning muzzle over tail as they plunged their talons into each other, ripping at bellies, backs, and wings.

Tau couldn't look away. The zealotry with which the two dragons slashed at each other had him transfixed, and he watched them spin through the sky like a boulder hurled by a giant until they came crashing down and into one of the walls of Palm City. They hit the barrier, built with quarried stone from the Central Mountains, and blew through it like it was the side of a canvas tent.

The expanse of wall they'd hit tumbled down like a landslide, coming apart in small pieces that brought larger sections after them. In turn, the larger sections were chased by entire columns of disintegrating rock, and in wave after wave of collapse, the wall north of Palm City's main gates came tumbling down.

A cheer went up from Kellan's Indlovu, who had yet to see

combat, but Tau wanted to tell them it hadn't helped. The wall that had fallen had collapsed in on itself. There was no way to pass it without climbing the mass of rubble, and the rubble was almost as great an impediment as the wall it had once been.

Meanwhile, behind the debris there was a bonfire of light, a howl from a dragon; then one of the two beasts drew itself back into the air, flying straight at Black Wrath.

Tau had no way to be sure, but somehow he knew that Black Wrath was the dragon Tsiora had called.

"Behind!" he yelled to the gargantuan as if it could hear him. "Behind!" But it was too late, and the dragon from the wall, legs and talons extended, smashed into Black Wrath's back.

Black Wrath snarled, contorted its serpentine neck, and took one of its attacker's legs between its teeth. Once the grip was firm, the dragon clapped its mouth closed around the appendage and shook its head back and forth, wrenching, tearing, then ripping the limb away. The lifeless leg still in its mouth, Black Wrath blew fire and turned it to dust.

The dragon from the wall threw itself from Black Wrath, frantic to flee the pain that had been dealt it, but Tsiora's monster was not finished. It turned back to the brute it had been fighting and blew enough flame to draw a screeching keen from that one, and then Black Wrath barreled for the dragon from the wall.

The wall dragon, bleeding corrosive blood from its amputated limb and having no desire to face Black Wrath alone, reached for the clouds, urging as much speed as it could from its damaged body, but Tsiora's dragon trailed it like a shadow, catching the wall dragon, digging talons into its rump, ribs, and then spine.

With its hold secure, it clawed and climbed its way up the back of the wall dragon, until in position and holding the helpless creature in its grasp, Black Wrath blew fire, coating its prey in a sluice of flame so hot and bright it turned night to day. The wall dragon writhed and screamed, but Black Wrath held it tight, blanketing it in a sheath of blazing suffering that burned the ensnared drake in a pyre of its own flesh.

"Tau, they killed it," Yaw said.

"What?" Tau asked, eyes fastened on Black Wrath.

"Our other dragon."

He made himself look, and there, in the waters of the Amanzi, two dragons ripped into the carcass of a third until it went to ash and disappeared.

"We've only got one left," Themba said. "Odili still has three."

"Champion!" It was one of the two Gifted who were set to watch the others in Isihogo. "It's time. The shrouds of those with the queen, they're failing."

"Tau," said another voice, Thandi's.

Tau stood, breaking the circle of Ayim. "What's happened?" he asked.

Thandi stumbled toward him, barely able to stand. "My dragon, she...she died at the wall."

Thandi fell and Tau caught her. "What's happening to you?"

"The break in the leash...it...I've never had a dragon die before....I felt...I felt her die."

Tau called to the Queen's Guard closest to them. "You there! Do you know the face of Priestess Hafsa Ekene?"

"I do, Champion."

"Find her or some other from her order. Bring them here as fast as you can. Our Gifted, they'll need Sah attention."

"I'm well," Thandi said, "it just...it felt like I died with her."

"Rest easy, you've done your part. It's our turn."

"Nyah is still in the underworld," Thandi said. "Her dragon died too, but her shroud is intact. She's—"

"I'll see to her. Rest." Tau waved over another of the Queen's Guard. "Watch her and tell the others to mind the Gifted. I think it'll be a bad time for them, when they return to Uhmlaba."

"Yes, Champion!"

Tau went back to the circle and sat down.

"Ayim," he said to the six. "Now we fight!"

CHAPTER THIRTEEN

SACRIFICES

Form the circle!" Tau bellowed, determined to be heard over the squall of Isihogo's winds.

The moment he landed in the underworld, the other Gifted, whose shrouds were a breeze blow from gone, began to leave Isihogo. They'd been asked to fly their dragons past the limits of their shrouds' protection, but with their dragons dead, the Gifted in Nyah's and Thandi's Hexes served no purpose and endangered everyone with the extra light from their souls' glow. So, the shroudless left Isihogo and the only Gifted who remained were those in Tsiora's Hex and Nyah, her shroud translucent and fading.

"Leave, Nyah," Tau shouted. "You've done your duty."

The vizier shook her head. "My dragon fell and I no longer need to draw power from this place. My shroud will hold for a while yet and I'm staying with the queen. "

The mists were not the place for drawn-out discussions, and nodding to the vizier, Tau ran to stand near to the opaque void that was his queen's armor. The shrouds of the five women in Tsiora's Hex were papyrus thin, and he could see the golden glow of the souls within. Unlike the others, Tsiora's defenses were strong as ever, and such visible evidence of her power was a comfort. But unable to see her face, Tau worried about the strain she was under.

"Eyes to the mists," he shouted at the Ayim. "Now that we're here and glowing like embers, the demons won't be far behind."

But it wasn't the Ayim's souls that called the monsters. Within a breath of Tau's last word, one of Tsiora's Gifted lost her shroud, and filled with power, she didn't glow; she shone.

"Cek!" said Themba as a demon soared through the mists, dragging the thick fog in its wake as it leapt for the glowing woman.

Tau's sword brother jumped into the monster's path and was joined by Auset, the two of them closing the gap through which the demon had hoped to dive. The creature hit Themba square, knocking him down, and Auset whipped it about the head and neck with her dirks, sending it into a snarling rage and giving Themba the chance to crawl clear. As one, they fought the thing, sword and dirks slashing and cutting, rending demon flesh from demon bone.

The Gifted, her features revealed without her shroud, held up shaking hands to her mouth as if to scream, but shock stole all sound from her.

"Trust in the Ayim!" came Tsiora's voice, booming out from the impenetrable dark of her shroud. "Trust them and stay with the Hex."

The Gifted, young and shaking like she were standing atop a mountain peak, slammed her eyes shut so she could not see the demon that wanted her blood. She turned away from it, trusting blindly that her defenders would keep the monster from her, and she returned her powers to the Hex.

She's right to be afraid, Tau thought. She'd lost her shroud first, marking her as the weakest among the Gifted in the queen's Hex. When it came time to leave the underworld, the other Gifted would force their power into her. They'd make her burn bright enough to become the focus of the dragon's ire, and it would latch on to her soul, trapping her in Isihogo with the demons. The young Gifted was moments from her own death. Knowing that, she still did her duty, and bearing witness to such courage made Tau feel like he'd taken a spear to the heart.

A demon came for him, and with his mind still on the young Gifted, he unleashed a barrage of attacks on the monster. The thing he fought was shoulder-high, stocky, and twice as thick as he was. It also had short arms and legs. It could not reach him easily and Tau punished it for its lack.

But before he could put the demon down, a second fiend joined it and the two of them began hounding him together. He kept them both back, and between blows, he could see that the rest of the Ayim were fighting skirmishes of their own.

To his left, Uduak laid waste to anything foolish enough to come near, while on his right, Jabari moved as ineludibly as death. In choppy glimpses gained only when his fight turned him round, he saw Yaw and Ramia on the other side of the circle, giving no ground to demons that loomed over them.

The Ayim were holding.

"Queen Tsiora?" Tau called, hauling his strong-side sword from the eye socket of the thickset demon.

"One more Guardian to fell," she said. "The big one."

The Dragon Queen had evened the score, and Tau, fighting one demon only, backed up a step, making space, and took a risk.

It was like moving each eye in a different direction, only more disorienting, but he did it. Tau split his vision and pushed a portion of his consciousness back to Uhmlaba, where, from his body's sitting position in front of Tsiora's tent, he caught a moment of the battle for Palm City.

Low in the skies, Black Wrath blew fire and dove down toward Odili's last dragon, its wings frozen in time like a painter's rendering. Wrath's prey was wounded, and though Odili's dragon's light-drinking scales prevented Tau from identifying where it had been cut, he could still see blood pouring from its side and out over the battlefield like obsidian rain.

The men below looked carved from stone. Tau saw swords raised to kill, soldiers cut down or dying on the ends of blades, and still, the most unfortunate were the few caught in the rain of dragon blood. Those few, though far from Tau, had expressions of agony so broad that even the distance could not soften them.

In Isihogo, the demon was moving and Tau let go of Uhmlaba to fight it. It swiped at him, misjudging the distance and missing. Tau thrust at it, connecting. It howled and jerked away, pain blooming, and with the circle of Ayim still holding, Tau split his mind again.

Little had changed or moved in Uhmlaba, and so Tau paid attention to the things he had not before. He saw that Kellan's Indlovu were only now entering the fray. He saw that the Ihagu and Ihashe had suffered a massacre at the hands of Odili's Nobles and enraged Ingonyama. He saw that Black Wrath was strides from catching the dragon, the one with its blood pouring down, in its claws and Wrath's target had no room to maneuver. Fighting back, Blood Pour had its maw open wide and Tau could see flame lighting its jaws as it sought to deluge Black Wrath in fire.

A new demon attacked. Tau let Uhmlaba fall away, defeated his enemy, and was about to split his mind again when he saw the strangest thing. From the mists, moving faster than should have been possible, came a dozen shrouded Gifted, running right for the circle of Ayim.

"Tau!" shouted Themba.

"I see it," he called back, swinging his head toward Nyah. "What are they doing?"

"Those are...they're Odili's Edifiers. I don't know what they're doing," she said. "If they try to breach the circle, cut them down."

"Nothing gets through!" Tau yelled to the others as the dozen shrouded Edifiers ran closer.

It didn't make sense. Though the Edifiers could use their Gifts to move through Isihogo at great speed, which was what allowed them to travel to one another and exchange messages in the mists, their use of power that night meant they were corporeal in Isihogo. It meant that, when they came close enough, Tau and the Ayim could either kill them in both realms or send them back to Uhmlaba with grievous psychic wounds.

It made no sense, Tau thought, as the first of the Edifiers stopped just outside the range of his swords and dropped her shroud.

The other eleven Gifted did the same. They surrendered their shrouds while holding as much of the Goddess's power as they could bear, turning themselves into a dozen blinding suns of golden light.

Realization and terror hit Tau together, and he held his swords tight. Odili had sent these Edifiers, loyal to the point of fanaticism, to sacrifice themselves and draw the demon swarm, and the tumult of howls that answered the glowing Gifted, the voiced hatred of a thousand demons was loud enough to drown out even the wailing of Isihogo's eternal windstorm.

Death was coming.

CHAMPIONS

The first of Odili's Edifiers to die did so in a grisly fashion. From beyond the mists, sucking and slicing tentacles lashed out and latched on to her glowing flesh to pull her screaming into the gloom. Another demon, eight-legged, scuttled into view, its bulbous compound eyes reflecting the glow from the souls of everyone present. With its forelegs it reached for the Edifier nearest Tau, and he stepped forward to greet it in kind.

"No! Hold the circle!" Nyah shouted to Tau and the Ayim. "They'll feed on the Edifiers first. It gives us time."

Tau hesitated, looked into the frightened face of Odili's Edifier, and rejected Nyah's words. He stepped forward to defend the Gifted, but another demon, this one winged, flew overhead and punched through her body with the hooked talons on its feet. Her mouth fell open, and without even the chance to call for help, she was taken into the air and the mists overhead.

Tau shouted in frustration, checking the skies. She was gone and things were bad. The fliers were dangerous, rare, and if they had been lured by the Edifiers' glow, then the worst of Isihogo was on its way as well.

"Protect the queen and the Hex!" Nyah shouted, this time to Tau specifically. "The Edifiers sowed their field. They know what harvest it brings."

Another Gifted was assaulted and destroyed.

"We can't just watch them—"

"Yes, you can!" Nyah shouted. "The demons will come for us next."

"Odili's Guardian has fled." It was Tsiora, speaking through the deep of her shroud. "It means his Hex has wearied its strength. They've abandoned the underworld, and you must do the same while we finish this."

"My queen, you need to leave as well," Nyah yelled over the winds, her voice frantic. "If Odili's Gifted have abandoned the underworld, then we must do the same. Already this battle has taken too much power from Isihogo.... It could be noticed."

"Then pray that the Cull aren't keeping watch," Tsiora said. "We can't leave until we finish this!"

If they said more, Tau didn't hear it. A demon attacked, he was forced to fight it away, and when next he had a spare breath, he stole a glance at the young Gifted in Tsiora's Hex, the one who'd been first to lose her shroud.

She looked terrified, and seeing her that way tore Tau in two. Relief ran through him that her sacrifice would save Tsiora, but pacing his relief was his shame at how easily he'd come to value the queen's life over another's.

Seeking some reprieve from the shame, Tau split his mind in two, flashing back to Uhmlaba, where he saw that Kellan's Indlovu were facing Odili's fighters. The time difference between realms meant that he could only view the battle in discrete moments, and watching a war fought in frozen glimpses turned the expected nightmare of battle into something even more ghoulish.

The killing fields were covered with the dead, lying like unearthed worms across the ground as smoke cocooned the air like massive spiderwebs. Men, their mouths yawning wide in endless screams, died for an eternity, and in the sky was Black Wrath, not far from the city, its domes, and...

Tau snapped the whole of his mind back into Isihogo. "Another dragon!" he shouted, calling to Tsiora and Nyah. "It came from the mountains and is flying over the city. Queen Tsiora, it's coming for your dragon!"

"Another..." Tsiora went quiet and Tau guessed she was seeing through Black Wrath's eyes. "Such vicious treachery," the queen said.

"Odili didn't use every Hex, did he?" Nyah asked.

"He did not," Tsiora said. "He was attacking us in phases."

Tau named them in his head, the surprise attack aided by dragon fire, the sacrificial Edifiers to overwhelm Tsiora's Gifted with demons, and the masterstroke, the dragon held in reserve to finish them once they'd lost the ability to call Guardians of their own.

"The Edifiers over here are dead," called Yaw from the other side of the circle of Ayim. "The demons are coming for us."

"We have to leave," said Tau as an Edifier in front of him fell and Nyah lost her shroud, her soul's glow seeming luminous, beautiful, and vulnerable. "We can't hold the circle against this many."

"We said we wouldn't leave before, and now we cannot, not if Odili has a Guardian," Tsiora said.

The shame Tau had felt earlier vanished, replaced by a worry so deep it shook him to his core. Tsiora was going to stay in the under-world past the point where her Hex could save her.

"Protect the queen," Nyah said. "Protect her and the Hex."

"I can't lose her again...," Tau said, his mind melding the past and present. "I can't—"

"Tau!" Nyah said, tearing him from the past. "Champion Solarin, do your duty."

He couldn't make it go away, the memories and the pain that came with them. He tried to do as he must regardless. "Ayim, tighten the circle. Nothing passes your blades."

In mere breaths, the Ayim did as they were bid, the light of the last Edifier went dark, and as if a balance was being struck, the shrouds of those Tau was meant to protect failed, sending out enough light to push back the encroaching dark, enough light to provoke the things that had been hidden in it.

Only the queen still wore her ebon armor, and though she was safe for the moment, the mercy was a small one. The demons, those within sight as well as the ones still half wrapped in the mists, crept closer, possessed with a need to snuff out all the lights they could see.

The first wave hit hard, and the Ayim's saving grace was that the demons sought to kill them in small skirmishes versus overwhelming them in numbers. Demons did not think in tactics like women and men, and it seemed random chance as to whether they worked together to secure a kill or resorted to dueling for one, fighting by themselves and for themselves only.

The Ayim had the advantage in that. Themba would fight to save Auset and Auset would fight to save him. Uduak protected Tau's back and Tau could team with Jabari to slaughter larger foe. Ramia and Yaw did the same, shoring up the other's weaknesses and bolstering their sword sibling's strengths.

And they held for a time. It felt like a season, but Tau doubted it was a hundredth of a sun span. The only thing he knew for sure was that he fought the demons with everything he had in his heart, spirit, and soul. The only things he knew for sure were that he could not give in and that they'd still get him anyway.

Unable to help them, he watched as Yaw, Themba, and Ramia died to demon talons, teeth, and torture. Unable to help, he watched as first two, then three, then four of the Gifted in Tsiora's Hex were killed, in Isihogo and Uhmlaba. He came close to watching Nyah die but pulled the demon off her and fought it back before it was able to tear out her throat.

"Tsiora!" he bellowed.

"We are trying," she said, and Tau wanted to flash back to Uhmlaba to see what that meant, but the throng of demons was too thick and then Uduak fell, dragged under by a foul sea of beasts.

"Back to back," Tau said to the Ayim, shoving Nyah up against the surprisingly solid bounds of Tsiora's shroud. "Auset, Jabari, back to back, protect that Gifted!" He pointed to the young woman whose shroud had been first to fail, thanking the Goddess that she'd survived when other Gifted had not.

We have to protect the sacrifice, he thought as she was wrenched from the circle, swarmed, and torn apart, taken from Isihogo and Uhmlaba both, equally dead in both.

That came close to breaking Tau, and his worry got worse when a light behind him flared so brightly it felt tangible, like it was pressing against his back. Daring death, he turned away from the demons and looked over his shoulder to see.

Tsiora's shroud had failed, and though she stood beside Nyah, he saw her alone. She was so beautiful. She was so…he'd lost Zuri this way.

"Odili's Guardian is dead," Tsiora said.

"Leave, then," Tau said. "Leave."

"We can't. Our Guardian will not release us, and there is no one to take our place."

With hopelessness clawing at him, Tau lowered his swords.

"Tau!"

Heeding Auset's warning, he wheeled away from a demon's bite and struck it three times in rapid succession, dropping it to the dirt. Turning to thank Auset for saving him, Tau saw a demon dragging what was left of her into the mists.

That left Tau and Jabari, standing against the legion of demons. Everywhere Tau looked he saw them and the hunger in their faces. They were waiting, sending in one or two to nip at them, hoping to catch them unawares and drag them off. It was misery, torturous misery.

"Queen Tsiora," Tau said. "The circle is broken. Leave now or never."

"We're being held here," she said. "But so too do we hold to our Guardian. We've sent it to burn down the city gates, compelling it so fiercely that, though the demons may take us before the work is done, she will not stop burning until the gates fall."

In a shout, the first sound he'd made in the underworld, Jabari was taken down and dragged into the mists. Nyah was closest to him, and she reached out. Their fingertips touched and they scrabbled to keep hold of each other, but then Jabari was wrenched back and out of sight.

Nyah moved forward, thinking she could still help him, and Tau yelled for her to get back. The vizier was corporeal in the under-world, and if the demons got her, she'd die in both realms.

"Your promise, Champion," Nyah said to him. "Will you keep them safe? Will you keep my girls safe?"

Tau's eyes went wide. The only reason Nyah needed him to take care of Tsiora and her daughter was because she wouldn't be there to do it herself.

"I swear it to you. I swear it to the Goddess," he said, grieving already. "I'll give my life before I'll surrender theirs. Just help her. Save Tsiora."

Nyah turned to the queen. "Before it's too late," she said. "Do what must be done!"

"No, we...I will not," Tsiora said. "I won't do this to you."

"Tsiora, it's not you I'm asking," Nyah said. "I'm speaking to my queen, the queen of the Omehi people, because she'll do whatever it takes to be there for her people. She'll do it, always."

Tsiora shook her head, staring at Nyah as if in shock.

"Goddess keep you, Tsiora," she said.

"Nyah...," whispered Tsiora, pleading with the woman who'd helped raise her. "Nyah...," said the queen of the Omehi as she shunted all of her power into her vizier.

The sudden burst of light was blinding enough to push the demons back, and, eyes burning, Tau shielded his face. Her power drained, and glowing faintly, Tsiora dropped to her knees, exhausted, defeated, stricken.

"Nyah, I love you," she said, winking out of Isihogo's existence.

With Tsiora safe, Tau moved as close to Nyah as he could, and, swords raised, he stood in front of her, hoping the demons behind them wouldn't come.

"I can give you some time," he said. "Maybe you can—"

"The Guardian has me," she said. "I'm done."

Tau shook his head. "As long as I stand, you will too."

Nyah didn't seem to hear. She was staring out around her. "They're not attacking. Tau, you have this chance. Exhale and leave this cursed place."

She was right. The demons were holding themselves back, and

Tau didn't understand why until he saw a group of them shift left or right, clearing a path so that, from the mists, the one with the ring of horns about its head had an unimpeded way forward.

It had no eyes but its steps were sure, and it was dragging its over-sized Guardian-scale blade in its left hand. Behind it, the blade's point scored Isihogo's blighted ground, cutting a furrowed line through its murk.

"You?" Tau asked it.

"Oh Goddess," said Nyah, her voice trembling. "Try to leave, Tau. Don't stay here with me. Don't stay here with it."

Tau shook his head, spat on the ground, and loosened his wrists. Nyah would not die alone.

POWERLESS

They were waiting for you," Tau said to the demon with the dragon-scale blade.

It came on.

"Tau . . . ," said Nyah.

"This is a duel, yes?" Tau asked it. "It's to be a contest between us?" He twirled his swords. "I'll play, but for stakes."

The horned one came on, sword splitting the ground behind it.

"If I win, you let her go," Tau said, pointing to Nyah. "If I win—"

The horned one swung its massive sword in an overhand arc with so much force the air around Tau sucked at him as he threw himself aside. Missing him, the weapon's edge struck the ground like a lightning strike, the blade blasting two or three handspans into the ground, and the horned one ripped it free like it was nothing, tearing up heavy gouts of muck when it swung the blade at Tau again.

Tau leapt back and the blade's point strafed past his midsection, three fingerspans from cleaving him open, and Tau shouted over the winds to it.

"If I win—"

The horned one sent the sword back the other way, and Tau had had enough. He dashed in, avoiding the heft of the swing, and, raising his weak-side sword to block the blow near its demented hilt,

Tau stabbed out with his strong side. The demon's blade connected with his blocking one and Tau's forearm snapped in two.

As his arm broke, Tau's strong-side sword, the stabbing one, was knocked aside by the horned demon's hand, the demon moving so quickly Tau had no time to react when it parried or when it reversed its motion to slap him across the head and neck, sending him spinning through the air to crash down several strides away.

Tau tried to scream when he landed. He'd fallen on his broken arm, and what was left of the bone had shattered on impact. But the only sound he managed was an agonized lowing. The demon's slap had crushed his jaw, leaving his tongue hanging helpless from the side of his mutilated mouth.

Tau turned to Nyah, trying to resist the pain exploding through him, and knew how bad the damage was when he saw her face. Her hand was over her mouth, her eyes were wide, and she was shaking her head as if to deny the hateful things she was being shown.

Refusing to be beaten, Tau staggered to his feet, moaning with the pain his every movement caused his mangled arm and jaw. He'd lost his weak-side sword but had held fast to his strong-side one. With it in hand, he stumbled his way to Nyah's side, standing in front of her, blocking the horned one's path.

He raised his sword, positioning it defensively, and the horned one attacked, dashing in and closing the distance between them before Tau could blink. His sword, held too high for the demon's incoming blow, wobbled uselessly when the horned one thundered a fist into Tau's chest, launching him back and off his feet, splintering his ribs, and caving his chest clean in.

He must have blacked out, because he didn't remember hitting the ground. He just knew he was coughing up blood, unable to breathe, and that he'd never known so much pain.

Still, drawing in air that felt thick as sludge, Tau rolled to his left, and using his good arm, he pushed his way to his knees. The horned one was between him and Nyah. The other demons were moving again, coming for her.

Tau, moaning and blubbering, making whatever noises he could from his dangling mouth, got to his feet, picked up his fallen sword, and, unable to bring air into the lungs he'd punctured by standing, realized he was drowning in his own blood.

"It's enough, Tau," Nyah said. "It's enough."

The demons, set loose by some unheard signal, sped for her, Nyah closed her eyes, and Tau stumbled to her defense.

He didn't see, sense, or know that the horned one had moved, but one moment Tau was running and the next he was lifted in the air, skewered on that massive, twisted black blade. The horned one tilted its weapon upward, and beyond the scope of more suffering, Tau felt nothing as his body slid wetly down the dragon scale, stopping when he hit the sword's hilt.

The horned one brought its eyeless face to his, coating him in the reek of rancid flesh burning, and Tau tried to turn away but didn't have the strength. The only grace in it, Tau thought with a dying mind, was that he was past the point of pain.

Then Nyah's screams, her voice filled with agony and fear, broke the fugue of Tau's ending, and her cries damned him. They damned his failures, his weakness, and as he listened to her die a true death, Tau Solarin learned that he had not been anywhere near the limits at which he could be hurt.

WAYWARD

Tau opened his eyes and looked up at Tsiora's face. She was holding him, cradling him, and crying. He tried to sit up, needing to tell her about Nyah and the horned demon, but his body and mind were not yet gathered and his limbs spasmed instead of obeying. His lips and tongue weren't working right either, and he found that there was little he could move besides his eyes. Unwilling to wait for his body to be his again, but afraid of what he'd see, Tau wrenched his gaze away from Tsiora and toward the place where the vizier had been standing.

Nyah was not standing. She was on the ground, her body riddled with ruptured boils, her face slack, and her eyes, unseeing and stained with red tears, unfocused.

She was dead.

"C-cover her," Tau said, the words spluttering from numb lips. "Cover her."

It was Jabari who did it. The rest of the Ayim were still recovering, the Gifted who'd left Isihogo before the slaughter seemed stunned, and the Queen's Guard were reluctant to go near the dead Gifted.

Jabari moved with gentleness and purpose. He closed Nyah's eyes, covered her face, and then did the same for the five Gifted who had belonged to Tsiora's Hex. By the time the Petty Noble was done with the dead, Tau was well enough to sit up.

He was still in Tsiora's arms, and he put his arms around her. They stayed like that, holding each other, and it hurt Tau to feel her body shaking as she cried. He closed his eyes, wishing the whole day and night were some horrible dream from which he could wake, and that was when he heard the flaps of the queen's tent rustle.

His heart dropped and he called to the Queen's Guard. "The tent," he said, but it was too late.

The flaps opened, and there was his mother with Chibuye.

"Queen Tsiora?" the girl said, recoiling when she noticed the bodies of the dead Gifted.

Tau saw the child's gaze move from body to body, Gifted robe to Gifted robe, and he saw the exact moment when she recognized her mother's robes. He saw it in her mouth, opening slightly, in her eyes, filling with tears, and in her body, stiffening, tightening, registering that the world had suddenly and irrevocably changed. He was there the moment a child knew her parent had died.

"Mama? Mama?! Mama!"

Tsiora left his arms, going to Chibuye. She went to her knees in front of the girl and tried to hug her. The child fought it.

"What happened to Mama? Why is her face covered? What happened to her?"

Tsiora tried to speak to her, tried to find the right words. She managed one. "Gone," she said, and the child, too small a thing to withstand the crushing weight of its meaning, collapsed into the queen.

Tau got to his feet and the world spun round him. They'd lost so many. They'd lost so, so many.

He heard the queen's voice, flat, uninflected. "General Buhari, our dragon felled the city's gates, and the way is open. Send in our army."

Hadith resisted. "My queen, yes, the gates are down, but Odili's fighters are retreating. If we hold back, we can regroup, tend our wounded. We can launch a planned and concerted attack come morning. Odili's forces can't repair the damage to the gates and walls, and by taking what's left of the night to recover, we'll spare lives on both sides. We'll spare—"

"Take the city, General," the queen told him, her flat affect replaced with bronze. "Take the city and send the Goddess back Her wayward children. Send them back to Her, one and all."

They had lost so, so many because of Abasi Odili, thought Tau, opening his eyes to find Hadith looking to him, waiting for him. His mother, facing him too, gave him an upward nod, telling him to go, and Tau would have sworn she could see him, see into him, even without her eyes.

Tau turned to Hadith. A decision needed to be made, he had promises to keep, and the queen had made her wishes clear. "You have your orders, General Buhari," he said. "Take the city."

Hadith's eyebrows pulled together, and he paused long enough for Tau to worry about what might need to come next if Hadith disobeyed a direct order.

It didn't come to it, and Hadith saluted stiffly. "Your words, my will," he said, going to order the assault.

"What have they made us do?" Tsiora asked him, holding Chibuye. "What have they made of us?"

"What we must be," Tau said, his mother stepping closer to him and the queen when he spoke, her hands clenched in fists.

"Win our capital, Champion Solarin," his queen said. "Save our sister and deliver Odili to the Goddess's justice."

It was Tau's turn to nod. The things his queen wanted, these were things Tau would do. "Your words, my destiny," he said, turning to call the Ayim to arms.

"Champion, you...you must come back to us," Tsiora said, and it muddled him to see her like that, so totally unmasked. She wiped tears from her face. "Above all else, Tau, we wish for you to come back."

So many had been lost to bring him here.

"There is nothing in Uhmlaba that could stop me," he told her as he left.

CONQUERORS

They crossed the Amanzi using the same ponton bridges that Odili's army had abandoned in their rushed retreat when Tsiora's dragon had been the last one in the skies. They didn't meet significant resistance until they were among the rubble of the great stone wall of Palm City. Before that initial engagement, Hadith had ordered a slow, methodical push. He wanted Tsiora's army to move into the city in waves, clearing paths, neighborhoods, sections. He wanted the army to announce that surrender would be accepted and that those wishing to do so would not be harmed. Hadith Buhari, grand general of the Omehian army, had many wants, but no one, woman or man, can control the Roar, and Tsiora's army swept the city like the ocean at storm.

Tau, at the head of the Ayim, led the way. He had his black blades in hand, a heart heavy with loss, and promises to keep, and he brought Odili's Ihagu, Ihashe, and Indlovu sharp justice. He stalked the midnight corridors of the capital, with its tall buildings of rich, smooth adobe, painting the walls with the blood of those who blocked him. He fought in tight paths, along vaulted archways, through shops, in a temple of the Goddess, and even in a home where an old Nobleman put a knife to the throat of a Lesser boy to keep the Ayim at bay.

Tau told the Noble that if he harmed the boy, he'd suffer for it.

Odili's men, many more of them than there were Ayim, broke into the house, hoping to make short work of Tau and the six with him. The old Noble, thinking the battle won, laughed in Tau's face and slit the boy's throat.

Tau saved that Noble for last. He and the Ayim killed everyone else. And when Tau had gone to put the old man to death, he'd gibbered, pleaded, and pissed himself. His screams came after that.

The next significant engagement came in a glorious circle large enough to hold the whole of Keep Onai. Fighting in it, Tau thought back to the Queen's Melee as he skirmished alongside his six Ayim, laying waste to Indlovu and tearing to pieces the world these Nobles had known and understood for so long.

Then, at the last, they came to a bridge spanning a thin tributary of the Amanzi that had been redirected to run through the city, providing Palm with needed water and desired beauty. The bridge was a wondrous work of sculpted stone, its sides depicting a frieze of Omehi warriors fighting a last stand against an enemy of far greater numbers. It showed a woman, Gifted, hand outstretched and calling a Guardian forth to bring fire to her foes as the outnumbered Omehi faced their fate without fear. It was very noble.

"Ingonyama," said Uduak as they stepped onto the arching bridge.

The man, running ahead of three units of Indlovu, was enraged, and even for one of them, he was big.

Tau licked away the blood spattered across his lips and turned to Uduak. "Mine," he said, spinning his blades and racing to meet his enraged enemy.

The Ingonyama had no shield and was holding his great sword in both hands. He swung for Tau, but he was no horned demon bred in the underworld, and fast as he was, strong as he was, empowered as he was, he was just a man. He'd lived only one life, and Tau had suffered through thousands.

Tau slipped the man's swing, battering him with both swords, and the colossus staggered, his stone skin and plated armor the only things keeping him alive. The Ingonyama lashed out with a leather- and plate-stitched glove, driving Tau back, forcing him to avoid each attack or be killed by the man's power.

Flowing with the Ingonyama's rhythm, timing his punches and sword swings, Tau countered every miss with dragon scale. He chipped away at the Noble like a sculptor seized by inspiration, and when the man began to cry out in pain, he cut deeper. He didn't stop when the Ingonyama's Gifted pulled her powers. He didn't stop when the Ingonyama collapsed. Tau kept going until the work was done.

"He's dead," said Uduak.

"What?" Tau rasped, standing over the pile of hacked-up flesh that had been a man.

"Him."

Tau stared down at the mess and recoiled. The dead man's face was moving, his features contorting, changing to become demon-like. Having a hard time blinking away the vision, Tau looked away.

The palace was close and he had to hurry. It was getting harder to keep the monsters and the men separated.

Speaking to the Ayim, he pointed to the domed palace with one of his swords. "The queen's sister will be inside, and Abasi Odili is with her."

CHAPTER FOURTEEN

ESI OMEHIA

Esi Omehia was on the balcony in the main hall in the Peninsulan Palace and she could hear her Queen's Guard dying. Moments earlier, to defend her, they'd left the main hall and closed the doors, leaving a few Indlovu behind to bar them from the inside.

She knew whom they were fighting out there, and the knowledge scared her. She knew it was Tsiora's champion and the Lesser wretches who clung to him like lice. She tried to take comfort in the sounds of Abasi Odili's voice. He was beside her, but every so often something or someone would hit the outside of the door, making it bang. She jumped every time it happened, and she hated it.

She was so anxious her palms were sweating. She would have wiped away the wet, but the only thing near enough to help was her gown, which was the color of purest alabaster, and the sweat would show on it.

So instead of using her dress, Esi rubbed her hands together, well aware that she wasn't doing much. She wouldn't filthy herself, though. If she was going to be taken to her sister, she'd go to her as a queen.

It didn't help her nerves that soldiers kept running in and giving Abasi reports or messages, and she tried not to listen. She didn't want to hear about the city being overrun. She didn't want to know the names of this inkokeli or that general who had been killed. She wouldn't even let herself imagine what else was happening out there in the city as Tsiora's army of wild Lessers infested Palm.

Her quiet voice whispered evil things to her, telling her that Tsiora would give her to the Lessers, telling her that Tsiora would give her to the savage she'd made her champion, and none of Esi's usual tricks would shut the voice up.

Needing to do something, anything, Esi hummed to herself, reciting the last song her bard had written for her. She loved the words, and saying them in her head helped drown out the quiet voice.

"Esi," Abasi asked, taking her hand in his, "is it bad?"

She gave him a smile. "I'll be fine, Bas. It's just hard when I'm tired."

"I think they're going to get into the hall, Esi," he said, telling her terrible things with his beautiful voice, the words dancing with each other like they were part of a melody just beyond hearing. "I thought we could trap them in the hall. They were stuck between the Queen's Guard and two dozen Indlovu. I thought we could stop them."

Esi blocked out the words, listening to their sounds instead. She adored the way he spoke, and long before his arms, it was his voice she'd reveled in. For his sake, she wanted to be strong, but the words slipped from her lips before she could leash them. "Is there truly no hope?"

He reached for her other hand, and lifting them both to his lips, he kissed her fingers. "She won't harm either of you, and that truth is worth so much more than hope."

The quiet voice scoffed.

Esi placed a hand to her stomach. "She will hurt me, Bas. She'll hurt me by taking away the man I love."

He lowered his head, shamed by her concerns. "I've failed you, my queen."

She put a finger to his chin, lifting his head, getting him to look at her. "You didn't fail me, and I don't want to be your queen right now," she said, leaning in and kissing him, pressing her lips to his, feeling the warmth of him, and not for the first time, wondering how different things could have been.

Her quiet voice chattered in her ear, telling Esi that she was going to lose everything and it was all because her sister had tried to surrender the Omehi to primitives.

"This isn't your fault," Esi said to Abasi. "We tried to save our people from Tsiora's cowardice and zealotry. We tried."

"Even knowing how it ends, I'd do it over again, if you asked me," he said to her.

Another messenger ran over, interrupting them, and Abasi stepped back from her, taking his fingers from hers.

The quiet voice told Esi that he was going to leave, abandoning Esi to her fate, but in saying that, the voice had gone too far and Esi could and did silence her.

"Champion Odili," the messenger said, saluting them both. "Queen Esi."

"Report," Abasi told the messenger.

"We no longer control the city," the soldier said, making Esi gasp.

And though she didn't approve of affection in public, it swelled her heart to see that, in that moment, Abasi knew her well enough to return his hand to hers. They were stronger together. They always had been.

"The hallway beyond these doors? Can we hold it?" Abasi asked the soldier.

The man shook his head.

Abasi nodded. "I haven't received a casualty report for the past span."

"I-I'll have someone with updated numbers bring them to—"

"We won't have time for that. Tell me what you know."

"Yes, Champion," the soldier said. "We've lost at least three scales of Indlovu, five claws of Ihashe, and the few cowardly Ihagu who didn't surrender at the first chance they got have broken."

"I see."

"Champion, the worst is our loss of Gifted. Including the Edifiers, Entreaters, and our Enervators and Enragers, we'll have to burn more than—"

"No more," said Esi, as the quiet voice screamed at her. "Bas, let's not hear any more."

"My queen," said the soldier. "Apologies."

She waved him away. "Leave us."

"Ah…"

Esi wanted the soldier to go, but she was also a queen. "Say it, then."

"My queen, Champion, the…the defense of the palace has not been finalized."

The soldier was trying to be respectful to her while seeking his answer from Abasi.

"I'm going to get them to stand down, Esi," Abasi said. "They can't hold, and asking them to try will kill more Gifted and Indlovu, all to grant us a quarter span or two."

"You want my permission?" Esi said as the quiet voice told her to withhold it.

"I need your permission."

"Should I do it, Bas?"

He nodded.

"You have my permission," she said. "Tell them to stand down."

"Tell the Gifted and Indlovu to stand down," Abasi said to the soldier. "Spread the word, weapons away, Palm City is Queen Tsiora's."

There it was, Esi thought. Just like that, Tsiora was a queen again.

"Thank you, Champion, my queen. It has been an honor to serve." The soldier saluted, turned smartly, and marched off.

"It won't be long now," Abasi said. "Esi, please do as we discussed. For me, please."

"What if you're wrong, Bas?"

"I'm not."

"What if you are? If you tell her that it's you who did this, that it's you who made me do this…" Esi's head was pounding. "Bas…she might kill you."

He smiled at her, and tenderly, as if he couldn't believe he was permitted to do it, he placed a hand against her cheek.

She leaned into his palm and fingers. "What if she doesn't believe you? I can't lose you. And Bas, the Edifiers…Tsiora knows no Gifted would take orders from a man. They wouldn't sacrifice themselves on your word alone. Let me own my actions. Let me help you, for once."

"Your sister is a traitor to her race, self-righteous in her wrongheadedness, and blinded by religion," Abasi said. "She's so weak she may actually rule over the end of the Omehi, but, Esi Omehia, your sister loves you. She loves you and she'll ignore the truth shouting in her face, if it means she can continue pretending that you feel the same way about her."

Esi shook her head, then kissed the palm of the hand he'd had on her cheek. "I won't live without you. Bas, the first chance I get, I'll put a dagger through her heart."

His smile grew rueful. "The Goddess knows how I feel about you, and you're stronger than anyone I've ever met. Esi, you're stronger than your sister could ever be, but I don't see you hurting her or yourself. You may not love her, but you do care for her."

"It's love that lets me do it," Esi said. "It's my love for you that lets me do it."

"Then you'll break my heart," he said, "because, after killing someone you care for, you'll be lost too."

"Look what she's done to us. I hate her."

"Don't say that. Don't even think it. In people like her there's a permanent war waged between love and loyalty, and if the scales ever tilt too far...Esi, Tsiora will punish disloyalty, even from you. So do it for me, my queen, for what we've made together, let her think she's loved."

"You want me to be a traitor. You want me to forget my dreams and make my heart hard."

"I want you to live," he said, kissing her forehead. "Goddess, Esi, I need you to live." His eyes teared up.

"We can run," she said, wishing that they could.

"We've nowhere to go."

"Bas..."

"I love you, Esi."

"Bas..."

"Shhh. They're coming."

PRINCESS

The great doors to the main hall in the Peninsulan Palace were forced open, and in marched more Lessers than Esi had ever seen up close. They searched the main floor, beat her unarmed Indlovu, and threw them to their knees. They terrified her, and they were nothing compared to the seven demons who walked in after them.

First of them through the doors was the biggest Lesser she'd ever seen. He had hands the size of drums, and they were drenched in blood. Beside him were what appeared to be two women, and for a breath, she thought they might have been Auset and Ramia, but it couldn't be. They were dressed for fighting, each of them holding two strange swords, and they looked too cold, too cruel.

Past them was another big Lesser, though this one was skinnier. He moved through the room like an inyoka, gliding across the floor as if the bottoms of his feet had been smeared with oil. Beyond that one was a Lesser who strutted into the room with a smile as wide as the Amanzi. He laughed and chattered, making mock of her captured Indlovu before stopping to gape up at her, his naked desire evident and disgusting.

The sixth through the door was something from a nightmare. He moved like a puppet on strings set too tight and had the size of a Noble, but she could see none of his features to confirm it. He wore a cloak too thick for the weather, the hood up, and his body was bandaged from head to toe with bleached cloth that had turned the color of copper, because whatever afflictions he had, they were bleeding through his bindings.

Then, at the last, she saw the one who led them all, and her fear grew so great her head spun, making the ground feel as if it were tilting and swaying beneath her feet. She reached for Abasi and he batted her hand away.

"We can't, Esi," he whispered, and she knew why they hid their love, but she needed him then. She needed him because they were stronger together and because the quiet voice was screaming at the sight of Tsiora's demon coming closer.

He moved into the hall, his gait a broken lurch that turned something as simple as walking into a ghastly sight. Esi tried to silence the quiet voice, to calm it, but Tsiora's demon looked up to the second floor where she stood, his gaze crashing down on them, and in it, in his scarred, wicked face, she saw so much hate and rage that she began to scream as well.

"Up the stairs," Tsiora's demon said to the six who stood with him, his voice a graceless rasp that took her mind to the sounds of bones cracked and crunched in the mouth of a glutton.

"Bas...," she said, her scream dying in a throat constricted by fear, and despite his caution and plans, he took her hand, holding it tight and close as the six came for them with her sister's twisted champion in tow.

"It'll be well, Esi," Abasi said. "Please, it will be well, my queen."

She was a queen, her authority derived from the Goddess Herself, but what was that worth when faced by the godless?

"It'll be well, Esi, please!"

The six were on the second floor, and up came Tsiora's demon. She saw his eyes then, burning with the intensity of dragon fire. Her knees buckled, and she would have fallen to the floor if Abasi had not been holding her.

"We surrender!" Abasi said.

"I don't care," the demon replied, pulling out two black swords and coming for them.

"Tau! No!" shouted a voice from the main floor. "Ayim, as grand general, I order you to stop him."

Esi saw the man who'd spoken. It was another Lesser, another big Lesser who wore the uniform of a general. Under any other circumstances, she would have found the pairing funny, but the Lesser in the uniform of a general was trying to save their lives.

"Ayim!" he said again, hurrying up the stairs as five of the six ignored him.

The only one who moved a muscle was the enormous Lesser.

"Tau...," the big man said, stepping between her and Tsiora's savage.

"Move or be moved, Uduak," Tsiora's champion said, and though the one named Uduak was head and shoulders bigger than the scarred champion, he did as he was bid, clearing the way for the demon.

"Stop it, Tau!" the Lesser general shouted from halfway up the stairs.

But Tsiora's champion did not stop, prompting Abasi to take Esi's wrist and pull her behind him. "I surrender, and will give the queen's sister into your care, if you promise she'll not be harmed."

That was not the plan. Abasi had said she'd be fine, that they might both be fine, but Esi understood how, standing opposite that madman, Abasi had to wonder if they were both about to be cut down.

"Champion to champion, tell me you will not harm—"

"You, a champion?" Tsiora's savage rasped, shaking his head. "No, Abasi Odili, you're a traitor, usurper, coward, and murderer, and I will have justice."

"This isn't it, Tau," said the Lesser general, holding a hand to his body, just below his chest, and coughing as he ambled over. "We're better than this."

Tsiora's champion licked his dry lips. "I am this."

"Give us the sister, Abasi Odili," said one of the warrior women, dressed like a caricatured cross between an Omehian handmaiden and a hedeni savage.

Goddess wept, Esi thought, it was Auset and Ramia. Esi couldn't believe it and wondered if they might help her.

Abasi, however, had his eyes on Tau and his body in front of Esi's. He didn't know the women were Tsiora's handmaidens.

"Can you guarantee her safety?" he asked Auset.

"I can," Auset said. "Give her to us, quickly. I do not think you have long to live, and if she is with you when this begins, she may not survive it either."

"I've surrendered and have no weapons," Abasi said, using his hold on Esi's hand to guide her away from him and toward the sisters. "Is this to be the way of the new world under Queen Tsiora?" He handed Esi over, and though she tried pulling away, Auset's grip was bronze and Esi's choices were to go with her or have her wrist broken.

"Is this an indication of how life will be?" Abasi asked.

"Leave those worries for the living," Tsiora's champion said, swords aimed for Abasi's chest.

"Stop him," Esi said, begging action from the sisters. "Stop him!"

"Look away, princess," Ramia said. "He can't be stopped."

SISTERS

S ister!" called a voice that had shadowed Esi her entire life.

"Tsiora, call him off!" Esi shouted, trying to step closer to the balcony so she could see her sister.

"Champion Solarin! Await us," her sister said.

"Queen Tsiora, if you will," said the Lesser general, "give us a moment before coming up."

The constant shouting seemed to have wearied the general, and he kept touching the same point below his chest. It looked, to Esi, as if the Lesser was breathing like he had to pull his air through a hollow river reed.

"A moment, my queen," the general shouted, having gathered his strength. "We have not yet searched Princess Esi and Abasi Odili for weapons or other danger."

"Search them, then, Grand General Buhari," Tsiora said. "We wish to see our sister."

"Tau, back off," the general hissed.

The champion moved neither forward nor backward, and the general pushed his way past him to stand in front of Abasi.

"Listen to me, Odili," the general said. "Listen very carefully, because—"

"You have an offer for me, Lesser?" Abasi asked. "Is it similar to the type of offers you made in the Queen's Melee, perhaps?"

Esi did not know why Abasi goaded the man. He seemed the only one with any reason among the Lessers.

"Search them," Hadith said to the smiling one and the oil-footed Lesser.

The smiling one went straight for her.

"Themba, you can search Odili with Yaw's help," the general said. "Leave the princess to the handmaidens."

Esi's quiet voice laughed when she heard the sisters called handmaidens and went silent when they began to grab and squeeze at her body, checking her over.

"Odili, the champion named you a traitor, and you are one."

"Am I now, Gener—"

"Don't waste my time or your life," the general said as the other two Lessers grabbed and groped Odili, searching him too. "The queen is going to come up here in a moment, and what you do and say will determine if you live or die."

"Hadith...," growled Tsiora's champion, but the general pressed on.

"No weapons on the princess," said Auset.

"I cannot tell you that you won't hang," said the general, "but if you chastise yourself, swear fealty to our true queen, and renounce your actions, you may spend whatever natural days you have left in a prison instead of dangling on the end of a rope."

"No weapons on the traitor," said the smiling Lesser.

"Why?" asked Abasi. "Why do you want this from me?"

The Lesser general squinted at Abasi. "The Xiddeen will be re-forming their alliance—"

Abasi's eyebrows lifted. "And you need my public support so that my soldiers, as well as the armies fighting in the Curse, will accept your leadership."

"I need them to accept their rightful queen."

"And for that, you need me," Abasi said.

"Hadith...," the champion growled.

"What of surrender to the hedeni?" Abasi asked. "Is that still Tsiora's aim?"

"It was never meant to be a surrender," said Hadith. "It was meant to be peace."

Abasi had that look he got when explaining something he shouldn't have to explain. "Buhari, you're young, but you've lived and achieved enough to know that the things we mean to do rarely match the things we actually accomplish. If she'd had her way, it would be the end of who we are. You must see that."

The Lesser general had no time to answer. Tsiora had climbed the stairs, and the balcony went quiet.

Queen Tsiora Omehia, Esi saw, was wearing black from head to toe, and as was her custom, she was in a formfitting dress. But to Esi's surprise, she also wore a cloak and hood that looked very much like a Gifted's robes.

Still, it was her dress that held Esi's attention. The material was layered and overlapping, simulating the appearance of scales, simulating the appearance of dragon skin. The effect was striking, and when Tsiora stepped onto the balcony, she didn't look like a queen—she was one.

Her sister's companion completed the air of regality that seemed to emanate from her. Tsiora was with Kellan Okar, and though Esi hadn't seen him in cycles and though he now had strange scars on the sides of his neck, she knew him on sight.

His was not a face that fell from memory, for the Goddess made few women or men who could draw the eye like Kellan did. It was embarrassing to admit it, but seeing them together made Esi feel as if she should bow her head. They were a perfectly matched pair and she couldn't understand how her sister could make a scarred and limping wretch her champion when men like Kellan Okar existed.

The only answer was that she really was the person Abasi feared her to be. Tsiora, queen of surrender, hewed closer to the path Ukufa had wrought than the one the Goddess made. Tsiora was on the wrong path, and as much as that thought sickened Esi, she did believe that women could change the direction of their lives but worried it might be too late for her sister.

Tsiora might be too far gone. She was so debased she let that Lesser touch her, had probably let him lie with her, and could it matter if

Tsiora changed who she was, when he would always be some part of who she'd been?

"Esi," her sister said, sweeping onto the second-floor balcony as if she were being drawn onto a dance floor. "Our Esi."

She was perverse.

"Tsiora," Esi said, the unadorned name causing her sister's smile to slip and her steps to slow. "Queen Tsiora," Esi added.

The smile returned, brighter than before, and Tsiora took Esi in her arms, kissing her on both cheeks.

"Esi, we were so worried, but it's over now. You're safe now."

Esi's quiet voice howled.

"Oh, Esi, your head," her sister said. "It's...it's happening right now, isn't it?"

They were all looking at her, and Esi's shame burned almost as hot as her fear.

"It's not," she said, barely able to hear herself over the quiet voice's clamor. "It doesn't happen anymore. I'm well. I'm well now."

"There's a priestess. Her name is Hafsa Ekene, she may be able to help."

"I'm well," Esi said, pulling back from her sister's embrace. "I don't need help."

"Queen Tsiora, please," Abasi said. "It makes it worse to speak of it, and—"

Her sister rounded on Abasi, stabbing a finger in his direction like it was one of her champion's blades. "Silence, you. Speak again without our leave and we'll have your tongue."

The speed with which Tsiora could become cruel had always startled Esi, and it had been that way since they were children. She still remembered every time her sister had become angry or upset and lashed out, telling her that she'd never be queen.

Tsiora used to tell her that all the time. She'd tell Esi that, though they looked alike, they were different in all the ways that mattered. She'd tell Esi that she wasn't special and she'd call her broken, mocking her and changing the words to her favorite songs to nasty poems about how Esi didn't speak to the Goddess, but just to herself.

The worst of it, though, was that when Tsiora had just threatened

Abasi, it had also smashed Esi's illusions. She'd known they were still in danger, of course she had, but seeing her sister, being held by her, it made some small part of the nightmare feel just a little bit safer. But Esi didn't feel that way anymore.

"Queen Tsiora," said the Lesser general, "I believe I have an understanding with Councillor Odili."

"Do you, General," Esi's sister said.

"Odili will publicly claim responsibility for endangering the Omehi queendom and submit himself to both your rule and justice."

"How very generous of him," she said.

"My queen, his crimes are great and the harm he's caused is immeasurable, but by accepting guilt he will invalidate any outstanding resistance to your rightful rule. It's a means to—"

"What happens to him?" asked Tsiora's champion.

"Beg pardon?"

"You heard me, Hadith."

Champion or no, Esi expected her sister to chastise the man for speaking out of place, but she did nothing.

"It's my suggestion that Abasi Odili's lands, titles, and wealth return to the queen and queendom," said the Lesser general, "and that the man himself be sentenced to imprisonment for the rest of his natural—"

Tsiora's champion laughed and Esi jumped. It was a dirty sound that maddened her quiet voice.

"No, Hadith," the champion said.

"Tau, there's so much at stake, and—"

"Queen Tsiora, I have done all that you've asked. I led those closest to me to the walls of Palm City, and we came with an army of Lessers at our backs. The rebellion is quelled and your sister stands safe next to you. But my task, the task you set for me, was one of vengeance, and I would see it finished."

Esi could see that Abasi wanted to speak, but he didn't dare. Her sister was as good as her word and she wouldn't balk at having one of the barbarians cut out his tongue.

However, the Lesser general was not under the same threat. "Tau, this won't bring any of them—"

"Ask us," Tsiora said to her twisted champion. "Ask anything of us."

The Lesser stared at her sister like no one else existed in all the world, and Esi saw it then. It was faint, but she could see it running horizontally between them, moving as if it were alive, spiraling like the pillars of fire the guardians spit. It was a dark and grotesque energy and it leashed them to each other. Her quiet voice saw it too and, in its dolor, came closer to overpowering her than it had since she was a girl.

Run, it told her, run, run, run.

"A blood duel in the Great Circle of Palm City with Lessers and Nobles filling it to overflowing," Tsiora's champion said. "I want to fight him to the death."

"And you will, my champion," the queen of the Omehi said. "You will."

FAITH

Run, run, run, her quiet voice shouted, when it had to know she wouldn't abandon Abasi. Esi loved him, and though her quiet voice was right that they were in danger, it was wrong about how to survive it.

They couldn't run, but they'd been handed a chance to fight, and for the sake of the Omehi, Abasi, and the life growing inside her, Esi would take it.

"You're allowing this?" she asked her sister. "A blood duel between two champions?"

"Two champions?" her sister asked.

The Lesser general was standing beyond Tsiora, and he was in her line of sight. Esi saw it when his eyes widened, as if, impossibly, he'd already grasped her intent. Seeing the danger before the others, he tried to stop her.

"Don't do it, Princess Esi," Tsiora's grand general said. "Things are not as they seem—"

She refused to be foiled by a Lesser. "I feel the Goddess's voice inside me, sister."

Tsiora turned to her and Esi could see the cruelty rising from wherever it was that her sister kept it hidden. "Esi, you're confused and don't know what you're saying."

"Oh, sweet sister, I know exactly what I'm saying."

"Stop it," Tsiora said. "You know the Goddess doesn't speak to you. She never has and never will."

"Because I'm not Gifted, sister? Because I'm not like you?"

"What does that mean?" Tsiora asked.

"He's right, you know that, don't you?" Esi said.

"Who?"

"Bas."

"Abasi Odili?"

"He's right about you. You're not fit to lead."

"How dare you," Tsiora said.

"Do the rest of them know that I was born first?" Esi asked.

"The stress has undone you."

"They don't know, do they?"

"Esi..."

"Do they know that the Gifted come to princesses when they're just little girls? Do they know that they sent us to the demons over and over again, pushing us to see if we could hide from them, calling it a game, and—"

"Stop it, Esi—"

"I couldn't hide, Tsiora. I couldn't hide and the monsters would find me and hurt me, and those evil black-robed slatterns kept sending me back to them."

"Shut up—"

"I was a child, Tsiora."

"Shut up!"

"A child. Remember, Tsiora? Remember how our dear mother wouldn't name us until after were tested? Our mother who called us 'girl' and 'child' until she could be sure that she was giving the right name and the right to rule to the right one."

"Esi..."

"That's not my name. You have my name. I was the firstborn, but here you are, Tsiora, queen of the Omehi, a thief who stole her sister's name and life because of a gift you did nothing to earn."

"Esi, you should be careful now," her sister said.

"Tell me something. You say you speak for the Goddess. Tell me, does She shape the world as She wishes it to be? Is that why you, second born, are queen, and I am called a usurper for taking back what's mine? What do you think, Tsiora the second?"

Her sister had her hands squeezed into tight, tiny fists. "Everything that happens, happens because She wills it."

And just like that, Esi had her. "If you believe that to be true, don't demean the Goddess by fighting your champion against mine with nothing at stake but their blood. Let it be known that the victor of the duel shall determine who among us is the rightful queen of the Omehi. Will you do that, faithful Tsiora?"

Abasi risked having his tongue cut loose. "No, Esi, I can't—"

And Kellan Okar, beautiful as he was, did an ugly thing. The Greater Noble slammed an elbow into Abasi's stomach, doubling him over. "Stay silent, Odili. You heard the queen."

Odili spluttered, working to draw breath, and Esi wanted to go to him, but she had to finish it.

"Let the Goddess decide which queen must rule," she said.

"There's only one queen," Tsiora told her.

"There will be, when Ananthi proves who it is, in front of thousands."

Tsiora leaned back on her heels. "You blame us for your childhood, when we were a girl too? You blame us and let a man use you to tear our people apart. Esi, what do you want from us?"

"Want? From you?" Esi asked. "I want to know if you're as faithful as you claim. I want, more than anything, to find out if the Goddess really holds you as close as you kept telling me She did when we were growing up." Esi took a step toward her sister and the handmaidens closed in. "What do I want? I want much the same thing your Low Common does. I want our champions to fight to the death, but I want it so that the Goddess can choose Her true queen and I can finally have the life She told me was mine."

Tsiora slammed a fist through the air. "It's not Her you hear speaking!"

"We'll see."

"Enough!" Tsiora said, rushing over to stand toe-to-toe with her, and, surprising herself, Esi didn't flinch.

She held her ground against Tsiora, who'd been so quick to hit when they were younger, and before her courage failed her, she let the rest of her speech tumble out. "A duel between champions to determine the true queen of the Omehi. No Guardian scale, bronze only, and one sword each."

Tsiora was angry and Esi's sister always did stupid things when she was angry.

"No Guardian scale, bronze only, one sword each," her sister agreed.

"And the victor is the champion of the true queen," Esi said, a teacher prompting a student.

"The victor is the champion of the true queen," Tsiora echoed, and Esi could have laughed and twirled and danced.

She'd done it. In a single step, she'd walked the whole of the path back to victory, saving herself, Abasi, and the peninsula, because her faithful sister was a faithful fool.

Tsiora moved away from her. "We feel sorry for you, Esi. You've been in Odili's clutches for so long you can't see that he is evil and forsaken, but we'll show you. Tomorrow, when our champions fight, you'll bear witness to the Goddess's will at work."

Esi swallowed a mocking laugh. Any woman comparing the two men could see that her champion—tall, strong, and royal—would crush the scarred Lesser in a fair fight. She looked to Bas, to share in the triumph that words had won over war and weapons, but what she saw on her lover's face seized her heart and set her quiet voice screaming.

On him, like a million insects crawling, Esi saw dread, despair, and death.

FIGHT

E si had not slept. After the confrontation with her sister, she'd been sent to rooms in one of the palace's towers and guarded. The guards, Lessers, had scoured the rooms, removing anything that could be used as a weapon against others or herself. They'd checked the windows too, to ensure they were too small for Esi to slip through. They'd even taken the thicker bedsheets, in case she thought to strangle herself with them.

They needn't have bothered. Esi would not send herself to the Goddess while Bas still breathed, and he who kept her world turning did still breathe.

She knew he did because he was, at that very moment, standing in the Great Circle, in the hot sun, on the far side of the roped-off area where the fight would take place. He was facing her and she wondered if he could see her, if he could pick her out among all the faces.

It was only the second time in her life that Esi Omehia found the Great Circle of Palm City to be too small for its purpose. The first had been the mourning ceremony for her grandmother, Queen Ayanna, and it had been unseasonably hot then too. Given the many parallels to that awful day, when her sister had become queen, it was no surprise that the memories came back to her. Esi was even sitting in the same red-canvas-covered pavilion that had been used then.

The pavilion, seating Tsiora, the Lesser general, and Kellan Okar, and guarded by Auset and Ramia, who, once cleaned and decently clothed, looked like themselves again, adjoined the fighting space and offered the best view of what was to come. It also managed to keep the worst of the heat away but could do nothing about the stink of thousands of sweating bodies. The smell in the circle was so thick it was palpable, assaulting her nose in much the way the riotous clash of colors worn by the citizens of the city, soldiers, Sah, Proven, and Drudge attacked the eye.

It seemed that, in spite of the oppressive heat, the whole world had come to watch a man die, when most of them wouldn't even be close enough to see it. The crowds in their gaiety, like multicolored walls of fetid flesh, were too thick to see through, and for other than those who had stood overnight in the circle or those who were privileged enough to be escorted to its center by armed Indlovu, the fight might be heard, but it would not be seen.

Esi knew it didn't matter. She didn't have to be of or among the people to understand their desire to present themselves. In one night, thousands had died, more were wounded, the city's walls had come down, and dragons had burned women, men, and even themselves to ash, yet two queens still stood. The city needed to make sense of its fear and loss. The people needed the night's carnage to have a purpose, and the Great Circle of Palm City stank and overflowed with people because if all the death they had borne wasn't given meaning, then the life the city had left would have none either.

At some signal he'd been waiting for, Kellan Okar stood from his seat and walked from the pavilion to the center of the fighting circle. Seeing him, the crowd hushed to an occasional cough or rustling of clothes, and Kellan's powerful voice carried through the space.

"We are here to ask the Goddess's blessing. We are here to see Her will done. We are here to satisfy the challenge that Princess Esi offers to Queen Tsiora, and in full faith that the Goddess's hand steers the swords of men, our queen agrees to this contest between the Royal Noble Abasi Odili and her champion, Tau Solarin."

The crowd erupted at the mention of the Lesser's name and Esi felt sick to see so many faces caught in the ecstasy of the moment, mouths gaping, hands raised, and feet stamping in approval of such a base and vile creature. The Omehi were losing their way, and the only thing offering her hope was the neutrality on the faces of the Nobles whom she could see.

The Petty, Greater, and Royals stood in staid silence, the only acknowledgment of the unwashed around them being the occasional handkerchief held close to diffuse the stench that sought to overrun them and replace everything decent and good with rot and wretchedness.

"This contest ends with death," Kellan said after the cheers had faded. "Its victor, in sight of Goddess, women, and men, shall confirm and substantiate the rule of the true Omehian queen."

Oh, how they roared at that. It was a thing for the history books, after all. Two sisters, spilled from the same womb, vying for one crown, and their men ordered to die for it on the hot stones of the Great Circle of Palm City.

The reckoning had come, and though she had everything to lose, Esi's blood rose, pumping so hard it stoppered her ears and made her fear fainting from its rush. Hearing only her heart beating in her chest and echoing in her head, she missed it when the young Gifted woman walked in from the rear of the pavilion.

"Thandi, what is it?" her sister said.

The Gifted leaned close and whispered in Tsiora's ear, and though Esi's sister tried to hold her expression steady, Esi had known her for too long. All it took was a slight parting of Tsiora's lips and the barest fluttering of her eyelids and Esi knew that a storm had rolled in. Something was wrong, and, smiling on the inside, Esi returned her attention to the fighting circle, wishing Tsiora the full brunt of whatever it was that came for her.

Eyes alighting on Bas, Esi forgot her sister, the Gifted, and their petty concerns. In front of her, not two dozen strides distant and looking determined, both Bas and the limping boor wore the black-and-red armor of an Omehian champion. Both men held a single bronze sword, with the Lesser holding his in the wrong hand, but only one of them bore a shield and helmet.

It should have been shaming to see her champion take more

protection than his opponent in a battle before Chosen, queens, and Goddess, but Esi felt none. Instead, she wished she could kiss the shield and helmet and pray over them to keep Bas safe.

She hadn't been able to shake the feeling she'd had the night before, and though she was not her sister, always ready to look to the Goddess, in the breaths before the fight began, Esi closed her eyes and sent Ananthi a prayer.

"He is a good man, he'll be a great father, and I love him," she whispered to the Goddess. "Spare him today and I will be a true queen who honors you and your Chosen," she said. "Keep him safe and I swear I'll spend the rest of my life doing the same for our people."

She opened her eyes, and in the light of a new day, her nighttime fears felt less real. In the light of a new day, she could look out at the fighting circle with clear eyes to see that Bas was head and shoulders bigger than the Lesser. She could see that he almost doubled Tsiora's champion in weight and that the bastard limped badly. In the light of a new day, Esi Omehia held hope that without his Guardian swords, the Lesser had lost his last advantage over a better man.

Kellan Okar walked to the front of the pavilion, turning his head from one champion to the other. "May the Goddess be with you," he said, raising his hand into the air.

"Spare him, Ananthi. Spare him," Esi breathed as Kellan's hand knifed down.

"*Fight!*"

MOTHERS

The contest opened with cheers and screams from the crowd as the two champions, one of them destined to die, approached each other. When they were close, the men exchanged words, but it was impossible to hear them over the roars of the Omehi there to see blood.

Esi tried to read their lips, but the way the two champions were circling each other stymied her efforts.

She thought she saw the Lesser say, "justice" and "father," maybe the words "at last." She thought she saw Odili say, "surrender," "queen," and "Noble." In a flashy and pointless show, she saw the Lesser swing his bronze sword in a circle, and then he advanced.

Bas let him come and Esi held her breath, waiting for him to strike the maggot down. The Lesser stepped into range and, without hesitation, Bas slashed at him. His helmet obscured most of his face, but Esi could still see his eyes as he focused on his victim.

"Yes!" she shouted, losing herself in the moment as Bas's sunlit-bronze blade careened through the air to meet... nothing.

His swing, so clean and true, passed through where the Lesser had been, and Esi's mind twisted in on itself as she tried to make sense of how Bas had missed. She tried to understand how the Lesser had come to be behind him, but her thoughts gave way to fear. The Lesser could attack.

But Tsiora's thrall did not strike. He spurned his advantage and walked off, demeaning Bas's nobility by treating him like he was a less-than-worthy adversary. The Low Common was making a mockery of a duel that could only end in death, and the Lessers watching roared in approval, loving his lowbred behavior.

Facing his opponent's back and being a better man, Bas chose to end the farce. He charged forward, bold and beautiful as a shooting star, his war cry and blade leading the way, but with his back still to Bas, the Low Common lurched out of reach.

The near hit had Esi's heart thrashing against her rib cage. "Kill him," she whispered, and it was like he heard.

With his shield raised and his sword flying left and right, the man who risked his life for her moved across the cobblestones with the grace of a grassland wind. Bas pushed his body to its limit, the muscles on his thighs and arms rippling beneath the bulk of his padded armor as he pressed forward without opposition, obligating his opponent to give ground before his onslaught.

Bas's charge and the sequence following it were blinding, brilliant, beautiful. He was a Royal Noble and a true son of the Goddess, but, somehow, his every move was thwarted. Tsiora's savage, behaving as if it were all a show, danced away from each strike, scuttling about like a scorpion soon to sting, making light of the real life on the line.

The Low Common seemed to want to make Bas look foolish, and Esi hated the half man for his dishonesty. She hated that the Nobles around the circle, who had begun to hang their heads, and the Lessers, who were raising theirs, couldn't see what it was that Tsiora's champion truly sought. Like Isihogo's demons, he wanted to destroy the way of the world, and like them and everything else evil, he had to be stopped.

But Bas was unable to land a single strike, and gulping down air, he ended his attack before having killed the Lesser. He still pursued his opponent, but it was slowly and on shaky legs. His assault had drained him.

Meanwhile, Tsiora's champion walked back and forth in front of

Bas, snarling and blathering like a madman. He limped and hopped and hunched, moving like some predatory insect. He cawed at Bas, pointing his sword at him, and Esi began to have trouble breathing. Her nerves—scrubbed raw—were getting the better of her; they made the crowd sound too loud, her mouth taste too dry, and the Lesser seemed to be transforming before her eyes.

She saw his face split and swell, his mouth becoming too large by far, and his teeth grew pointed and dripped saliva. His hands became clawed, the fingers ending in talons meant to strip flesh from bone, and then there were his eyes. They'd frightened her before, but glowing red with rage and violence, they terrified her.

The worst of it was that no one else saw him as he really was, and Esi, feeling fixed in place, could do nothing but watch what was to come.

Tsiora's demon attacked, and Esi's dread built as she watched the man she loved struggle to defend himself against it. Steps behind the creature's pace, Bas stumbled, looking sluggish against its inhuman speed. His blocks were mistimed, his counters erratic, and he couldn't hold the monster back. It slashed him once, twice, and then a third time, the last strike sending his blood spraying skyward in a thick stream of red that reaped startled screams from several onlookers.

It was seeing Bas bloodied that broke her; he was being overwhelmed, and unable to hide from that fact, Esi's faith fled. What could two people do in the face of so much wrongness? They had love and right on their side, and she'd wanted to believe them enough, but in the harsh light of day, she could tell that they were not. Just like when she'd been a child, nothing would stop the demons.

Feeling tears coming, Esi blinked, and when her eyes opened, she found herself reliving her firmest memory. She was a little girl, wearing the new dress her mother had given her. She remembered that she'd been holding her favorite wooden toy horse when the women in black robes came. Telling her to be brave, Esi's mother pushed her into their arms, letting the women tear Esi's mind from the world. Her mother had given her to them so that they could send her to that cruel place where the monsters waited.

She'd try to hide from them, the women and then the monsters, but both would find her, and the monsters, they would tear her apart, the pain and agony of it crashing through her small frame and into her head, ricocheting through every memory and moment until she'd be lost for days, stuck in a body she couldn't move and a mind she couldn't control.

For as long as Esi could remember, the demons had stalked the edges of her life, but Tsiora had done something to change that. Her sister had given them a way to enter the world completely, and one of them, Tsiora's creature, was hurting Bas, and Bas was screaming.

Out there, in front of her in the circle, Bas was crying and bloody and hurt and begging, begging for mercy, but no one could see that it was a demon that cut at him, and even if they could have seen the truth, Esi had been through enough to know that none of them would have the decency to stop it.

She watched as Bas's helmet was bashed in until it did more harm than good and he had to snatch it from his head, casting it aside. His shield was battered until he let it fall to the cobblestones and the arm that had been holding it was a mass of welts. The fight went on, he could barely keep his head up, and the demon beat him about the legs so badly that Bas had trouble moving.

"Stop," she wanted to say, "stop it," but watching her friend and lover tortured had stolen her voice, and Esi sat in silence as he was mutilated.

"End it, my queen," said Tsiora's general with tears in his eyes. "You have to make him stop."

Her sister turned to the general and then turned away. Tsiora was so much like their mother, Esi thought, but Esi was not. She was no longer a helpless child, and she would never let someone suffer as she had been allowed to do.

Springing to her feet, Esi ran for the fighting circle. She was fast but not fast enough, and one of Tsiora's handmaidens grabbed her, holding her back.

"Let her go," her sister ordered, and the hand on her wrist vanished, and Esi ran.

"Get away from him!" she shouted at the demon. "Get away!"

It spun to face her, locking red eyes on her, its lips quivering in rage over pointed teeth. "He's mine," it snarled, turning back to Bas so that it could hurt him more.

She pounded her fists on its back, and she shouted at it, but she couldn't stop it.

It stalked its way over to Bas, who was lying on the cobblestones of the Great Circle and taking shallow, desperate breaths.

"Why won't you help us?" she said to the faces around her. "What made you so cruel that you'd let this happen? That you'd let monsters tear away everything we are? Why won't you help?"

Surrounded by thousands, Esi was still alone. They stared back at her, blank Noble and Lesser faces, unmoved and unmoving, all except the demon.

"You call me a monster because I won't let you treat me like my life is worthless, a thing to be used and thrown away?" it said. "You call me a monster because I refuse to live like you think I deserve? If that's what you mean by monster, watch me be monstrous!"

It raised its twisted sword to keep hurting Bas, but Esi would not let it, and she stood between it and the man she loved.

"Goddess's mercy," she begged, bringing her hands together and intertwining her fingers.

"I'll grant you as much as She's always given to me and mine," it said, stepping forward and bumping into her.

Although she was frightened beyond reason, she held her ground against it. "His name is Abasi," Esi said. "He's the son of Ayanda and Lungile Odili. He was born and raised in this city, and when his sister died giving birth, he gave a third of his estates to the Sah so they could find a way to prevent what happened to his sister from happening to more women. He's spent his life fighting for our people's safety, and he is the man I love." Esi put her hands out to stop the demon's advance. "Goddess's mercy."

The demon watched her with its red eyes. "That's not everything he is or all that he's done," it said. "He put so much pain and grief inside me, it's driving me mad." The demon showed its teeth and drummed a clawed fist against its chest as if it would rip its heart free from the cage of its body. "He gave me this rage that consumes me, and I will finish this so I can finally have peace."

It stepped closer, its body pressed against the palms of her outstretched hands, and Esi dropped to her knees.

"He's going to be a father," she said, looking up and into the demon's cruel face as she let go of their secret. "Goddess's mercy, please."

The demon stopped, its sword dipped, and, slowly at first but increasing in speed, it changed, becoming more human until even the red in its eyes, the last sign of its true nature, disappeared.

"He's going to be a father," she said.

Tsiora's scarred champion paused, then shook his head. "No, he won't," he said, his voice a violent rasp that was still, somehow, melancholic, and then he turned and left.

From her knees, Esi crawled to Bas. He was on his back, facing the hot sun, and she used her body to shield his face from its harshness.

"Bas," she said softly.

His neck and chest were pulsing as he gasped for air he couldn't hold.

"Bas," she said.

He heard her the second time, and his eyes jerked toward her as she hovered her hands over him, not knowing what to do or where to touch or how to help. And then he lifted his hand, blood dripping down fingers wrapped round the hilt of a small golden dagger. Slowly, so slowly, he moved his hand to hers and pushed the dagger at her.

"No," she said. "I can't."

His lips moved without sound and he pressed the dagger into her hands, conveying with his expression what he could not manage with words, and Esi cried, sobbing hard enough that it set her whole being heaving. Bas's body was destroyed, her hands were covered in his blood, and there was only one mercy left to give.

"I love you," she said, pointing the blade at his chest. "I love you so much."

She stabbed down as hard as she could, and when the dagger plunged into him, Abasi's back arched, his mouth flying open to wail at the harm she'd done. Esi had missed her mark.

She came close to collapsing. The Goddess wanted too much from her, but Bas needed her too, and it was him who she could not fail. In shaking hands, she drew the dagger from Bas's flesh, lifting it high into the air before slamming it down on the place where she laid her head at night to hear his heart beat.

Her aim was true and Bas's body spasmed before going still. Esi had broken his heart, and she watched as the life left the eyes of the man she loved.

She curled over him in grief, and her tears fell onto his cheeks as her face touched his. She'd lost everything, and the real war was just beginning. The demons were coming, and they could not be stopped. They'd remake the world, and she knew that, when they did, no one and nowhere would be safe.

So, Esi Omehia, the giftless, went to Isihogo and took from a "mother" too weak to do what must be done to protect Her children. She stole as much power from the Goddess as she could hold, and glowing like a new sun, Esi braved the demons one last time so that her unborn child would never have to.

CHAPTER FIFTEEN

REWARD

Tau was limping to the pavilion and had his back to Odili when the man died. He waited to feel different. He'd balanced the scales, and that had to count for something, but his father and Zuri were still gone, and it didn't hurt less because the man responsible was dead.

Instead of relief or a sense that justice had been done, Tau felt tired, hollow, and he kept picturing the things he'd done to Odili in the circle. It made him feel sick, and Tsiora had borne witness to it all.

He had to get to her, because he needed some kind of absolution, and she was the only one who could offer it. After seeing the hate her twin had for him, Tau needed Tsiora to look at him without Esi's revulsion.

But each step was hard. He didn't know what he'd do if Tsiora saw him as a monster, and he was torturing himself with that thought when Esi screamed.

Hearing her sister's scream, Tsiora stood and stared past Tau, her expression telling him more than enough. He didn't need to look back to confirm it. He could guess what Esi had done, and though it was probably too late already, Tau flung himself to the underworld to save her.

Isihogo welcomed him with its shrill winds and perpetual twilight, but something wasn't right. Princess Esi was screaming so loudly she could be heard over the underworld's winds, and even that wasn't it. It sounded as if she shouted with two voices.

Tau turned to look at her, thinking that he'd left too much of his mind in Uhmlaba, thinking he was hearing an echo of her terror reflected in the underworld, but what he saw was so horrifying it smothered his other concerns.

Esi was a few strides away, kneeling in the murk, shining like a small sun. She'd taken energy from Isihogo into herself, courting the demons, and they had set upon her. She was swarmed, and the monsters, eager to release the power in her veins, ripped at her.

Tau ran to fight them, aware of how little it would matter. Esi had been mauled, was close to death, and he didn't want to think how things would be for her back in Uhmlaba with psychic wounds that deep.

Guardian swords to hand, he swung at the nearest demon, his blade burying itself in its temple at the same time that he felt the pressure of a new presence behind him. He didn't look back. He moved faster, desperate to get to Esi before it got him, picturing the horned one running him down with that bastard blade it carried, and for the first time in lifetimes, the mists and the things it hid scared him.

Reaching Esi, he stabbed one of the creatures digging its claws into her and swung his other sword to keep the others back. He was struck then, and as much as he'd expected to be caught, the force of the blast surprised him.

Knocked aside, Tau lost control of his underworld body, and his mind splintered.

He felt himself falling until his knee smacked the stones of the Great Circle back in Uhmlaba. He was badly shaken and had dropped to the ground, but glancing up, he saw Tsiora with her hand outstretched. It'd been her, not the horned one. She'd hit Esi with a wave of expulsion and caught him too.

His senses and orientation coming back to him, Tau heard the crowd react. He heard the gasps, cries, and rising panic. He heard it, prayed Tsiora had been in time, looked over his shoulder, and found his prayers unanswered.

Princess Esi, rocking on her knees, was a unique ruin, and Tau had seen demon-deaths before. The oozing blood, corrupted skin, boils, and rashes were familiar, but the extent of them and seeing them on Tsiora's twin hit hard. He stumbled to his feet, and for the second time in breaths, he went to her.

At the last, Princess Esi, blood pooling in her eyes and blinding her, reached out to him before collapsing into his arms. She was light as a leaf, and Tau held her as she died. Her last words were about a little girl and the name they would give her the moment she was born.

Shadows extended over them then, and Tau heard footsteps. He looked up, and the heaviness in his heart was enough to push him into the stones beneath him. Tsiora was there with Kellan, Hadith, Auset, Ramia, and Thandi, and the expression on the queen's face, the sorrow and loss in it, made him relive the day his father died.

"I'm so sorry," he said as she went to her knees in front of him and touched her sister's face.

"Esi?" Tsiora asked, calling out to her sister.

"She's gone," said Tau.

"Esi?"

"At peace."

If Tsiora heard, she didn't show it.

"Kellan," Tau said.

The Greater Noble nodded and called over the Queen's Guard. They formed a ring around them, giving Tsiora what privacy could be had in the middle of the Great Circle of Palm City with thousands and thousands watching.

"Shall I put guards on Odili's body?" Kellan asked Tau.

"Have him taken and prepared for burning with the others who died in the battle for the city," Tau said, finding it strange to be saying such a thing and thinking that, after everything he'd done that day, it was the one mercy he could offer.

He hadn't struck the final blow, but the last man responsible for the death of his father was gone. He'd expected that the Royal

Noble's death would change things, but looking around the circle, Tau saw hundreds more women and men just like Abasi Odili.

As Esi made clear, those Nobles all had lives and loves, duties, aspirations. They could be kind and a comfort to their friends and families. But there was another truth about them as well. Nobles granted themselves a humanity that they did not extend to people like him, and because of that, they thought little of ruining or even ending a Lesser's life.

It made him wonder if anything other than killing them all could prevent the harm they seemed determined to keep causing. He'd already lost his father to their whims, and living each day without him felt impossibly hard. He'd lost Zuri as a result of Noble betrayals, and along with her life, they'd stolen everything she could have accomplished and everything she could have been.

After the things the Nobles had done for generations, Tau didn't think the Goddess would call him evil if he chose to visit more vengeance on them. But kneeling near Tsiora, close enough to feel her grief as she kissed her dead sister's forehead, Tau found that, though his own pain had not been vanquished, much of his stomach for vengeance had.

"Tsiora," he said, and she lifted her head, her face despair-stricken. Not knowing if she'd reject him, he reached for her. She saw him do it, dropped her eyes, and placed one of her bloodstained hands in his.

"We're tired, Tau," she said. "Every fight leaves us with less to love in this life. Do we even have time to burn and mourn Nyah and Esi?" she asked. "Tau, Kana is coming."

The news rattled him, but if he was truthful with himself, he'd known Kana would come. Tau had killed his father.

"Thandi told me before the fight," Tsiora said to him. "It was an edification from General Bisi. They were attacked on their march here and were forced to flee, but Kana is pursuing them with his army." Tsiora bent down to kiss her sister's forehead again, and when she sat up, there were tears in her eyes and blood on her lips. "We're so tired."

"Then you'll rest and you'll mourn, and whatever comes, I'll be here with you," Tau said, realizing how much his promise to Nyah meant to him.

The day had taught him that there was little justice to be found in dealing death, but he'd do whatever it took to keep Tsiora and Chibuye safe.

"Let Kana come," he said. "He won't like what he finds here."

PYRES

Night had fallen and Tau was at the burning. He stood behind his queen but in front of the damaged walls of Palm City and in front of a crowd larger than those who had come to see him fight Odili. He counted it an obvious but notable mark of hope that more people attended the ceremony to wish their loved ones good-bye than had been present to see a man killed.

As one, they faced out toward the point where the Amazi River's two forks came together. The waters, rushing over the rubble of the Trident Bridge, had flowed beyond the riverbanks at that joining. They had flooded a little of the land there, making the night seem brighter because of the many points of firelight reflected in the shallow swathe of the false lake.

In front of Tau and past Tsiora, who had an arm around the softly crying Chibuye, there were hundreds of mass pyres extending out to the newly forged water's edge. Each pyre was watched over by a soldier standing at attention with a lit torch held at their side. It was pretty to see and hard to look at. It made Tau feel like he was in Kerem again, but with the dead having multiplied many, many times over.

Wearing ceremonial masks of nickel, sculpted in the likeness of the Goddess with Her foreign features, Sah priestesses and priests were spread throughout the area. It was the only way that more than a few of the living would be able to hear any words spoken for the dead, and when the Sah began to talk, Tau didn't listen to much that was said. He was watching Tsiora's back and thinking about what Nyah had told him. He was thinking about how she'd warned him that Tsiora could only take so much before she'd break.

Nyah had known the queen better than anyone else still living. Tau knew that. He also knew what it took to stay standing when the whole world wanted you on your knees, and he believed that Tsiora would stand until she had hold of the things she wanted or she was cut down.

Her strength, clarity of vision, and determination were unyielding. They kept her upright during the speeches and for the length of the ceremony. Then, to help the dead on their way, Tsiora and Chibuye took a torch to the pyre that held the wrapped bodies of Nyah and Esi. The pyre caught fire and burned bright, sending their loved ones home to the Goddess.

The crying, once a blanket of murmurs, became louder and disjointed as emotions peaked and valleyed while the flames rose to free the dead. Tsiora had Chibuye standing in front of her then, and she had both arms around the child as they stared at the flickering pyres.

Hadith, whom Tau had not spoken with since before the duel, came to stand at his side along with Kellan and Gifted Thandi.

"Yes?" asked Tau.

"It's General Bisi," Hadith said. "We need to join our strength to the soldiers under his command."

"What is our strength, Hadith?"

"We're trying to mesh two armies who, very shortly ago, were killing one another. We're trying to bring them together, and the only reason it hasn't failed entirely is because we're facing a common threat." Hadith ran a hand halfway over his scalp. "Tau, I'm not sure we can wage any kind of war with what we have. We've needed to imprison nearly every inkokeli in Odili's army. We have soldiers in scales, claws, and wings with junior leadership and confused loyalties. I can't even be sure we won't take swords in our backs from those we're trying to fight beside."

"It's fight with us or die to the Xiddeen. Make the stakes clear," Tau said.

"I'm trying," Hadith said.

Kellan cleared his throat. "Champion, I'd like to second the grand general's thinking. Our best chance is to combine our military with the rages under General Bisi's command. There's a valley north and east of Palm City. It has a high ridge on its north side and it runs right up against the Central Mountains on its southern side. It's a tight space for a fight, and being outnumbered, it'll suit us better than anything else we have."

Tau moved his eyes between the two men. "You're arguing that we should fight in a valley and not from the city?"

"The walls are down and the river's easily passable," Hadith said. "If we let the fight come to Palm, we'll be pinned in it and putting every single citizen at risk."

"So you say, knowing well I'm no military strategist. Tell me what you want," said Tau.

"We need to speak with the queen," Hadith said.

"The queen is mourning."

"Champion, we know, but this is urgent," Kellan said. "If we're going to make it to the valley in time, we must march at first light."

"In the morning?" said Tau. "I thought I was supposed to be the impulsive one. Hadith, you're telling me that you haven't been able to replace the inkokeli you've removed from duty, that the army is one or two incidents from open revolt, and you want to march that same army in a few spans? You want to take that army to war?"

"There's not much choice in it," said Hadith, "and we need to tell the queen the options."

"Options? You've told me one thing," Tau said.

"It's what we have."

"No," Tau said. "She's strong, but she should at least have this little time to mourn the loss of those she loved."

Gifted Thandi, sighing, pushed her way between the two men. "She should, Champion. She should have the time, but she doesn't. Bicker with each other, if it makes you feel better. I'll tell her what she needs to know."

She marched over to Tsiora and spoke with her. Then the three, Tsiora, Thandi, and Chibuye, walked back to Tau, Hadith, and Kellan. Tsiora's eyes were red from having cried, but when she spoke to them, her eyes were dry.

"Prepare the army to march at first light, Grand General," she said.

MEASURES

Back in the palace, Tau waited while Tsiora put Chibuye to sleep. She'd had an extra bed brought into the royal apartments for Nyah's daughter, and though the apartments were made up of many large rooms, the bed was placed in the same one in which Tsiora herself would sleep.

Tau was with them, keeping his eyes on the floor and holding himself still as Chibuye went from muted weeping to ragged sniffles to deep breathing. Tsiora sat at the edge of the bed, a hand on the child's back, waiting for her to come to a complete rest. It took more than a span for the little one to do so.

"She's asleep," Tsiora whispered. "Where's Hafsa?"

"In the adjoining room with the others," he said.

"Good. If she wakes, we'll send Hafsa to her." She stood up.

"You're sure you want to do this now?"

"We'll be fine," she said.

Tau slid the door to the bedroom open. It didn't swing in or out. Instead, there was a gap in the wall in which the door could be hidden, and Tau marveled at the ostentation of splendors that sought to turn even basic concepts like doors upside down. The queen walked past him, and he followed her into the room where the others were waiting and slid the door closed.

Everyone was sitting around a circular table. Most of them held hot cups of rabba, using the drink's heat and bitter taste to stave off the weariness of a long night. When they saw the queen, they rose. Acknowledging the women and men in the room, Tsiora took a seat at the table. Tau took the chair on her right, and once he was settled the others sat too. At the table were Thandi, Hadith, Kellan, Uduak, Auset, Ramia, and Hafsa.

"Only one Noble," Tsiora said.

"I know, Your Majesty," Hadith said. "We do not reflect the composition of the army well enough, and the Nobles in it will not think on that kindly. I'll look to remedy the situation as soon as I can, but for now, and with your approval, I'd like to give Kellan Okar command over all the Indlovu, ours as well as the men who were under Odili's command."

"Approved, General," the queen said. "Now, tell me how we win."

"Our best hope is to engage Kana in the valley north of the Central Mountains," Hadith said. "I don't think we come out of this successfully any other way, but I worry that we're being baited."

"Baited, how?" she asked.

"The edifications from General Bisi set the count for Kana's army at far fewer than I'd expect, but the fact that he has an army at all means that his slaughter in Kerem did remake the warlord's alliance. So, where are the rest of Kana's fighters?"

"You think they're coming for us from somewhere else?" the queen asked.

"I do."

"Where, the water?"

Hadith nodded. "It would make sense. We've never moved so many fighters from the interior of the peninsula before and I think Kana knows or has guessed that we called up the Ihagu and Ihashe who usually protect our mountains and beaches."

"Hmm..." Thandi said, thinking it through. "He could be hoping to occupy us with a battle in Palm City while the other Xiddeen come from the water to take the rest of the peninsula."

"And if it's so, how do we stop him?" Tsiora asked the room.

"Split the army again," suggested Auset. "Send some to the beaches and the rest to fight in the valley."

"Don't they already outnumber us?" asked Ramia.

"They do," Hadith said. "With Bisi's army, we'll have twenty thousand, but Kana has more than sixty."

"Rather win one than lose two," said Uduak.

"What?" asked Auset.

"Uduak would rather win one battle than lose both of them," said Hadith. "And I think he's right."

"Am right," Uduak said.

Tau couldn't hold his tongue any longer. "Are you certain we're not better served waiting for Bisi to join us in Palm City? We can fight from here."

"I'm as certain as I can be," Hadith said. "The walls here are breached and the river is traversable. If we allow Kana to come to Palm, we'll be letting him trap our army in this city with our people, with hundreds of thousands of mouths to feed." Hadith looked around the room. "He won't even need to attack. He'll just starve us out, killing us slowly as news of cities, fiefs, and hamlets being overrun all across the peninsula comes to us in desperate edifications crying for help we can't provide."

Hadith's words were followed by silence.

"We'll make our stand alongside General Bisi's soldiers in the valley," the queen said, her decision made. "One army, one push, one fight. No half measures."

Tau glanced in Hadith's direction. He didn't like the look on their grand general's face. Hadith was determined but also grim, and Tau had seen that look in skirmishes. It meant the plan had merit, but not much of it.

"Agreed?" the queen asked.

They were.

"Then there is one thing we must do before we continue." The queen stood and the rest hurried to do likewise. "Gifted Thandi, if you would?" Tsiora said.

Thandi moved to stand in front of the queen.

"We regret that there isn't time to do this in the traditional manner and hope you won't hold that against us."

"My queen?"

"The Gifted have need of a leader, and this queen must have a KaEid whom she can trust."

Thandi's eyes went wide. "My queen?"

"Thandi Tariro, will you honor us by serving in that capacity? Will you lead our Gifted in peace and war?"

"Ah...Queen Tsiora, I-I'm..." Thandi's lips were trembling. "Queen Tsiora, it would be the honor of my life to serve as your KaEid."

"We thank you, KaEid Tariro."

Thandi lowered her head, looked up at the queen through her lashes, and smiled. The way she looked, Tau thought she might hug the queen, but Thandi settled for looking around the room at the others, her eyes stopping and holding on Kellan Okar, who returned her smile.

"Well, we've filled the positions we wanted to with the best of our people," Tsiora said. "General Buhari, if we're not mistaken, you need to do more of the same." Tsiora walked back toward the room where Chibuye was sleeping, speaking over her shoulder. "We have faith, faith in the Goddess and in all of you. Do not fear, because we walk in Her light, and in it there is nothing to fear."

But where there was light, there was shadow, and Tau had something he needed the queen to know. "Queen Tsiora, may I have a word?" he asked.

She was at the door to the other room. "Of course," she said, "come in."

He'd wanted to wait for the right time but realized the right time would never come. He had to tell Tsiora about the demon that held a sword like a man. He had to tell her what he knew about the horned one that had set the other demons on Nyah and defeated him.

THIEVES

Tau followed his queen into the room where Chibuye was sleeping. Tsiora put a finger to her lips, then beckoned to him, asking him to come with her into the next room over. Tau did as he was bid and they moved through that room and onto an outdoor balcony overlooking the city.

The balcony was enclosed by a bronze railing shaped like a series of interwoven climbing vines. On the balcony's floor and hanging from its jutting ceiling were colorfully painted adobe pots with plants growing in them. Tau didn't recognize the greenery.

"A garden?" he asked. "What food can you harvest here?"

Tsiora went to the nearest plant, letting her fingers play across its leaves. "They grow neither fruits nor vegetables. They are for beauty."

"I see," Tau said, thinking about the time and effort that would be needed to bring water to these pretty but pointless plants.

"Come," the queen said, showing him to a matched set of cushioned chairs that were long enough for a Noble to lie down on comfortably.

The overly long chairs faced each other, and between them was a short table ladened with bowls of berries and nuts. Tau walked past the long chairs and the food table, interested in the bronze railing and what was beyond it.

Laid out before him, like a detailed miniature, Tau could see most of the capital. Some parts of the city were still smoking from the battle, and the light from the funeral pyres still burned bright, but the thing that surprised him was how vast, peaceful, and normal Palm seemed after what had befallen it. In thousands upon thousands of windows he saw the flicker of candles or torches as Omehi women, men, and children made the best of the lives they had.

From the balcony, he could also tell who lived where as surely as he knew his left hand from his right. To his left, there was a section of the city that had to be filled with Lessers, perhaps Harvester or Governor caste. To his far right, where the houses rose two and sometimes even three floors above the ground, were the places where Nobles lived. Straight ahead and farthest from the palace, huddled beneath the walls, were ramshackle huts, pilfered military tents, and tiny adobe houses that could be knocked over with a hard blow from a Greater Noble's shield.

The Omehi in all their glory, Tau thought, turning to see Tsiora slide the balcony's door closed behind them.

"We don't want to wake her," she said. "You wished to speak with us, Champion Solarin."

"Tau. It's...if you please, you can call me Tau."

"Tau," she said, sitting on one of the long cushioned chairs.

He sat in the one opposite. "Queen Tsiora, I think there's something I need to tell you."

She tilted her head, looking at him gravely. "Shall we take a moment to pray first?" she asked.

He wasn't quick enough to school his expression. "Pray?"

Her cheeks dimpled with a mischievous smile. "Apologies. You just looked so serious, and everyone thinks we have to be so serious too. That's what Esi thinks. She thinks we're dour and mirthless and that everything is about the Goddess for us, but it's not. We were more than just a princess and we're more than just a queen. We're a woman, a daughter...we're a sister."

Tau wasn't sure he had anything worth saying to that, so he listened instead of speaking.

"We care about Nyah and Chibuye and we loved our mother

and...and Esi...." Tsiora's smile slipped as she choked up. "We loved her too. We love her so much, Tau."

Goddess, she was crying. She'd been about to laugh two breaths ago. "My queen..."

She put her head in her hands, pressing the bottom of her palms to her lips, trying to hold in the sounds of her sobs. Tau went to her immediately, sinking to his knees in front of her so that their heads were at the same height.

"Did she always hate us so much, do you think?"

"I don't know that she hated you at all," he said.

"Let her go..."

"My queen?"

Tsiora lifted her head from her hands. "Those were the last words Esi heard us say. 'Let her go.'"

"It's not your fault."

"Whose, then?" Tsiora asked, opening her hands to him. "The Goddess's, because everything that happens is Her will? Is this Her will, my sister's death and my pain in it?"

"I don't know," Tau said.

"How is that good enough?"

He took her hands in his. "It isn't. It isn't good enough and nothing will be for a while, because that's part of what loss is, an absence of goodness and happiness that can't be reasoned with or diminished."

"When does it end?"

"In time."

She shook her head. "Not good enough."

"No," he said, "it's not."

More tears came, and she leaned into him. He placed his arms around her, holding Tsiora as close as he could, and she cried into his chest, her pain cutting at him until he could take no more, and with the whole of his heart, Tau Solarin made his queen a promise.

"For as long as you'll have me, I'll be here for you," he told her. "For as long as you want me to, I'll fight for you."

Tau woke up a short while later. His left arm was numb, he was on his back, and it felt like he was lying in deep mud, but, he realized, that was because he was on one of the long chairs. It was dark, which meant the sun had yet to rise, and he wondered where the queen was right as he heard her sigh.

The moment that followed was as much of an out-of-body experience as anything Tau had encountered in Isihogo. The queen was lying beside him, and partially on him. His left arm was numb because it was under her and she had her head on his shoulder and chest.

Craning his neck away from her, Tau spied his sword belt and blades on the other long chair, and feeling naked without them, he tried to extricate his arm without waking the queen.

Tsiora's eyes drifted open right away. "Tau?"

"My queen."

"Tsiora."

"Queen Tsiora."

"No," she said. "Just Tsiora."

"Tsiora?"

"Yes," she said. "Are you too hot?"

"Neh?"

"Is that why you're moving away? Is it too hot?"

"Ah no. I'm ... I was going to get my swords. They're on the other long chair."

"The suffah?"

"Suffah ... yes."

"And you want to bring your swords to this suffah?"

Tau didn't know how to answer that. "I ... Perhaps I'll leave them where they are."

"Yes, they're probably more comfortable on that suffah. There's more room."

"What?"

She laughed, and in spite of his confusion, her laughter made him smile.

"Apologies, Tau," she said, eyes roaming his face. "We love to tease, but there's so few we can do it with."

Tau didn't know if he loved being teased, but seeing her smile made him like it well enough.

"Do you ... should we get up?" she asked.

The long chair was too soft, and staying on it would mean being stiff for the rest of the day, but Tau did not want to get up. "Maybe we could stay a little longer?"

"Mm–hmm," she said, shifting and ending up closer to him, the tight curls of her hair tickling the bare skin on his neck.

It got quiet, and not wanting to do it, Tau admitted to himself that being near Tsiora gave him peace.

"Tau, do you know why we haven't been able to win the war against the Xiddeen?"

Well, most of the time it gave him peace. "They outnumber us too greatly," he said, trying to offer a decent answer.

"In part," she said. "The other part is that, though we can call down Guardians, we could never hold them long enough to truly defeat the Xiddeen armies, but with enough Gifted, we could now."

"The Ayim?" he asked.

"The Goddess meant for us to meet. We're certain of it."

He grunted. He didn't feel Goddess sent, but if they could use the Ayim and the dragons to stop Kana from killing them all, he'd take it. In any case, he'd been looking for the right time to tell the queen about what he'd seen in Isihogo, and though it still wasn't it, he had no illusions that he'd find a better one.

"There's something I want to tell you, before it's too late," he said.

She bit her lip gently and looked up into his eyes. "Yes, Tau?"

"There's something in the mists."

Pulling her eyebrows together, she squinted at him. "Beg pardon?"

"The mists of Isihogo."

She rose onto her elbow. "That's what you want to tell . . . wait, what's in the mists?"

"A demon, but it's . . . different. It's stronger and faster than the rest. It knows more than they do, and I think it can control the others."

"They don't . . . that's not how they are."

"I swear it, Tsiora. I know what I'm saying and I know what I saw. It has horns on its head, no eyes, but it sees. It has several holes in place of ears and long talons on the ends of human–like hands. It . . . it carries a weapon. It wields a twisted guardian sword."

She sat up. "You're scaring us."

He sat up with her. "That's not my intent."

"Have you fought it?"

He nodded.

"And?"

"It scares me very much."

She looked wide awake. "What do you think it is or means?"

"I don't know. Are there any stories about something like this?"

"If there are, we don't know them," she said, wrapping her arms around herself.

It wasn't cold, but Tau placed his hands on her arms and ran them up and down, to warm her.

"What are you doing?"

"Warming you."

She tilted her head at him. "We're not actually cold."

He stopped. "Ah..."

"It feels nice though, and since you've just told us an unpleasant story in the dark, we won't deny ourselves a little nice right now."

He continued to run his hands up and down her arms and she closed her eyes and leaned back into him. The sun was rising, and it was growing brighter on the balcony.

"Why now?" she murmured.

"The demon?"

"No, not that. Why would we meet now? Like this?"

"How could we meet any other way?"

"Hmm?"

"I'm a Lesser and you're a queen."

"You're our champion."

"Do queens usually have champions who are Lessers?"

"What if we weren't a queen and you weren't a Lesser? What if we were just Tsiora and Tau?"

"If we were, we wouldn't be the same people we are now."

She sat with that for a while. "So, queens and champions, Nobles and Lessers, war and loss, and we're permitted no happiness other than what we can steal from moments like these?" She sighed. "Can we lie down again? Just until dawn?"

They lay down, he held her, and she slept. He stayed awake, watching the world continue to brighten as the sun rose behind them. He watched the sky change colors from black to blue-red to the golden-yellow of a soul's glow, and he tried to understand how it was possible to feel as if everything was both beginning and ending all at the same time.

A span later, as Tau was doing up his sword belt and walking through the room where the war council had met the previous evening, Thandi opened the far door and spotted him. He froze, hands on his belt buckle.

"Champion..."

"Thand—KaEid Tariro," he said. "I was just leaving."

"Yes, so I see."

"No, no," he said raising his hands and having to scramble to catch his sword belt before it fell to the ground. "I'm not leaving like that."

"I don't know what you mean."

"I was...I slept on the long chair."

She squinted at him. "The suffah?"

"Yes, that. They're horrible."

"You didn't sleep much, then?" she asked, eyes twinkling.

Tau's mouth was open and he seemed to have forgotten how to close it. "It's been a difficult time for her, for everyone. I was just there to..."

She inclined her head toward him. "You're the queen's champion."

"I'm not...I'm not that kind of champion."

"Indeed?"

He was more at ease on the battlefield. "She's sleeping, resting undisturbed, like she did the entire night."

Thandi's face softened. "I believe that she is and I'm glad you were there with her. I wish she could continue to rest, but we're out of time."

The door slid open behind Tau. It was the queen.

"We march for the valley?" Tsiora asked.

"We do," the KaEid said.

CHAPTER SIXTEEN

SIDES

The march to the valley was tense and the army moved like twin inyokas, winding their way over the northern fork of the Amanzi and tromping across the grasslands at the foot of the Central Mountains, which loomed over them on their right. Kellan marched at the head of the soldiers who had fought for Odili and Esi. Hadith, Tsiora's grand general in charge of the entire army, led the march for the soldiers who had fought for the queen.

Tau rode beside Tsiora and Thandi. The Ayim marched behind him, and Hafsa sat in a tottering wagon with Chibuye, who couldn't bear to be apart from her or the queen.

Jabari, unable to manage long marches, was in the wagon as well. He was slouched down, every part of his flesh covered against the sun's hot touch, and sitting as far from Hafsa and Chibuye as he could, likely thinking he was doing them the favor.

Behind them, for a couple of thousand strides, the army's soldiers, supply wagons, service Lessers, Proven, and Drudge stretched into the distance until the curve of the world swallowed them whole. The tail of the twin inyokas was hidden from sight, making it seem as if the army was a creature long enough to wrap its length around the whole world.

It was hard for Tau to look back and see the unending line of Omehi and not remember the stories Tsiora had told of the flight of their people from their ancestral lands. More, it was difficult for his mind to properly accept that several military rages, filled with full-bloods, were in a rapid retreat, fleeing the Xiddeen, who outnumbered both Omehi armies combined.

The scope of events in which Tau found himself embroiled made little sense to him, and each time the war council met, it was filled with facts and figures, food-supply numbers and weapons-readiness discussions. There was constant talk of the soldiers who had taken ill, the herbs and medicines they had available, and the flared tempers between Nobles and Lessers.

Worst of all, he thought he might develop a permanent slouch from having to lean over hand-drawn maps of the valley as Hadith and Kellan and the other inkokeli moved triangles and squares over the top of the coal-marked parchment. In one instance, he watched them sweep several shapes from the map after considering the merit of one or another defensive posture, counting up the losses as if they were coins fallen from a torn purse instead of a prediction of lives lost in battle.

It was a busy few days that left Tau with the impression that there was more to being a good champion than swinging a sword. The problem was that, for these other duties, he was ill suited and poorly prepared. Adding to his discomfort, his relationship with the queen had changed, and after a whole season spent getting to know her, he felt like they were working out how to behave around each other all over again.

It wasn't brave, but the tumult of emotions he felt whenever she was near made him stay away. Only, that didn't help either. Whenever he was away, he wondered about her.

Most recently, he'd taken to being around her as much as he could while saying next to nothing. That had gone worse than absenting himself, and the queen had begun saying less and less to him as well. It was what he thought he wanted, and yet, inexplicably, it upset him. He felt wild relief, then, when their army met up with the rage of the famed General Bisi. It was something to help take his mind off his queen.

They first appeared as a haze on the horizon that turned into a dust storm kicked up by tens of thousands of pairs of feet. When they were several hundred strides from the head of Tsiora's army, General Bisi's Rage came to a halt, and every single man in their front line snapped to attention and raised the black-on-black flag of the Indlovu.

"Good Goddess, I'm not Governor, but that looks like more soldiers than there should be in a rage," said Themba.

Tau, Tsiora, Thandi, Kellan, Hadith, the Ayim, and a few of Hadith's inkokeli were lined up at the head of their army. Tau kept his eyes faced front, but he could picture how pitiful their one flag, the royal black and red, looked in comparison.

"He has more than one rage with him," Hadith said. "They were being overrun and Bisi took command of two others."

"Why would the other generals let him take charge?" asked Tau.

"Because it's Bisi," Kellan said, as if that explained it.

"Here he comes," whispered Themba.

A small contingent had broken from the rest of the army. There were three of them, riding horses.

"Should we go out to meet them?" Tau asked Hadith, still avoiding talking to the queen.

"No," Hadith said. "He comes to us. We are with the queen."

"Of course," Tau said.

As the three men drew closer, Tau was able to make out more detail. Tau guessed that Bisi was the man riding in the middle, and at first, Tau thought that he was coming to them enraged, but as he got a better look, he realized that Bisi wasn't enraged; he just looked it. General Bisi was the biggest Noble Tau had ever seen.

"Oh," said Themba, "I see why the other generals let him take charge...."

Tau felt pity for the man's horse. It had to be a struggle to carry that much weight. General Bisi was a boulder of muscle, with a jaw so broad it made his full lips look small by comparison. His nose helped balance him out. It was flat and broad and gave off the impression that it was a symbol, pointing up toward his lined forehead.

"No wonder we have so few animals in the peninsula," Themba muttered. "They had to kill half of them to get enough leather for that one's armor."

"Hush, you," Auset said.

And then Bisi was with them. He and his men pulled up a respect-ful distance from the queen and dismounted their horses at the same time, as if the action had been choreographed in advance. As one, they dropped to a knee, heads bowed, the triad of shaven pates glis-tening in the hot sun.

"Queen Tsiora," said the general, spacing the two words evenly in a voice as deep as an earthquake's root.

"General Bisi, rise," Tsiora said.

"My queen, it has been too long since I have seen you."

"We were a girl."

"That long, then," he said. "The front line does not know or respect the passage of seasons or cycles. In any case, this general is privileged to live long enough to be in your presence again and to see, for himself, that the rumors of your great beauty have been unable to do the truth any decency."

Tau was annoyed. They were here to defend their lands against Kana, not play pretty with words.

"If I may introduce my companions?" Bisi said.

Tsiora inclined her head, giving him permission.

"These men are Generals Itro and Enitan. They have supported my leadership over the three military rages."

"Well met, generals," Tsiora said.

"Now, my queen, though I regret that we will not have more time with one another, I should begin the process of bringing your military leadership into my own, if we are to ready our defenses in time for the Xiddeen."

Tau moved his eyes to Hadith, then Tsiora.

"General Bisi, there is a misunderstanding. We have our own grand general."

Bisi looked right at Kellan. "Little Okar, you've grown."

"General Bisi," Kellan said.

"You lead here as grand general?"

Kellan shook his head. "I am inkokeli of the queen's Indlovu. It is Hadith Buhari who leads us."

"Buhari?" asked Bisi.

Hadith was nervous. Tau knew it. Hadith hid it well, though.

"I am Grand General Buhari."

To his credit, Bisi's face moved about as much as a slab of stone.

"I see," he said. "You lead this army?"

"I do."

Tau realized that Bisi hadn't so much as looked at him yet.

"How large? I estimate it to be roughly two rages."

"It is almost that," Hadith said.

"I lead three rages and the men are accustomed to my command. As a general, would you agree that it would be faster and simpler to bring your men into my command?"

"It will not matter if he agrees or not, General Bisi," the queen said.

"My queen?"

"Hadith Buhari is our grand general, and until we excuse him from that role, his thoughts on his holding it are immaterial. General Bisi, you will hand control of your forces into Grand General Buhari's care, and you will report to him."

Tau's left hand drifted to his hilt, and he gazed at the massive force standing at attention only a few hundred strides away. He could kill Bisi, he thought, but he could do nothing about the thousands behind him.

Bisi dipped his head. "Your words, my destiny, Queen Tsiora. The Bisi Rage is yours to command, and now they shall be Grand General Buhari's, until he is excused."

"Thank you, General. Your loyalty is a source of great comfort."

"We have always been loyal to the Omehi," he said.

"General Bisi, what do we face from the Xiddeen?" Hadith asked.

Bisi, stone-faced, gave his report. "Per our last edification to you, Kana is half a day's march behind us and he heads a host the equivalent size of ten to twelve rages."

The thought of that many fighters set against them got Tau's heart beating faster.

"Any idea where the rest of the Xiddeen might be?" Hadith asked.

"Twelve rages isn't enough for our grand general?"

Hadith ignored that. "The concern is that the Xiddeen come at us in force but not in full force. They'll outnumber us three to one, and though on their face, the odds favor Kana, they're still risky odds against an army of Omehi. Where are the rest of his warriors?"

"I'm no Sah priest, seer, or soothsayer, Grand General," Bisi said. "My recommendation is that we face the fight we have. If we survive it, we can worry about where the rest of the savages have wandered off to."

"I see," Hadith said.

"Perhaps you don't," Bisi said. "These are not ocean or mountain raiders. These are Curse-blooded savages. They're coming with their beasts of war, their best fighters, and not a one of them gives any quarter. I warn you, even their women are good enough to kill your Ihagu and Ihashe."

Tau thought he'd been bothered by all the meetings, the planning, and the oddness between him and the queen, but Bisi was bothering him so much more. "We've faced the Xiddeen before," he said.

Bisi's eyes clicked over to Tau. He looked him up and down, noting the champion's armor, before turning back to the queen. "It saddened us greatly to hear that a champion as great as Abshir Okar was gone. His like will never be replaced."

"I was there when he fell," Tau said, annoyed that the general had dismissed him so easily.

"Lucky thing he wasn't the queen, then, if your presence affected the outcome so little."

That was a step too far from a man with such ephemeral loyalties, and Tau moved to dismount so that he could say as much to the general's face.

Hadith coughed and spoke. "Champion Solarin, you have the sharpest eyes and I would be indebted to you if you could offer them to us."

Tau had gotten down from Fury. "What?"

"General Bisi tells us that Kana's army is not far behind his own, and I've learned that in this section of the Central Mountains there's a rough but usable path that leads to a lookout point. With your eyes, you could provide us with valuable information."

Tau knew what he was doing. Hadith was trying to stop Tau from confronting Bisi.

"Grand General," Tau said, "there's just one small thing I wouldn't mind doing here first."

"We'll accompany our champion," the queen said, causing every head in earshot to swing to her.

"Up the mountains?" asked Bisi. "My queen, is that wise?"

"We'll be with Champion Solarin, and, believe us, General, there is no one living or dead with whom we'd feel safer."

As with Hadith, Tau knew what she was doing, but he didn't want his friends to have to defend him. He could do it himself.

"Shall we leave now, Champion?" Tsiora said.

He looked from Bisi to her. He had no choice. "My queen," he said, bowing his head.

"Do you mind if we bring our handmaidens?" she said, smiling at him. "Do you think you could protect all three of us women?"

Ramia was smiling too, but Auset looked like she'd swallowed a bee, and she was giving Themba a side-eye sharp enough to cut. With uncharacteristic wisdom, Themba kept his mouth shut.

"Of course, my queen," Tau said.

"Good, we've spoken so little recently, and though war threatens, that has bothered us."

He clenched his jaw, trying to mimic Bisi's stone-faced trick. He couldn't believe she was so openly talking about them not talking.

Tsiora gave the reins she held a slight tug, getting her horse to move toward the mountains. "Are you coming, Champion? We're very curious to discover what secrets the lookout point has ready to reveal to us."

NEVER

Their horses made it halfway to the lookout point before the path became treacherous for the animals. To keep them safe, they tied them to a tree circled by stunted grazing grass and continued on foot.

It had already been an entire span and Tau and Tsiora hadn't said a single word to each other. To avoid adding to the awkwardness, Tau kept his eyes on their surroundings.

The Central Mountains, or at least this part of them, were much greener than the mountains of his home. The grass grew taller and greener and the trees and bushes were healthier too. It was pretty.

"What did you say?" the queen asked.

"My queen?"

"You said something was pretty."

"Oh, the mountains, my queen."

"The mountains?" She looked at him like he'd stepped in Fury's droppings.

Tau checked for Auset and Ramia, hoping for a distraction, any distraction, but they'd let themselves fall behind and were out of earshot.

"Why are you doing this?" she asked him.

"My queen?"

"Why are you doing this, Tau?"

He didn't have a good answer for her.

She stopped walking and he had to as well. "So much hangs in the balance and nothing as small as this should matter." She waved a hand at herself and at him when she said it. "Yet, it feels like it does. We wish we could stop it from feeling so, but we're not sure we can, and that's . . . unsettling." She was breathless when she finished.

Tau forced himself to admit it out loud. "I feel the same," he said.

"Then . . . then, why not say so?"

"Because it feels like a betrayal," he said, thinking of Zuri.

"A betrayal . . ."

It made him feel impossibly small to see her hurt. It made him feel as if everything the Nobles had ever called men like him was true.

"I'm sorry, Tau," his queen said. "I'm asking too much."

"No . . . I just don't know if I can . . ." He tried to work through the knot inside him, hoping to unravel even a little of it. "I can't survive losing you, and there's not much left in the world that scares me like the thought of that does."

He saw Tsiora's eyes grow wide when he said it, but the time for talking was done. Auset walked into view, Ramia behind her, dragging her feet.

"I can't walk any slower," Auset said to them. "I really can't." She looked at Tsiora's and Tau's faces, shook her head, and called back to Ramia. "They're not done."

"I told you," Ramia said, not meeting anyone's eyes.

The four of them stood in silence.

"Well, if no one is talking, can we finish the climb to the lookout point?" Auset asked. "The path is right there."

Tsiora was staring at Tau, and he didn't know how to read the many things he could see in her eyes.

"Champion?" Auset said.

"Of course," he said. He needed time to deal with the thing he'd just told Tsiora. He needed time to think. "Can you stay with the queen? I'll climb the rest of the way up."

"Mm-hmm," said Auset, running a thin twig under one of her nails.

Tau bowed to Tsiora, who hadn't said a word since he'd said what he'd said to her, and feeling her eyes boring into his back as he left, he trudged up the rest of the path.

The way quickly became steep, and the last few strides to the lookout point were a proper climb, requiring his attention.

"This better be worth it, Hadith," Tau said as he finally stepped out onto the ledge of the lookout point.

The view stole his breath and sense. Tau had grown up in high places, but what he saw from the lookout point in the Central Mountains was a wholly new beauty. It wasn't the power of the Roar or the endless stretch of beach winding its way up the coast, but from where he was that day, he could look back and see the topmost tips of Palm City's towers, while above him, the Central Mountains soared up and into the clouds. Looking straight ahead, he could see all the way to the Northern Mountain Range, the flatlands before him giving way to rolling hills of green and yellow, and there, dividing the Central Province from the North, was the Amanzi Amancinci River, its waters sparkling like they were the sky-blue scales of some infinitely long inyoka.

He breathed deep, tasting the cool mountain air and marveling at the land that was his home, the land that was all of their homes, if they could keep it.

Sobered by the thought, Tau looked down at the valley below him and immediately agreed with the decision to fight there. It was the ultimate battleground for a smaller army that needed to stop a larger one.

The north side of the valley rose rapidly, making the ground there difficult to traverse and near impossible to fight on. Similarly, the south edge of the valley ran right up to the mountains, and given the natural barriers to the north and south, there were just two reasonable ways to move soldiers into the valley.

An army could come in from the west, as his army had done, or they could come in from the east, as Bisi's Rage had done and as Kana's Xiddeen were about to do. And once in the valley, the army wishing to push forward would need to do so through the rocky choke point at the valley's middle. It was, Tau noted, a natural killing field.

He lifted his eyes, shifting his gaze to the east and toward the enemy. He was too far to see much, but what he could see awed and worried him.

As he'd been told, Kana's army was many times the size of theirs, and he could see Xiddeen riding those war lizards as well as bigger beasts that seemed to have more than four legs, though it could be the distance playing tricks on his eyes.

One thing was clear: The fight would not be easy. In truth, even with dragons and the valley's choke point making numbers less of a factor, Tau couldn't say it looked winnable.

So with worry making a nest in his guts, Tau took note of anything that Hadith might use, finally finding a purpose for all the things he'd been forced to learn in all those Goddess-awful strategy meetings. He remained in place for a half span before deciding that there was nothing more to get from being there but a headache.

He'd been crouching and stood up to stretch his bad leg when he heard someone step on and crack a stick behind him. He turned, expecting it to be Auset come to ask what was taking so long. The hunching demon, then, was a surprise, and stumbling back, Tau almost sent himself over the cliff's edge.

Cursing, he caught his balance and pulled his swords free as the monster, long snouted, with sharp teeth, tusks, and pointed ears, stalked toward him on all fours, snarling and snapping its club-like tail behind it. Tau knew it was looking to leap on him, and he didn't have much room to avoid it, if it did.

Unwilling to wait for it to attack and send them both careening off the mountain, Tau raised his blades and jumped at it, roaring as he did. With a snarl, it sprang to meet him, they collided in midair, and Tau was knocked back.

He shouldn't have jumped. Once his feet were off the ground, he couldn't dodge or reposition. Thankfully, his forward momentum meant the beast didn't have the power to plunge them off the cliff, and instead of open air, the demon slammed him into the ground, blasting the air from his lungs. His head ringing from where the back of it had struck stone, Tau wrestled the writhing mass on top of him as it snapped its jaws in his face, its foul-tasting spittle running into his mouth when it splattered on him.

It couldn't tear into him, not yet. He had the hilt of his sword shoved beneath its chin and was pushing back, but his blocking blade wasn't in a position to cut, and the demon was stronger. He couldn't hold it off for long.

Baring his own teeth as he strained to shift his other sword for a strike, Tau pulled the blade back as far as he was able and rammed it forward, stabbing the creature in the stomach and feeling his dragon scale slip inside it like oiled hands into a leather glove.

The demon howled, reared, and came down fast, trying to crush him beneath its forelegs, but Tau was rolling, and when its legs hit the stone, he was already clear. Skittering around on his ass for a stride, Tau scrambled to his feet and readied his weapons. Only now, it was the demon that had its back to the ledge.

It growled and snapped at him, raising its barbed tail over its back like a scorpion's sting. Tau didn't know if it could use the tail like a maul and didn't want to know. Blades whirling, he attacked, cutting and slicing at anything the demon put in range.

"This is my home!" he screamed.

The demon roared, Tau roared back, they came together matched in murderous intent, and the moment it could hit him, the monster whipped its barbed tail down, flying it in like an ax, but Tau skipped away from the chitin-wrapped barb, dodging it and coming close enough to stab the demon in the shoulder of its left foreleg before moving away.

It swung for him with its other foreleg, and Tau blocked with his strong-side blade. The block was good and true and didn't matter enough. The demon knocked him down and off his feet. He lost sight of it, heard it charging, and sprang up, swords leading the way. They engaged, separated, tangled again, and spun away from each other.

It hadn't cut him and couldn't break his defense, but Tau had been bashed about and was bruised all over. His head was still pounding too.

Bad as he was, the demon was worse. It was bleeding from a dozen open wounds and panting. It had its oversized maw hanging open, the black-and-blue tongue within flapping up and down as it eyed him.

"I don't know where you go when I kill you in Uhmlaba," Tau said as they shadowed each other, "but if you return to the mists, tell Ukufa how much it hurt when I sent you to him."

The demon, growling, raised the spiked barb on the end of its tail, and Tau attacked.

The breaths that followed were a frenzy of claws and blades. The demon swung its tail and Tau severed it below the barb. The demon shrieked and reared to its full height, standing taller than Tau by a full stride, and it snatched at him with both front legs. Tau vaulted forward before it could bring its claws together and drove both blades deep into its neck.

The demon clubbed him on the shoulders, its claws cutting into his armor, and Tau marched the dying monstrosity back. It tried to resist him, but he forced it to the cliff's edge by wrenching his swords around in its neck like they were dragon-scale reins. The demon, one step from oblivion, flailed as it hissed and spit at him, its alien eyes full of malice.

"Die, nceku," Tau said, lifting his good leg to kick the under-world's spawn from the mountain.

It made no sound as it fell or when it smashed into the rocks below, bouncing once into the air, its body splayed, limp and lifeless, before falling to the rocks again and bursting into ash that floated in the breeze like motes of vanishing dust.

Body aching, Tau backed away from the ledge. He wanted to sit, to rest, but he worried that there might be other things lurking in the mountains, waiting for him or . . .

The realization hit him like a rogue wave, drowning him in fear, and, swords out, he ran recklessly down the mountain, desperate to get to Tsiora before it was too late.

TRY

Tsiora!"

Tau's thigh had long since seized up, and he almost turned his ankle on the path's last turn. It didn't matter. He didn't slow down until he saw Tsiora and the handmaidens. Only then did his heart unclench.

"Tau?" she asked.

The handmaidens had their dirks out and had circled the queen as best as two people could.

"Demon, in the mountains," Tau said, sucking air.

"Demon?" Auset said. "In Uhmlaba?" She was looking for confirmation.

"Yes!"

"Are there more?" Ramia asked.

"I don't know," Tau said, running over to them and scanning the mountainside. "Have you seen anything?" he asked, the hairs on the back of his neck rising.

"Nothing," Auset said.

Trying to shake away the sense that they were being watched, he turned to the queen.

"We're well," she said.

"I shouldn't have left you."

"We're well. We're with Auset and Ramia."

"I thought something might have happened to you. I thought I might have lost you. Goddess, I can't do it. . . . I can't. . . ."

"We're here."

He sheathed his swords and stepped closer to her, shaking his head. "You don't know how it felt. You have no idea how it felt."

"How can you say that?" she asked. "We felt it when you went into Palm City after the battle. We felt it when you fought Odili. We feel it every time you're in harm's way, and we're always the one putting you there. Don't you dare say we don't know how it feels, Tau Solarin. We do."

"Goddess," Tau said, "I swear to the Goddess . . ."

"Yes?" she asked, lifting her hands to his face.

"What if I lose you?"

"We're here," she said, stepping into him.

"But, what if—"

She kissed him, and he wrapped her up in his arms, lifting her from the ground and kissing her back, his whole being alive with the feel of her.

"We're right here," she said.

"So are we," said Auset.

Tau and Tsiora moved apart.

"Don't be shy now," Auset said. "Not after all that."

"Auset, leave them be," Ramia said. She looked as embarrassed as Tau felt.

"Auset, Ramia, apologies," Tau said.

"Apologies?" Auset asked. "I think I would have gone mad if it'd taken even one more day for you two to do that."

Tau looked at Tsiora. She gave him one of her small smiles, no mask in sight, and it was the most beautiful thing he'd ever seen—until the worry hit, crashing over him in tidal waves that swept him up and over, drawing out the joy in the moment.

"Tau?" Tsiora asked.

"I'm fine," he said.

"You don't look it."

"It's the demons. It keeps happening. Maybe Nyah was right.

Maybe what I've done, the things I've done…maybe they're sinful. What if I am weakening the Goddess and Her powers? What if I'm letting them in?"

Tsiora held his hands. "You're a good man and what you've done isn't sinful." She gave him another smile. "In any case, we think that the Goddess is not so frail that Tau Solarin, fierce and incredible as he might be, can weaken Her."

Her gaze shifted to his lips and back to his eyes. "Since we were old enough to understand our destiny, we wondered if all we'd ever have was blood, fire, and death, but maybe, just maybe, the Goddess will allow us a different path."

Tau wanted to believe her, but he'd spent so long letting life lead him to Odili that he wasn't sure what else it could be.

"Maybe She'll give us our tomorrow," Tsiora said. "We need to believe that there will be time to heal, to live, to be."

"That sounds like peace, but can people like us ever have it?" Tau asked, wanting nothing more and nothing as much from life.

She touched his face again, her skin soft, cool, no matter the heat of the day. "Can we try to find out?" she asked as Ramia shouted a warning.

Tau swung round, pulling Tsiora behind him, just in time to see a short, heavyset Xiddeen shaman appear from thin air, alongside two armed Xiddeen warriors.

TSIORA OMEHIA

Tsiora's lips were still tingling from her first kiss when Tau stepped out in front of her, pulling his swords free and moving to stand with Auset and Ramia. Protecting her, the three of them had their weapons aimed at the shaman and the warriors that had appeared with them.

Tsiora hadn't met many of the Xiddeen's shamans and couldn't be sure if the one in front of her was typical or not, but they were covered in curse scars, their flesh corrupted in places, like boils that had been popped and had the extra skin scraped away. The scars were common among the Xiddeen, though it was unknown why it seemed to afflict some of their kind so much worse than others.

Besides that, the shaman's hair was unkempt and knotted, they wore leather rags and had bone and bronze bangles fitted tight to their wrists and ankles, but none of that was what held her attention. What did have her attention, Tsiora thought, glancing at the warrior woman and man beside the shaman, was that she couldn't tell if the shaman themselves was male or female.

"Peace," the shaman said. "I come as peace."

Tau had his swords pointed at the two Xiddeen. "Come in peace? Where did you come from at all?"

The shaman pushed the Xiddeen male toward Tau as if he was an offering.

"What are you doing?" Tau asked.

"Justice, yes?" the shaman said, their voice a high croak. "We give you justice for one of your dead."

"How do you come to speak our tongue?" Tsiora asked.

The shaman bobbed their head. "I'm shaman in the...Curse, yes?" They grinned, showing yellowed teeth. "I learn from Ihagu. I learn from Ihashe. I learn from Indlovu. Yes?"

"From prisoners you capture and torture," Tau said.

"Justice," they said, offering up the frightened-looking Xiddeen male again.

"Justice for what?" asked Auset.

She and Ramia had moved their way around the shaman and their warrior companions until they were standing behind them.

The shaman looked over their shoulder to see Auset. "Your fighter. Justice for the fighter this one kill," they said, poking the Xiddeen male in the back.

"Who? Who did that one kill?" Tau asked.

"In Omehi war camp. We need food, yes?" the shaman said, making the motion for eating. "We take food, but an Omehi fighter, see us, yes?" The shaman poked the male warrior again. "This one, he hit the fighter in back of head. Break head, and the fighter..." The shaman clicked their tongue and ran a finger across their neck. "The fighter gone, yes? Gone to the gods."

"Gods? Do not be blasphemous in our presence, shaman," Tsiora said, drawing herself up to her full height.

The shaman watched her, ducking their head in a motion mimicking a bow. "We come as peace," they said. "Not to kill. We must give justice, yes? So you know it is peace." They locked their eyes on Tsiora. "The first Omehi queen to come to Xidda, she always want justice, yes." The shaman was not asking a question that time.

"You're talking about the soldier that was found killed in camp," Ramia said. "We never found the killer and thought a demon had done it."

Auset shot Ramia a hard look and Ramia clamped her mouth shut.

The shaman cocked their head at the two women, trying to make sense of the interaction, when Tau drew their attention back to him.

"The soldier in camp? How long ago was that?" Tau asked the shaman. "How long have you been following us?"

The shaman made a boat-on-water motion. "Water, yes? Sand, yes?" They made a walking motion.

"What does that mean?" Tau asked.

"They came here on a ship and landed on our beaches," Tsiora explained.

The shaman nodded vigorously. "Kana."

"You were with Kana? You're spies? Messengers?" she asked.

The shaman shook their head. "Not from Kana, no. Not from that one. He no more peace."

"We know that much," Auset said.

"I don't understand," Tau said. "You came on Kana's ships but you're not with Kana."

More head shaking. "We come with Kana. We not with Kana. We come with food, water, supply, yes?" The shaman pointed a fist at Tau. "You take this. You take our supply."

"What?" asked Tau.

"When you look for Kana, yes? Kana not there. Kana gone. He leave ship, but I am there. I am there with this one"—they pointed to the warrior woman—"and this one," they said, poking the Xiddeen male. "Then you come," the shaman said to Tau. "You come and do not see us. You take supply."

"On the beach when we went to scout Kana's ships," Tau said to Tsiora. "We found abandoned supplies there." He turned back to the shaman. "They were yours and you were there?" Tau asked, moving his sword point closer to the shaman.

"Yes, yes."

"You saw us take them and we didn't see you? How?"

"How, yes? How?" The shaman grinned, closed their eyes, furrowed their brow, and disappeared along with the two Xiddeen warriors.

Ramia yelped in surprise. Auset swung her head, looking for the pair of them, and Tau scowled, twirling his swords in a single circle.

Before he had the chance to kill anyone, Tsiora took herself to the mists. She'd never heard of gifts powerful enough to move a Gifted through Uhmlaba, so, whatever the shaman had done, they hadn't gone far.

The mists swirled around her, and through the weight of her shroud, Tsiora saw what she was looking for. Directly in front of her, where the Xiddeen had been standing, she saw the shrouded shaman as well as the faint glow from the two Xiddeen warriors' souls.

The warriors glowed faintly because they were not actually in Isihogo. Instead, the shaman's powers were keeping all of them hidden from eyes in Uhmlaba.

To confirm her suspicion, Tsiora split her mind, forcing a piece of her consciousness to remain in the mists while the other part looked out at Uhmlaba with her real eyes. It was disorienting, and negotiating the time difference between the two realms always felt like it threatened her hold on sanity.

"I see you, shaman," she said in the mists, raising her hand, drawing power from the Goddess, and blasting them with expulsion.

The shaman and their shroud exploded, vanishing from Isihogo, and the illusion they'd made in Uhmlaba collapsed, revealing them and two warriors to the naked eye.

Tsiora let go of the mind split and drew herself out of the underworld. The shaman was reeling and then fell to a knee.

"Powerful queen," they muttered, nursing their head and shuffling back to a stand. "Very powerful."

"Where did they go, just now?" asked Auset.

"Nowhere," Tsiora said. "The shaman used their gifts. They can hide themselves and others in plain sight."

"This is how you followed us," Tau said.

"Yes, I follow," the shaman said, squinting at Tsiora as if they could figure out what she'd done just by looking at her. "No one see, yes."

"Why did you follow?" Tsiora asked.

"Why?" the shaman said as if it should be obvious. "Kana come to this stolen land to fight, but he does not come with all tribes. Only a few are with Kana, yes?"

"Yes," said Tsiora.

"Other tribes already fighting," the shaman said.

It sent a shock through Tsiora, and she wondered how much of the peninsula they'd already lost. "Where are they fighting, Kigambe, Jirza?"

The shaman didn't answer her directly. "Other tribes tell Kana he must make peace. We need peace so all on Xidda fight the same enemy, yes?"

"The same enemy?" Tsiora asked, relief flushing through her. Her people were still safe, for the moment. "Who is our common enemy?"

"Tribes cannot make Kana stop." The shaman pointed a knobby finger at Tau. "Because of you, yes."

Tau didn't say anything. He had a habit of doing that, and she usually felt like she wanted to shake an answer out of him when he did it, but the shaman's accusation had been leveled at the wrong person. She was the reason Kana was determined to have his war. She was the one who'd sent Tau to kill Kana's father.

Thinking quickly, Tsiora pulled the pieces together. "We have a common enemy, that's what you're saying? Then, we can help each other. Make Kana leave our land and we can discuss working with the Xiddeen."

"No, no, no," the shaman said, shaking their head as if she'd misunderstood a simple problem. "Kana no stop." They pointed at her this time. "You must kill Kana. He stop then, yes?"

"Whose side are you on?" Tau asked.

Not a bad question, thought Tsiora.

The shaman waved their hands and came at the discussion another way. "Kana has feud and will not stop, but Kana will always love Xiddeen, yes. He let me come on ship because if Kana kill you, he help Xiddeen with his fighters. If I come to you and you kill Kana, maybe you help Xiddeen. Both ways, Xiddeen get help, yes?"

"Help you do what, exactly?" asked Tsiora.

The shaman's face grew serious, and the change chilled Tsiora.

"Strangers come to Xidda. More strangers with big ships and many people, yes," the shaman said. "They fight us with warriors like him, yes." The shaman was pointing at Tau.

"Like him?" Tsiora said, her voice faint.

"Yes," the shaman said. "They come to Xidda, the ones with the silver skin and the ones who fight like him. They come to Xidda, not for Xiddeen, but when they see Xiddeen have Omehi magic, they start to kill everyone."

"Silver skin...," said Tsiora. Her fingers were trembling. She hated when they did that. It was such a show of weakness.

"You know them, yes." The shaman was not asking a question.

Tau turned to her then, but for the moment, she couldn't bear to face him. She lifted her face until it was full in the hot sun overhead, and she closed her eyes.

"Tsiora?" her champion said.

"We may not be strong enough...," she whispered. "We may not have our tomorrow."

"Tsiora, what is it?"

She opened her eyes and looked at Tau, wishing that they'd had just a little more time together. "It's the Cull," she said. "They've found us."

GLOSSARY

Ananthi, the Goddess—The one true deity, the creator of Uhm-laba, Isihogo, women, men, and all that exists. She is the source of all gifts, and the Omehi are Her chosen people.

Aqondise—A leading warrior's most trusted companion; a second-in-command.

Cek—Soulless.

Citadel City—The first true Omehian city on Xidda, Citadel City sits at the westward base of the Fist and is home to the Indlovu, Gifted, Sah, and Guardian Citadels. It is the primary training grounds for the Noble warriors, the Gifted, the priesthood, and it is the traditional base of power for the Royals who sit on the Guardian Council and lead the military effort.

Claw (military unit)—Three scales operating together under a single command.

The Crags—A large plateau in the Fist mountain range that has been divided into several fighting areas that are used to train the Gifted, Indlovu, and Ihashe. The Crags are the location of the Queen's Melee.

The Curse—The massive and unexplored desert territory beyond the front lines of the war. The Xiddeen live out in the Curse, though how they can survive in the poisonous wasteland is a mystery.

Cycle—One rotation through all four seasons (Seed, Grow, Harvest, and Hoard).

Demon-haunted—A woman or man whose mind has been broken by time spent in Isihogo.

Dragon (military unit)—A dragon is three wings operating together under a single command.

Dragon's Span—A hand symbol meant to ward away evil thoughts, demons, and faithlessness.

Drudge—A Lesser made casteless for failing to serve the Omehi in combat.

Edifier—A Gifted capable of moving quickly through Isihogo to pass messages to other Edifiers in distant locations.

Enervator—A Gifted capable of temporarily incapacitating others by forcing their souls into Isihogo.

Enrager—A Gifted capable of pulling power from Isihogo and moving it through the blood of a Greater Noble or Royal Noble, making the target bigger, stronger, faster, and more resilient.

Entreater—A Gifted capable of binding her will to the will of another.

The Fist—The smallest mountain range on the Omehi Peninsula, it starts at the ocean and runs a short way down the center of the peninsula. Citadel City sits at its westward base. The Fist holds the Crags training grounds.

Gambeson—A padded defensive jacket.

Gaum—A potent intoxicant made from the poison in a scorpion's sting.

The Goddess's Curse—For fighting against Her chosen people, the Goddess afflicted the Xiddeen with a curse that corrupts their skin and bodies, giving them weeping sores and seeming to rot them from the inside out.

Guardian—The Omehi name for a dragon.

Hedeni—Women and men who have no faith in the Goddess and live outside of Her grace.

Hex—A group of six Entreaters who work together.

Ihagu—The Omehi militia that makes up the front lines in the endless war against the Xiddeen. These men are not granted military status.

Ihashe—The elite fighters and soldiers of the Lesser castes. They are granted military status after graduating from the one-cycle training provided at either the Southern or Northern Ihashe Isikolo. They must serve six active cycles to complete their service.

Indlovu—The elite warriors of the Noble castes. They are granted military status after graduating from the three-cycle training provided at the Indlovu Citadel in Citadel City. They must serve six active cycles to complete their service.

Ingonyama—The Chosen's deadliest fighters, selected from the very best of the graduating military initiates. If the Ingonyama is a Greater Noble or Royal Noble they are teamed with an Enrager, who will use her gifts to empower the Ingonyama in combat.

Inkokeli—Leader of an Indlovu unit or Ihashe scale.

Inkumbe—A small grass-eating and four-legged creature from Osonte with small horns and cloven feet.

Intulo—A salamander/lizard. Also a description of a slippery person who won't stay still in an argument—their thoughts are loose, fluid, not substantial.

Inyoka—A poisonous serpent.

Isihogo—The demon world—a colorless, mist-filled prison, where time flows differently and Ananthi's powers are found.

Isikolo—A school or academy.

Jirza—The capital city of the northern province.

KaEid—The leader of the Gifted. Typically of Royal Noble blood.

Kigambe—The capital city of the southern province.

Kora—A stringed musical instrument.

Kudliwe—A small scurrying and flying insect that burrows into bags of grain and is difficult to kill.

Masmas—A frothy intoxicant made from fermented cactus juice.

Mka—The particular pungent and unpleasant smell of winds produced after having eaten bean- or onion-heavy meals.

Nceku—Soulless one.

Neh—An Omehi interjection commonly used to indicate a statement of opinion or fact, a command, an exclamation, or a question, or to indicate that something went unheard.

Nkosi—An honorific used when addressing Nobles.

Olu—A pricey intoxicant made from crushed and fermented fruits.

The Omehi/The Chosen—The people, Nobles and Lessers, chosen by the Goddess to lead all the races of men.

Osonte—The original homeland of the Omehi.

Palm City—The capital city of the Omehi peninsula and the central province, and the seat of the queen and her royal family.

Preceptor—The one who instructs Gifted initiates in their training.

Proven—A warrior who has proven their mettle and worth in combat by sacrificing enough of their body to no longer be combat-ready. Proven maintain their military status and are required to serve out all time remaining in their six cycles of military service. Most Proven sign up for additional service.

Rabba—A fruity, bright, and floral aroma'ed stimulant drink made from wet-processed beans grown in the highlands of the Southern and Northern Mountain ranges.

Rage (military unit)—Three dragons (military unit) operating together under a single command.

The Roar—The unsettled ocean.

Sah Priesthood—The women and men who preach the word of the Goddess, maintain the Omehi's religious traditions, and help guide the Chosen ever closer to the Goddess's grace.

Scale (military unit)—The Omehi's most common and basic fighting unit, made up of fifty-four men.

Seasons—The Omehi make note of four seasons: Seed, Grow, Harvest, and Hoard. Each season lasts approximately three moon cycles.

Shul—The Xiddeen word for "great chief"—a leader whose powers transcend tribe.

Uhmlaba—The world of the races of men.

Ukufa, the Insatiate—Ukufa the thief, liar, corrupter, divider, enslaver. Ukufa the creator of death, suffering, war, and hate broke the world with his hunger for more than the world could give. He is held in Isihogo by the body and spirit of the Goddess.

Umbusi—A fief's governor.

Umqondisi—A teacher, trainer, master, leader.

Wing (military unit)—Three claws operating together under a single command.

Xidda—The land the Omehi discovered after fleeing Osonte.

Xiddeen—The name the aboriginals of Xidda use for themselves.

NOBLES

THE
OMEHI
PEOPLE

LESSERS

THE CHOSEN CASTES

QUEEN AND ROYAL FAMILY

ROYAL NOBLES

THE GIFTED

INGONYAMA
(ACTIVE AND INACTIVE)

GREATER NOBLES

PETTY NOBLES

IHASHE
(ACTIVE SERVICE)

HIGH GOVERNOR
(ADMINISTRATORS)

LOW GOVERNOR
(CREATORS/EDUCATORS)

HIGH HARVESTER
(FARM ADMINISTRATORS)

LOW HARVESTER
(SKILLED FARM WORKERS)

HIGH COMMON
(WORKERS CAPABLE OF
MANAGING OTHER WORKERS)

LOW COMMON
(WORKERS)

DRUDGE
(INDENTURED SERVANTS)

THE
RULING
AND
GUARDIAN
COUNCILS

INDLOVU
(ACTIVE SERVICE)

IHAGU
(ACTIVE SERVICE)

GRATITUDE

To **Lurlene Winter**, my mother, you named me after a writer, showed me how joyful a life lived in love with books could be, and raised me to be unafraid of walking the unbeaten path. Everything I do and everything I am springs from you.

To **Diala Winter**, my wife, who shares the days when the greatest joys come into my life and who has stood with me when the losses felt too big to bear—there's not much I'm afraid to face with you by my side, and there's little that would be as good, exciting, or memorable if I didn't get to do it with you.

To **Koa Winter**, my son, you're eight and in school as I write this, and already I know that you're a gift not just to me and my life, but to the whole world. I'm lucky to be your father, I'm so incredibly proud of you, and the universe will have heard me if only you have health and happiness in this life. Please believe in yourself, because you will always be more than enough. Please try to leave people better than you find them, because the world can be hard, and we're all in this together. Koa, I love you with all my heart and I always will.

To **Anthony**, who incessantly demanded that the story's stakes always be clear, being held accountable for doing one's best work by a friend and reader like you is a blessing that every creative person should beg to be cursed with.

To **Joey**, my high school friend who is all grown up now and spends his days negotiating, closing, and managing multibillion-dollar deals, but still makes time to give me story notes at night.

To **Malik**, whose advice, encouragement, and insight are priceless—there are so many levels to…to everything, and bearing witness as you see and operate on damn near all of them lifts me up and makes me want to do and be better.

To **Aunt Pansy**, **Uncle Carl**, **Uncle Steve**, **Uncle Melville**, **Aunt Cheryl**, **Uncle Bertie**, **Michelle**, **Anika**, **Sheyamba**, **Tshaka**, **Richard**, **Susie**, **Kyle**, **Lily**, and **Gisela**, though we may not always be together, every time we meet it's like we've never been apart, and having you and yours as family is a blessing.

To **Khaled**, **Fadia**, **Dia**, **Ange**, **Mia**, **Dominic**, and **Alexia**, who turn every day brighter and can somehow, inexplicably, always make leaving the house to spend time together seem like a far better idea than staying in it, you have completed my family.

To all of you, thank you from the bottom of my heart!

THE SCALE

If this page exists, know that it and all the others in this book do so only because the following people helped bring them to the world . . .

To **Brit Hvide** (my editor), whose passion for stories, empathy for those who write them, and way with words inspire me—it's rare to talk about just how large a role fortune plays in bringing a story successfully to its readers, but after watching my father buy lottery tickets every week for years, I think I know good fortune when I see it, and I'm so very lucky this story ended up in your talented and caring hands.

To **Tim Holman** (Orbit's publisher), I'm in awe of the house you've built. It's a place filled with people of principle and integrity who act on their ideals, taking action when, sometimes, even the awesome power of words is not enough. You built a home for good people doing their best to tell incredible stories, and as a guest in that home, I can't imagine a better welcome or a more comfortable place to stay.

To **Erin Malone** (my literary agent), who helps guide this thing that I'm still hesitant to call a career, who offers comfort when the wild west that is this industry feels a little too out of control, and who has no idea how much joy I get from seeing all the pictures of little Charlie growing up.

To **Eric Reid** (my film/TV agent), what a magnificent world of contracts, financing, scripting, casting, crewing up, and distributing it is in which you move. Now, I don't say this lightly, but your world may almost be as cool as I feel when I'm sitting at home in my pajamas with nothing else but a laptop and the voices in my head (maybe).

To **Emily Byron** and **Jenni Hill** (my UK editors), your support, kind words and warm emails were always enough to remind me that, even in the depths of *The Fires of Vengeance*'s first draft, I was never all alone.

To **Nivia Evans** (the editor backing up my editors while also handling a crew of unruly and unreasonably talented authors all on her own), I see you out there doing the work of three people at a level that would make five proud. I see you.

To **Lauren Panepinto** (creative director), you've given my stories a face with which to greet the world, and that can't be overvalued because, in my humble opinion, books *are* judged by their covers. True, it's only an initial judgment, but it can be a fatal one, and your work keeps this story from a lonely death on a dusty back shelf.

To **Karla Ortiz** (artist), your cover for *The Rage of Dragons* made me so proud, and unbelievably, you've outdone yourself with the cover for *The Fires of Vengeance*; it gave me shivers the first time I saw it. With your mind and skill, you capture the spirit of the story that's being told, and I've been a reader for long enough to know just how rare and precious a thing that is.

To **Anna Jackson** (publisher Orbit UK), having your support for this story means it will be read by countless readers. It means that this book will be on the shelves and in the stores of the country of my birth, and I am very grateful for absolutely all of that.

To **Alex Lencicki** (associate publisher), looks like you're now tasked with melding business and art, a bizarre and hazardous alchemy. Yet, with every new book Orbit releases, your alchemical binds seem to hold. So, next time we meet, we're going to sit down, and I'm going to pry all your secrets from you.

To **Laura Fitzgerald** and **Ellen Wright** (marketing and publicity), at a time when hundreds if not thousands of new books are traditionally and independently published every single day, your jobs are both daunting and critical. Without the work that you do, readers have little chance of even knowing that a book exists. The saying used to be "If you build it, they will come," but I prefer "If you build it and tell the right people, you might be able to get a decent-sized audience to pay a little attention." Well, you brought more than a decent-sized audience to what we built, and that is a power as mysterious and as wonderful as anything the Gifted in this story wield.

To **Nazia** (senior press officer), your warmth, kindness, generosity, and passion for all things SFF are like a ray of multicolored light in the dark underworld that bookselling can often inhabit. You make every space just that much better.

To **Megan Fitzpatrick**, **Nita Basu**, and **Prentice Onayemi** (Hachette Audio and the audiobook's narrator), every day, more and more people, who may not always find the chance to sit down with a book, are listening to books, and there is something so wonderfully human about stories returning to their beginnings as a connection between the voice of the teller and the mind of the listener. I'm so happy that this story can be heard as well as read, and that's because of you.

To **Bryn A. McDonald** and **Eileen Chetti** (managing editor and copy editor), your attention to detail and tireless eyes make my sentences flow, my fight scenes make sense, and my war wounds consistent. With gentle and nonjudgmental guidance, you've shown me that I have absolutely no idea how commas work (at all), and I'm glad that you did. But what I'm most grateful for is that you treat these words and worlds with as much consideration as you would your own, and it would be a difficult task indeed to find the right way to thank you properly for that!

WWW.EVANWINTER.COM

Dear Reader,

Life is the spans we're given and the choices we make in how to spend them, and I cannot thank you enough for choosing to spend a few with me.

Wishing you and yours happiness, health, love,

Evan Winter

Visit www.evanwinter.com to be the first to learn more about Evan's books—past, present, and future.